TAKE ME HOME

BETH MORAN

Boldwood

First published in Great Britain in 2023 by Boldwood Books Ltd.

A CIP catalogue record for this book is available from the British Library.

Paperback ISBN 978-1-80483-360-5

Large Print ISBN 978-1-80483-359-9

Hardback ISBN 978-1-80483-361-2

Ebook ISBN 978-1-80483-358-2

Kindle ISBN 978-1-80483-357-5

Audio CD ISBN 978-1-80483-366-7

MP3 CD ISBN 978-1-80483-365-0

Digital audio download ISBN 978-1-80483-363-6

Boldwood Books Ltd
23 Bowerdean Street
London SW6 3TN
www.boldwoodbooks.com

For Asher
A whole book couldn't express how blessed I am to call you my son

1

I'm no stranger to tears. In my line of work, they're unavoidable. Big, fat, honking sobs soaked up with mounds of tissues. A frustrated swipe at grief spilling over reddened eyelids. The hardest to bear are the silent streams, unnoticed by the person weeping, as if the pain is so deep, so all-encompassing, it is merely who they are now.

They don't just cry, of course. I've encountered simmering bitterness. Rampant rage. Fear, twisted up with anxiety. The fog of lingering shock. Heart-wrenching loneliness.

So, why would I put myself through this, day after day? Why choose to spend my life submerged in the kaleidoscope of strangers' sorrows?

Because I know that behind the tears, curses and questions is love.

And I, too, have navigated the river of loss. Surviving its swirling, murky depths was hard enough. Everything else that accompanied it – the house, the paperwork, the practicalities – became a burden so heavy that without help, I would have surely drowned.

So, here I was, walking with Alice Dumble's family through the aftermath of her death, providing hugs, hot drinks and a listening ear as we packed up eight decades of accumulated clutter. Three weeks of tears, stories and sharing this most precious, intimate of tasks.

Yet after all that, I still couldn't quite summon up an appropriate response to a sixty-something woman peeling off her top to reveal her eighty-four-year-old mother's face grinning at me from her crepey chest.

A woman of few words at the best of times, I stuttered, 'Wow, Denise, that... really expresses your devotion,' before mercifully being interrupted.

'For goodness' sake, Mum.' Denise's son, Scott, held a hand in front of his eyes, causing one of the mugs of tea he was carrying to slop onto the beige carpet. 'Seeing you half naked is bad enough. If I have to see that tattoo of Gran one more time, I'll be traumatised for life.'

'Oh, stop being such a drama queen,' Denise said, fondly patting the top of her mum's head. 'I've got a bra on.'

'Nevertheless...' I took a mug from Scott with a nod of thanks. 'If we're hoping to get everything tied up today, we'd best get on with it.'

Alice Dumble had passed away after a long illness, so in theory, there'd been plenty of opportunities to sort things out – or at least find out her bank details. However, her family had grown so used to the doctor telling them Alice didn't have long, they'd stopped taking it seriously. Consequently, by the time they contacted me, a week after the funeral, Alice's home, her affairs and her family were a complete mess.

The four children, nine grandchildren and assorted partners began arguing as soon as the eldest daughter claimed the wedding ring, and were still squabbling yesterday afternoon about a chipped vase. I'd had my work cut out to help the Dumble family deal with the varied tasks accompanying their mourning. This included sifting through mountains of stuff, readying the house to be sold, wading through bank accounts, credit, store and discount cards and dealing with so many random online subscriptions, I was surprised she had any savings left.

In eight years of running my business, providing a house-clearance and administrative support service to people following bereavement, this project had required more diplomacy, tissues and chocolate biscuits than any other. I was itching to sign off the final few documents before leaving the Dumbles to scrap over the house sale. More to the point, I wanted to finish up before Kenneth, another sibling, arrived. He was still questioning how little I'd sold the television for, and trying to insist I forfeited the 10 per cent of profit that was part of our contract. Depending upon what my various clients could afford, I'd either agree commission on any items sold, a fixed fee, daily rate, or a combination of all three. For the Dumbles, I'd be lucky to cover the cost of biscuits.

Once Denise had pulled her top back on, we sat on the sagging sofa and went through a printed summary, including all the completed admin, the allocation of various items in line with Alice's will and the bits and bobs I'd managed to sell or otherwise redistribute. Denise and Scott both signed on the dotted lines, and after one last hug, I opened the front door to find Kenneth standing on the other side.

'Ah, Sophie. I'm glad I caught you,' he said, eyes bugging beneath a thick, white fringe.

'Hi, yes. Um, I'm actually all done here. Denise has the completed folder.' I offered a quick smile and made to move past, but he wasn't budging. 'If you've any queries, you can email me.' Once I'm a good hundred or so miles away, that is.

'Oh, no. I'm sure everything's in order.' Kenneth's voice caught, causing me to look at him properly. His eyes were brimming with tears. 'I just wanted to say thank you. And to give you these. You've got us through three nightmare weeks with no bloodshed, and, believe me, that's a Dumble first.'

He whipped his hand from behind his back, brandishing a bunch of flowers. I kept my eyes on his face, managing to smile and mumble my thanks as I gingerly took hold of the stems.

Yep – my finger pressed against a thorn and I caught the waft of familiar scent even as I lifted my chin and forced my breathing to shallow. He'd brought me roses.

Nausea surging in my stomach, I garbled another goodbye, resisting the urge to run as I rounded the end of the driveway and hurried down the street before dumping the flowers on a random doorstep.

It wasn't personal. If they'd have been lilies, carnations or any other flower, I'd have kept them. But roses? Those, my mangled heart could not handle.

* * *

It was a twenty-minute walk through crisp, February sunshine to the campsite that for the past three weeks had been home. I usually parked my motorhome much nearer to the house I was clearing – where possible, on the driveway. For larger properties, I tended to be offered a spare room, which I would accept depending upon the weather, how comfortable I felt with the family and whether Muffin, my dog, was also welcome. After one conference call with the Dumbles, I'd booked into a local campsite. The added bonus being electric hook-up, a walk home at the end of each day to clear my head, and no chance of a Dumble hammering on the motorhome door once I'd clocked off. The time of year also meant that I'd practically got the campsite to myself, which was precisely how I liked it.

The second I stepped up into the motorhome, Muffin scrabbled to her feet, planting her front paws on my waist, her whole body wagging with joy. My heart gave a bittersweet squeeze as I rubbed her silky ears in return. I had tried my utmost not to fall too hard for this animal. While helping two sons sort through their father's bric-a-brac shop eighteen months ago, I'd found myself with a knee-high chocolate fluffball for a shadow. Muffin had been grieving her owner, and she'd chosen me as the replacement. It had become increasingly impossible to resist the hope in those soft brown eyes. So, I'd got myself a housemate.

About ten minutes into the first night, she'd scrambled over the makeshift barrier I'd erected around her cushion bed, then burrowed her way under my duvet and into my heart.

I didn't know how old she was. Other people might not worry about this kind of thing, but with my past, in my job, it was hard to stop every snuggle, every fun-filled walk being tinged with the certainty that, one day, it would come to an end.

After reassuring my dog that, despite having left her alone for a whole three hours, I still loved her, I shut down the morbid thoughts stirred up by the scent of roses and settled down on the sofa. I'd time for lunch, a chapter or two of a book and a skim through my emails before readying everything for our next journey. The strain of the past few weeks started to ebb as I heated some soup and reminded Muffin that we were about to set off on a new adventure.

The only thing I needed to decide now was which adventure that was going to be.

* * *

Once we were safely tootling up the near-empty M1, Muffin strapped into the passenger seat, I called Ezra using hands-free.

'Sophie! We just got back from school. Hang on.'

I waited for a few seconds until his gaggle of children burst onto the line.

'Hello, Auntie Sophie!' they called, the two girls overlapping each other so it was hard to distinguish between them, while thirteen-year-old Ishmael sounded more like his father than his younger sisters.

'Are you coming home?' Aaliyah, who was nine, asked. While I rarely stayed longer than a few days at their farmhouse, and only two or three times a year, it served as my official address when I needed one and was therefore technically my home.

'Not just yet. I'll be back for Easter, though. Only a few weeks to go.'

I chatted for another minute or two before Ezra announced that there were snacks waiting in the kitchen, allowing us to talk in peace.

'You survived the feuding family, then?' he asked. 'You aren't calling from A&E?'

I spent a few minutes filling him in on the past weeks. Ezra was a silent partner in the business, the only person on earth apart from his wife, Naomi, who I trusted. His mother had been my parents' solicitor since before I was born, and he'd taken over the role when I was a teenager. He'd been there when my world crumbled into ashes, given me a safe haven where I could slowly piece myself back together, and, as an added bonus, taught me everything I knew about inheritance law. I wasn't Auntie Sophie by blood, but having changed dozens of nappies, spent endless hours cuddling babies in the rocking chair while we both cried, and witnessed their eldest daughter, JoJo's, first steps, I was happy to accept the title.

I'd been living with Ezra when the idea for my business began. A friend asked for advice after her mum died, which ended up with me staying for a couple of weeks while we sorted everything out. She then passed my number to a colleague who'd lost his wife. His sister happened to work in a retirement village, and so it went on.

Why did they ask me, a twenty-five-year-old ex-floristry apprentice?

Because I'd learned far too many unwelcome, yet horribly necessary, lessons about how to keep on living, carry on breathing, and slog through the mountains of debris left behind when everyone you love the most has gone.

'So, where next?' Ezra asked, once he'd also filled me in on the latest goings-on at the farmhouse.

'That's partly why I was calling.'

'Okay, but if this is going to require a long discussion, we might be better off waiting until this evening. I need to clear up the snack-time carnage before Naomi gets home. If I don't up my game, she's going to make me go back to working full-time.'

'No, it won't take long. I've only got two options. A woman in Sheffield whose dad died suddenly. There's ex-step-siblings circling and some complicated and not necessarily legal business ties with two other countries. Plus, the woman is severely allergic to dogs so I'd be in the motorhome, and there's snow forecast for next week.'

'If that's genuinely an option, I can't wait to hear the second.'

'Option two is a place called Riverbend, on the edge of Sherwood Forest. It's an Edwardian country house with a guest suite including the added luxury of a bath, central heating and a log fire. The client, Harriet Langford, has offered a daily rate that will set me up for the rest of the year. Meals and other expenses included. She's even got a dog. Called Flapjack. Who would apparently love to have Muffin to stay.'

'I don't understand the dilemma here. I know you want to help people wherever you can, but this is also your life, and your livelihood. You can't risk getting embroiled with something illegal.' He paused to tell the kids to pick their coats up off the floor. 'You haven't mentioned who's died at the fancy hall. Presumably this is the issue?'

A sign up ahead informed me that the next turning was for Sherwood Forest. I had half a mile to decide.

'That's the thing. There isn't anyone.'

'I don't follow.'

'Harriet Langford owns the whole lot. Why does a fifty-five-year-old woman want help clearing a house she's still living in, and to tie up all her affairs, when she's very much alive?'

'Well, I guess there's only one way to find out, isn't there?'

'By moving in? That could be riskier than the first option.'

'A grand, old house with miles of countryside for Muffin to explore, no troublesome family to deal with? Sophie, these past few clients have really taken their toll. I can hear how tired you are. Why not choose the easier, nicer option for once?'

Ten seconds later, we were heading off the motorway and into the forest.

* * *

The nearest village to Riverbend was Middlebeck, which appeared to consist of not much more than a central green surrounded by a few shops, a primary school and tiny church. I pulled over in the one spot that would comfortably accommodate the van and called Harriet Langford to arrange an introductory meeting. If I picked up any bad vibes, or she turned out to be a brazen weirdo, I could always back out before signing anything.

'How soon can you get here?' she asked, with a warm voice that was instinctively reassuring. 'Are you anywhere close by?'

'I'm not far at all. I could be there first thing in the morning.'

'Well, if you're not far, how about supper tonight?'

'Oh.' After a moment's hesitation, I decided I might as well get it over with rather than potentially wasting a night here. 'Okay, yes. Thank you. That would be lovely.'

'As you enter Middlebeck, go straight past the pub, a hundred metres or so, and the turn-off is on the right. You won't miss it. Once you've reached Riverbend, you can park in front of the main house, then follow the signs to the studio and let yourself in.'

'Right. Thank you.'

'Thank *you*. I'm very much looking forward to meeting you.'

It was just after five. At the grander places I'd visited over the past few years, I'd learned that supper would not be served any time soon. Deciding it was best to give Harriet an hour to prepare for my arrival, I poured a mug of tea from the flask I'd made earlier, then tipped some kibble into Muffin's bowl after a firm nose nudge reminded me that *her* supper was due ten minutes ago. I sent an apologetic reply to the potential Sheffield client, with links to some websites they might find useful, then killed half an hour looking up Sherwood Forest dog walks before swapping my jeans and jumper for a navy trouser suit and cream blouse. Stuffing my dark-blonde hair into a bun, I added a swipe of mascara, slipped into brown ankle boots and was about as ready for Riverbend as I was going to get.

2

I chugged past the pub, craning my neck until I spotted the turn-off Harriet had mentioned. It was a one-track lane tucked between thick hedgerows, that I probably would have missed in the dark if it hadn't been for a wooden sign lit up by solar lamps, pointing to 'Riverbend' in turquoise script styled to look like a river. My headlights caught glimpses of trees lining the road as we bounced over potholes and puddles, but it had started raining a few minutes earlier so I couldn't make out what lay beyond them. Just as I'd convinced myself I must have missed another sign, a brick wall loomed up ahead, the lane continuing through a high archway. Concentrating on not scraping the sides of the motorhome on the wall as we crept through, when I did look up again, the house standing in front of me took my breath away.

'Wowzers, Muffin. Take a look at our new home.'

I stopped for a moment, taking in the Juliet balcony above curved steps leading up to a broad front door. It was more of a hall than a house, but the squat – almost square – shape and the fairy lights entwined in the clematis clambering up the wall made it appear more homely than grand. An enticing glow shone through the rain from several floor-to-ceiling windows and my stomach gave a soft growl at the thought of the supper we might find within.

I could just about make out another signpost to one side. Parking up on the large semicircle of gravel in front of the house, I hopped out to take a closer look. More fairy lights wrapped around the hand-painted arrows pointing to the boathouse, kitchen garden and the studio. I released Muffin from her seat belt, clicked on her lead and we dashed through the downpour, around the corner to where another sign for the studio pointed up an external flight of wooden stairs with patterned pots of greenery perching on every step.

'I guess this is where we'll be staying,' I said as we climbed towards the turquoise door, lit up by a carriage lamp fixed onto the wall above it. Harriet had said to let ourselves in, but if this door led straight into the guest suite, then I wasn't sure how she would know that I'd arrived. Instead, I gave a tentative knock, followed by a louder one a short while later. When that yielded no result, I resorted to following her instructions, twisting the large, brass handle, opening the door and stepping inside, Muffin tugging on the lead in anticipation of getting out of the rain.

Oh, boy. I froze, one step inside the door.

I really hoped this wasn't the guest suite.

Partly because one frantic glance revealed no bed, wardrobe or any other bedroom-type furniture.

Mostly because the room contained half a dozen technicoloured, feathered, sequinned and seemingly otherwise naked women.

The flutter of trepidation that always accompanied an initial client visit, already magnified by the strangeness of this partic-

ular project, expanded into full-blown flapping. I'd have immediately turned and fled, if it hadn't been for Muffin yanking the
lead out of my hand and scampering past the naked bodies to
the huge, curly-haired dog lumbering to its feet in one corner.

Everyone stood there in stunned silence, the only sound two
dogs spinning around each other, wuffling in delight.

'Can we help you?' a tall, thin woman painted from head to
toe with rainbows said, after what felt like an eternity of them
staring at me and me trying not to stare at them.

'I'm so sorry to interrupt. I must be in the wrong place. I'll...
try another door.'

I most definitely would not try another door. Who knew
what I might stumble upon behind that one?

'Are you the journalist?' another person asked, folding her
arms across a stomach slathered with silver glitter. 'I thought
you were coming next week. I don't mind you taking my photo
as long as you don't print my name.'

'Ooh, Kelly. You don't need to be ashamed of people seeing
you like that. You look fab!' A completely blue woman, like a
naked Smurf, tutted.

'I know that!' Kelly replied, tossing her silver bob. 'But if my
boss knows I've been here, it's another excuse for him to fire me,
and I'm on a final warning after the Christmas party.'

'That's outrageous!'

'He can't fire you for being here! It's hardly a crime. Oy, journalist lady. You'd better make sure this article is an accurate
account. It's about time people stopped being so judgemental.'

'That's a good point!' the tall woman added. 'How can we
trust that you'll not misrepresent us?'

'Um...'

'Well?' she demanded, taking a few steps closer, hands on
her rainbow hips.

'I'm not the journalist.'

'You're not? Are you sure?'

'Very sure.'

'Well, then what are you doing here, in a private, confidential group?'

Trying to leave?

'I was told to let myself into the studio. The sign pointed up here.'

'Well, who on earth would tell you to do that, given that this is personal invitation only?'

Panic started rising up my throat.

'I did,' a rich, warm voice answered through an open doorway at the back of the room. 'Sophie?'

'Yes,' I breathed in relief. 'Harriet?'

'Hattie, to my friends.' She strode into the middle of the room, carrying a large pot of paint in each hand. Her tiny frame was dressed in faded, patched-up jeans and a simple, grey T-shirt. Her feet were bare and her hair was a mass of salt and pepper curls, eyes shining the same turquoise as the paint decorating the door and signs. Despite her diminutive size, she radiated vibrant energy. I'd never seen anyone look so alive.

'I'm so sorry, I got my timings a little mixed up. Morag's right, this is a private group. I thought it would be over before you arrived. Everyone, please accept my sincerest apologies for inviting a stranger to intrude upon your session. I know Sophie will keep your identities confidential. If you can start finishing up, I'll show her to the main house and be right back.'

'Who is she, then?' a woman covered in black feathers asked.

'Yeah, you've put us in a vulnerable position here, Hattie. We have the right to know who she is,' someone painted in caterpillars on one side, butterflies the other, said.

Hattie glanced at me, faltering for a split second like a light bulb flickering. 'Sophie's a historian. A publisher asked me to write a book about Riverbend, and I thought it was a brilliant idea, but I haven't got the time or the brains for that, so they sent Sophie to help me out.'

'So she's writing a book, not an article? Does that mean the journalist isn't coming?'

'Ooh, are we going in the book, Sophie? Will it have pictures? Can we have some warning before you take them, so I can get my wings just right?' The black-feathered woman flapped her arms like a crow.

'Um... I'm not writing the book.' Hattie's eyes flashed in panic until I pressed on. 'It's Hattie's book. I'm merely helping her decide what to put in it. And it's going to be a history book. None of you look ready to be confined to history just yet.'

'Too right we're not!' The chorus of jokes and giggles continued as Hattie whistled for the dogs and ushered me back outside, not breaking her stride until we'd hurried around the house, through the front door and into the kitchen.

'I'm so sorry. I'll explain everything. Give me half an hour to clear up and shoo them out. Oh, and if you can cook fajitas, the ingredients are in the fridge. I think Lizzie left instructions.'

* * *

For want of anything else to do except jangle with nervous energy, once I'd given the enormous kitchen – including a gigantic range oven, professional coffee maker and walk-in pantry – a good ogle, I found a stack of plastic containers in the fridge with a recipe stuck to the lid, and cooked a meal in a strange kitchen for a woman I'd only just met, trying not to completely freak out about what on earth I'd got myself into.

I was mashing an avocado when Hattie returned. Muffin shared none of my qualms, having curled up with her new best friend on a giant dog bed in front of an old fireplace.

'I'm mortified.' Hattie whipped open a forest-green cabinet and took out two glasses, adding a generous slosh of gin and some tonic before handing me one, not bothering to ask if I wanted a drink, or even whether I drank at all.

'It's taken over a month to get this group relaxed enough for the body session, and now I've blown their trust with one mistimed judgement. When will I learn to lock the studio door? If anyone blabs, it'll make it so much harder with the next lot.' She held her glass up in my direction. 'If *you* blab, it'll be just as bad. But I'm hoping to woo you into working with me, in which case you'll need to sign a non-disclosure form.'

I took a large sip of my drink.

Hattie broke into a grin, reminding me of the sun coming out from behind a cloud. 'How am I doing so far? Am I wooing you well?'

I gave the pan of chicken and vegetables a feeble poke. 'Umm...'

'Oh, my goodness.' My host gave a startled laugh as her bright eyes widened in horror. 'Here you are, having been suddenly exposed to six semi-naked women decorated like toddlers let loose in a craft shop, and now you're cooking dinner while I stand here rambling on about my reputation! You must think I'm crackers.'

'Um, no, it's... I mean...'

'No!' She held up one hand. 'I'm counting on us spending a lot of time together over the next few weeks. Sharing a home. I'll be trusting you with precious memories and the objects that hold them. Family secrets. Private information. If this is going to work, we need to be honest with each other. I don't expect you to tell me anything more than the job requires. But I do ask that what you tell me is the truth. If that's too much, then let's enjoy a lovely meal and you can be on your way first thing in the morning.' She wrinkled her nose. 'But I liked you the moment I saw you. And I *love* your dog. I'm very much hoping you'll stay.'

I had to admit that I liked Hattie, too. Honesty was a crucial element to my work, and I was intrigued by her, and her project. Her house was idyllic. And while some might interpret being asked to cook the dinner you'd been invited to as rude, I was very short on people who treated me as one of the family. It was becoming increasingly difficult to ignore the nagging whisper that never letting anyone really get to know me outside Ezra's family, always moving on before I risked growing attached to a place – or its people – maybe wasn't so perfect for me after all.

I took another sip of gin, then turned to face her, forcing my shoulders straight and my chin up.

'I don't mind cooking. I usually live in a motorhome so this kitchen is my idea of heaven. But while I can keep what I saw earlier to myself, I am wondering exactly what it was, and whether I'm likely to stumble across anything else like it, if I do stay here.'

Hattie's eyes glinted. 'What do you think it was?'

'I'm guessing – *hoping* – some sort of art class? Although that wouldn't explain why it's so private and confidential.'

'Apart from the fact that most of those women were wearing nothing more than their underwear?'

'They were wearing underwear?' The smallest of smiles tugged at my mouth. 'Well, that already makes me feel better.'

'Really?' Hattie peered down her pert nose at me. 'They're grown women. It's only bums and boobs. All of us have them. We've spent weeks creating a safe space to be open and vulnerable. To go beyond the surface. I was disappointed how many of them kept their knickers on.'

'So, not art, then?'

She pulled her chin back in surprise. 'You didn't think that was art?'

'Honestly?'

'I already said, I'm insisting upon it.'

'I've had a long day. A difficult few weeks. At this point, I barely know my own name.'

Hattie's mouth dropped open. 'Oh my. This is why I have Lizzie. I'm a terrible host at the best of times, and it's only going to get worse. Please, sit down. I'll serve up dinner, and while you eat, I'll tell you all about it and me. And why I asked you to help me. Then if you have any more questions, you can fire away.'

She shooed me towards the enormous table, grabbing plates from a rose-pink dresser and serving dishes from an orange shelf. Once we'd helped ourselves to tortilla wraps and the chicken mix, added sour cream, guacamole and a generous sprinkling of cheese, I felt brave enough to ask another question.

'Why did you tell the women that a publisher had sent me?'

Hattie put her wrap down. 'I will come to that. But it would be easier if I started at the beginning.'

'Okay.'

'Are you ready, or do you want to finish eating first?'

'I'll eat, you tell me everything,' I said, my echo of her earlier words producing a smile.

'Right. I'm Harriet Langford.'

I nodded. That was about the one piece of information I already knew.

'Otherwise known as Hattie Hood.'

I sat back. 'The artist?'

She nodded, unable to hide her pleasure at me knowing the name.

'I love your designs.'

Hattie Hood was well known for her forest prints used in high-quality homeware and soft furnishings – including the duvet and pillow cases in my motorhome that were covered in tiny monochrome deer. Other designs included acorns, berries and woodpeckers.

'Thank you. I love them, too. As well as creating the design, and having input into the merchandise, I also work as an art therapist. This includes individual clients, and group sessions. I work with recovering addicts, people struggling with mental illness, grief or other traumas. The group you met today have called themselves the Changelings. I won't go into any more details but let's just say they're all around fifty and have a tendency to sweat a lot. They also feel stuck, stressed out and at times so angry, they could decapitate their loved ones for breathing too loud. We're arting out the feeling like a drab old has-been. Replacing it with some fierce and fabulous.'

'Hence the caterpillars and butterflies.'

'Zinnia's come a long way.' She sighed. 'But you can understand why being interrupted by a stranger was unwelcome.'

'I'm so sorry.'

Hattie glanced up at me, sharply. 'No. *I'm* sorry. It would never have happened if... Well. Let's just say, I've got a lot on my mind. Which is another reason I need your help.'

'Can you tell me more about that? My services are for people who've been bereaved. I help clear houses, complete admin. Bring everything to a close, as painlessly as possible. Why do you want my help when no one's died?'

She gave a rueful smile. 'I'm only fifty-five but that's two years older than my mother when I lost her. I've got a big house here, crammed with history and memories. I don't want to wait until I'm doddery and decrepit before I start sorting through it. And if anything happens to me, I loathe the idea of strangers pawing their way through my possessions. I also want – *need* – someone to know the story. Of this house. Of my family. Now feels like the time to tell it.'

'To put in a book?'

'Goodness me, no. I tell my stories through pictures, not words.'

'So why didn't you explain to those women that you're hiring me to help you sort through the house, get things ready in case the worst happens?'

'Because it's none of their business.'

'Okay.'

She shook her head. 'And because some of this story isn't pleasant, or easy to remember. I don't want people sniffing about, asking questions or spreading gossip. I don't want Harriet Langford's story intruding onto Hattie Hood, and the lovely life I've created for her here. I want to sort it, then neatly pack it away once we've finished, and carry on. That's why I haven't asked Lizzie or Gideon to help. They've got enough to do.'

'You've mentioned Lizzie a few times. Is she family?'

Hattie smiled. 'I wish. Although if she was, she might not get away with bossing me about so much. Lizzie is my assistant. She sorts my schedules and classes, emails and admin, as well as cleaning, shopping and making sure I remember to eat. She relishes a long to-do list, is an all-round genius and I'd be lost without her. She also loves to talk, especially about her famous employer, which is another reason I don't want her knowing why you're here.'

'She thinks we're writing a book as well, then?'

'She does.'

'And Gideon?'

Her whole face lit up. 'He *is* family. My cousin. His mother, Agnes, was married to my uncle, Chester. Chester died a long time ago, but Agnes and Gideon live in the boathouse.'

I remembered the arrow pointing to the boathouse on the sign near the entrance.

'You don't think they'd want to help? Or to hear the family story?'

'Potentially. But Agnes is seventy-eight, and suffers from terrible arthritis, amongst other ailments. On top of caring for his mother, Gideon runs his own business.' She stood up, taking our now empty plates and loading them into the dishwasher. 'Besides, Chester was my father's brother. Riverbend belonged to my mother's family. My father chose to be the villain in this story. Gideon won't hear that pathetic tale until he has to.'

She opened the fridge and stared at the contents until I got up and pointed out the individual pavlovas that had been sitting beside the fajita containers. Once we'd refilled our glasses and were savouring the chewy meringue, topped with vanilla cream and what Hattie informed me were local bilberries, she got down to business.

'So, now that you've had a chance to recover from the Changelings, what do you think? Will you stay and help me? Do you need to ask more questions first, or negotiate a contract? I'm open to offers. Money isn't really an issue.'

I had a dozen more questions simmering in my brain. None of them about the project, or the contract. If Hattie had intended to lure me in with a mysterious story, it had worked. And the prospect of spending a few weeks in a place not drenched in sadness and loss was a powerful draw.

As for Hattie, money wasn't really an issue for me, either. I'd bought my motorhome outright, and had a nice cushion of savings, thanks to Ezra's advice. While working with wealthier clients allowed me to help people who couldn't afford to pay me, it certainly wasn't going to make or break my decision.

'I'd love to stay and am happy to accept your terms. I'll email a draft contract tomorrow for you to go over, and you can send your non-disclosure form. I've signed them before, it's not a problem.'

'Oh, now that's perfect. I'm so pleased.' She looked me right in the eyes. 'I have a feeling Riverbend is just what you need.'

3

I was greeted the next morning by soft rays of late winter sunshine, peeping around the edge of Hattie Hood pheasant-print curtains as if hoping to be invited in. Muffin opened one eye from her usual position, curled around my feet, but the bed was so deliciously cosy, the surroundings so restful, that I couldn't resist snuggling back down under the enormous quilt.

While showing me around the house the night before, Hattie mentioned that she had therapy sessions throughout today, Friday, so I had the luxury of some time to settle in. We'd arranged to meet once she'd finished, at five-thirty. After a quick peek in the living room, she'd continued the tour with a spacious office containing two desks, floor-to-ceiling shelves displaying a vast array of Hattie Hood merchandise, and all the usual office equipment. There was a formal dining room, a sunroom with a grand piano and a boot room, utility room and a snug. One staircase led to the main therapy studio and a smaller space where Hattie worked on her designs. Another flight of stairs in the middle of the house ended in a hallway leading to both Hattie's bedroom and the guest suite, including a bathroom bigger than my entire motorhome. A narrower flight of stairs led from this floor up to the attic rooms, which Hattie promised to show me another time.

After fetching in some essentials, I'd spent an hour in a sunken Jacuzzi bath before climbing into the four-poster bed. I'd stayed in several large houses over the years. Some of them draughty, or stuffy, or somehow both at the same time. Others full of sleek, shiny edges, or creaky and crumbling. One or two had been lovely, the kind of house I might dream about if I ever dared to dream again. But Riverbend was different from all of those. It was like a hug in house form. Peaceful and comforting. Light and fresh yet cosy and sumptuous. My bedroom was full of welcoming touches – a patterned bowl brimming with chocolates on one bedside table, a matching one containing dog treats on the other. Not just the basic toiletries but a whole hamper including face packs, skin treatments and scented candles. Beside a kettle and coffee machine on an oak chest of drawers, a tin of homemade shortbread was tucked in with the tea, coffee pods and luxury hot chocolate.

Once I'd dragged myself out of bed, I sat in a squishy tweed armchair wearing the fur-lined socks I'd found on the bed, a soft, woollen blanket over my knees, and wept, clutching a mug of Earl Grey as I gazed through my tears at the fields and forest beyond the sash window. Why did this haven cause me to cry, for the first time in so long? Perhaps it was the bone-deep weariness from years spent trying to ease other people's suffering. Or because this place had dislodged memories of the time when loneliness was an alien concept and home was taken for granted, along with yet another jolt of awareness that my current way of living was not normal, or easy. I had missed being loved and cared for with an ache that reverberated deep inside.

I wondered if the warmth of this beautiful place could start to melt the sheet of ice I'd carefully constructed around my heart.

That thought was terrifying and wonderful at the same time.

For the first time in forever, I dared to think I might be brave enough to linger long enough to find out.

* * *

I couldn't linger too long today however, despite how much I savoured the fluffy robe, fancy tea and moment of emotional self-indulgence. Muffin had been increasingly restless, wondering whether there was going to be any breakfast. She had now resorted to resting her head on my knee, staring up with a look that conveyed how utterly, wretchedly starving she was.

I changed into jeans and a dark-red jumper and headed downstairs, cringing slightly at how formal I'd looked the night before compared to Hattie's jeans. I'd left Muffin's food in the boot room, beside Flapjack's things. By the time she'd gobbled down her bowl of kibble, the house was still quiet, so we slipped through the front door and I fetched my walking boots and a grey corduroy jacket from the motorhome.

'I know!' I grinned at my dog, who was skipping with excitement at the thought of meeting a Sherwood Forest squirrel. 'Isn't this amazing?'

The air was clear and still, carrying the faintest hint of spring, and it was impossible not to feel a fizz of anticipation at the potential adventures ahead.

We walked across the gravel at the front of the house in the opposite direction to the archway we'd driven through, towards the treeline in the distance. Beyond the driveway, a footpath led across a lawn to an iron gate in another wall. A sign by the gate read that this was the kitchen garden, which didn't seem like the best place to take a dog bursting with pent-up energy, so we continued on. After a minute or so, the wall curved around, leading us past a large greenhouse and a rickety outbuilding. As soon as I rounded the curve, I had to stop at the view in front of me. With it being February, the trees were mostly bare and the undergrowth scrubby, the ground more mud than grass, but winding through the midst of it all was the river. Not great or grand but sparkling and burbling with joy as it carried along the rain from the night before in a wide arc that must have inspired the house's name. I let Muffin off the lead and she raced to where the bank formed a small beach area. While she spent a glorious few minutes splashing in the shallow water lapping against the sandy dirt, ignoring the ducks quacking at her from the safety of the deeper water, I took the opportunity to soak up the surroundings and take a few deep breaths of countryside air.

Once she'd got herself thoroughly sopping, I called Muffin on, and we turned to see where the river would take us. The forest lined the far bank, so we'd need a bridge or a boat to reach it. The riverside footpath led in either direction and I assumed that one of them must end up at the boathouse that Hattie had mentioned. I'd prefer to avoid stumbling onto her aunt's property, but the bushes and trees prevented me from seeing anything beyond the river's bend.

'Which way next, then?' I asked Muffin, her guess as good as mine. Better, given her powerful nose. She trotted off and I ambled behind, watching my step as I squelched along the muddy footpath, while also trying to keep one eye on the stunning river and trees beyond.

It was so peaceful here, the only interruption the occasional bird call, the only creatures in sight a squirrel darting up the trunk of a chestnut tree to escape Muffin, and another cluster of ducks sailing past. The questions about Hattie's project and the more troubling ones that had surfaced during my crying session earlier softly sank back into my mind's murky depths as my senses relished the wonderful feast of nature.

As another bend emerged up ahead, I decided we should probably turn around and start heading back. However, at that same moment, Muffin stopped her detailed investigation of a clump of reeds, stuck her nose in the air, then suddenly darted forwards, whizzing down the path to where it veered out of sight. I tried calling her back a couple of times, but once her hunting instinct locked onto something, it was almost impossible to change her mind.

Praying she'd merely sniffed another squirrel or a rabbit nearby, but aware it could be something else, I followed, picking up speed until I ended up hurtling around a large rhododendron bush too fast to spot the giant puddle hidden on the other side. Or to see the man, sensibly skirting around the edge of it.

It took three galumphing strides before I skidded to a stop, right in the deepest part of the puddle, my arms windmilling as I fought to stay upright.

Of course, three strides were more than enough in half a foot of water to splatter both me and the man with thick, brown sludge.

I sploshed around to face him, cringing in embarrassment, but before I could utter an apology, two dogs came racing out of the undergrowth, the smaller one jumping up at the man, covering his jeans in pawprints, the larger one launching itself at me, knocking me straight onto my backside in the freezing water.

'Flapjack!' the man ordered. 'Get off her!'

Flapjack was about as obedient in that moment as Muffin, who, having said a thorough hello to the stranger, proceeded to join her enormous friend, now pushing his nose into my face while trying to climb onto my submerged lap.

I was a micro-wobble away from tumbling flat on my back when, to my relief, the man grabbed Flapjack and somehow managed to yank him out of the puddle. A moment later, he did the same for me, only holding my hands rather than the scruff of my neck.

It was as I lurched to my feet, taking a few stumbling steps onto slightly drier land, that it happened. I jerked to an abrupt stop about eight inches in front of him, his hands still gripping mine. He was a fair bit taller than my five foot five, but was bending slightly, presumably for balance, and as my head tipped up, our eyes met.

Honestly? If he weren't holding my hands, I might have toppled back into the mud.

I'd never believed in anything as fanciful as love at first sight.

Lust at first sight – I knew what *that* felt like, and it wasn't this.

The jolt that ripped through me when this person's eyes – the exact same blue and brown flecks as the February river behind us – hit mine was far deeper than a physical reaction, mere chemicals spurting into my bloodstream.

This was everything the sappy paperbacks that my sister had devoured as a teenager described. My knees turned to water. Breath stuck in my chest. My heart began pounding like a jackhammer. But my head? My head felt clearer than it had in months. Years.

It was a *knowing*. A realisation. As if I'd been waiting to look into those eyes all my life.

And in that crazy, all-consuming moment, I could swear that those eyes had been waiting for me.

We stood there, for endless seconds, until the stranger suddenly snapped back to reality, dropping both my hands and taking a swift few steps back until he bumped against the rhododendron.

'I'm so sorry... the dog... you're covered...' He waved one hand at my legs.

I glanced down before looking up again, but didn't need to confirm that I was, indeed, covered from the waist down in freezing cold, filthy water. It had already seeped through my jeans and, if I wasn't mistaken, soaked right on through my knickers. I took in his dark, slightly reddish hair, short at the sides but long enough on top to form thick waves. He looked a few years older than me, perhaps late thirties, and his face bore rugged features that gave the impression he'd spent his whole life up and down this river. He wasn't blandly handsome, at least in the classical sense, but the curve of his mouth and the creases framing his eyes were kind. It was a gentle face. I could have stood there staring at it for hours.

'You haven't come off much better.' I nodded to his own legs, almost black up to the knees, and it was his turn to glance at the splotches all over his dark-green jacket and his dirt-streaked hands.

'Besides, I think we started it. Muffin must have caught Flapjack's scent and gone to find him.' I turned to where both dogs now sat watching us, their heads cocked in curiosity. 'This is Flapjack from Riverbend? Hattie's dog?'

A slightly daft question, considering the likelihood of two giant, curly-haired dogs having the same name.

He nodded. 'And you must be Sophie?'

For a fraction of a moment, I half wondered if he knew my name by some sort of divine destiny, before rationality reasserted itself and I realised that if he was with Flapjack, then Hattie must have told him about me.

'Yes.' I tried to smile, but the discomfort of an ice-cold backside meant it turned into more of a grimace.

'You're the historian, come to help Hattie write a book?' he asked, sounding genuinely interested. I was managing to maintain a smidgin of composure by avoiding his eyes, but his voice was almost as bad – or should I say, as good. Deep and mellow, it was a story-teller's voice. A lullaby voice that lapped over me like a warm bath.

I didn't want to lie to that voice, those eyes. I might never see this man again, but I didn't want a single word I said to him to be marred by deception.

'We're going to look at Riverbend's history together, yes.'

Before he could reply, my phone rang. Wiping a hand on my jumper, I retrieved it from the tiny shoulder bag I used on dog walks. It was Ezra. I was tempted to let it ring, but the man smiled, nodded goodbye and started walking away, so I figured I might as well answer, rather than leave my friend worrying.

'You're still alive, then?' he asked, with a hint of grumpiness because I hadn't messaged him yet, and it was nearly midday.

'Just about.'

'What? What does that mean?'

'Hang on.' I sent a quick selfie, focussing on my waist down.

'We met Hattie's dog Flapjack on our walk along the river. He's like an overenthusiastic grizzly bear, and I happened to be in the middle of a puddle when he decided to say hello.'

'I hope she was suitably apologetic!' Ezra, who was understandably protective towards me, didn't see the funny side. 'And will replace the clothes if you can't get them clean.'

'Oh no, Hattie wasn't with him. It was... a man.'

'What man?'

'Um...'

My stomach concertinaed as I realised I didn't know who he was. That was better, though. I'd carefully curated my whole life around not developing strong feelings for anyone beyond Ezra and his family, who it was too late not to love. Seeing that man again, getting to know him, could only complicate things in the worst possible way. I was happy to go on the odd date or three if I met someone I found fun and attractive. But if there was even a hint that things could end up deeper than a casual fling, I stayed well away. It was too risky. My battered heart simply couldn't take it.

'Anyway, the house is amazing, and in the most incredible setting. It's so tranquil. Exactly what I need after three weeks in the Dumble warzone.'

'And the client, Harriet, she's okay?'

I gestured to Muffin and we started walking back towards the house, my jeans squelching with every step. 'She's Hattie Hood!'

'Hattie who?'

'The artist who makes all those expensive designs for pottery and things. Ask Naomi – you've got a Hattie Hood teapot. She seems really nice, though. Very open and friendly.'

I went on to describe how Hattie wanted to get her affairs and possessions in order, in case anything happened to her, that she was conscious of her mother's early death and didn't have any family apart from an elderly aunt and her son, so preferred to use someone impartial.

Reassured, Ezra made me promise for the millionth time to keep in touch.

'Let me know when you find out who that man is.'

'Excuse me?'

I could hear him laughing down the line. 'And whether he's single. I've not heard that tone in your voice for a long time.'

'Oh, go away. You're not my dad.'

'I prefer older and much cooler brother.'

'Fine. I'll speak to you soon, then, bro.'

'You do that, little sis. Take care.'

I hurried up to the house as fast as was possible when caked in mud, and opted for the boot-room entrance, rather than the front door. Slipping off my walking boots, I hovered for a second, wondering if I dared remove my trousers as well, but as my hand drifted to the jean button, the door to the main hallway whipped open, revealing a young woman brandishing a stapler.

'Who are you?' she barked. 'And what are you doing in here?'

While I took an instinctive step backwards at the sight of her fierce glare and aggressive stapler snapping, Muffin had no such qualms. The woman couldn't help but be seduced by the soggy ball of fluff bestowing her the honour of a full-body wag. Once she'd lowered her weapon and given Muffin's floppy ears a good scratch, I'd recovered my composure.

'I'm Sophie. I'm staying here at the moment.'

'Sophie!' The woman's eyes widened in recognition. 'Hattie said you'd be here at five-thirty. I thought you were a deranged fan. We get them from time to time, but Hattie refuses to fix the main gates, because at least then we can see them coming. She thinks that otherwise they'll sneak through the garden. Which did happen once, to be fair. Gideon wants her to get a proper fence all the way around, but apparently that would block the view and stifle her creativity. And at the end of the day, that's what pays our salaries, so we can't argue.'

'Right.'

'I thought you'd be older, to be honest. I was imagining that woman who does history on the telly. The one with long, grey hair.'

'I don't have a television.'

'She's a lot... frumpier. You're...' she paused, as if seeing me properly for the first time '...in a right state. Did you fall in the river?'

'Flapjack knocked me into a puddle.'

She gave a loud huff, rolling her eyes. 'That dog! Hattie's arty-farty, "be wild and free" philosophy is all very well when it comes to people, but dogs need discipline. If you wait, I'll fetch a robe and we can stick your clothes straight in the wash. There'll be a towel in here somewhere for this gorgeous girl, who I'm sure is far better behaved than our wildebeest.'

'Are you Lizzie?' I dared to ask as she took a faded towel out of a cupboard and started rubbing Muffin's coat, my dog nuzzling closer in ecstasy.

'The one and only.' Lizzie grinned up at me.

'To be honest, I'd assumed you'd be older, too.'

'What, like one of those old-school, busybody secretaries that keep everything running behind the scenes, and know far more than their boss does?' Lizzie was anything but frumpy. Her jet-black hair was cut in a blunt bowl chop, so bad it must be ultra-fashionable. She wore a tiny, leather skirt, a furry, pink jumper revealing a bellybutton piercing in the shape of a spider, and fishnet knee-socks. I'd guess her age to be about twenty-five.

'I just got the impression you'd been around forever.'

'I've been around since I was fourteen, so nearly half my life.' Her vigorous rubbing eased to a gentle pat. 'I got sent here for art therapy, with the full intention of raising hell so Hattie would be forced to give up on me, just like everyone else had. I spent weeks trying to fight her, but she refused to engage, simply turned every attack into an opportunity to "art it out" as she calls it. By the end of the course I was back in school, off drugs and almost managing to keep out of trouble. She offered me a job, helping her with social media and stuff like that.' She shrugged. 'It turns out I was awesome at organising, so the rest is history. And yes, I am like one of those secretaries. I know Hattie Hood better than she does.' Lizzie straightened up, her eyes sharpening with a look that appeared far more perceptive than her chattering implied. 'Harriet Langford is a whole other matter. Which is why you're here, I suppose.'

'She said you were too busy to help with the house project.'

'That's true. She could have told me about it before this morning, though. Anyway.' She shook her head, her smile returning as quickly as it had vanished. 'You're shivering. I'll get you that robe.'

4

Once I was clean and dry, I joined Lizzie for giant Hattie Hood mugs of butterbean soup and crusty bread. She talked about her husband, Joss, who she lived with in Middlebeck, and their rescue hens, Cher, Celine and Whitney. I didn't mind her stream of chatter. It avoided too many questions about me. Some of them I might be willing to answer. Most of them I definitely wouldn't. I might be living here for the next few weeks, but this was business, not a holiday or friends hanging out, and, as always, I would keep things professional.

After lunch, I spent half the afternoon researching both Harriet Langford and Hattie Hood on the Internet, and reading the forms she emailed over. The other half was an unplanned nap thanks to conducting the research on my ridiculously comfy bed.

At five twenty-five, I hurried downstairs to meet Hattie in the living room. Passing the open kitchen door, I couldn't help pausing for a second when I thought I saw the man from this morning in there. I'd be lying if I said he'd not been loitering in my head. A swift second look revealed that I hadn't imagined it

– he was leaning against the worktop, talking to Lizzie. Our eyes met, and it happened again. A zap of electricity that locked our gaze into place while those blue eyes dived into the very depths of my being.

Dammit.

Whatever this attraction was, it had to stop. Immediately.

I gave my rebellious hormones a sharp slap and hurried on to the safety of the living room.

'Ah, Sophie. How was your day?' Hattie was already there, sitting on a wide sofa with a tray of drinks and cake on the table in front of her. Flapjack was snoozing in a patch of sunshine by the full-length window, so Muffin mooched over to join him. 'Apart from my terrible dog mugging you, of course,' she added, pouring coffee from a silver pot. 'He can't resist a beautiful woman, but that's no excuse in a court of law, is it?'

'Muffin wasn't any better. It's only because she's a third of Flapjack's size that she got away with it.' I accepted the offered mug, declining milk or sugar, and took a seat on the opposite sofa. 'But it was lovely to meet Lizzie, and I appreciated a quiet afternoon.'

'Quiet only once Lizzie got back to work, I imagine.' Hattie smiled as the door opened again. 'And here she is. Are the others with you?'

Lizzie came to sit beside her boss, allowing 'the others' to enter behind her. I wasn't surprised to see the man from the kitchen, or the elderly woman leaning on his arm. It hadn't struck me immediately because of the age difference but seeing him in the kitchen had convinced me that this was Hattie's cousin, Gideon.

'Gideon, Aunt Agnes, this is Sophie, the person I told you about.'

'Hello again,' Gideon said, with a smile that made my toes

curl up inside their furry socks. He wore a checked shirt with the sleeves rolled up, and when he reached past to pour his mum a coffee, for the first time ever, I found a wrist sexy.

Ugh.

I hated this. I hated him being Gideon. Or at least I wished I did. It would be a lot easier.

'Thank you everyone for taking the time to be here,' Hattie continued, once we all had a drink and a slice of lemon cake. 'I didn't want to bore you with the details until I knew for sure it was going ahead, but I'm delighted that Sophie has agreed to stay for a while to help me put some thoughts together about Riverbend's history. She'll have full access to the whole house, so please be prepared to assist her in whatever way she needs.'

'The whole house?' Lizzie asked, a hint of stiffness behind her smile.

'Yes.' Hattie met her gaze head-on. 'We'll be working on the top floor, but you can message if you need me.'

'Right.'

'Are you sure about this?' Agnes asked, her brow furrowed. 'It's going to be painful, opening up that door again. You don't have to do it just because some book people want a juicy story. It's not as if you need the money.'

'I know it won't be easy,' Hattie replied. 'But I'm ready. Those rooms have loomed above my head long enough. Don't forget I'm a therapist; I do know a bit about processing memories. It's time I took my own counsel. Besides, Sophie's here to support me.'

'I'm not sure how a historian can help with bad memories.' Agnes sniffed. 'I really don't think this is a good idea.'

'Ah, but Sophie isn't any old historian.'

'We're just worried about you,' Lizzie added, chewing a mouthful of cake.

Hattie raised an eyebrow. 'I appreciate your concern, but remembering this can't be as difficult as living through it was. I will be fine. Now, tell me what you think of the cake. The gals are coming over on Sunday and I always feel nervous serving cake to a professional baker.'

To a mixture of my dismay and delight, it became apparent that everyone was staying for dinner. I'd hoped to be finding out more about Hattie's story, which was particularly intriguing now I knew we had painful family memories in common. Instead, the next couple of hours were another sore reminder of quite how unfamiliar fun, friendly conversation had become. Apart from my brief visits home to the farmhouse, I ate my meals alone. Even when I was staying in a client's house, I kept a firm line between work and my personal time. I had no idea how to participate in this lively back and forth.

Three things I discovered over the course of that meal.

Food tasted infinitely better when eaten in good company, surrounded by laughter and witty comebacks.

Hattie loved her family, including Lizzie, who she called 'my heart's daughter', with a passion that stabbed in my guts like a carving knife.

The terrifying, heart-melting longing I felt for gentle, charming Gideon Langford was going to be a big problem.

I gobbled up a slice of leftover lemon cake for dessert, gulped down a decaffeinated coffee and got the heck out of there as soon as was decently possible.

Hattie had one more clanger to drop as I left.

'Oh, Gideon, I'm tied up with a meeting all morning tomorrow. Can I trust you to show Sophie around the grounds without her coming back encrusted in slime?'

'It would be my pleasure.' Gideon smiled his ten-thousand-watt smile, his perfect, river eyes sparkling on mine. I whipped my gaze to Hattie, certain that if anyone caught me looking at Gideon, they'd instantly spot his effect on me.

'You really don't have to. Hattie told me how busy you are with your business,' I mumbled, making no sense due to staring at Hattie while speaking to him. 'I don't mind exploring by myself.'

'It's Saturday tomorrow, I'm not working. I'll meet you here at ten.'

'Perfect!' Hattie said, winking unashamedly at Lizzie and Agnes.

Oh, dear.

5

I slept the fitful sleep of the horribly infatuated, finally giving up and watching the sunrise with a mug of tea, curled in the tartan chair with Muffin on my lap. After another foolish hour or so getting ready for a guided tour with a man I vehemently didn't want to like me, swapping my jeans for practically identical jeans more times than any woman should stoop to, it was nearly eight-thirty, which I decided was a not-too-unsociable time for a guest to be up and about.

I was eating raisin toast with butter and distracting myself with a local newspaper I'd found on the worktop when Hattie appeared an hour later. She wore skinnier, less scruffy jeans today, along with a plain white T-shirt and patterned headscarf to hold back her grey curls. She looked effortlessly stylish.

'Morning!' After jabbing impatiently at the button on the coffee machine, she began dolloping yoghurt into a bowl while waiting for the liquid to appear. 'I don't mean to be rude, but my Zoom started five minutes ago. I'm allowed to be a little late, given my artistic temperament, but keep this big-headed twonk of an account manager waiting too long and he'll become extra contrary. I wouldn't care, except that everything he says makes me want to jab a paintbrush up his hairy nostril and I want this over with as soon as possible.'

She sighed, deftly sprinkling raspberries on the yogurt. 'I hate it when Lizzie schedules in meetings on the weekend. She did it on purpose because she loathes the twonk even more than I do. Anyway, enjoy your guided tour. Let's meet back here for lunch, and after that, we can venture to the top floor.'

Hattie whirled out of the room with her breakfast.

At ten to ten, the front door opened and a moment later, Gideon walked in.

'Hey.' He broke into a grin when he saw me fidgeting at the table. 'Have you been waiting for me?'

'Enjoying a leisurely breakfast while I catch up on the Sherwood Forest gossip.'

'A perfect start to the weekend. Are you all caught up, or should I get a drink while you finish off?'

'No.' I got up, clearing away my empty pots. 'Reading about those stolen goats is more than enough drama for one day. Let's go.'

We started by heading to the kitchen garden I'd walked past the day before. It was overcast today, with wisps of early morning mist still lingering, the shimmering droplets clinging to our hair. Gideon paused to open the iron gate.

'This is one of my favourite places in Riverbend. It's not much to look at in February, but if you're still here in the summer, it's more colourful than Hattie's studio.'

We wandered up and down the raised beds, past clusters of pots and patches of peaty earth. Gideon pointed out the different plants, and the bare spaces where bulbs and seeds slept beneath the soil. There were leeks and cauliflower, and he slipped a handful of herbs into a paper bag then tucked them into his rucksack. A greenhouse stood in one corner, although the anaemic sunshine barely made any difference to the temperature inside. In here were salad leaves, rows of baby seedlings and a shelf containing seed packets.

'You know a lot about these plants. Do you spend much time here?' I asked as Gideon added a sprinkle of water to a tray of tiny shoots.

'Well, yes.' He stuck both hands in his jeans pockets and scanned the greenhouse like a king surveying his kingdom. 'I work here.' He squinted. 'That's why Hattie asked me to show you around.'

Ah. Okay. Of course that's why.

'You're a gardener?'

He nodded. 'I take care of the whole estate, and a few other gardens in the village. Do some landscaping from time to time, too.'

'When did you move to Riverbend?'

We left the greenhouse and made our way to another gate, on the opposite side of the garden to where we'd entered.

'About six years ago. We were in Lancaster before that. I worked for a landscaping firm, but didn't get much pleasure from short-term projects. I always wanted to be a farmer. Tending the same patch of earth for decades. Seeing the seasons come and go, and working on plans that take time, and patience, but yield the most satisfying results when they come to fruition.' He pulled a wry smile. 'I had this dream that I'd create a place I could leave to my kids one day. That they could live and work and raise families on the same land, surrounded by the trees I'd planted and fields I'd farmed.'

'That's incredible.' I had to turn away as we crossed a scraggly meadow, startled by the tears in my eyes.

'Yeah, well. The dream ended with a spectacularly bad break-up, so when Hattie offered us the boathouse, given Mum's health, it seemed like the next best thing. I still get to tend family land, even if it's only family through marriage. Hattie gives me pretty much free rein, for fear of "quenching my creative gardening spirit". It's pretty special, helping things thrive and flourish.' He ran a hand over his head, as if embarrassed. 'Anyway. I've clearly spent too much time with an art therapist. I like growing food, the end.'

'I understand completely. Planting a seed, watching it sprout and shoot and then, one day, become something beautiful. Or tasty.' My words grew softer, as I remembered. 'I used to love that, too.'

'Used to?' He looked at me, waiting for me to elaborate, but my throat was too clogged up with grief to say any more. All I could do was shrug and dab at my eyes, offering a watery smile so he didn't think I was completely pathetic.

'Where next?' I croaked, after an awkward moment of struggling to pull myself together. Not that Gideon seemed awkward; he merely watched with that gentle face, forehead creased in concern.

'The chapel.' He turned, taking the hint that we were moving on, and nodded at the tiny building up ahead, nestled between weeping willows, the river coiling behind it.

'It's gorgeous.'

It really was. A pretty, pale-pink brick construction, about the size of a double garage, with a white roof and a stubby, slightly crooked spire, it looked like a baby chapel, still needing to grow into itself.

'Is it old?'

'Built around the same time as the house, in 1920, so by rural chapel standards, it's brand new.'

The heavy door opened with a creak and we crept inside, the dogs padding across the stone floor behind us. The gloomy day cast the five rows of pews and simple table and chair in shadow, but, despite a carved wooden picture being the only adornment, the atmosphere wasn't dour.

'It's so peaceful.' It was impossible not to speak in a hushed voice. 'As if the simplicity stops it feeling heavy, or too sombre.'

Gideon nodded. 'Hattie calls it her saving grace.'

'She still uses it?'

That explained the lack of dust and the set of charcoal pencils on one windowsill.

'It's a great place to hide from overenthusiastic assistants.' He gave a brief smile. 'Or let go of a day spent immersed in other peoples' traumas.'

'I can imagine.' I could have done with a saving grace once or twice.

He frowned. 'She's been here quite often lately. I keep suggesting she needs a holiday, but she insists there's no place she'd rather be.'

We moved on, turning back along the river until we reached the boathouse, a quaint cottage with a small garden surrounded by a waist-high hedge.

'This is our place,' he said, stopping to point at a turquoise door, decorated with a tiny rowing boat. 'That's the front door. Please come and knock on it whenever you like.'

'I thought you were supposed to be busy,' I said, staring at my feet, the hedge, my dog... anything but those eyes.

'I can be. But my mum isn't. She had to give up driving and struggles to walk as far as the village. She knows I'm happy to take her, but she's always felt a bit reticent with the villagers, like the Langfords' impoverished relative, forced to accept their charity, and she can be the same with Hattie.

Someone new to have a cup of tea with would be really good for her.'

'Okay. When I have time, I'd love to visit.'

'Really?' He glanced at me, eyebrow raised.

'In my line of work, I spend a lot of time with older people. Most of them sad or struggling. I've got quite good at helping lift their spirits a bit and enjoy hearing their stories.'

'I'd have thought a historian spent more time researching old documents than with actual people.'

'Well... I do a lot of that, too.' If old documents included birth certificates, and wills, or faded love letters.

'Why are they sad and struggling? Do you specialise in tragedies? I know Hattie's had her ups and downs, but her story has a happy ending.'

I pretended to be distracted by Muffin, who was innocently sniffing a tree stump, feeling a rush of frustration that Hattie insisted I lied about all this.

In the end, I merely shrugged. 'I suppose that's just how it's seemed lately.'

We were almost back at the kitchen garden, although here Gideon followed the wall further away from the river. We passed a scruffy tennis court then cut through a wooded area with a fire pit and various structures that Gideon informed me were the sculptures some of Hattie's clients had created. These ranged from a miniature house made out of woven twigs to what looked to my uncultured eyes to be a lump of rocks piled in a random heap.

'And lastly, my absolute favourite corner of Riverbend.' He picked up his pace. 'Again, it's nothing compared to later in the spring, but I've been working on it for a few years now and have managed to make it worth a look all year round.'

We came to another high brick wall. This time the door was

solid wood, painted in what I would forever think of as River-bend blue. That was how I didn't realise until it was too late.

'After you.' Gideon held the door open with one arm, bowing slightly.

I expected to enter another garden, but instead, the door led into a sort of large summer house, what was sometimes called an orangery. Both walls stretching off either side and the roof consisted of panes of glass held in wooden frames, with square pillars down the centre. But I barely noticed that.

While most of the raised beds contained mere stems, or bare branches winding up trellises and wooden arbours spaced along the smaller aisles, I recognised them instantly.

February should have been safe. I should know; I was once a professional, after all. But the gardener standing behind me had somehow, in the humid warmth of this summer house, created an environment where my deadliest enemy could flourish even in winter.

There. A few metres away. A row of palest pink, peach, and yellow roses.

A second later, the scent hit me and with it, as always, the memories, rising like bile in the back of my throat.

I spun around, pushing past Gideon's confusion, and fled, my chocolate-coloured shadow right behind me.

I inherited my love of flowers from my father. We spent countless hours throughout my childhood, shoulder to shoulder in the borders of the garden surrounding our grand Victorian home in Birmingham. It was our time, time that my older sister had no interest in being a part of, preferring to stay indoors with a book or Super Mario. We grew all sorts, from grumpy-looking pansies to merry sunflowers, but our favourites were the roses.

Dad used to tell me, as we planted and pruned, how he brought my mum a bunch of white roses from his garden on their first date. He'd clutched them so tightly when he first saw her that he'd bled onto the cuff of his best shirt. As she'd dabbed at the scratch with her tissue, their eyes had met and that was the moment they knew it was forever. She dreamed of tending to all of his wounds. He pictured a garden full of roses that he'd gather into bouquets on her birthdays, anniversaries and simply because he loved her.

So it was an obvious step at eighteen to get a job with a local florist. I enjoyed working in the little shop, walking to work and coming home to my family at the end of each day. But my passion was for bigger things. I spent hours poring over everything from botanical encyclopaedias to wedding magazines. Larger businesses were starting to set up websites back then, and I would hijack the family computer, searching for inspiration to fill my sketchbooks. A week before my twentieth birthday, I got an apprenticeship with an exclusive event florist, and it was the best present I could have wished for.

The only downside was that it was based in Leeds, a three-hour drive away. Leaving behind my parents, the sister who was also my best friend, and our beloved garden was a wrench, but moving into a crumbling terrace with three students was totally worth it. I spent the next two years working six, often seven days a week. When a lavish event was coming up, we toiled well into the night in order to produce the most stunning, intricate arrangements with only the freshest of blooms. I visited flower farms, and both the New Covent Garden Flower Market and the famous Royal FloraHolland in Amsterdam. I attended lectures and practical tutorials on botany, business and design, soaking it all up like a peony in the sunshine.

Occasionally, I found time to squeeze in a social life. I had a couple of relationships, one with an intern at the florist's, another a friend of my housemates, but I was far too focussed on my career for them to last.

Life was busy and exhausting but I loved every second of it. The only downside was constantly missing my family. We spoke several times a week and visited each other whenever we could, but it wasn't nearly often enough.

Then, to top it all off, my sister, Lilly, got engaged. And while, yes, I was happy that she was going to be married to Chris, who we all adored, and looking forward to being a bridesmaid, what kept a smile on my face for eight months straight was being asked to do her wedding flowers.

My first independent commission. I wouldn't earn any money from it – both because it was my sister, and also my contract forbade any paid work on the side. But I would get to create the loveliest, most beautiful bouquets to grace St Gilbert's church. I would design them to match Lilly and Chris perfectly.

And I would use white roses, grown in my family's garden, nurtured by my father and inspired by my mother.

Until one morning, as I gathered my ideas together, every surface in my shabby kitchen piled high with flowers, the whole house drenched in the fragrance of my fondest memories, of my sister's future, waiting for my family to arrive, so eager to show them the love I'd poured into the designs filling my sketchbook, my phone rang.

My hand gripped an Avalanche rose as I listened to the words that in one horrific, heart-shattering moment changed everything. This time, there was nobody to blot the blood that trickled down a thorn-pierced palm.

That summer, I weaved together three bouquets. I blended lilies with pink astrantia and softest baby's breath, watered with my tears.

I laid them on three coffins.

There were no roses in St Gilbert's church that day.

6

With a deliberate effort to keep my chin up and stride purposeful, I left the sanctuary of my bedroom and made my way to the kitchen. I'd waited until one o'clock, working on the basis that, after having breakfast at well past nine, Hattie wouldn't be eating lunch too early. I was banking on Gideon having lunch with his mum, dreading the thought of seeing him after running away earlier. It had taken a good hour in my bedroom to shake off the panic and compose myself, forcing my mind to focus on an antiques podcast.

I made a coffee, opened the fridge and wondered about helping myself to leftover soup from the day before, but when thirty minutes later Hattie hadn't arrived, I decided to go and look for her. After scouting around most of the downstairs, I eventually came to the office, tapping on the door before poking my head in.

Hattie was slumped over her desk, face completely hidden in the tumble of curls. I would have been alarmed, if she hadn't immediately produced a hearty snore and Flapjack weren't peacefully snoozing on a futon in the corner. Deciding that we weren't well enough acquainted yet for me to wake her up in person, I employed an old trick I first used with one fiercely proud older man who found it impossible to sleep in bed after his wife passed away but seemed to find the tone of my voice perfect for dropping off to.

Moving quietly back to the kitchen, I pulled out my phone.

'Hello?' Hattie's voice was croaky with sleep, but I pretended not to notice.

'Hi, it's Sophie. I was wondering what time you wanted to meet.'

'Oh. Um. We said lunchtime, didn't we?' She stopped to clear her throat. 'Is one okay?'

'It's actually almost two, now.'

'What?'

There was a short pause with some rustling in the background. 'I lost track of time. Sorry, Sophie. It's my most annoying habit, getting absorbed in my ideas.'

'No problem. I'm at your disposal, and it's no chore to wait in such beautiful surroundings.'

'That's very kind of you. Oh, and speaking of which, how did your tour go? No! Don't answer that. I'll see you in the kitchen asap.'

After another apology, we heated up the soup and made sandwiches with thick slices of rustic bread and crumbly cheese.

That's not quite true. I made lunch, Hattie faffed about rearranging the fruit bowl, did a quick sketch of a hare on an old envelope, and set the table.

We chatted about the grounds, and the projects Gideon had been working on, and she asked a dozen questions about living in a motorhome, all of which I answered factually, and to the point.

'How long have you lived like this?'

'Seven years. Once I went from helping out friends of friends to a proper business, visiting strangers, I needed a car and a place to stay. Finding hotels or an Airbnb was a pain when I didn't know how long I'd be there, and living out of a suitcase soon grew frustrating, so a motorhome seemed like the perfect option. Even better once I'd got Muffin.'

'Hmm.' She picked up her sandwich. 'You must have been young. You did very well to be able to make such a significant purchase.'

I knew full well what she was hinting at. However, unlike the usual prickle of discomfort, there was something about Hattie that made it easy to answer her.

'I'd inherited some money.'

Her aquamarine eyes watched me for a few seconds, as if taking in far more than my words. 'Well, it sounds like you made a very solid investment. In my wandering days, mobile homes used to turn me green with envy. I hope you'll let me have a snoop inside at some point.'

'Of course.' I smiled, grateful for her tact. 'I'm not sure Flapjack would squeeze in there, though. He might have to watch us through the window.'

'Oh, that monster always finds a way!' She laughed.

Once we'd eaten and made a pot of tea, Hattie invited me to follow her up to the top floor.

We climbed a creaking wooden staircase with a faded carpet running down the middle. At the top was a heavy door with an iron lock that Hattie opened with a key clasped in a quaking hand.

'Are you okay?' I asked as she gripped the door handle before pausing, chest rising sharply as her eyes squeezed shut.

After a weighty moment, she gave a firm nod, eyes opening

again with a glimmer of determination. 'I've not crossed this threshold since the renovators moved everything up here, when I first came back in 2006.'

'How long had you been away?'

She sighed. 'Sixteen years. In many ways, a lifetime. But that story is for another day. If we don't start at the beginning, none of the rest will make sense. Come on, let's do it.'

She twisted the handle and the door swung open with an ominous squeak.

Entering the room was like stepping back through time, the only clue the room had been abandoned for so long being the clouds of dust motes swirling in the beam from the open doorway as Hattie squeezed through piles of boxes to hurriedly pull thick drapes open. I followed suit with the other side of the room, the pale afternoon light shimmering through grimy panes of glass, revealing velvet-effect wallpaper in deep purple and cream, dotted with paintings featuring scenes from the Riverbend grounds.

There was a bedframe with a yellowing mattress, a wardrobe, chest of drawers and dressing table made of ornately carved mahogany that I instantly recognised as valuable. Hattie pointed out two doors on the far side of the room that led to a bathroom and dressing room, and the remaining space was stacked with wooden crates, trunks and plastic boxes, their modernity jarring with the antique furnishings.

'Was this your parents' room?' I asked as Hattie stood motionless, her eyes darting across the contents.

Her mouth twisted up at one side. 'My father considered the attic room for servants. Not that any still lived here when he moved in. His room was below us. After he died, I knocked through into two other bedrooms and a bathroom and rebuilt them as the studio. This was my mother's room.' She moved across to the dressing table, gently stroking her finger through the thick layer of dust. 'She died in this bed, so it was the last place I saw her.'

'I'm so sorry.' If Hattie had been here when her mother died, given how long she'd been away, Hattie must have been fairly young when it happened. How young, I supposed I would find out soon enough.

She turned to me, smile wavering, her face pale. 'Yes, I believe you really are.'

'Would you like a few moments to yourself? I can fetch us both a drink.'

'Oh, my goodness, no! The last thing I want is to face this alone. That's why I invited you here.'

'Okay. Where do we start, then?' I asked, switching to my practical, professional-yet-compassionate work mode.

'Like I said, at the beginning.' Hattie walked over to the trunks, inspecting all three before giving one a decisive pat. 'Here, I think. If you don't mind, I'm going to sit down for a minute. You go ahead and open it up.'

She pulled out the chair that had been neatly tucked under the dressing table, wiped off the worst of the dust with her headscarf and repositioned it in a relatively clear section of patterned carpet beside the bed. I dragged the trunk over so we could both see what I found inside.

After carefully undoing the cracked leather straps, I slowly lifted the lid. Resting on the top was a roughly whittled owl, a pair of binoculars in a stiff case and a small bow with a quiver of arrows. I passed the owl to Hattie, and she cradled it on her knees.

'Ah, yes. This is the one.'

'Did these belong to your father?'

A quick shake of her head.

'Oh, no. His part in the story comes much later. The binoculars were my grandfather's, Cornelius Albert Hood, but we need to go further back than that. What else can you find in there?'

The top layers were knitted blankets, although as I kept digging, I uncovered neatly folded layers of women's clothing, which I laid on the bed for Hattie to inspect closer. It was a mix of practical wear, including jodhpurs and a riding jacket, and elegant dresses and petticoats, all of them very old. Then, about two thirds of the way down, was a package wrapped in tissue paper, crisp with age. Clearing a space on the bed, Hattie tenderly unwrapped and unfolded it.

It was a floor-length, ivory gown, the empire waist and three-quarter-length sleeves embellished with fine lace and intricate beading. More lace edged the ruffled skirt and high neckline.

'Is it a wedding dress?'

She nodded, smoothing out a crease in the bodice. 'It was made for Millicent Hatherstone. The woman who should have been my Grandpa Cornelius's aunt. I'm afraid this whole story is interwoven with heartbreak and loss. But is there anything sadder than a wedding dress doomed to never be worn?' She paused to glance up at me, a rueful smile creasing one corner of her mouth. 'Well, I suppose that depends on who you were going to marry. But again, that's a whole other chapter. *This* is where Riverbend's story begins.'

* * *

Riverbend

Millicent Mabel Hatherstone was born in 1896, in the heart of the forest, at Hatherstone Hall. An only daughter preceded by four brothers, she immediately became the sparkling diamond in a house full of hunting boots and cricket bats. Both her father, Lord Hatherstone's, greatest joy and her mother's closest confidante.

It was perhaps also inevitable that when required to be working on her embroidery or piano practice, Miss Millie-May was generally found by her frazzled nanny up a tree, on a horse or knee-deep in the river. Always accompanying a gaggle of brothers and other boys from the village, to whom she was determined to prove herself equal, despite being at least two years younger and six inches shorter than most of them. And while she could never run quite as fast or throw a ball as far, she won universal admiration for trying.

As one by one her brothers were dispatched off to boarding school, this did nothing to tame Millie-May's wild spirit. She point-blank refused to submit to her highly recommended governess. Instead, she employed increasingly elaborate schemes to sneak off to the village school. The first few times, she perched on a tree branch and spied on the lesson through the window, but was quickly discovered by the schoolmaster, Mr Buckle. There then ensued a heated discussion by the end of which, to Mr Buckle's confusion, he appeared to have been outwitted by a nine-year-old girl. Before he knew what was happening, he'd given up demanding she return home and offered her a seat beside his son, Edgar.

'I don't care if that dullard of a governess canes me every day between now and Christmas,' she pronounced to her parents at breakfast the following morning, the wince as she sat down implying otherwise. 'I won't stay in the house all day. I especially won't if it means listening to her droning on. I'm going to school with my friends and none of you can stop me.'

In the end, they agreed that as long as she achieved top marks, was well mannered in class and otherwise kept out of trouble, Millie-May would attend Hatherstone school. To be fair, she did come top of the class in science, mathematics and history, and Mr Buckle declared her a delight to teach. As for keeping out of trouble... Well. Two out of three was better than nothing. And she'd surely grow out of all this undignified behaviour, wouldn't she?

* * *

'What are we going to do?' Lady Hatherstone wailed, when once again, a fifteen-year-old Millie-May appeared for supper with twigs in her honey-blonde hair and grass stains on her skirts. 'Why hasn't she grown out of this by now? What on earth will become of her?'

'What are we going to do?' Her father would chortle. 'Millie-May is perfectly capable at deciding what she will become, and if you haven't yet learned that nothing we do will make a blind bit of difference, then you're not half as clever as you pretend to be.'

What Millie-May decided to become, she announced on her seventeenth birthday, was the wife of Edgar Buckle, whom she'd been sitting next to in class since that fateful day eight years earlier. It took a full ten days of ranting and raging, a stern letter being sent to Mr Buckle and a very expensive vase thrown through the morning room window before Lord Hatherstone conceded defeat.

Accepting that the marriage would take place either with or without his blessing, confirmed when his wife found two tickets for a passage to New York in her daughter's bridal trousseau, Lord Hatherstone decided that he'd rather give his daughter to a local pipsqueak than lose her forever.

He did, however, quash any ideas about crossing the Atlantic by purchasing Millicent's favourite section of the forest, including the perfect spot for a new house, gifting it to her as an early wedding present.

She would call the house Riverbend.

A week after the final plans were completed, Britain entered the First World War.

Of course her brave and valiant fiancé went off to do his duty, along with all four of the Hatherstone sons and so many of the other boys she'd once scrambled about the forest with. In his absence, Millie-May pressed on with the plans for River-bend, her father helping to oversee the construction of the house while negotiating the numerous obstacles that were the inevitability of war. The main house was finally completed in the spring of 1916.

Millie-May was supposed to be supervising the draperies in the drawing room when the news came from the village. Her father found her on the little riverbank beach, fishing.

Edgar had been injured on the battlefield in France and died the following day. 'Tell Millie I'm sorry I'll not be back for the wedding,' were the last words on his lips.

Of course her parents, the two brothers who made it home and everyone else with an opinion demanded Millicent sell the new house and remain at Hatherstone Hall with her parents until she found another suitor. Preferably one with a title and some land of his own this time.

She moved into Riverbend on her twenty-first birthday, the day she had intended to marry. The first thing she did as mistress of her own estate was to hold a service of remembrance for her beloved in the chapel she'd designed for their wedding.

Six months after the war ended, in May 1919, Millie-May bought another ticket to New York and handed the deeds of Riverbend to Edgar's nephew, Cornelius Hood. The accompanying note read:

Riverbend was built for joy and family, not a heartbroken wife and mother who never was. Fill this place with a lifetime of love and happiness, and all those children whom my beloved and I never got the chance to bear.

Cornelius and Louisa moved in on the day of their wedding: 11 July 1919. Their first son, Edgar, was born a year later, Michael and his younger sister, Verity, in the next few years. Riverbend was at last the family home bustling with joy that Millicent and Edgar had dreamed of. But, while we must hold onto the hope of a happy ending, in this story, tragedy is only ever a chapter away.

7
___

Hattie paused, the hand that had caressed the fabric of the dress throughout her story now coming to rest in her lap as she looked up at me. 'It must be time for a cup of tea and some cake.'

'What about these things?' I asked, feeling uneasy at the thought of leaving such priceless objects scattered across the mattress.

'Oh.' Hattie stood up, but turned to look at them, frowning. 'I don't have the energy to do anything else today. What do you think we should do with them?'

'How about I itemise everything we've looked at so far, and then pack them up again? I'll start a database and make sure I label the trunk so we know where to find them when you're ready.'

'Perfect! I knew there was a reason I hired you.' She attempted a grin, but the toll of spending time up here was evident in the creases around her eyes. 'I'll put the kettle on.'

A few minutes later, I brought my drink upstairs and got straight to work cataloguing the items from the trunk. As well as listing each one, adding brief notes including their probable age and potential value, if any, I also added a longer note on a separate page, detailing the story as Hattie had told it to me. While I had no intention of ever writing a book, Hattie wanted Riverbend's history to be remembered, and this seemed the best way to do that, for now.

It was nearly eight by the time I made my way back to the ground floor, my stomach reminding me that getting lost in the past was all well and good, but in the present day, I was long overdue a decent meal.

I found Hattie on the living-room sofa, a fire in the grate and a dog curled up on each side of her tiny frame.

'Sophie, how's it going?'

'That trunk's all packed up, the contents catalogued. I've added some potential suggestions for what you might want to eventually do with some of Millicent's things, but that can wait until we've finished looking at everything.'

'An excellent idea.' Hattie raised her eyebrows over the top of cerise glasses. 'It's Saturday night; a young woman like you should be having fun, not sorting through old gowns.'

I smiled. 'I actually find that quite enjoyable.'

'Then it's a good job you found Riverbend. We'll soon show you what fun really looks like.'

'What would be good is some dinner. Have you eaten yet?'

Hattie glanced at the clock above the mantlepiece. 'You won't be surprised to hear that I lost track of time.'

'Really? I'm starting to wonder if this is a ploy to ensure I always end up cooking.'

She burst out laughing, a guffaw from deep in her belly that made it impossible not to join in.

'Oh, Lizzie is going to love you once she stops sulking about not being allowed on the top floor.' Hattie stood up, stretching.

'That was a big moment for me, heading up there. I've been doing some therapy, arting out some of the traumatic memories threatening to creep back in. If I don't pace myself, I'll never be able to get through the whole project.'

She held out a sketchbook, opened to a drawing of an older girl kneeling by a bedside, her hands gripping the quilt, face twisted to the side with a harrowing look of desolation across her features.

'That is stunning.' The heat of tears pressed against the backs of my eyes. That girl could have been me, eleven years ago. And far too many times, since.

'I'm calling it *The Empty Bed*.'

'Are you going to do something with it?' I hesitated, not sure how to ask. 'I mean, if not, could I buy it from you?'

Hattie jumped up and grabbed the sketchbook back. 'Absolutely not!' She ripped out the page and threw it onto the fire before I could process what was happening.

'I'm so sorry!' I stepped back, flustered. 'I didn't mean to offend you.'

'You didn't,' she said, hands on her hips as she watched the paper crumple into ashes. 'That picture encapsulates one of my saddest, loneliest moments. What possible good would it do for you to have that? You could hardly frame it, hang it in your motorhome.'

I shrugged, my embarrassment lessening thanks to her kind smile. 'I don't know. I guess I could relate to it. Maybe I'd find it therapeutic to look at.'

'Oh, no, no, no.' Hattie began walking towards the kitchen, gesturing for me to follow. 'That's not how it works. You can't hijack my therapy for your wounds. You'll need to do your own work. Don't worry, though.' She beamed, opening the fridge with a flourish. 'We've plenty of time. All that pain and regret will be well and truly arted out before we're done here.'

Not if I had anything to do with it, it wouldn't.

* * *

After cobbling together some pesto pasta, we ate at the kitchen table and then, sensing Hattie was still tired, I politely declined her invitation to watch a film and took Muffin upstairs with me to read in what I already thought of as my tartan chair. We'd agreed to meet up for Sunday lunch and then resume work in the afternoon. Hattie had apologised for working me on weekends but explained that she had therapy sessions spread throughout the week, and so I'd easily be able to take a couple of days off then. I didn't mind at all. It wasn't as though I had any other plans, and often found that clients needed to fit around their jobs.

I had another lazy morning with my book, and Hattie wasn't around when I went downstairs for breakfast, or an hour later for Muffin's walk. The sky was a sheet of slate-grey hanging low above our heads as we set off but as always, this did nothing to dampen my dog's enthusiasm. Once I'd skirted past the rose garden, we spent a blustery hour exploring the wider grounds, eventually curving back towards the river, where we finally found a bridge leading over to the forest.

'Yes, it looks very exciting, and full of fascinating smells,' I agreed, when Muffin padded halfway across the bridge before stopping to look back at me with a pleading expression. 'But can you see that horrible black cloud? If we don't turn back now, we're going to end up soaked.'

Reluctantly, she joined me on the path that followed the river, the first few raindrops starting to fall. As we hurried along

– or rather, I hurried, then stopped to call Muffin, who'd found yet another irresistible clump of leaves to sniff – the sprinkle soon became a downpour, the winter rain whipping into our faces.

We battled on until, just when I'd accepted that for the second time since arriving at Riverbend, I would be ending a walk in soggy underwear, we rounded another curve and spotted the chapel up ahead. Muffin immediately headed for it, as fast as her little legs could fight against what was rapidly intensifying into a storm.

Hurrying after her, I came to a stop in the porch, Muffin looking up at me with her head cocked to the side, wondering what on earth I was waiting for. 'Porch' was a little generous. It was an overhang about two feet wide, and no match against the icy darts coming at us from all angles.

Holding one hand up in a 'wait' signal, I tentatively pushed open the door, not expecting to find a Sunday morning service going on, but still cautious about entering without asking permission. The faint creak of hinges was easily masked by the wail of the wind, the whole room cast in gloom thanks to the stormy clouds. It was only once we'd slipped inside and Flap-jack padded down the centre aisle to greet us that I spotted Hattie, kneeling in the second pew from the front, her clasped hands resting on the back of the seat in front of her, head bowed. I would have coughed, maybe said her name or waited for Muffin to nudge her knee in hello, except that her shoulders were heaving, and in a momentary lull of the wind I heard her gasping, desperate sob.

'I don't know if I can do this. Please... please help me. Give me the strength to face it. Please...'

I grabbed Muffin's collar and slunk back outside before I could hear any more.

8

When I found Hattie in the kitchen a couple of hours later, there was no trace of the distress she'd displayed in the chapel. She'd added a soft grey cardigan to her pale-blue top, and her make-up-free face was clear and bright as she bopped along to ABBA while chopping up tomatoes for a salad.

'Sophie, good morning!' She beamed. 'Or is it good afternoon already?'

'It's one, like we agreed. Good lunchtime?'

'Oh, it will be!' She winked before turning back around to start on a cucumber.

'Can I help at all?'

'There's not much to do, really. A farm-shop lasagne in the oven, fresh bread ready to warm and wine in the cooler. Oh – you could see if the table's all set?'

The table was covered in yesterday's newspaper, a pile of drawings and an empty milk carton.

'No, not that one. We're eating in the dining room. Oh, could you check how the lasagne's doing?'

After seeing the size of the lasagne, I wasn't surprised to find the plates and cutlery laid out for more than two people. My first thought was Gideon and Agnes, but there were five settings, so that left one unknown, unless Lizzie was eating here on her day off. Before I had a chance to decide how I felt about more time with Gideon, the doorbell rang, sending both dogs into a flurry.

'Can you grab that, please?' Hattie called. 'Just make sure Flapjack doesn't jump up at Kalani – she loathes dog hairs on her clothes.'

I opened the door to find three women squashed together under one umbrella, before they burst into the hallway like those joke snakes-in-a-can.

'You must be the historian,' one of them said, while simultaneously shrugging out of a dark-red, leather jacket and shaking the rain from her black bob.

'I thought she was an author?' another asked, unwinding what seemed like an endless scarf from her neck, the end that was visible sporting two googly eyes and a forked tongue.

'Well, yes, if you want to be picky,' the first woman replied, rolling her eyes as she offered me the jacket. 'A historical author. I am sorry, though, the Middlebeck grapevine didn't pass on your name.'

'Sophie.' I decided to leave the proper introductions for Hattie, instead waiting while a navy cagoule, a yellow mackintosh covered in pink elephants, the scarf and a hat knitted in the shape of a frog completed the pile in my arms, turning to put them in the boot room just as Hattie appeared.

'Wow, you almost made it on time!' Hattie laughed.

'Well, your guest has a reputation for turning up early, so we hoped she'd help you be not so rudely late for once,' the woman who'd handed me the jacket replied.

Hattie hugged and kissed each of the women in turn.

'Sophie, these are the Gals. Laurie, Deirdre, and the one with the attitude is Kalani.'

'She means me,' the woman with the jacket added, with a dismissive shrug. She looked to be somewhere in her mid-forties, but her chic shirt-dress and immaculate make-up could have fooled me into thinking she was younger. 'Someone's got to tell it how it is around here.'

'So, you're Laurie?' I asked a woman with an auburn plait wearing leggings and a beige hoodie, assuming the fifty-something one who'd come in the giant scarf was Deirdre.

'That's me,' the older woman said, offering her hand to shake, before realising that was impossible due to my hands being buried under a mountain of wet fabric. She had straggly, ash-blonde hair and a round face devoid of any cosmetics, a black knitted jumper with a horse on the front and skinny jeans.

'I know, not many thirty-five-year-old Deirdres about,' the younger one added, smiling. 'My mum's a big Corrie fan. Thankfully, my life is a lot less eventful than my namesake's.'

'You can say that again,' Hattie said, slipping her arm through Deirdre's and leading her towards the dining room. 'But we'll keep working on it.'

* * *

I ended up spending another meal surrounded by the unfamiliar buzz of vigorous conversation, spirited hand gestures and raucous laughter. At times, the discussions grew positively boisterous, the affectionate teasing and amusing stories growing wilder as the wine continued to flow.

'Well, Hattie. Your reputation is in tatters,' Laurie announced, banging her glass on the table once her host had passed out plates of dessert. 'Lindsey told everyone in the bakery queue that you invited a stranger to her naked therapy session.'

'I might have known she'd be the one to blab.' Hattie sighed.

'I don't know if people are more bothered about a randomer walking in on them – no offence, Sophie – or hearing that you make people do therapy naked,' Kalani said, topping up everyone's glasses.

'Ian Watkins was asking where he could sign up,' Deirdre said, shuddering.

'I don't make people do anything!' Hattie huffed, before taking a large swig of wine.

'You might not wrestle them out of their clothes, but you can be very persuasive,' Laurie said. 'Michelle told me she's thinking of pulling Kaylee out of the Shine course.'

'No!' Hattie cried. 'Kaylee needs this more than anyone. And I've two more who said they'd only do it if Kaylee did. Once those three cancel, then the rest will topple like dominoes. These girls have spent far too long already waiting for some professional help. It's that or back to CAMHS for another ten-month wait.' Her face twisted up in frustration. 'I can't believe I was so stupid as to mix up the times. No offence, Sophie.'

'You didn't actually tell me a time, so it wasn't completely your fault. I should have checked.'

'What, checked that I might have naked therapy going on?' Hattie shook her head. 'No. This is completely my fault, and I'm furious at myself. I don't care about whatever wild rumours people spread about me, but it took me years – *years* – to build people's trust in what I do here, so that I could help them. And I do help – people who'd never dream of going to counselling or find the confidence to talk to a stranger about their problems on Zoom. Ugh!'

She dropped her head onto the table, narrowly missing her plate of cake crumbs.

'Is there anything we can do to help?' I asked.

Hattie lifted her head an inch, one eye gleaming.

'No!' Kalani said, straight away. 'I can't believe you'd use this as another ploy to manipulate us into letting you art us off.'

'Art it *out*,' Deirdre added, helpfully.

'I don't art anyone!' Hattie said, pushing her hair back off her face as she sat up again. 'Like I said, you're the one doing it, and what you do and how you do it is completely up to you. That's how creativity works.'

'Well, if you think you can ply us with wine, lasagne and amazing cake – this is amazing, by the way, almost as good as Laurie's – and then trick us into signing up for therapy we don't even need, then you're delusional.'

'Everyone needs an opportunity to express themselves.'

'I agree. I think I just expressed my opinion on your therapy perfectly!'

'How about we call it an art class?' Hattie went on, undeterred. 'Lots of people would love to have an opportunity to be taught by a famous artist.'

'Oh, so now you're resorting to playing the famous card.' Kalani snorted. 'You must be desperate.'

'What if I am?' Hattie asked quietly. 'I am absolutely, heartbreakingly desperate that these girls get a chance to heal from the terrible things that they've been through. I can't tell you what they're dealing with, because despite Michelle having no respect for her daughter's confidentiality, I do. But I promise you that if it was your niece, Maya...' she turned from Kalani to Laurie '...or Flora... then you would do whatever it took to get them any help you could. And however much you might poke fun at what I do here, you know that I'm good at it, and it works.

If nothing else, then just those girls knowing that somebody cares and that they aren't facing this horror alone will make a difference.'

'You could try talking to Michelle,' Deirdre suggested. 'Explain what happened, and that there's no way you'd allow a teenage girl to get undressed.'

'I can. And I will. But if my own best friends pooh-pooh my work here. When the people who know me most in the world don't trust me to help them deal with their issues... you know that this gossipy, pernickety village listens to you Gals. And, well. I'm not going to beg.'

'Is Amber Jackson signed up?' Laurie asked, her face tight with tension. 'I know Marnie and Doug are at their wits' end with how to help her after what that man did. They're talking about a secure unit if she tries to... you know... one more time.'

'You know I can't answer that,' Hattie said, but she didn't bother to wipe away the tear now trickling down her face.

'Come on, Gals.' Deirdre folded her arms. 'Hattie needs help here. All it's going to cost us is a few evenings. That is right, isn't it? Because you know I'm beyond skint right now, Hattie.'

'All my courses are free of charge,' Hattie said, a glimmer of hope in her voice.

'Laurie, you said it yourself, our friend's reputation is hanging in the balance. Remember when that rumour was going around about you accidentally poisoning everyone at the Christmas market? Hattie filmed herself eating your mince pies and posted it all over social media. Your sales tripled in two days.'

'You did save my business,' Laurie admitted. 'Thanks again, Hattie.'

'You're more than welcome.' Hattie patted her hand.

'And, Kalani, you didn't have a single friend for a whole

year when you moved here. Everyone was intimidated by your London fashion and snarky sarcasm. They had you pegged as a snooty cow. Now look at you, Ms Chair of the Middlebeck Fete Committee. More coffee dates than the characters in *Friends*. I heard you've been meeting Tye Devon for dinner. If Hattie hadn't purposely sat you at her table at the school auction, you'd still be in your swanky house watching Netflix alone.'

'I won't do anything weird.' Kalani narrowed her eyes. 'Or discuss anything personal.'

'Of course.' Hattie's voice was breezy, but the way she looked Kalani right in the eyes and offered a discreet nod said that she'd heard the tremor of fear behind Kalani's bravado, and she promised to be careful with it. 'Sophie, you'll join us for a few art sessions, won't you?'

'Um...'

'I've got a brilliant idea. How about a taster this afternoon? If after that you aren't interested, then no pressure, subject closed, I'll find another way to save the Shine course.'

'How long will it take?' Laurie asked, still not convinced. 'I need to call in to Dad's later on.'

'Twenty minutes?' Hattie shrugged. 'Maybe a little longer if you really get into it. You never know, it might be fun.'

* * *

'Fun' was not the word I'd have used to describe us, an hour and a half later, as we huddled around Kalani, currently crumpled on a beanbag in the studio, sobbing her eyes out.

'You're a frickin' witch, Hattie Hood!' She gasped, burying her head in Laurie's soft shoulder. 'I haven't cried about this since the day it happened.'

'Because you haven't talked about it?' Deirdre asked, gently patting Kalani's back.

'Because I've tried not to *think* about it! Let alone make it into a bloody collage after quaffing half a bottle of wine.'

'To be fair, Hattie didn't make you choose that particular person,' Laurie said, stroking her hair.

Kalani sat up, wiping her nose on the tissue I offered her. 'No, but she said there was no point doing it if we weren't going to be honest, and, apart from my dad, he was the man who's influenced my life the most. Partly because, since him, I've never given another man that kind of power.'

'Who is he?' Deirdre asked.

We all looked at Kalani's collage, which she'd made following Hattie's prompt to create something depicting a man who'd had a major impact on us. I'd spent an hour cutting pictures out of magazines and sticking the tiny pieces on a sheet of card, trying to capture Ezra. I'd made a huge heart with lots of pinks and purples, a wide white smile surrounded by a jumble of toys, household items and flowers (not roses!) to represent his chaotic home. Driving out of the middle of the page I stuck a motorhome, and then added a length of string to show how the motorhome was still connected to Ezra, no matter where it travelled.

Kalani had ripped up several sheets of tissue paper. She'd glued a rainbow of scrunched-up colours around the outside, then started coiling them towards the middle, gradually adding in the odd piece of black, then increasing the black as she worked inwards, until the centre of the page was a three-inch square of black tissue paper. Right in the centre of that was a circle of crumpled red, and on top of that she'd stuck a picture of a knife.

'Because what he did to me felt like being sliced in two,'

she'd said, when we'd sat in a beanbag circle to share our artwork, and Deirdre had casually asked what the knife meant. 'Not physically. Into two Kalanis. Before and After.'

Then she'd suddenly started to howl. And I mean the kind of howl that sounded as if she were being sliced in half all over again. The hairs on my arms sprang up. Once it petered into a haunting silence, she spent the next fifteen minutes silently sobbing.

Deirdre asked her question again. 'Who is this man?'

Kalani took a long, slow breath. 'He was my tutor at university. I really liked him. Everyone did. He was funny and charismatic and ridiculously clever. So, when he started paying me attention, I was thrilled. Coffee in the Student Union café, an evening in the wine bar where real grown-ups, not students, drank. A private tutoring session in his study. Where he assaulted me. Like anyone with half a brain could probably have seen coming a mile off.'

We all went very still for a moment.

'Oh, my darling, that's awful. I'm so sorry that happened to you,' Laurie said, her arm tight around Kalani's shoulders.

'Yeah, well.' Kalani sat up a bit straighter. 'It worked out for the best because I dropped out, joined a flat-share in London with my cousin and met a guy at a party who gave me an internship in PR. I ended up making a bloody fortune, moved here and met you lot and never wasted another second falling for a man's lies.' She let out a twisted cross between a sob and a laugh. 'You could say he did me a favour. I mean, the assault wasn't even that serious...'

'No.' Hattie, sitting on a beanbag beside us, spoke softly but her voice was granite. 'We could not say that, Kalani. Despite you doing such an incredible, courageous job of moving on and creating a new life for yourself, being assaulted is not for the best. Every assault is serious and that evil man did not do you a favour. He stole something extremely precious. Behind that portcullis guarding your heart is a young woman petrified of allowing anyone to betray her like that again.'

'Yeah.' Kalani sniffed. 'I've worked pretty hard to keep that girl dead and buried. Looks like you've managed to resurrect her.'

'She doesn't need to die, just to heal so that she can be free to grow up.'

'And that means more of this?'

Hattie sat back, her arms wrapped around her full skirt. 'What do you think?'

Kalani scanned the rest of us, one hand automatically reaching out to grip Deirdre's.

'Absolutely.' Laurie gave her friend a squeeze. 'I totally haven't got time for this, you know how hectic things are with the bakery, two teenagers driving me round the bend with their dramas, and now Dad being so ill. Never mind those chuffing pigeons. But I think you need this, Kalani, and if a Gal needs me, you know I'm there.'

'I don't want you to be scared inside,' Deirdre said to Kalani, swiping at her own damp cheek. '*I* don't want to be scared any more. Please let's do this.'

'You soppy pair.' Kalani laughed, shaking her head. 'How on earth did I end up friends with you?'

'We're the only ones willing to ignore your offensive remarks,' Laurie said.

'Sophie?' Deirdre asked. 'You'll art it out with us, won't you?'

I took a couple of shaky breaths. The very thought felt as though I were tumbling down a cliff. The last thing I wanted to do was start poking around at my inner feelings. If Kalani and Deirdre had a scared young woman inside them, then mine was absolutely petrified. But being a part of this, witnessing Kalani bearing her private pain, I could hardly be insensitive enough to say no, could I?

'If you don't mind me tagging along.'

'The more the merrier!' Laurie said. 'Or should that be, the more the sadder?'

Either way, I was here to do a job. If that now included once a week sticking magazine scraps onto card and finding a vaguely plausible reason for it, then no problem. No one needed to know that I'd be keeping my real pain, my genuine issues, buried deep down inside where they belonged.

* * *

'Sophie needs a gorgeous gal,' Laurie said, after Hattie had taken Kalani into her other studio for a longer conversation while the rest of us cleared up.

'She's not the only one.' Deirdre was rinsing the glue sticks. 'Are you sure you're ready for that though, Sophie? It's a serious commitment.'

'I've no idea what you're talking about, so, no, I'm not at all sure.'

Fifteen minutes later, I had my first gorgeous gal in my hand. They'd swept me out of the studio and back to the kitchen, Muffin and Flapjack bouncing ahead of us, and proceeded to plonk me down at the table while Kalani and Laurie flung open the fridge, rifled through cupboards and sloshed and glugged various items into a glass jug, finishing it off with a sprig of mint and wedge of lime.

'It's our signature cocktail,' Deirdre explained, once Hattie and Kalani had joined us. 'We invented it at what became our first meeting of the Gals. Laurie had invited us to her house for cocktails, but we weren't very good at sticking to the recipes. It's not actually that nice, but it'll make everything else we do seem a bit less bonkers.'

Laurie proudly placed a glass in front of me. 'Behold, the gorgeous gal.'

A murky, dark-green colour, it certainly didn't look (or smell) gorgeous.

Hattie waited until everyone was holding a full glass. 'This is it, Sophie, your official initiation into the Order of the Gals. Membership is for life unless you turn out to be a man-stealing weasel like Heidi Sprag.'

'May her knickers forever show through her trousers,' Laurie chipped in.

'And her mascara always be gloopy,' Kalani added.

I glanced at Deirdre, but she just clenched her jaw and blinked furiously.

'Anyway, apologies for bringing up the weasel, Deirdre,' Laurie went on. 'But once you've drunk, Sophie, there's no going back. You must stick to the Gal Code: always laugh at our jokes, keep our stories to yourself and never embarrass another Gal in public unless it's for her own good. Are you in?'

'Of course she's in!' Kalani cried, raising her glass in a toast.

'To the latest addition to the Gals!' Hattie cheered.

'Um...'

What on earth was I doing? How had this happened? Me, Sophie Potter, who constructed her entire life around not making real friends, forming lasting connections or belonging to anyone, anywhere, ever, now about to enlist in some sort of lifelong sorority for grown women?

I looked at the four Gals, their glasses poised, waiting. What on earth were *they* doing, these audacious women, inviting me of all people to join their treasured friendship group?

Oh, to hell with it, half a bottle of wine, an afternoon arting it out and eight years of voluntary loneliness yelled inside my head. *Why not say yes, for once?*

So I took a big sip of my really-not-gorgeous gal and said yes. Yes to laughing at jokes, sharing stories and what I suspected could well involve a lot of embarrassment that just, quite possibly, might end up being for my own good.

9

The other gals left around six. Hattie was clearly flagging, despite us not making it anywhere near the attic. I remembered her anguish in the chapel, which seemed so long ago now, and wondered if that had something to do with the strain creasing around her eyes and sagging shoulders. The rain had finally stopped and the clouds cleared, the sunset bathing the River-bend lawn in a fiery glow, so I decided to give her some space, taking out Muffin for a quick walk to clear the last of the cocktail fug from my head, and try to process an eventful day.

We took the shortest route to the river, planning on hanging around on the bank for a few minutes before heading back to the house. Had I been here alone, I might have felt nervous about being caught in the deepening dusk, but having a dog padding alongside me, however ineffective she might be if we encountered any danger, always somehow provided the reassurance I needed.

That was, until we reached the river, when the dark shape of a person loomed up ahead. My instinctive reaction was to stop and turn back, quickly and quietly enough so that whoever it was didn't notice me, but Muffin scuppered that idea by bounding up to greet them with an excited bark.

As soon as the man turned to give her ears a scratch, I could tell it was Gideon. My heart decided to thump even harder than if it had been a stranger, but it was going to be impossible to slip into the shadows, so instead I did my best to stroll up and say hello as if the last time I'd seen him, I hadn't run away for no discernible reason.

'Hey.' He nodded, eyes creasing with a smile.

'Hi.' It was all I could think of to say but seemed to be enough. Gideon got up from his camping chair and offered it to me, as if this were the most natural thing in the world.

'No, it's fine. We're just having a quick walk. I don't want to be caught out in the dark.'

'I'll walk you back,' he said, calm as anything. 'Sit for a few minutes. This is too good not to share.'

'I don't want to take your seat.'

'Too late.' Gideon shrugged out of his puffer coat, dropped it on the muddy ground and sat on it.

I sat down, huddling up in the chair for warmth. My raincoat was still damp from the morning's walk, and the grey jacket I'd worn wasn't thick enough for a February evening.

'Here.' Leaning forwards to a pile of supplies in between us, Gideon poured a flask of thick liquid into a travel mug and stretched over to pass it to me.

I held up my hands to decline, despite the cloud of steam having the most enticing aroma.

'I'm not taking your coffee as well as your chair.'

'Oh, no. I have another one.' He gestured to a second mug.

'Were you planning on someone joining you?'

He gave a secretive smile, meeting my eyes head-on. 'Just hopeful.'

I accepted the drink with a thank you, savouring the delicious warmth as I took a sip.

'I'm guessing it's a step too far to offer you my hat?'

'You guessed right.'

He grinned, every angle on his rugged face highlighted in rose-gold evening light. I hastily turned away, my eyes landing on a fishing rod set up near to Muffin, who was nosing about on the bank.

'You're fishing?'

'In theory.'

'What does that mean?'

'Some would say after a storm is the best time to fish, but it's too cold to stay out here for long. Really, I'm here for that.'

He nodded in the direction of downstream, and my breath caught in my throat as at precisely that moment, the sun hit the surface of the water. The trees either side were stark silhouettes against a sky ablaze with pink, amber and crimson, but the river itself was liquid gold.

We sipped our coffee and soaked up the dazzling glory in reverent silence, my cold toes and the dank air insignificant in comparison.

'Do you often come and watch this?' I asked, when only a sliver of copper was still visible where the water met the horizon, the forest and fields now draped in shadow.

Gideon's gaze remained on the view. 'It depends on the time of year. In the winter, I can time it to the end of my work day. Other months, I might take Flapjack on a walk. Or go pretend-fishing.'

'Pretend?'

He gave a rueful smile. 'I like the peace, the enforced sitting and waiting, the excuse to hang about on the riverbank, but I hate catching fish.'

'There's no one else about. Why do you need an excuse to sit here?'

'My mum. I can't persuade her to come with me, and if it's cold like this, she couldn't cope with it anyway. I just feel a bit less guilty if she thinks I'm doing a hobby, rather than choosing to be here instead of with her at home. That's the main reason I'm not out here more frequently, because it means leaving her alone.'

'And how often do you make use of that second mug?' I asked, a smile tugging at my mouth.

Before answering me, he paused to point out a bird soaring higher and lower as it flew across the river and back. 'A wood-lark. It means spring is coming.' Then he turned to me, one eyebrow raised. 'This is the first time I've needed a second mug. But then.' He shuffled on his coat. It must have been absolutely freezing down there. 'This is the first time I've brought one.'

While I tried to process that revelation, he asked about my day and we chatted for a few more minutes about the Gals, who he knew well. The topic of my fake job thankfully didn't come up, and Gideon was kind enough not to mention me bolting from the rose garden the day before. However, it was too cold to keep sitting here, and Muffin had resorted to clambering onto my lap rather than lie on the soggy ground. At a suitable pause in the conversation, we both stood up and, after Gideon had propped the chair against a tree and gathered most of his things into a rucksack, we began walking towards the house.

'You really don't need to escort me. I've got Muffin, and isn't this all private Riverbend land?' I asked, trying to sound as if I meant it.

'I want to.' He shrugged. 'Even if I didn't, I'm not the sort of man who lets a woman walk home in the dark.'

When we reached the door to the boot room, he stopped to

check his watch. 'It's only seven-thirty. You could invite me in for another coffee.'

It was almost impossible to resist his smile.

'I could, but one coffee is plenty for me this time of night.'

'Hattie's got decaf. Or tea. Hot chocolate.' His smile grew. 'I'm not really interested in a drink. But I'd love to keep talking.'

'Talking?' I asked, feeling a prickle of potential disappointment that he was pushing this. 'Because I've met plenty of men who after walking me home and asking for a coffee they don't really want, it's not talking they're interested in, either.'

He stepped back, quickly, his face plummeting, mine burning with embarrassment as I realised I'd misinterpreted his intentions.

'No. That's not what I meant. At all,' he said, shaking his head in alarm. 'Hattie's my cousin, and my boss. Even if I was the type of guy to try to charm his way inside for that, which I'm absolutely not, I wouldn't disrespect her by trying to seduce her guest. Or someone who's working for her. No. Honestly. I really like talking with you. I really like... you. That's all I meant.'

'Right. Well. Now I'm totally mortified for assuming the worst.'

He broke the tension with a burst of laughter. 'I hope me being interested in you wouldn't be the *worst*.'

'Either way, I will respectfully and apologetically decline. It's been an eventful day and I'm not going to keep you from Agnes any longer.'

Gideon nodded. 'Fair enough. Thank you for sharing the sunset with me. It was far more beautiful than if I'd watched it alone.'

'Thanks for inviting me. It was really special.'

He turned and started to walk away down the side of the house before coming to a stop as I shooed Muffin inside.

'So, out of interest, what would be the best?'

'Excuse me?' I looked at him, confused.

'If me worming my way in for... not a coffee... is the worst. What's the best?'

'I don't understand.'

He grabbed the rucksack straps with both hands. 'I'm asking what you'd like to do on a date. With me. Well, I suppose the first question would be whether you'd like to go on one. The next question is what kind of thing you'd like to do.'

I stood there for a moment, my brain in an internal tug-of-war with my heart, currently flip-flopping like one of the fish Gideon hated to catch.

'I don't date clients. Or their families.'

'Why not their families?' he asked, sounding genuinely interested rather than annoyed.

'Because there's too big a chance the family ends up being involved in my work.'

'And that's a problem?'

'It can be.'

'Okay. How about we hang out on a non-date?'

'Um... really?'

He laughed again. 'I think I can handle seeing you just as a friend. Or a temporary neighbour?'

Gideon might be able to handle it, but I wasn't at all sure that I could. While it was true that I didn't date clients or their family members, the bigger reason for me saying no was that I only ever dated on a casual basis. There was nothing casual about my attraction to Gideon. I'd thought far too long and hard about the intensity of connection I'd felt the first time we met, but I still had no idea what it meant, let alone how to handle it.

'I'll think about it.'

Well, that was honest at least. I'd find it almost impossible to think about anything else.

* * *

On Monday, Hattie had a start-of-the-week meeting with Lizzie in the morning, then retreated to the studio until three, when we met in the attic for our next session. She already appeared tired – I imagined that therapy could be draining – but she insisted we press on and tackle another container. I opened the trunk nearest to the one we'd already looked through, but, after glancing inside, Hattie closed it again. The third trunk was the one she wanted.

Like the first, this also contained a mixture of toys, personal items and clothing. There was a careworn, knitted elephant tucked in with a matching giraffe. I found three boxes engraved with initials that I now recognised as belonging to Hattie's grandfather Cornelius and his sons, Edgar and Michael, each with a neatly stashed shaving kit inside. There was an ornate box stuffed with costume jewellery and a fabric doll with a missing arm.

The clothes ranged from a carefully wrapped christening dress through increasingly larger childrenswear up to two hand-tailored morning suits and a graduation gown. There were also a gas mask and a ration book from the Second World War.

'This belonged to my mother, Verity,' Hattie said, cradling the doll. 'She called her Penelope. I can still remember when I was especially miserable, or ill, she'd ask if I could take care of Penelope for a while. It always worked. Somehow, remembering that my mother – who I viewed as something akin to an angel – had once been a little girl like me helped me to feel a little stronger, and more grown up. It was just the two of us, you see, in so many ways. She was much older than most of my friends' mothers, and I assumed that was why she had no family, why the stories she told about my uncles Edgar and Michael and Grandpa Cornelius were all from so long ago. It was only later on that she told me the real reason why, for the second time, the sole inhabitant of Riverbend was a young woman with a broken heart.'

Riverbend

Verity Abigail Hood had an idyllic childhood. In a similar fashion to its original owner, during her earlier years, she relished the freedom of Riverbend, roaming the acres of forest either with her brothers or alone. School was a tedious necessity, her mother's never-ending list of chores a constant frustration, but the hours she spent amongst the trees or on the water more than made up for it. However, as she grew older, her focus began to shift from the forest towards more sophisticated things. She started to notice how the village girls smirked at the scabs on her knees, prompting her to regret her insistence on wearing scruffy short-trousers, however practical they might be. For the first time, she felt a prickle of shame when the boys ignored her at the harvest dance, clustering around the prettier girls while she sat alone beside the lemonade table, no longer interested in joining the younger children having fun in the hay bales.

To her irritation, she couldn't stop her eyes from drifting

over to one particular boy, Jonathan Townsend, who stood several inches above the others, with broad shoulders, thick, dark hair and eyes the perfect green of an oak leaf. When she stammered hello after bumping into him outside the bakery, he looked down on her skinny four feet eleven inches with a look of such pity that she turned and fled, getting a scolding from her mother when she arrived back at the house without the bread she'd been sent to fetch.

She sobbed into her pillow that night, not least because she'd had to stay at home and bake the missing bread herself as penance, meaning she couldn't accompany Edgar and Michael to their cricket match, where she knew full well that Jonathan would be the star bowler. And things only got worse.

The week she turned thirteen, as if the challenge of being stuck in a body that refused to grow in any of the directions she wanted it to, alongside brothers who insisted on still calling her Baby V, weren't enough, a giant spot erupted on her nose, Jonathan proposed to her cousin, and Neville Chamberlain declared war on Germany.

She'd been imagining her teenage years as a carefree whirl of dances, pony shows and picnics. Instead, while she still had to keep up the dull things such as school and piano practice, now she also had to help her mother dig for victory, chop old curtains into dresses and transform rations into a decent meal. But that was nothing compared to saying goodbye to her brothers. When they were replaced by four Lumber Jills, working in the forest for the Women's Timber Corps – including the noisiest, messiest, scariest one of them sharing her bedroom – try as she might, Verity found it difficult some days not to feel a tiny bit sorry for herself.

Oh, she knew she had the easy job. Staying at home, ensuring the chickens kept laying and the vegetable patch was weed-free. The only things being shot at in Sherwood Forest were the deer and pheasants, and there were no bombs dropping overhead. The closest they got to actual war was the three Polish airman who died when their plane crashed near a local village.

But she missed her brothers with a constant, anxious ache that churned up her insides and made it impossible to force down the vegetable soup some days. When her father left, too, for some mysterious job that a fifteen-year-old wasn't allowed to ask questions about, the houseful of intimidating women, grubby bathrooms and an empty pantry made her want to scream. When she stumbled upon one of them kissing her latest infatuation in the rose garden, she did scream. Long and loud, in the deepest part of the forest where no one could hear.

Only afterwards, when first one telegram arrived, and then the other, and, as if that weren't enough to destroy her mother, a bomb hit the building where her father was working, killing him instantly, did she look back with bitter contempt at that spoiled young girl who'd thought she had something to complain about.

She never did grow much taller, but she ploughed all her energy into becoming stronger, and wiser. While her mother faded into the shadows of grief, Verity had no choice but to grow up. She stopped bothering with school, knowing there was precious little of any use to be learned there, and set out to educate herself on everything she'd possibly need to know about running a country estate. She hung her dresses back in the closet, chopped the bottom ten inches off her brother's dungarees, and got to work.

* * *

It was again early evening by the time Hattie had talked me through the highlights of the trunk. She'd been tired before we started, but by now looked positively haggard. Lizzie had messaged earlier to say that she was leaving for the day, and dinner was keeping warm in the Aga, so we ventured downstairs to ladle fragrant lentil curry into bowls decorated with woodpeckers.

Hattie ate three mouthfuls before declaring herself whacked and heading upstairs to bed.

I was starting to wonder whether there was more to my client's exhaustion than a busy life and draining job. However, it wasn't my place to ask. Clearly, Hattie liked to keep a lot of things private. And the less I knew, the fewer potential secrets I had to keep from people like Lizzie and Gideon.

I cleared up the kitchen, spent another couple of hours cataloguing some more items, and resolved to keep my questions to myself.

10

I spent Tuesday adding the rest of the items from the second trunk into the growing database, setting to one side those Hattie was happy to donate to a museum or otherwise pass on. Hattie was speaking at a conference on Wednesday so, finding myself at a loose end, after a long conversation with Ezra, I decided to keep my promise to Gideon. Still convinced that spending time with him wasn't wise, I did the next best thing and took Muffin the long way round to the boathouse.

The air had cleared since the weekend storm and, despite it still being the last week of February, there was a discernible change in the season. A few of the trees displayed a distinct tinge of green at the ends of their branches. Some of the bushes were covered in velvet buds and when we ventured through the woods near the fire pit, the ground was sprinkled with clusters of primroses. Back along the riverbank, I watched the sunlight dance across the surface of the river, inhaled the sweet, springlike air and couldn't think of anywhere I'd rather be.

Agnes opened the boathouse door a good inch and a half

when I knocked, once Muffin had grown tired of watching the ducks and I felt ready for a cup of tea.

'Oh. It's you. I'm very sorry, I can't remember your name.'

'Sophie.'

'There was a girl in my class called Sophie. She was a horrible thing. I didn't like her one bit.'

'Okay. Well, I'm not her. So, I was wondering if you fancied a cup of tea and a chat.'

'Now?'

'Yes. If you're free. Or I can come back another time.'

'I don't know anything about Riverbend. Or Hattie's family. I barely knew her mother, and the rest of them were dead long before I married Chester.'

'I'm not here to work.' I tried to rustle up my friendliest smile.

She squinted one eye through the gap in the doorway, which was, if anything, growing even smaller. 'Why are you here, then?'

'I don't really know anyone else in the area. Hattie's working away today, and I could use the company. But I understand if you're busy. I didn't mean to spring myself on you. I was just walking past and wondered if you might be free...'

The door opened a whole other inch. 'Is your dog here?'

'Yes. I wiped her paws, though. She's not muddy.'

The door had flung open before I'd finished the sentence. Muffin barged forwards, knocking her nose against Agnes' knees, and she beamed at the dog in delight. 'I can't pet you standing up. Come on, let's find the sofa.'

She disappeared inside, Muffin wagging her way after her. Presuming that I was included in the invitation, I followed them.

The cottage was nothing like I expected. I'd imagined musty, cluttered rooms with faded wallpaper and bad lighting. Instead, I stepped into an open-plan living space including a stunning, dark-brown kitchen, pale floorboards and fresh, colourful décor.

'This is amazing.'

Agnes didn't bother looking up, engrossed in rubbing Muffin's belly. 'It's all right. If you like the trendy, minimalist look. Personally, I prefer bit of floof and a pretty net curtain.'

There was nothing minimalistic about the wall of patterned picture frames displaying photographs of Gideon, Agnes and a man I presumed to be her late husband, Chester. Or the shelving jammed with dog-eared books, vibrant Hattie Hood prints everywhere and the painting of the bridge I'd come across a couple of days ago.

'I think it's very homely.'

'Well, Gideon likes it and he did the decorating. Of course, he had to stick his cousin's merchandise all over the place. Not that I like to complain. I'm just grateful for a roof over my head.'

Somehow, I suspected those last statements weren't entirely true.

'Shall I put the kettle on?' I asked, hoping to change the subject.

'We don't have one, so no, you can't. I'm quite capable of making my guest a drink,' Agnes huffed. 'If you're here to patronise me, young lady, then you can leave me and the dog to it.'

'Her name's Muffin.'

Agnes bumped past me into the kitchen area. 'I already told you, I don't remember names.'

Watching her hand wobble as she clutched first one mug, then another, while holding them under a boiling water tap, it was difficult to resist intervening. Having worked with a variety of elderly and infirm clients over the years, from those who cried with gratitude when I handed them a hot drink, to those who'd rather go thirsty than let me impinge on their independence, I could respect where Agnes stood on that spectrum.

'So, are you going to tell me why you're really here?' she asked, once we were sitting in the living area, Muffin's chin on her lap.

My brain stuttered for a few seconds, getting caught on Hattie's story about my reason for being at Riverbend.

'Did my son ask you to call in?'

Releasing a surreptitious sigh of relief, I took another sip of tea while figuring out how to answer that.

'He didn't, but he did mention that you weren't able to get out much. I've not ventured into the village yet. Hattie and Lizzie are almost constantly working. I was hoping you might have time to show me around? We could pick up anything you need while we're there.'

'I'm sure Gideon would love to give you a Middlebeck tour.'

'Maybe, but he's also working. And I wondered if you might enjoy shopping for your own food for once. You could choose whatever you wanted rather than what Gideon picks up.'

'Careful. We're teetering back into patronising again.'

I ignored her steely words and focussed on the glimmer of interest in her dark eyes. 'If we go soon, Gideon could come home to dinner in the oven. I'll help you cook, as a thank you for showing me around. What's your favourite?'

She pursed her lips, fingers idly fondling Muffin's ears. 'Gideon used to love my hotpot. They don't make it the same down here.'

'Hotpot it is, then. If we make double, I can take some for Hattie.'

Agnes snorted. 'Aha! The truth comes out. Had enough of her haphazard cooking already, have you?'

I gave her a sidelong glance. 'I might have done, if she didn't keep engineering things so that I'm the cook.'

'Sounds about right. Come on, then, drink up and we might stand a chance of getting to the butcher's before the best cuts of lamb have gone.'

'I'll need to fetch my motorhome if we're going to drive.'

'Not if we take Gideon's car.'

Two hours later, we'd visited the butcher, the greengrocer and Middlebeck Minimart, as well as stopping off at Laurie's bakery and café for a restorative cup of tea and a late lunch. I spotted one of the Changelings from the art-therapy class there, who flapped her now imaginary crow wings at me and winked. Agnes had shown me the village landmarks, which seemed to total the green, the pond on the green, the church, and a statue of a farmer whose name no one could remember. She'd had a whale of a time pointing and barking instructions while I'd fetched, carried and paid for everything.

I had to admit, I'd enjoyed myself, too. It had been a long time since I'd been shopping with someone, especially someone who squeezed every tomato in the grocer's and accused the butcher of fiddling with the scales, putting up such a fearsome argument that he knocked off fifty pence, even though we all knew Agnes was bluffing. Once back at the boathouse, we found he'd snuck in a joint of ham.

Instead of being pleased, Agnes shoved it forcefully back into the bag.

'This is why I don't go into the village,' she snapped, visibly trembling as she pushed the bag into my hands.

'Because people might slip you an extra piece of meat?'

'Because everyone thinks I'm a charity case, treating me like I can't pay my way.'

I didn't mention that her dispute over the scales implied precisely that, shrugging instead.

'From where I was standing, it looked as though he liked you, and found your haggling entertaining. The ham is a reward for a battle well won.'

'You wouldn't understand,' she muttered, but her scowl eased slightly as she took the bag back and put it in the fridge.

Agnes decided we needed another cup of tea before we started cooking, and as we drank it, she told me about her life before Riverbend. How her husband, Chester, was diagnosed with multiple sclerosis only a couple of years after they got married, then suffered a series of debilitating relapses until he died when Gideon was four.

'It was always a risk, of course, that he'd not be there to see Gideon grow up. Chester was seven years older than me, and I was forty when Gideon came along. We'd been told children wouldn't be possible, so it was a huge surprise for both of us.'

'A good one, I hope?'

Her eyes softened. 'How could a baby be anything else? He's the best thing that ever happened to me. Who knows where I'd be without him?' She snorted. 'Not gallivanting around Middlebeck with the likes of you, that's for certain. Probably stuck in some run-down, cabbagey old people's home. Or dead.'

'You don't think Hattie would have invited you to Riverbend, without Gideon?'

Agnes put her cup on the coffee table with a decisive thud. 'Hattie wouldn't have known anything about us if Gideon hadn't insisted I went to Leonard's funeral. And he only knew about *that* because Leonard left him money in his will.'

'Leonard?'

'Hattie's father.' She struggled to her feet with a sharp wince. 'You're the historian. Shouldn't you know these things?'

I wanted to ask more, starting with why Hattie knew nothing about her father's family, but as Agnes creaked over to the kitchen, telling me to find the big black pan in the bottom cupboard, I could sense that the topic was closed for today. No doubt I'd hear the rest of it from Hattie, in time.

A painstaking hour later, a Lancashire hotpot was bubbling away on the hob. I washed up while Agnes dozed on the sofa, Muffin's head in her lap. Unlike Hattie, she'd been more than willing to chop, stir and sprinkle, despite the challenges of wielding a knife with such swollen, arthritic fingers, they could barely grip the handle.

Around four-thirty, Gideon arrived, coming to an abrupt stop when he saw me wiping down the worktops.

'Hello.' A huge smile began spreading across his face, which, alongside his dishevelled hair, healthy glow and well-fitting T-shirt, flooded my insides with warmth.

It was ridiculous how my chest caught every time I saw him. Ridiculous, and terrifying. I could not – *would* not – allow someone to affect me this powerfully. I sucked in a deep breath, wrestled those feelings back down, and adopted a much smaller, more sensible, *friendly* smile in return.

'I came round to see your mum,' I said, just to be clear.

'Was she asleep the whole time?' His smile, if anything, grew even wider.

'We've been into Middlebeck, actually. Done some shopping, had a leisurely lunch and cooked dinner.'

'And drank about a dozen cups of tea, I'm guessing?'

'Maybe half a dozen.'

'No wonder she's exhausted.' He walked over to her, pausing at the side of the sofa, the smile softening into something more serious as his eyes met mine. 'Thank you.'

'No thanks necessary. I've had a great day.'

'You're staying for dinner, seeing as you cooked it?'

I picked up my bag and Muffin's lead. 'Agnes cooked. And I need to feed Muffin, so no, not this time.'

'Another time, then?' He glanced up, eyebrows raised in question. 'Tomorrow? Friday evening? A friendly, non-date dinner with my mother?'

I pretended to be busy snapping on Muffin's lead, hiding my face so he couldn't see the battle between my head and my hormones. I'd already stepped over my professional boundary with Hattie and her Gals, and I'd strayed even further today. But I knew full well that part of me had come to the boathouse half hoping it would lead to an invitation like this. This place, these people, made me want to throw my rulebook in the river.

But the rules were what kept me safe, protected. What enabled my defective heart to keep on pumping. However lonely it might be.

'Still thinking about it?' Gideon asked, his eyes crinkled in kindness, and maybe a hint of hope.

'I'd need to check with Hattie about our schedule,' I stammered.

'No problem. Just let me know.'

He placed a gentle hand on his mum's shoulder, causing her eyes to flutter open.

'Gideon. You're back already. Is the historian still here?' she asked once he'd kissed her on the cheek.

'I'm just heading off, Agnes,' I answered. 'Thanks for a lovely afternoon.'

'Wait.' She started the arduous task of standing up. 'I promised the dog a piece of ham.'

'No, honestly, it's fine. Please don't get up.' I tried not to wince as Agnes sank back onto the cushions.

'I want to get up! I'm not an invalid.'

After another unsuccessful attempt, she reluctantly accepted her son's hand, wobbling on seized-up joints as he helped her to her feet.

'Mum? Are you all right?'

She didn't look all right. Agnes swayed, eyes tightly closed as Gideon tried to steady her.

'I'm just... can you...? I need to sit down.'

'I'm just a bit dizzy,' she breathed, following a tense couple of minutes after Gideon lowered her back onto the sofa, pressing an anxious hand to her pale cheek, his eyes assessing every twitch. 'You pulled me up too fast.'

I fetched a glass of water and passed him a blanket from the back of a chair. 'Funny turns', as some of my clients called them, were something I'd witnessed often enough to prompt me to complete a first-aid course. Over the years, I'd got better at spotting the difference between something needing medical attention, like a potential mini-stroke, and what was simply too much stress or becoming overwhelmed. After a few more minutes, Agnes appeared to rally, insisting on shuffling to the bathroom, with a detour to check the dinner wasn't drying out.

'I'm fine,' she snapped for the dozenth time, catching Gideon loitering by the bathroom door when she came out. 'I'm old. I had a busy day. Drama over. Can we please eat now? Starving me won't help.'

With one glance at the strain behind Gideon's smile, I took plates from the open shelving unit and spooned out three portions while Agnes took a seat at the kitchen table.

'Well, if we're having a guest then the least you can do is open a bottle,' she said, with a twinkle that caused Gideon's shoulders to visibly relax a couple of inches. 'Now, with all that nonsense, I haven't had a chance to tell you what we've been up to.'

Gideon listened patiently as Agnes gave a blow-by-blow account of our trip into the village. By the time she'd finished telling him about the butcher, the ham had become a thoughtful gift from a friend rather than a backhanded insult. She also insisted that I gave Muffin not only a generous slice to take back with us, but a bowlful of hotpot, seeing as her dinner was back at the house. As soon as Agnes finished eating, she declared that she was finishing off her glass of wine with a book in bed. I cleared up while Gideon lit a fire in between pretending not to be making sure Agnes was safely settled in her downstairs bedroom, then I topped up our glasses while he checked on her again, under the pretext of bringing her medication.

'I'm sorry,' he sighed, collapsing onto the sofa. 'When I asked if you'd call in, I didn't think it would end up being the whole day.'

'It's fine. I didn't have anything else to do and, like I said, we had fun. Well. Mostly.' I braved a careful glance at him. 'That couldn't have been at all fun, seeing your mum like that.'

Gideon shook his head. 'It's kind of par for the course these days. It's why I worry about her, being home alone so often. I've tried to get her to have one of those emergency wrist alarms in case she falls while I'm out. Or at least to spend more time at Hattie's. She can sit in the sunroom by herself and not feel as if she's bothering anyone, but Lizzie would be around to fetch her a cup of tea and check on her.'

'She said everyone in the village treats her like a charity case. Finding the ham really upset her.'

He furrowed his brow in frustration. 'Do you think that's why the butcher did it?'

'Not at all. Is there a reason why she might feel that way, though? Has she been made to feel inferior in the past?'

Gideon took a sip of wine while he considered that. 'Dad had to give up his job when his health deteriorated. I'm pretty sure my uncle Leonard, Hattie's father, used to send us money, long after Dad died. Mum was a medical receptionist, so we could get by, but it wasn't Riverbend. And for some reason, we never visited. They didn't even swap Christmas cards, let alone a phone call. Maybe Mum felt we weren't welcome. I only knew about the money because I found a cheque when I was a teenager. There's a lot I don't know, and once Mum's gone, I never will.'

'Have you asked Hattie? She might know more about why they didn't keep in touch.'

'Hattie's even more closed off about it than Mum, if that's possible. To be honest, I was shocked when she said you were coming.'

'If it was me, I'd have been upset that Hattie was prepared to talk to a stranger and not her own cousin.'

'Yeah, I was a bit.' He gave me a sideways glance. 'Until I met the stranger.'

'Is this what asking me on a date was about, then?' I asked, confident enough, due to the crackle between us, that it wasn't. 'Trying to worm your way into my affections so I'll blab the family secrets?'

He smiled. 'I'm a patient man. I can wait until the book comes out. For the secrets, and a date.'

Sitting here with Gideon, my dog snoozing on the sofa between us, the fire glowing, wine fuzzing my senses, I wanted nothing more than to do this again. But how could I, when Hattie had made me into a big, fat fake historical author, writing a book that would never exist?

'Though, like I said, I'd love to spend more time with you, before then. As friends. With or without Mum joining us.'

Would it be that big a deal if we hung out a few times, went on a couple of walks, and then he discovered that my job wasn't quite how Hattie had explained it, and there wasn't going to be a book?

Yes! the functioning, non-lust-addled part of my brain yelled. *Lying to a friend is a big deal!*

I'd speak to Hattie and insist on explaining to Gideon I was helping her catalogue the attic contents. Problem solved. Friend made. Heart recklessly bouncing about in my chest.

I took a deep breath. 'Did you have anything particular in mind?'

'It would be remiss not to give Muffin a proper tour of Sherwood Forest.'

'Oh?'

He'd answered quickly enough to reveal that he'd definitely had this in mind. I tried to ignore how it made my stomach flutter.

'We can head over to the main forest. Find the Major Oak, nosy round the visitor centre. See if we can spot an outlaw or two. There's a great place to eat at one of the nearby campsites that's dog friendly. If Muffin doesn't have strict rules about who she dates, then we could bring Flapjack, too.'

'That sounds great.'

He shrugged, but his eyes shone with pleasure. 'I thought you'd be interested in exploring some local history that goes beyond Riverbend.'

'Okay, I'll speak to Hattie then we can arrange a date.' I pulled up short. 'For our friendly *non*-date.'

Gideon grinned into his wine glass.

Who were we kidding?

11

When Gideon walked me home, once we'd finished the bottle of wine and talked for another two hours about everything and nothing, I found Hattie in the kitchen with a mug of chamomile tea and a sketchbook.

'Sophie! How was your day? I heard you and Agnes were running rampant around the village.' She got up and fetched another mug, pouring tea from the pot as she spoke.

'We did some shopping, yes, and she showed me the local sights.'

Hattie laughed. 'Well, that couldn't have taken long. The statue with no name and a few ducks.'

'Oh, she took her time about it.' I smiled.

She chewed the end of her pencil. 'Well, you must have something special I don't, because I can't persuade Agnes to come out with me. That dinner last week was the first time she's been here in months. I've tried everything, thrown all my Hattie Hood charm at her, but I can't convince her to like me.'

'I wouldn't take it personally.' I sat down opposite her.

'I didn't, until Deirdre told me she was gallivanting about with you.'

'Yes, but I'm not her niece. If my job's taught me anything, it's that families can be complicated.'

Hattie peered at me over the top of her pink glasses. 'Is yours?'

I clutched my mug, tears suddenly prickling the backs of my eyes. 'No.'

Then the image of Ezra, Naomi and three fabulous children filled my head. 'Mine is different. But not complicated. Not any more.' I took a sip of tea. 'What are you drawing? More arting it out?'

Hattie smiled. 'The whole time I was speaking at the conference, I could see a murder of crows – that's what you call a group of them together, I looked it up on the train back – strutting about the lawn.'

She showed me a sketch of over a dozen crows all wearing different things like hats, waistcoats and glasses. One carried an umbrella in its wing, another a shopping basket.

'They're fantastic. But not at all like your usual designs.'

She sighed, adding a stripy tie to one of the crows. 'Things are changing. *I'm* changing. I suppose it's inevitable that I'd need to create differently, too.'

'You're changing?'

Hattie carried on adding to the picture. 'It's impossible to relive your past without it affecting you. A past like mine, anyway. That's half the point. I've spent all this time speaking to people about the need to confront painful memories before they can grow and move on from them. I'm sick of feeling like an awful hypocrite. I know I have to do this, but I also know that by the time we're finished, nothing will seem the same.'

'In a positive way, I hope?'

She looked at me. 'I hope so, too.'

We drank our tea, Hattie still working on the picture, until she put down her pencil and closed the sketchbook. 'Tomorrow, then. I've got a private session first thing, and I'm hoping most of the Changelings will brave it back, so let's meet for lunch, then get back to business. For now, I need to go to bed.'

'I did want to ask you something, quickly, if that's okay?'

'Go on.' Hattie had stood, but she leant on the back of her chair, waiting for the question.

'Agnes and Gideon keep mentioning the Riverbend book, and how I'm a historian. I'm not a good liar and find it quite stressful. Would it be okay if I mentioned to them that I'm really here to help you catalogue and decide what to do with the contents of the attic, as long as they don't tell anyone else?'

Hattie pursed her lips.

'I think we can trust them.'

She straightened up. 'Sophie, can I remind you that the non-disclosure form you signed included my aunt and cousin. If anything, they're the people I most want to keep this from. If it's too stressful, then stop spending time with them. I don't have to explain myself to you, and if you can't handle it, then I'll find someone who can.'

Oof.

I sat back, stunned by her response. As I'd already mentioned, I'd experienced first-hand how the goings on in many families were a mystery to the rest of us, and I wasn't going to be rattled by her insistence on secrecy. However, in the week I'd spent at Riverbend, Hattie had never spoken harshly to anyone. It seemed as though I'd touched a very raw nerve, and I wondered for a moment whether Agnes was right to feel as if Hattie's welcome wasn't as all-encompassing as she made out.

'Understood.'

She gave a brusque nod, then quickly left the room, Flapjack padding after her.

'Not understood, actually,' I told Muffin as I tidied up the mugs and rinsed out the teapot. 'Although I've a feeling that by the time I've finished this project, things might be clearer. The bigger issue, for now, is having to keep up the pretence with Gideon.'

Muffin cocked her head, eyebrows arching. Deceit was an unknown concept to her.

'I'm wondering if the only answer is to write the stupid book.'

Needless to say, I'd been a total wreck the summer my exuberantly warm-hearted family died on their way to visit me in Leeds.

Chris, my sister Lilly's fiancé, had survived the impact of an eighteen-tonne lorry jack-knifing into the side of his car. He'd spent three weeks in hospital then moved back to his mum's house in Devon. I'd visited him before he'd been discharged, but an ocean of mutual grief was the only thing we had in common, and the funeral was the last time I'd seen the man meant to be my brother-in-law.

After Chris's dad had told me the news, I'd stumbled upstairs and started throwing random things into a bag, knowing I had to go home even though the people I needed weren't there any more. I was trying to remember how to breathe when there was a knock on my bedroom door and an angel walked in.

I knew Ezra from Christmas parties, summer barbeques and all sorts of occasions in between. My parents had bought, sold and merged several small businesses over the years, and Ezra's mother had grown from a trusted solicitor to close friend through all the complicated wranglings and roadblocks. With my parents having no siblings between them, at some point this friendship had morphed into family. Once his mother had retired, Ezra had taken on her clients. I'd seen him evolve from the lanky youth who'd humorously tolerated my childish adoration, through serious student, to confident young professional.

And now, there he was, standing in my scuffed bedroom doorway holding a mug of tea.

'I need to go home.'

'Of course.' Ezra nodded.

One hand clutched a pair of knickers, the other pressed against my disintegrating heart. 'I don't know how to get there.'

Ezra put the tea down on my bedside table and gave me the biggest hug.

'I don't know what I'm supposed to do. The kitchen's full of roses and I don't know where to put them,' I sobbed into his shirt. 'I made all these designs, got samples and everything and now I don't know what... how...'

'It's okay. I'm going to take you home now. You don't need to worry about any of it.'

'But the flowers!'

Because, of course, having a meltdown about flowers was so much more bearable – *fixable* – than all the rest of it, which was too hideous to think about.

Ezra held me for a long time until my breathing settled and I felt able to carry on with the next few feeble steps of packing up some things and crawling into the passenger seat of his car.

And that was how it went on. With every panic attack, administrative task or agonising decision I had to make, he was there to steady me, explaining things at a pace gentle enough to penetrate the trauma clogging my brain, holding my hand through sleepless nights staring at mindless rubbish on Mum and Dad's television.

After the funeral, his pregnant wife, Naomi, helped me move again. I couldn't bear to stay in the house I'd grown up in, suffocating in shadows and silence. Returning to my old life in Leeds was beyond me. The only person I wanted to arrange flowers for was gone. The thought of doing that for anyone else felt abhorrent, like the worst kind of betrayal. So, with a compassion that I was too numb to comprehend back then, Ezra and Naomi welcomed a broken husk of a human being to their farmhouse on the edge of the Peak District. They helped me sell my childhood home after sorting through its contents, made sure I ate, showered and wasn't completely consumed by the grief. When their second child, JoJo, was born, I cuddled her in the rocking chair when she woke at night, and read stories to their toddler, Ishmael, while Naomi fed the baby or snatched a few minutes' peace. Somehow, slowly, these precious little lives gave me the courage to try to live again. Then one day, while I was still half-heartedly trying to figure out what living might look like, I got a message from a friend I'd worked with in Leeds. Her mum had died and she didn't have a clue how to handle it. I ended up visiting her for the day, then going back for two weeks. For the first time in over a year, my life had a purpose beyond the boundary of my own pain.

So, while Ezra, Naomi and their three children would never replace the parents and sister I had lost, they were my home, and my heart, and I was so utterly grateful that they'd chosen to be my family.

* * *

'We won't stay up here too long today,' Hattie informed me as we climbed the attic steps the following day, with no trace of her annoyance the night before. 'I've got to prepare for another class with the Changelings at six, and then the rest of the Gals are heading over for your next session.'

I wasn't sure how I felt about that. While I'd managed not to dig too deep while completing our trial art therapy, and I was determined to keep it that way, I knew that Hattie had other ideas. But there was that phrase – *the rest of*. I was one of them now. Part of something. It filled me with awe and dread in equal measure.

'The final trunk.' Hattie pointed it out, from where she now perched on the end of the bed. 'Once we've done this, only a few thousand boxes to go!' Her mouth curled up in a smile, but it was the only muscle in her face that moved.

'Are you ready?'

'I am.' She blew out a watery laugh. 'I just wish someone would tell that to my quivering guts.'

I slowly opened the trunk. This time, the contents were clearly female. There were layers of formalwear, the skirts widening then narrowing again as they reversed from the early sixties through the fifties. There were books, personal items like silver-plated hairbrushes and a jewellery box containing a sparkling array of necklaces, brooches and earrings. Near the bottom, I found a wooden case that contained paintbrushes and a dried-up palette of watercolours.

'I'll take that,' Hattie said, tears glistening on her eyelashes. 'It'll be perfect for arting out all this exposed grief later.'

As she reached forwards to take the case, she stopped, ignoring it in favour of what lay beside it, a corner of which was showing where the tissue-paper wrapping had come open.

'What's that?'

I carefully unfolded the rest of the paper, lifting out a stunning, forest-green ball gown, packaged up with satin gloves and, in a velvet pouch, a matching tiara.

'Oh, I remember these,' Hattie said, reverently placing the tiara on her head. 'Every now and again, my mother would open up her wardrobe and show them to me. Once, when I was, ooh, maybe thirteen, she let me try them on. This dress was verging on scandalous at the time, but she said it was worth it, because my father couldn't resist a scandal.' She sighed. 'Although, if she'd known how that turned out, maybe she'd have stuck to something more respectable.'

12

RIVERBEND

When the war finally came to an end, Louisa Hood couldn't bear to stay in a house that felt as though it was waiting for the men who would never come home. She packed up the shards of her shattered heart, kissed her daughter, Verity, goodbye and moved in with her widowed sister-in-law in Bristol.

The last thing Louisa did before saying goodbye to Riverbend forever, having accepted that, no matter how vigorously she begged or bullied, Verity would be staying put, was ensure that her daughter would not dwindle into eccentric spinsterhood, drifting about in that big house alone.

'I've lost a husband and two sons; my only hope now is grandchildren,' Louisa lamented one breakfast. 'We've no time to waste.'

'Mother, I'm nineteen.' Verity tapped the top of her boiled egg with a teaspoon. 'I've got plenty of time for all that. As convenient as you might find it to have me married off before you go, I'm in no hurry to grab myself a husband.'

'Well, you should be! If you hadn't noticed, eligible bachelors are in even shorter supply than stockings. If we're going to stand any chance of finding a man capable of running River-bend, we need to act quickly, and we need to be clever.'

'Please, Mother. If the past few years have shown anything, it's that I'm quite capable of running Riverbend myself.' She deftly dipped her toast in the perfectly cooked egg, as if to prove it.

It had been a steep learning curve, with plenty of mishaps along the way, but once she'd realised that being responsible for their land also included the freedom to run it how she wanted, she'd relished the challenge. This, alongside her tenacity and an impressive cabbage crop, had earned her a reputation amongst the local landowners as a competent farmer. In the aftermath of the war, she prized that far more highly than being considered pretty. The only time her short stature bothered her nowadays was when she needed a step to reach the top shelf in the barn, or struggled climbing up into her new tractor.

'Perhaps. But as out of touch as I may be, even you modern women haven't figured out a way to make babies by yourselves. Don't you want to be a mother, fill our home with children again?' Louisa's voice cracked on the words, sending a familiar ripple of guilt through Verity that she'd been the child to survive, and her brave, brilliant brothers – the rightful heirs of Riverbend – had not.

'If good men are so scarce, then how on earth do you expect me to find one?'

While Verity knew she wasn't excessively plain, she'd rather muck out the chicken coop than attempt to flirt and had no idea how to talk to the type of people her mother would deem suitable.

Louisa arched one eyebrow, forefingers gripping her porcelain teacup. 'Simple, we'll do it the old-fashioned way.'

'What, are you going to arrange a dowry, attract the local

gentry with the promise of three good horses and ten acres of cabbage?'

'No, my darling. We're going to have a party.' She lifted her chin. 'Sherwood's finest, most fabulous party since Robin wed Marian.'

And that was that. Louisa temporarily set aside her mourning and plunged into party preparation as if the lives of her unborn grandchildren depended on it, and once Verity's initial resistance had crumbled, she joined her mother with all the gumption of a girl who'd never been kissed.

News soon buzzed through Sherwood Forest that Riverbend was planning a grand ball, with the sole intention of finding Verity Hood a husband and, like a reversed *Cinderella*, single men of all ages from far and wide were invited. Louisa had to reiterate that there was, in fact, a strict guest-list, although Middlebeck villagers were all welcome. This local girl hadn't forgotten where she and Cornelius came from before Millicent Hatherstone's outrageously generous wedding gift. The village responded in kind, ensuring the Riverbend Ball would be as elegant and enchanting as if rationing or the ravages of war had failed to penetrate the heart of the forest. For days prior to the party, people trooped down the lane bearing barrels of beer, crates of apples and three of Jack Pollard's prize hogs, ready for roasting.

Louisa hired several girls and strong youths to help cook, clean and tidy up the grounds. She borrowed chairs and tables to place on the lawn. Verity strung up bunting left over from the VE Day celebrations and they sold one of Cornelius's cars to pay for a professional swing band.

But in all the frantic back and forth, Louisa never forgot that the glitz and glamour mustn't detract from the true focus of the night. Like all good mothers, she considered Verity to be the most beautiful young woman a man could wish for. However, she was under no illusions that everyone else could spot this beneath the battered straw hat and patched-up overalls. So, in order to help those attending come around to her point of view, she dug out an old dress that Riverbend's original owner, Millicent Hatherstone, had stored in one of the attic rooms. Louisa sharpened her scissors and got to work.

The result was stunning. Shocking. Spectacular. While many young women were hoarding their clothing coupons, others repurposing old curtains or the suits their fathers and brothers had grown out of, Verity Hood shone like an emerald in comparison. With most of the rural population still dressed for wartime practicality, Verity's dress was pure, forest-green silk, with ruffles, ribbons, a full, sweeping skirt and a decadent row of buttons running up to the salacious neckline.

For the first time in her life, Verity felt like a woman. And it showed. Suddenly, she understood the Lumber Jills' knowing glances and confident bearing. Aware that she was attracting no small amount of attention, she decided that, after everything she'd been through, she might as well enjoy it. Verity pranced and danced. When she found herself catching the eye of the same stranger for the third time, she downed her champagne cocktail and gave him a downright wanton wink.

He was by her side within seconds, introducing himself as Leonard Langford, son of Sir Charles Langford.

'I hear you're looking for a husband.'

Verity hid her shock behind a whoop of laughter. 'I think you've mistaken me for my mother.'

'Darling, your mother was the last thing on my mind when I saw you in that dress.'

'Oh?' She ducked her head, cheeks flaming. It was all very well pretending to be forward, but on the inside, she was nothing but fluster.

'Why is she so keen to marry you off?'

She rolled her eyes. 'She wants a grandchild to fill each empty bedroom.'

'How fascinating. I was hoping for five children myself. Will that do it?'

'It would, but five sounds like a lot of work for the poor soul who ends up their mother.'

'I'm rich. I can afford help. Leaving you to enjoy the blessings of our offspring, while someone else gets on with the hard work. From what I can gather, you've done more than your share already.'

'Haven't we all, these days?' Verity found the courage to throw him a coquettish look. 'And since when did I become accomplice to your future plans?'

He tipped his head back and guffawed, sending a thrill of pleasure across her bare shoulders, then fixed her with a wry smirk. 'Since you winked at me across the dance floor, my love. Our fate was sealed. Now, how about you show me around this charming estate of ours?'

Three months later, Middlebeck chapel finally held its first wedding. Verity filled her side of the aisle with villagers and farmers who eyed up Leonard's smooth hands and slender frame with furrowed brows while across the divide, the Langford family prayed that this strangely capable woman might be enough to hold the attention of such a notoriously charming rogue.

As soon as they'd returned from a brief honeymoon in Rome, Leonard had Verity's brother, Edgar's, bedroom converted into a nursery. Louisa had promised she'd be back for the first christening, and the newly-weds eagerly awaited some good news to share.

On their first anniversary, they were still waiting.

'Not to worry,' Leonard drawled, having prised Verity away from the fields and whisked her off to lunch at an expensive restaurant in London. 'We're still young. Plenty of time, and we might as well enjoy ourselves while we wait.'

Two years later, Verity discovered quite how much Leonard was enjoying himself, when, at the fourth Riverbend Ball, she caught his hand up another woman's skirt.

And so it went on. Verity channelled her energy into her beloved Riverbend while her husband channelled the profits into revelry, gambling and, she suspected, more mistresses. This included frequent trips away to places that Verity hardly bothered to ask about. Leonard would generally return contrite, with gifts in hand and declarations of how much he'd missed his pretty, independent wife. Verity would pretend to believe his assertions that this time it would be different, he was done with 'all that', whatever 'all that' was. She ignored the rumours, prayed that he was the one unable to conceive so she never had to deal with the complication of another woman's child, and poured her affections into this man who still made her laugh like no one else, while captivating her body with one touch.

Verity offered him plenty of reasons to stay, filling the hole created by the empty bedrooms with dinner parties and day trips, holidays in Europe alongside involving him in her new projects on the estate. Yet every time, after maybe a couple of months, perhaps a year, she would detect the drawing away, the emotional distance that inevitably became geographical, too. Ten years into their marriage, she threw herself against the front door, blocking him from leaving for yet more 'business' in Antwerp. He responded by grabbing her upper arms so tightly, he left bruises, thrusting his face up against hers as he cried that he couldn't bear to remain another night in this cursed house of shattered dreams.

Verity decided then and there that she'd had enough. Better to offer both of them the chance for happiness, for children, with someone else than continue this poisonous cycle of love and despair. They were still young; it wasn't too late. Only, when Leonard returned, for the first time, he professed an interest in the land he'd declared doomed to another generation of misery. He spent hours learning how the estate ran, what was profitable, and when. With this new, shared interest came renewed energy and enthusiasm that crossed over into every part of their marriage. More than one person commented on how Verity's eyes shone, and cheeks bloomed, with a not-so-discreet glance at her waistline.

The glow was soon extinguished when her husband sold two good fields to a neighbouring farmer.

Eight years later, and every acre of farmland was gone, along with the livestock and equipment. Anything beyond the main grounds, lost to pay off unknown debts and cover up countless lies. On her fortieth birthday, Verity celebrated her miserable life by getting drunk enough to allow her wastrel husband into her bed for one last time before she packed his bags and banished him forever.

Then, a month or so later, the whiff of eggs at breakfast caused her to throw up for the third day on the trot. After Leonard had sold, stolen or sabotaged almost everything that mattered to her, Verity was finally able to give him the only thing he'd ever truly wanted.

* * *

'She was pregnant with you?' I asked, having sorted through most of the trunk while Hattie told her mother's story.

'She was. I was born 1 May 1967. But you don't have the time, and I definitely don't have the energy, to get into that today. Come on, we can squeeze in a strong coffee before I head to the studio.'

I repacked the trunk ready for cataloguing another day and followed Hattie down to the kitchen. It was on the lower staircase that she stumbled, slipping a good few steps before grabbing onto the broad banister and jerking to a stop.

At least, I thought she must have stumbled. From my angle, a few steps above her, it appeared more as if she *crumpled*. There was nothing on the stairs to trip over, not even a runner with a potential wrinkle for her white pumps to catch on.

'Are you okay?' I asked, hurrying to put an arm around her shoulders.

Hattie's eyes were closed, her face grey. 'Whew. I knew this project would be taxing, but, after all these years as a therapist, I had no idea how quite how exhausting digging into the past could be.'

'Maybe that's why people like to art it out instead, because talking can be so hard.'

'A very good point!' She offered a weak smile. 'I'm tempted to add a dash of something stronger to my coffee, but I need my wits about me with those Gals.'

Reassuring me that she was startled, but not injured, Hattie gingerly continued down the remaining stairs and into the kitchen. I followed behind, adopting my professional attitude of calm as Lizzie made us both a drink and sliced up a fudge cake, reeling off some new sales figures, but I was now certain. A wan complexion, irregular naps, frequently distracted, and now an unexplained stumble... add that to suddenly needing to sort out three generations of possessions. Let alone the insistence on confidentiality.

I wondered how long it would be before Hattie told me she was seriously ill.

13

I'd made the conscious decision to arrive at the studio five minutes late, avoiding any chance of interrupting the Changelings, but Hattie thwarted my plan by relocating their session to outdoors.

I was taking Muffin on a quick walk through the woods, hoping to settle my pre-therapy nerves, when with unfortunate timing, I strolled into a clearing at the same moment a figure all in black charged towards me through the darkness, releasing a teeth-rattling scream while brandishing an axe above their head.

I dodged to one side at the same instant they also veered to avoid me, so for a dangerous few seconds, it looked as though something terrible would happen. Mercifully, we both skidded to a stop a metre or so before a collision could occur.

'It's you!' The figure flicked their hood off, revealing the woman I'd last seen dressed as a crow. 'Are you spying on us again?'

'Who's spying?'

When I turned in the direction of this other voice, the dim light from the house enabled me to detect who I assumed to be the rest of the Changelings, clustered beneath the trees.

'I'm walking my dog,' I stammered, scanning around for Muffin, who'd inconveniently disappeared.

'A likely story!' one of them scoffed, folding her arms. 'She's hoping for another peep at our fabulous, fifty-something figures!'

'If you wanted a look, darling, you only had to ask.' Another one laughed.

'Um, speak for yourself, Marg; my physique is for my husband's eyes only! Well, apart from you lot last week, of course, but after everything we've shared, you don't count.'

'Please, ladies, Sophie lives here!' Hattie interrupted, stepping out from the shadow of a bush. 'She had no idea you wouldn't be in the studio today. No one did, because I keep the details of our sessions confidential, as you know full well.'

'She's right.' I started to back away, eyes still on the crow's axe, which she now held over one shoulder. 'I have no clue what's going on here, and I really don't want to.'

'We're expressing our unhelpful hormones via woodcarving,' the woman who'd been covered in caterpillars and butterflies last time said. 'Jen has rather strong feelings about hers.'

'She was aiming for the tree, not you,' Hattie explained.

'Because *she* wasn't supposed to be here!' Jen retorted.

'It goes without saying that Sophie will keep this to herself,' Hattie added, soothingly.

'It also goes without saying that next Thursday evening, between six and seven, I'll be in my bedroom with the curtains closed,' I added, before getting the heck out of there, trusting my dog would follow me when she was ready.

* * *

Thirty minutes later, Laurie, Kalani and Deirdre burst into the studio in a flurry of hugs, discarded jackets and jitters.

'Remind me again why we agreed to this,' Laurie asked, scanning the plastic sheeting set out underneath four tables and central pile of, amongst other things, newspapers and plastic buckets.

'Because for the first time in years, Kalani revealed that she's actually human,' Deirdre replied, although her expression was also wary.

'Yes. And I expect no less from the rest of you. It's someone else's turn on the beanbag of blubbering.' Kalani pointed her finger at each of us in turn.

'Blubbering is by no means compulsory,' Hattie said, with a shrug. 'This is your session, Gals. What you want to get out of it is up to you.'

'Yeah, right.' Kalani rolled her eyes.

'Now, today we're going to keep it simple, acclimatise gently, as it were, to the process of art therapy.'

'Aren't these wire clippers?' Deirdre asked, picking a pair up off a table. 'That's not my idea of keeping it simple.'

'Simple as in we aren't going to splatter our deepest, darkest emotions all over the so-called artwork,' Laurie said.

Hattie responded to that with a raised eyebrow before turning to Kalani. 'Didn't you get my message about wearing tatty old clothes you don't mind getting ruined?'

Kalani smoothed her hands down her faux-snakeskin dress. 'This is old.'

'Kalani, you bought yourself that for Christmas. It cost a fortune,' Laurie pointed out.

'Were we supposed to wear something old and tatty?'

Deirdre gasped. 'I didn't see that message. I've worn my best jumper.'

'Perhaps she didn't bother sending it to you,' Kalani muttered out of the side of her mouth. 'If you ask me, that outfit needs to be ruined as soon as possible.'

It was a harsh comment, but accurate. Deirdre was wearing a fuzzy, peach polo-neck that made her appear to have no neck and a very uncomfortable bra. It suited her auburn hair and pale complexion even less than the beige hoodie she'd worn last time. Her jeans were sagging in all the wrong places, with a damp ring around each hem from where they'd dragged on the wet ground.

'Deirdre, I love you, but if that's your best jumper then you need therapy more than I thought,' Laurie said, with a sympathetic smile.

'Hey!' Hattie exclaimed. 'That is not a therapeutic approach to another Gal's outfit. If Deirdre prefers to focus on her internal beauty, choosing clothes she's comfortable in rather than hiding behind a ridiculously expensive, glossy image, then she shouldn't be judged and definitely not shamed for it.'

'Ouch!' Kalani smirked, seemingly in no way offended by this non-therapeutic dig.

'I don't mean to shame her!' Laurie put her arm around Deirdre. 'But I don't think Deirdre dresses like this because it makes her feel comfortable. She never used to wear this stuff *before*. She dresses like she doesn't care about herself because that's how she feels. She's forgotten that she's the loveliest person anyone could meet. Hopefully by the end of this, she'll have remembered who she is, again.'

'Thanks, Laurie,' Deirdre sniffed, tilting her head to rest against her friend's.

'Oh, come on. We've not even started and you're already

welling up!' Kalani shook her head in mock horror. 'Hattie, you'd better hurry up and explain what this pile of junk is for.'

We were making papier mâché animals, representing ourselves this time, rather than other people.

'Ourselves how?' Laurie asked. 'Who we are, or who we want to become by the end of all this arting?'

'Or who we used to be, before someone smashed up our self-esteem and stomped on the pieces?' Deirdre asked.

'That's up to you.' Hattie smiled back. 'But take a few, careful moments to think about it first. Which you do you *want* to recreate today?'

'The me that is assertive enough not to spend my evening making an animal out of soggy newspaper,' Kalani said, with a toothy grin to show she was joking.

'Hopefully not. But the being-sarcastic-to-mask-her-vulner-ability you will be fine,' Hattie replied, blowing a kiss.

* * *

'How's it going?' Deirdre asked, stretching her arms up as she wandered over to my table an hour or so later.

'Wow, Soph!'

I froze for a microsecond. The second time we'd met and I was *Soph*.

'This is amazing!'

I stepped back, unable to hide my smile. I'd spent a lot of time making sculptures from chicken wire, a very long time ago, in that other life, when creating beautiful things had been my passion. Today, I'd crafted a wolf, ears pricked, mouth hanging open to reveal sharp teeth and a lolling, friendly tongue.

'What does it mean?'

'I think we'll maybe share that when everyone's finished?'

'I'm finished, and Kalani finished ages ago. How about you, Laurie; are you done yet?'

A few minutes later, the Gals convened on the Beanbags of Blubbering to showcase their animals, which we would be painting another time, once they were fully dry.

Laurie went first.

She'd done a plain sort-of round shape. Dangling off the bottom of it was a tangled mass of ribbons, in a multitude of colours.

'This is me.'

'It looks like a round blob,' Kalani said. 'With a mess hanging off the bottom.'

'Well, it was meant to be a jellyfish, but you've got the point.' Laurie flicked at the clump of ribbons. 'All this stuff. People. Work. Money. Hot flushes. Yet another email from school demanding an explanation for why my daughter insists on wearing her uniform the wrong way round, walking backwards down the corridors and calling herself, "Arolf". I don't know why she flips everything back to front, all right? I also don't know what lethal fungi and bacteria are breeding in the pit that used to be my son's bedroom. Right now, I don't have time to care thanks to being too busy helping my dad up and down the stairs, because he "feels funny" about having a stairlift put in. I'm too knackered after getting up at four to run a bakery, and chasing my darling husband's ruddy pigeons, because apparently that's his hobby now, so it's become my part-time, unpaid job. So, who am I? I don't even know. Where have I gone? Suffocating somewhere beneath everyone else's needs and problems. Can I do anything about it? Probably, but my brain is too fried to figure out what that might be. I'm a jellyfish, blobbing about with no backbone.'

'Wow. That's a lot.' Deirdre nodded.

'Too much.' Kalani looked horrified.

'Brilliant, Laurie. Thank you for sharing.' Hattie smiled. 'Perhaps you'd like to take your sculpture home to show Howard?'

'He thinks I'm taking Dad to the chiropodist. He wanted me to help install some new perches in the pigeon loft so I made up an excuse.'

'Right.' Hattie looked thoughtful. 'We'll move on, then. Kalani?'

'Is that a worm?' Laurie asked, looking at Kalani. 'Because I think that's a bit harsh, even for you.'

'What do you mean, *even for me*? And no, it's a snake. Shedding its skin, as you can see, here. Revealing the fresh, soft Kalani underneath. Leaving the crusty, cold Kalani skin behind. This is the me I'm starting to become.' She glanced up, hesitation in her eyes. 'I hope.'

'It's perfect,' we all agreed, until she was almost able to believe it.

I went next. 'I decided to make a wolf. I suppose I see myself as kind of a loner. Travelling around from place to place. I don't know if that's what wolves do, but it seemed apt.'

'Wolves live in a pack,' Deirdre said. 'They only go it alone when looking for a mate or a place to start a family. Soph, you've finally found your pack!'

'Now all you need is a mate,' Laurie added, eyes lighting up with excitement. 'We could help you find them, too, if you like?'

'Thanks, but I'm very happy being single.'

'Hmm.' Hattie gave the wolf a nonchalant pat on the head. 'You also seem pretty happy hanging about with my cousin.'

'What?' Everyone else leant forwards, nearly toppling off the beanbags.

'Is that your professional, art therapist's opinion?' I asked, cheeks flaming even as my traitorous lips insisted on curling into a sheepish grin. 'Because I thought we were here for that, not to discuss my love life.'

'You're right!' Hattie grabbed my hand. 'It was completely wrong of me to mention it in a therapy session.' She met my gaze, making sure I knew she was being serious before she broke into a smile. 'Next time, I'll wait until we're onto cocktails. Although, something tells me that your therapy journey is going to need to face up to the love, or lack of it, in your life.'

'Can we start cocktails now?' Deirdre asked. 'I have so many questions about Sophie and Gideon.'

'What, and miss you getting to showcase... *that*?' Kalani replied, eying up Deirdre's animal.

'No judging other people's art,' Hattie scolded. 'Deirdre, would you like to explain?'

'Can you guess what it is?'

'Um...'

I thought I could spot a pointy nose, maybe a paw. But that didn't do much to narrow down the possibilities.

'Is it a cat?' Laurie asked, hesitantly.

Deirdre shook her head.

'A... slug?' Kalani guessed.

'What?' Deirdre pulled her head back. 'Why do you think I'm like a slug?'

'Okay,' Hattie intervened. 'I don't think guessing is helpful. Would you mind explaining to us, please?'

'It's a sloth.' Deirdre pointed out the ears, what she claimed were four paws and a pair of eyes.

'It's harder to tell because it's not painted yet,' Laurie said.

'It's harder to tell because it looks nothing like a sloth.' Kalani giggled. If she carried on like this, Hattie would have to put her in art-therapy detention.

'Why a sloth, Deirdre?' Hattie asked.

'Because it was the most boring animal I could think of. All they do is sleep, or just hang about, being boring.'

'Deirdre!' Laurie and Kalani cried together.

'You are *not* boring!' Kalani went on. 'Not at all. Would I be friends with a boring person?'

'To be fair, beggars can't be choosers,' Laurie said.

'Well, yes, but how dare you call one of the Gals boring?' Kalani was twitching on the beanbag, getting irritated at how hard it was to sit up straight. 'You're hilarious, and great fun, and, and...'

'And I'm boring,' Deirdre said, seemingly unconcerned. 'I have a boring job that I hate. I have three – now four – friends, who I love to hang out with, but that's all I ever do. Since I broke up with Gavin, I live by myself, work by myself, talk to myself – like, all the time! I eat the same meals, plod along the same running route, live in the same village I was born in, and never go anywhere else. My last holiday was a weekend with Gavin in Mablethorpe.'

'That doesn't make you boring, though!' Laurie said.

Hattie held out one hand to stop her. 'Let Deirdre explain.'

'I've been feeling bleurgh for a while now. Once I got past being upset and angry about what happened. I've been stagnant. A little bit depressed, if I'm honest.'

'What? How did we not spot this?' Kalani reached across her beanbag.

'Because being with the Gals is the highlight of my week. You make me feel amazing. But an hour or two back in the house I've not bothered to redecorate since I moved in, and I'm flat as stale shandy again. Back in sloth mode. I don't know if Gavin cheated on me because I was boring, or I became boring because of what he did with Heidi Sprag, but now I'm stuck and I don't know how to fix it.'

'You should sign up for a dating app,' Kalani said. 'It's been over two years.'

Deirdre shrugged. 'Who wants to date a sloth? Maybe only other sloths. Otherwise, they'll ask you to marry them and then have sex with your best friend in the disabled toilet at your engagement party.'

'May her shopping bags always rip halfway between her car and the front door,' Kalani snarled.

'I'm so angry they did this to you,' Laurie said, her voice breaking as she shuffled her beanbag close enough to wrap an arm around Deirdre's shoulder. 'I'm so sorry you've been feeling like a sloth and we never noticed.'

'Well.' Deirdre sniffed as tears dripped off her cheeks. 'I wanted to do a sculpture of nothing, because that's what I really feel like, and I didn't want to be mean to sloths, but I thought Hattie wouldn't let me do nothing.'

'Now, look! You've got me started again.' Kalani pressed her palms against her eyes. 'If you were nothing, would you be able to make me cry?'

'It's the snakeskin coming off,' Laurie said. 'All your tears are coming out now. You were right to wear that dress today, Kalani. You should rip it to shreds or burn it when you get home.'

'It's not the snakeskin!' Kalani shook her head. 'It's Gavin. Being stupid enough to fall for Heidi Sprag; may her tea always be tepid. I can't bear that they made you feel like nothing. You're everything to us.'

'The hardest thing...' Deirdre stopped to take in a shuddering breath. 'The hardest thing is knowing that if I wasn't enough for Gavin then, when I was still happy and confident and *fun*, what hope have I got of anyone wanting this nervous, miserable wreck? I'm thirty-five. I thought I'd have a baby by now. I wanted to blame Gavin and Heidi for ruining my chances of becoming a parent, but they aren't responsible for me being a nothing, nobody sloth. I am.'

She pressed her cheek against the wet papier mâché of her sloth, shoulders slumping as she sobbed. Hattie gently put the sculpture to one side and then held her while the rest of us quietly tidied up and left them to it.

* * *

I'd been hoping that the Gals might have forgotten Hattie's comment about Gideon, but I should have known better.

'So,' Kalani said, while we waited for Deirdre in the living room. 'Gideon's pretty gorgeous, isn't he?'

I took a sip of coffee, coming up with no better strategy than to pretend I hadn't heard her.

'Been hanging out with him much?'

'I had dinner with Agnes, and he happened to be there,' I said, inspecting the ceiling.

'Oh, my goodness!' Laurie gasped. 'Look at your face. You really like him!'

'He seems... nice enough,' I stammered.

'He's very nice,' Kalani said, 'for a man. You should ask him out.'

'I'm not... I don't...' Utterly out of practice when it came to these kinds of conversations, I crumbled under their scrutiny. 'He already asked me.'

'What?' Laurie was practically bouncing up and down on the sofa. 'What did you say? Where are you going? When? You should wear that jumpsuit you wore last week. It really suits you.'

'I told him that I don't date my client's family members. I don't want to risk things getting messy and awkward.'

'Now that *is* boring!' Kalani groaned.

'So he asked me on a non-date to the Sherwood Forest visitor centre and I said yes.'

Kalani broke into a grin. 'Call it what you want, but that's totally a date. You do know that, right?'

I did know that. I knew that labelling it a non-date was fooling nobody, least of all me. Instead, I'd decided to focus on how one date, maybe a couple more, even a kiss, was perfectly within my casual, carefree, pain-free dating rules, so it didn't matter whether this was a date or not.

What I was definitely *not* focussing on was how in the one day since I'd seen Gideon, I'd missed him.

* * *

It was nearly nine when Deirdre and Hattie joined us, and by the time everyone had left, Hattie appeared grey with exhaustion.

'Shall I see what Lizzie's left for dinner?' I asked.

She leant back into the sofa cushions, eyes closed. 'To be honest with you, I'm still full from her fudge cake.'

'Are you sure?' I kept my tone gentle. Tentative. 'It would probably do you good to eat after such a tiring day.'

She sighed. 'I know. You're right. I'll get a piece of fruit later on. You help yourself, though.'

'I really don't mind fetching us both something.'

'Thank you, Sophie, but your job description doesn't include waiting on people.'

'Actually, you'd be surprised how often it does. Besides, I was offering as a friend. If... I mean... I think being one of the Gals means we're friends now?'

She opened her eyes, her gaze softening when it met mine, as I hovered by the door. 'It most certainly does. And you've probably gathered that while my friends are few, they mean a great deal to me. I get the impression you feel the same way?'

'More than you can imagine.'

A short while later, when I was nibbling on an omelette, she apologised again for her comment about me and Gideon. 'If it had been any other client, I would never have brought it up in a group. But, well, I'm so used to us Gals oversharing. And, honestly, I really like you, and I absolutely *love* that man, and I have a feeling you're both as lonely as each other, however hard you try to pretend otherwise. I'm a silly romantic attempting to live vicariously through other people's love stories and I got carried away. I promise I won't bring it up again in a therapy session.'

'Thank you.'

She waited a few moments before continuing. 'Having said that, we aren't in a session now... and we are friends... so if you did ever want to talk about it...?'

'I enjoy hanging out with Gideon, but that's all it is. There's no love story.' I took a deep breath. 'Especially while I'm having to lie about my real role here.'

She gave a thoughtful nod. 'Fair enough.'

'So, why is an incredible woman like you living vicariously through other people's love lives?' I asked, attempting to breach the awkward silence that followed. 'If you're such a romantic, why not have some romance of your own?'

'What, apart from the fact I'm old and odd and can barely manage to take care of myself, let alone anyone else, even if I did have the time?'

'Apart from those things, yes, why not?'

She put down her fork, her eyes fixed on something – or perhaps someone? – far off in the distance. 'Because I am a Riverbend woman.' Her head gave a slight shake. 'Our lives are love and then loss.'

14

I found Lizzie in the boot room the next morning, pulling wellies on over her silver tights.

'Hattie asked me to walk Flapjack,' she said. 'As if I didn't have a million other things to do. She was in the studio until stupidly late last night, so could barely function this morning.'

'I can walk him with Muffin,' I offered. Hattie had gone to bed as soon as we'd finished eating the night before. I'd stayed in the living room with the dogs until well past eleven, and she'd not come downstairs again.

'That would be amazing.' Lizzie hurriedly handed me a lead. 'Hattie's been so distracted with all this book stuff lately, she's really pushing the boundaries of a personal assistant in expecting me to pick up everything else. She's always been disorganised, but I shouldn't have to be reminding her to sleep and eat.'

'Are you worried?' I asked as she kicked off the boots. 'Do you think she's okay?'

Lizzie stood for a moment, the boots dangling from her hand. 'I'm not the one in the attic, poring through the horrible history she refuses to talk about to anyone else. You tell me, should I be worried?'

I didn't know how to explain that it wasn't going through the attic that I was concerned about, so instead I mumbled something about us both keeping an eye on her and left it at that.

By the time I got back, Hattie had messaged to say that she was already on the top floor. I found her beside a box, a stack of photographs in her hand and a baby's blanket draped over her knees.

* * *

Riverbend

Harriet Langford always thought of her earlier childhood in two halves. Not before and after, but Him or No Him. The periods her father was away, which varied from days to months at a time, were idyllic. As soon as his car sped out of the gates, it was as though the whole house, and certainly her mother, Verity, could breathe properly again.

During her younger years, every day with No Him felt like an adventure. School was an ordeal to be endured before racing home to find her mother and discover what delights they would be getting up to next. Weekends and holidays were even better. Whole days were spent with their rowing boat on the river, pausing when they felt like it for a swim, or a sunbathe, to pick bilberries or say hello to the sheep grazing near the bank. Other days, they'd cross the bridge and spend hours roaming the forest. Of course, with money often running short and the house and grounds to manage, there was always plenty of work to be done – mending and making, planting and pickling. But Verity's enthusiasm made it joyful, rather than a chore.

Harriet's favourite days were when, after a sticky morning digging up vegetables in the kitchen garden or stirring her mother's giant jam pan crammed with wild blackberries and pounds of sugar, they'd pack up the produce and walk into the village. They'd visit up to half a dozen houses on these trips, exchanging a punnet of fruit or a jar of chutney for a cup of tea and a glass of milk for Harriet. She learned that they weren't going to stop by the pretty cottages with the neatly trimmed privet hedge and snow-white net curtains. Verity preferred the run-down, neglected homes that appeared to be slumped over with exhaustion, much like their inhabitants. Harriet would sit and cuddle grubby, gangly infants while her mother stood at a cracked sink washing pots in tepid water as if it were a perfectly natural thing to do. Often they would return to Riverbend with a bagful of dirty washing, returning it the following day neatly ironed and darned where necessary. In other houses, they would simply sit, and listen to someone talk, Verity offering a hand to hold if there were tears.

Harriet began to understand that theirs wasn't the only family with secret sorrows.

As well as their trips into Middlebeck, the local children would venture up to Riverbend for summertime cricket matches in the meadow. Verity and Harriet would make gallons of lemonade to serve alongside scones laden with locally churned cream and Riverbend strawberries. On especially warm days, they would head to the water, the less daring girls lounging on blankets in the sunshine while the others paddled in the shallows, risking splashes from the boys showing off on the rope swing.

In the autumn, they gathered wood from the forest and built

giant bonfires, warming their bellies with sausages donated by a local farmer's son, and cracking teeth on toffee apples from the orchard.

Riverbend was bursting with life again. Verity would sigh with contentment and ask Harriet, 'Can you feel it? The house is happy now. This is what it was built for. Mess, mayhem and muddy footprints.'

'I wish it could always be like this,' Harriet would sometimes whisper, but her mother's face would go hard, like the statue by the rose garden, and she'd turn away as if she hadn't heard.

Because, like summer evenings and snowy days, eventually they would be replaced with a dark cloud. With Him. Pulling into the drive and thudding up the front steps, dispelling the peace and light with one glare, or snarl of displeasure.

Harriet learned at a very young age how to creep along a skirting board unnoticed. Never to leave a stray pencil or a hair ribbon outside her bedroom. To discern a mood via the tilt of someone's head, or the weighted pause before they spoke. To keep her answers short, and her questions to herself.

She learned the places she could linger after school and on a Saturday. Places like the café or the church hall, where she'd be warm and welcome. She also learned that if she crawled into her wardrobe and pulled the door shut, she could sometimes muffle the sound of her mother's tears, or her father's temper.

Most importantly, she learned how to escape into a drawing, or a watercolour. That stepping into these other worlds, faraway places on the pages of her sketchbook, she could leave behind the horror of her mother's bruises. Alternatively, some days the only way she could deal with the fear and anger was to get it out onto the paper, with slashes, scrawls and splatters. She could never tell her parents how she felt, knowing that invisibility was her best means of survival. But her pictures said it for her. The misery, the guilt. The confusion. The longing. The times she hated Him for coming back. The times that, even as she loved her more than her own life, she hated her mother for always letting him.

As she grew older, Harriet moved from Middlebeck primary school to a private academy, several miles away. There was talk of boarding school, but then another card game, or reckless investment, another woman demanding luxury in return for discretion, and the funds were inevitably diverted elsewhere.

So, she stayed at Riverbend and did her best to embrace the good days, and to endure the bad. She spent more and more time in the forest, sketching the animals and birds, who cared nothing for money or whisky, for women who laughed too loud and stayed too long.

Then, one day, Mother went to bed and didn't get up again.

And that was when things went from bad to horrible.

* * *

We spent the rest of the weekend taking our time as we sorted through reams of old documents, many of them highlighting the financial devastation that her father's lifestyle had wreaked across the Riverbend estate. Sunday night, as the sun began to set behind the treeline, the stars emerging unhindered by clouds or city lights, we carried boxes stuffed with papers down the two flights of stairs, across the lawn and behind the kitchen garden to the fire pit. Protected from the spring chill in warm jackets and woolly hats, we built a fire using a pile of pre-chopped wood, and fried local sausages and onions as the papers burned, the dogs observing from a careful distance.

'For the first time these documents have helped people feel better,' Hattie said, tucking the meat inside a soft roll and adding a generous squirt of mustard and relish. 'Even if it is in their dying breath.'

'Are you feeling okay about it?' I asked, handing her a glass of the champagne she'd insisted we brought with us.

She lifted the glass up to where a twisting column of pale-grey smoke mingled with the twilight. 'I feel as though years – decades – of resentment and hurt are floating off me, up into the sky, carried along with those ashes and sparks. I hadn't realised how heavily that attic was pressing down on my shoulders until you started helping me. Honestly, Sophie, therapists can be the worst people at listening to their own counsel. But this.' She took a long, slow sip of her drink. 'This is definitely okay. Cheers, Leonard Langford. You were a pathetic man and a dreadful father. You took from me everything that mattered, but it's time to stop allowing you to keep taking my peace and happiness, too. So, off, up into the sky you go. I forgive you for selling my family's land, and so many of their valuable posses-sions. For forcing your wife and child to scrimp and save while you gorged on the stolen profits. Maybe if you'd had the benefit of a decent therapist, things would have been different. However, my inner jury is still deliberating on the rest of your abominable deeds.' She turned to me, raising her glass again. 'Cheers, Sophie. You being here, preventing me from having to face this alone, is priceless.'

'Cheers.'

I didn't know how to say that, while sitting on a tree stump in the deepening dark with this woman, the glow of the fire warming my cheeks, I also felt more okay than I had in a very long time. I looked up at the coil of smoke, disappearing into the indigo haze, and I did my best to unclench my tattered heart and allow some of the ancient pain and grief to drift away with it. I watched them go, and I breathed in some of the peace and happiness that had been stolen from me by an overtired lorry driver trying to get home to his family.

As the last streaks of sapphire darkened to ebony, the bats flittering in and out of the branches behind our heads and the fire dwindling into embers, a figure approached along the edge of the trees.

'Good evening, cousin,' Hattie said with a smile, before I'd identified the face amongst the shadows. 'What has you sneaking about in the dark?'

He took a seat, removing one of the hands huddled in the pockets of his coat to pet Flapjack's head, now pressed against his knee. 'As estate manager, I consider it my duty to investigate the smell of smoke.'

'Thought you might be missing out on a party?'

'Either that, or some village kids were having the kind of party we can do without.'

'You smelled this tiny fire all the way from the boathouse?' Hattie asked.

Gideon turned his head to look at me. 'I was fishing.'

It was too dark to see his expression, but those eyes burned into me all the same.

He shrugged off his rucksack and pulled out a flask. 'I thought you could probably do with a coffee, given how cold it is.' He cleared his throat. 'Although I've only got one spare mug.'

It felt as though some of the bonfire sparks had ended up trapped inside my chest. In the days since we'd eaten together, it had crossed my mind that he might bring an extra mug to watch the sunset. I'd tried not to mind that I didn't have either the time, or the courage, to find out.

The non-date invitation had been loitering in my thoughts, and after my conversation with the Gals, I was wittering about whether I could handle a day out with Gideon and keep my growing feelings in check. It was new territory for me, the solid weight behind my ribs that ached with a constant need for something I'd never known I was missing until now.

In eight years meeting different people, other men, any attraction had complied with the rules to keep things simple, shallow, safe. Now this man, and the offer of a cup of coffee, had thrills tumbling through my veins.

I made a jumbled excuse about fetching another mug, and when I returned, Hattie was asking Gideon about his weekend.

'I was working today.'

'Working on a Sunday?' Hattie pulled a face. 'Not here, I hope.'

He shook his head, taking the mug and pouring me a drink. 'Reuben asked if I'd help clear a fallen tree up at Hatherstone. It was blocking the drive so he needed it doing as soon as possible.'

Handing back the full mug, he glanced up, eyes smiling. 'It does mean I'll be taking Friday off in lieu.'

'Good.' Hattie nodded in approval.

'Would Friday work for our visit to the forest?' he asked, just as I took a sip of coffee, the jolt sloshing painfully hot liquid into my mouth.

'Are you asking me or Sophie?' Hattie asked, with a faux-innocent smile. 'Because this is the first I've heard about a forest visit.'

'I was meaning to mention it,' I said, unable to hide my fluster. 'Gideon offered to show me around Sherwood Forest, but I wasn't sure what days you wouldn't be needing me.'

'On Friday, Lizzie and I have a meeting with someone, some-where, that's going to take all day. We're catching an early train and there's a dinner in some fancy place, so we won't be back until late. It's perfect. You can enjoy the whole day to yourselves.'

'That does sound perfect.' Gideon grinned, raising his eyebrows at me in question.

'Yes. I guess that's a... non-date.'

'That reminds me.' Hattie stood up. 'Thanks to the Gals' carefully spread propaganda about our sessions, the Shine course is back on. I've got to be up early to start prepping, so I'll bid you both goodnight.'

She started trudging away, Flapjack's trot a sharp contrast to her stooped shoulders as they disappeared into the shadows.

'How's your mum?' I asked as Gideon got up and used a stick to coax some life into the dregs of the fire.

He moved to sit on the stump beside mine. 'She had another dizzy spell yesterday. I wouldn't be surprised if there's been more while I've been out. She refuses to see the doctor, but I've booked a phone consultation, so maybe he can persuade her to get seen properly.'

'Are you sure you don't mind leaving her, on your day off?'

He sighed. 'I was hoping Hattie or Lizzie might call in, but that won't be happening if they're out.'

'Is there anyone else you could ask?'

He nodded. 'I can find someone to pop in. I wasn't expecting us to be out longer than I'm usually at work for, though. Were you planning a grand day of adventures?'

I ducked my face behind the coffee mug. 'I wasn't planning anything. You're the Sherwood Forest expert.' I paused. 'Maybe *half* a day of adventures?'

'How about a late morning until mid-afternoon of adventure, although please don't get your hopes up, it's pretty rare to catch a glimpse of Robin Hood or a Merry Man these days, and then dinner back at mine, seeing as Hattie's away? Hopefully that part will be adventure-free, despite Mum being with us.'

'That sounds...' Like a really long day for a first non-date with someone. But the thought of spending a whole day with Gideon was alarmingly *un*alarming. And whenever I was with him, what I *should* do felt increasingly irrelevant. '...perfect. How about I pack a picnic, if you're providing dinner?'

He grinned, the shine of a rogue remaining flame dancing across his cheekbones. 'Perfect.'

We continued chatting until the fire offered no more protection from the night nipping at our fingers. Gideon sorted the ashes while I collected the remains of our feast, and then he walked me back to the boot-room door, my heart skittering in my chest the whole way.

'Goodnight, then. Thanks for letting me join the party.'

'It was Hattie's party, not mine.' I cringed at the hint of breathlessness in my voice.

'I'll see you Friday. Or maybe earlier. You know where to find me.'

He leaned forwards then, every cell in my body standing to attention as he slowly, carefully, so softly I had to convince myself later that it had really happened, brushed his mouth against my cheek.

I was still standing there, wondering how on earth a minuscule peck on the cheek could be the best kiss of my life, and then he'd gone.

15

My second week at Riverbend continued in much the same manner as the first. While Hattie was busy with clients or holed up in her half of the studio, I explored more of the surrounding countryside with the dogs, delighting at how spring unfolded all around us on the beautiful, sunshiny days, squelching home to a hot shower and change of clothes on the mornings we encountered a March shower. I also had time to research some of the more collectable items we'd discovered in the attic and do plenty of reading.

I visited Agnes on Tuesday, when Gideon was working too far away to pop back for lunch, resisting the invitation to hang around until he'd finished for the day. I spent a lot of time, especially when pacing through the fields and forest, thinking. About Gideon, inevitably. My family, as always. More so about the choices I'd made since I'd lost them. Choices I'd made to protect myself. To create a life that was manageable. Meaningful. Or so I'd thought.

On Tuesday evening, I video-called Ezra.

'Do you think I've got it wrong, living like this?' I asked once Naomi had herded the children off to bed.

'Choosing to stay in a fantastic house in the countryside, working with a famous artist?' He looked at me sideways.

'No, I mean my whole life. Living in a motorhome, moving every few weeks.' I paused, blinked a few times. 'Not having any real friends or family apart from you guys.'

'It's your life, Soph. How you live it is up to you.'

'No. Don't do that. You've been giving me advice my whole life, and it's never been unwelcome.'

'Really? Back in your David Bowie from *Labyrinth* phase, every suggestion I made, you made a point of doing the opposite.'

I couldn't help laughing. 'I'll have you know I was going for Britney, not Bowie. And I was trying to prove how grown-up and independent I was. Even back then, I knew I'd be better off listening to you. You've got every right to have an opinion. You and Naomi understand why I needed to live like this, why having a home was too hard for me. Why I won't risk giving my heart to another person again. But what if I'm wrong? Or at least it's not necessarily what's right for me now? What if it's just keeping me miserable and lonely? What if love – or some proper friends – are worth the risk of losing them?'

'Is this that guy Gideon?' he asked, dark eyes scrutinising me through the screen.

I blew out an irritated sigh. 'Seriously, Ezra?'

He leaned closer. 'Yes. I'm serious. This isn't me teasing, like when you had a crush on the postman. The first time in years you want to talk about how the death of your family might have impacted your major decisions? Of course I'm serious. Have you finally met someone who could help you to see that there is life after loss?'

I gripped my head with both hands. 'I don't know... I don't know if I can think anything real about him yet. It's more this place. Hattie, and her friends. Agnes. I've got to know some wonderful families, who responded to their grief with love and care. But I've always seen that as *their* love, *their* family. Nothing to do with me beyond the job I was paid to do. Here, I don't know. Outside the farmhouse, this is the first place since leaving Birmingham that I've felt a part of.'

'And how does that feel?'

'Like I'm crouching in the doorway to a plane at ten thousand feet, wondering whether to jump.' I stopped, swallowed back the crack in my voice. 'What do I do, Ezra? Should I jump?'

Ezra spoke carefully. He knew how big a deal this was. 'You've been there less than a fortnight. It sounds like there's a lot to think about. My advice is that you take a few breaths, give yourself some time, keep doing your job, taking it all in and, most importantly, that you give me the surname and date of birth of this Gideon bloke so I can do a full background check before deciding whether he's good enough for you.'

'Okay. Yes to all of those except the last one.'

'Did you not hear me say that's the most important?' He pointed at me. 'That one was an order.'

'Thank you, Ezra. I love you. Give the kids a goodnight kiss from me.'

'Um, hello? Name and date of birth!'

As always, my friend left behind a smile on my face.

Hattie had told me only a little more of her story as we'd worked through boxes of paperwork, old books and other leftovers from her early childhood. She'd offered the odd anecdote relating to a particular stuffed animal and a sketchbook we found, but for the most part had remained focussed on the business side of our mission.

On Wednesday afternoon, we prised the lid off a scuffed, wooden crate, about a foot square. Hattie sat back so quickly, she almost fell.

'I'd almost forgotten about this,' she whispered, blue eyes round with wonder. 'I found it in the chapel after my father's funeral.'

'Do you know what it is?' I asked as she reverently lifted out a velvet bag, wondering if this was some much older history.

'It's what she hid from him. Before he moved her permanently upstairs, into here. Most of it won't be worth anything to anyone else, but these are all that remained of her most precious possessions, so they're priceless to me. I only braved a quick peek when I uncovered it; the pain was still too raw. Even knowing she felt compelled to hide this says everything. It broke my heart all over again.'

* * *

Riverbend

Harriet didn't understand, at first. How could she, a twelve-year-old girl in 1979, with no one to explain it to her? Her mother was gravely ill, she knew that much. She lay there in bed, eyes fixed on the ceiling, cracked lips twitching. Had she gone blind? Deaf? Because she didn't seem to know anyone was there. Even when Harriet climbed up onto the bed, stroking the pale face, murmuring her name, before resorting to shaking limp shoulders, crying and begging her to answer, her mother never flinched.

'Is it a stroke?' she asked the doctor, through panicked breaths. Her friend Mary's dad had suffered a stroke a few months ago. He'd forgotten how to talk and could barely move afterwards. Then he'd had another one and that was that. 'Will she die?'

'I need to speak to your father.' The doctor peered down at her from where he towered in the doorway. This new doctor didn't understand that speaking to Him was the last thing Verity – or Harriet – needed. Harriet wondered if she could get hold of Dr Parsons, who knew better.

'He's away. He left last night.'

Harriet couldn't help wondering if he'd done something before he went. Did he poison her mother? Or hit her over the head and damage her brain? Should she have called the police, instead of this useless doctor?

'When will he be back?'

She was about to answer honestly – even her father couldn't have answered that question. But then she stopped, her survival skills kicking in.

'He'll be home in time for supper.'

'Right. Good. Ask him to give me a ring, will you?' He picked up his bag and looked as though he was about to leave. Harriet felt relieved and petrified at the same time.

'But what about my mother? What's wrong with her? Aren't you going to help?'

He gave an impatient huff. 'I'll explain everything to your father.'

'What am I supposed to do while I'm waiting? I need to know how to take care of her.'

'I suggest you leave your mother be.'

And with a whirl of brown coat stinking of stale cigars, he was gone.

Of course, Harriet did not leave her mother be. She brought her tea, and when that went untouched, a bowl of soup. She patted Mother's brow with a damp cloth, straightened her blankets, and lay beside her on the bed and read aloud.

There was one glimmer of hope that evening. As Harriet recited their favourite Emily Dickinson poem, a solitary tear trickled out of the corner of Mother's eye and down her cheek. Harriet blotted it dry while ignoring her own. Mother was not dead inside her head; she could hear and understand. Whatever the matter, she was still her mother.

The following morning, when Harriet crept inside her mother's bedroom, breath trapped behind her ribs, she saw that the blankets were rumpled and the water she'd left on the bedside table was now empty.

Rushing over, she expected to find her mother's eyes clear, mouth curving in a smile, however weak.

But no. The empty, lifeless mother was still there. Vacant eyes. Hands limp and cold. Only the slow, unsteady rise and fall of the blanket proving that she hadn't died.

Harriet wanted to stay and watch in case her mother moved again. Or stopped moving altogether. But she also didn't want anyone finding out what had happened and taking her mother away. Or, worse, carting Harriet off to some children's home because there surely wasn't anyone else who would take her in.

So she ate breakfast, only realising as she buttered the toast that it had been nearly twenty-four hours since she'd eaten anything. She left another glass of water, a mug of tea and a sandwich by her mother's bed, and spent the day at school, pretending everything was perfectly normal.

The phone was ringing as she arrived back home, the bus

having dropped her off at the end of the drive. The doctor. Why hadn't her father called?

'He tried, but you were engaged,' she said, her years living in survival mode allowing the lie to fly easily off her tongue. 'He also tried again this morning.'

'Can I speak to him now?'

'He's gone to fetch his sister so she can help take care of the house. And me. But I could give him a message if you like? I've got a pencil and paper here, so I can write it down.'

'Tell him to telephone me as soon as he's returned. Otherwise, I'll call round in the morning.'

It was a risky move, and she wouldn't have done it if she weren't desperate, but she called back the surgery an hour later and adopted her gruffest, deepest, most arrogant-sounding tone.

'Doctor? Leonard Langford. What the devil is wrong with my wife?'

'Yes, hello. I'm sorry I didn't catch you yesterday. I'm afraid, Mr Langford, Verity is having a nervous breakdown.'

'What does that mean?' Harriet's hands started to sweat. She almost dropped the handset.

'It means her mind has given up on her. Taken itself away for a while because something in her life was too much to bear. Have you any idea what that could be?'

Harriet held the phone away from her face while she gulped down what felt like dangerously thin air. 'How do I help her recover?'

'Give her time,' the doctor drawled. 'Encourage her to eat, drink, get up and go for a walk. If she doesn't snap out of it in a few days, call me back and I'll get a referral to Highbury, if you like.'

'Highbury?'

'It's easier than having her languishing at home indefinitely. The psychiatric hospital provides reasonable care. Of course, if a man such as yourself preferred to pay privately...'

'I'll let you know.'

She dropped the phone back into the cradle, before sliding down the wall until hitting the floor, feeling as though her bones were collapsing in on themselves.

Nervous breakdown?

Mind given up?

Hospital?

Harriet had no idea how to get her mother to snap out of it. But she would do everything it took to find a way.

In the end, this included almost a week of replacing the half-empty mugs and nibbled plates of food by her bed with fresh ones. She brushed her mother's greasy hair one evening, pathetically thrilled by how this caused Verity to close her eyes and release a faint sigh of pleasure. Troubled by the scent of decay on her breath, she urged her mother to brush her teeth, to no avail. But then, on the sixth day since Verity escaped into her mind, Harriet found a way to coax her back again. She'd got the idea from the book she'd found in the library on psychiatric ailments, which talked about the power of the senses.

After getting everything ready, she opened the door to allow the fragrance of jasmine to waft over to the bed, mingling with 'Somewhere Over the Rainbow' from the record player she'd lugged upstairs earlier.

'I've run you a bath,' Harriet said, in a cheery voice with only a hint of a tremor. 'It's lovely and warm, and I've used your favourite bath salts. Can you smell them?'

Verity tipped her chin up, slightly.

'Doesn't that sound nice? A long, hot soak in the bath? You

can lie here and listen to your favourite showtunes album for as long as you like.'

To Harriet's amazement, her mother slowly pushed back the covers and started to haul herself upright. Harriet hurried to offer a helping hand to stiffened limbs. Without saying a word, Verity allowed herself to be shepherded over to the bathroom, where Harriet gently undressed her and helped her into the clawfoot tub. She sank into the water, eyes closed.

'I'll leave you to it, shall I?'

Verity didn't look at her, but her mouth creased up in a smile.

Harriet waited until she was back in her own bedroom before burying her sobs in her pillow. When she'd finally run out of tears, an hour or so later, she found her mother dressed, hair blow-dried and applying a slash of lipstick.

'I thought we'd have eggs for supper.' Verity snapped the lipstick lid on. 'All of a sudden, I fancied an omelette. Is there any cheese, do you know, darling?'

'I... I think so. Why don't I see what I can find?' There might be a stale rind of cheese left, but there was only one egg, and no butter. Or much else. Panicking that her mother would retreat back to the mind-place if she found nothing to eat, Harriet gripped the door handle, preparing to race to the kitchen.

'No, it's fine. I'll do it.' Verity stood up. 'If not, I'm sure we can come up with something. It's what we Hood women do, isn't it? Make the best of things.'

She paused to pat her daughter's cheek as she left the room in a haze of jasmine and clean cotton.

Harriet decided the best thing she could do was copy her mother and pretend the past six days had never happened.

When her father came back the following week, nobody mentioned it.

The next time, a couple of months later, her mother stayed in bed for three days. Where a bath hadn't succeeded, Harriet had come home from school to find Verity rolling out pastry for an apple pie.

The third time, after ten anxious, desolate, lonely days, her father came home and found his wife in bed in what he described as 'a disgraceful state'. He ranted and raved to a blank face, until eventually, she shocked all of them by sitting up in bed and screaming at him to shut up while launching her alarm clock at his head.

The in-between days were also far from perfect. Sometimes, Verity acted like her old self, gardening and baking, singing as she dusted the cabinets. Other days, she was up and about, but Harriet could tell she was still in the mind-place. She wasn't really listening and completed a hotchpotch of random tasks as if in a dream.

Occasionally, she stayed in the same, grubby dressing gown for days at a time, hair unkempt and barely lasting an hour or two out of bed before disappearing again. She would cry those times, rivers of silent sorrow that caused Harriet's stomach to shrivel in anguish.

It stopped making a difference whether or not He was home. As the months drifted into a year, Harriet got used to cooking and cleaning alone, never knowing whether her mother would be at Riverbend, or lost inside her head. Her father refused to contact the doctor, barking that he wouldn't have that quack prying into their business, her mother would be fine and, for pity's sake, stop snivelling about it.

At the start of the summer, he decided Verity would be better off upstairs, in the attic. He did her the courtesy of hiring a local man to decorate, adding the furniture from her mother,

Louisa's, bedroom, and installing a full bathroom suite so she didn't have to face the effort of the stairs on bad days. He lured her up there as if enticing a wild animal into a trap.

The next time, he went away it was for six weeks. When he returned, it wasn't alone.

Over the next two years, Harriet liked to think she lost count of the number of women who spent time in Leonard's bed but she knew full well that it was eleven. Some of them stayed a weekend. One moved in for a full month. Her mother got up on one of those days, breezed into the kitchen, took one look at the imposter sitting at her kitchen table, sipping tea from the porcelain cup Verity's own mother had given her as a wedding present, turned right around and went up to the attic again, where this time, she stayed.

She spent so long in bed that her ungoverned body began to fail. With little nourishment, or movement, the dry skin soon hung off her bones, her lips cracked and bled. After a few weeks, Harriet found clumps of hair on the grubby pillow. The bed sores were worst of all.

Still, Leonard refused to call the doctor. The one time Harriet tried, the current woman imposter overheard and cut off the call. Later that night, her father removed his belt and reminded her that what happened at Riverbend was nobody else's business. As soon as the welts on her backside and thighs allowed it, she walked to the surgery herself.

But the doctor ignored her insistence that he came when her father was taking the imposter out for lunch, instead arriving first thing in the morning. Father instantly switched on the charm, laughing with the doc, his drinking pal, about young girls with overactive imaginations that bordered on hysteria.

'She's been reading too many novels about Victorian waifs

dying of consumption.' Leonard shook his head in wry amusement. 'Verity has a migraine, that's all. I keep telling her she's working too hard, but will she listen? With a place like Riverbend, there's always more to do, but my sister's come to visit, and she'll help ease the load.'

This time, he didn't bother with the belt, simply pressing his daughter up against the coat closet where she'd been eavesdropping and leaning in so close that his enraged spittle landed on her cheek.

'If you speak to any more doctors, one of your teachers, friends, or anybody else about your mother being ill, I will kill her. Do you understand?'

Harriet nodded, pressing her legs together tightly so she wouldn't wet herself.

'Not you. Her. I'll feed her so many pills, it will look like an overdose. She'd probably take them willingly if I offered. And then your childish meddling will have killed your mother.'

'Why would you do that?' Harriet whispered. 'She's dying. Why won't you help her?'

He threw her a scornful glance after rattling her one last time against the door. 'No one's forcing her to stay in bed.'

'She's your wife,' Harriet pleaded as he strode away, too softly for him to hear. 'My mother. A person.'

Harriet was fourteen when, one day, her mother simply didn't wake up. Her heart gave out, they said, due to the extreme malnourishment caused by her eating disorder.

'Her heart was broken!' Harriet wailed, to the deer and the rabbits in the middle of the forest. 'Her heart gave up! It wasn't an eating disorder; it was a Him disorder! He did this! He killed her, just like he said he would.'

If it took one year, eleven months and six days to kill someone, did that mean it wasn't murder?

The two years following her mother's death were the bleakest Harriet had known. The imposter left but was soon replaced after what Leonard deemed a respectable mourning period. Worst of all, the trips stopped. Whether her mother had been his real reason for going away, a smidgen of conscience prevented him from leaving his child to fend for herself, or he was afraid that if he did, she'd tell someone the truth about how he'd sent Mother upstairs and let her wither away to nothing, Harriet didn't know and didn't care. Her childhood was no longer one of two halves, light and dark, good and evil. It was misery and fear, without end. Her beloved Riverbend had once again been overrun by grief and despair. The bad guy had won.

Harriet learned to wait until her father was asleep and then creep into the study to rifle through his pockets for cash, knowing that he'd prefer to believe he'd mislaid it rather than drinking himself into such a state, he could be robbed in his own home. She would add this to the thin wad of notes she hid under a loose floorboard at the start of each week. The couple who ran the post office were well aware that the state-awarded Child Benefit was safer in this child's hands than her parent's.

Sometimes, her father would arrive back from a day out flushed with success, grinning as he emptied carrier bags bursting with nonsensical indulgences such as partridge, tins of smoked oysters or preposterously expensive cheese on the kitchen table.

She grew used to feeling hungry, especially in the garden's scarcer months when the harvest produced little more than a murky soup.

The second winter, her father neglected to pay the gas bill, forcing her to scavenge the forest for firewood, reminiscent of the days prior to her mother installing central heating.

She went back to finding excuses to linger in the warmth of

her school's stuffy classrooms or volunteering at the community centre. For the first time, she wished there'd been the money for boarding school. The warmer months were easier, when she could spend hours in the woods, or on the riverbank. Drawing, dreaming, keening for her mother.

It was here, while sketching the wildflowers in a meadow her father had sold off, that she saw him: a tall boy leaning on the gate, watching her.

And nothing would ever be the same again.

* * *

'Whew.' Hattie blotted her eyes with the end of her gold headscarf, after a phone ping had interrupted her flow. 'That's Lizzie off home. I think it's time we called it a day, too.'

'It's nearly six. Has Lizzie sorted dinner?'

Hattie checked her phone again. 'Mac and cheese. You help yourself when you're ready. If you don't mind tidying up here, Flapjack and I will spend a couple of hours in my studio.'

I opted to stay and catalogue the contents of the crate – we'd found birthday and Mother's Day cards hand-drawn by Hattie, the talent obvious even as a young child. There were a dried posy of flowers, a wonky clay pot and a straw dolly. Tucked in one corner was a velvet case containing Verity's engagement and wedding rings. Beside it was a tiny Bible, full of notes scribbled in the margins and verses underlined in red ink. Only the rings had any monetary value, and we had both wept that Verity had been so convinced her husband would destroy these treasured possessions she had felt compelled to hide them in a chapel.

After a quick meal, with no sign of Hattie, the shadow of the afternoon's work still hung heavy around my shoulders, and I knew I needed to find something to help me shrug it off. I toyed with watching a romcom, or seeing if my honorary nephews and nieces were free for a chat, but in the end, I pulled on my jacket, called for Muffin and followed my heart.

16

'Hey!' Gideon almost bumped into me, the sun had long since sunk beneath the bend in the river, and it was almost fully dark under the trees.

'Hi.' I couldn't think of anything else to say.

His eyes crinkled at me from beneath his hat. The last time I'd seen someone that happy to see me, I'd turned up to JoJo's birthday party with a kitten. 'I was just heading back, if you fancied coming over to the boathouse for a drink.'

In lieu of a normal answer, I burst into tears.

'Oh!' Gideon looked at me, his face stricken, before pulling me up against his soft jacket.

I nestled in there for a minute or so, soaking up the solid warmth and how his arms steadied me. Then I shifted, unable to resist pressing up tighter against his chest, and became aware of the thud beneath my cheek. Steady, but not at all calm.

I held my breath, savouring the thumps and what they might mean, until reluctantly pulling away.

'A drink would be nice. Thank you.' I groped for a tissue in my coat pocket and wiped my face.

'Has something happened?' Gideon's brow was creased with concern.

'Just a tough day in the attic.'

We began walking along the path towards the boathouse. 'Do you want to talk about it?'

'Yes,' I replied, with a wry grimace, 'but I can't.'

He looked at me.

'I've signed an NDA.'

'Including speaking to me?'

I nodded as Gideon took hold of my hand to guide me around a puddle. It felt so lovely wrapped around mine – a gardener's hand, rough and calloused from years of nurturing other living things – that I made no attempt to let go once the path turned to dry gravel.

'Wow. Surely we'll find out anyway, once the book is published.'

'*If* a book is published. It's Hattie's story to tell, not mine, either way.' I shook my head, feeling even worse than usual about the deception while my hand was in his. 'But a mug of tea and conversation about something completely different will help just as much, I'm sure.'

We talked for a while about his work transforming an elderly man's backyard into an 'eco-garden', designed to attract birds, bees and all sorts of wildlife.

'He insists on helping, dragging bags of compost and water butts about. It would be far quicker to do it myself, and I can't help stressing about him injuring himself, but seeing the look of satisfaction on his face... well. I guess doing things together can be more important than getting things done.'

I thought about that as we walked along the river. Who I'd done things with. How usually, after a horrible day, drenched in tears, I'd go back to my motorhome and wallow in the grief, with no companion to help me clamber out of it.

How, perhaps, doing things alone had caused as much sadness as it was designed to protect me from.

'Look who I found, wandering about in the woods,' Gideon said as he gave his mum a kiss and adjusted the blanket slipping down her knees.

'Ah, the nice Sophie who doesn't push me over in the playground. Have you offered her a drink, Gideon? She looks cold. And tired. You are staying for a drink, aren't you? There's some of that fancy cheese from the farm shop in the fridge.'

'Tea or coffee?' Gideon asked, opening a cabinet door.

'Is that the best you can do? Look at her!' Agnes snorted. 'White or red, Sophie? Or how about a G and T?'

'White wine would be fantastic.' I smiled, already feeling some weight sliding off my shoulders as Gideon busied himself in the kitchen and Muffin settled herself around Agnes' feet.

'Taking its toll, then. The secrets in the attic?'

My smile faded. 'Some days are longer than others.'

'It's not the ghosts, stopping you from getting a good night's sleep?'

'There are ghosts?'

'Well, if any departed spirits had reason to linger, it'd be Verity Langford. Who knows what you've stirred up, poking around up there.'

I felt a prickle of unease scamper up my spine. I didn't officially believe in 'departed spirits' hanging about, but I'd spent enough time with their families to know that atmospheres were more persistent, and peculiar things did happen.

She raised her eyebrows. 'Has Hattie told you about her?'

I gave a non-committal shrug, but she carried on anyway, shuddering as she pulled the blanket tighter.

'We didn't even know she died, at first. Missed the funeral completely. Then we were passing one day, and decided to call in. Leonard was drowning his sorrows with whisky. We were shocked to hear Verity had suffered heart failure. Weakened from a nasty pressure-sore infection. When Chester asked why she hadn't gone into hospital, Leonard explained how she'd locked herself away in the attic and refused to allow him entry. He was devastated. Distraught. We'd have worried about leaving Hattie with him, but he'd hired a housekeeper, and she seemed very pleasant. Still, it was a terrible business.'

'What was?' Gideon asked, returning with three glasses and a plate of cheese and crackers.

'Your Auntie Verity's tragic death,' Agnes said, accepting a glass. 'No doubt all will be revealed in due course. Or sooner?'

'Sophie's here for a change in subject, not to go over it even more,' Gideon said, assembling two platefuls.

'Fair enough,' Agnes said, taking a slurp of wine. 'How about a game of Buckaroo?'

We ended up playing a board game that didn't require a steady hand, only an ability to impersonate people, compose poetry on the spot and lie through your teeth. I've no idea who won, but I laughed so hard, my face still ached when Gideon walked me back to the house a good while later.

'Better?' he asked, taking my hand as we wound through the shrubbery, his torch lighting the way.

'That was perfect.'

He paused for a second. 'Perfect? Me, Mum and a silly board game?'

'Friends, an open fire, *amazing* cheese and the funniest evening I've had in ages. The only downside being I'd forgotten that laughing too hard makes me snort.'

He bumped into me playfully as we resumed walking. 'I thought it was very cute.'

'Cute? Sounding like a pig? Is that your inner frustrated farmer talking?'

He beamed, teeth and eyes glinting as the lights from the main house loomed up ahead. 'For what it's worth, I thought it was pretty much perfect, too. The snorting was just the icing on the cake.'

'Seriously,' I said, once we'd reached the boot-room door. 'That might be normal for you. But apart from my brief visits to Ezra's farmhouse, I spend far too many evenings with only a book and Muffin for company. And it feels weird laughing at a book when you're sitting on your own in a motorhome.'

I'd told him about Ezra, Naomi and the kids, but not yet shared anything about my own family, or lack of other friends.

'Well, then I'm glad you came.' He tugged on my hand, so at home in his, I couldn't imagine letting go. 'Come again. Whenever you like. I think we've got Twister in the back of a cupboard. Mum's great at it.'

'I will come again.' I hesitated, trying to find the right words. 'But not too often. And it won't be for long. Another two or three weeks and I'll be finished here, moving on to a new client.'

'Hmm. But will this new client, who I hate already, give you such great cheese?'

'Some of them do, actually. But that's not my point.' I emphatically removed my hand from his. 'I'm really enjoying your company. Yours *and* Agnes'. I'm really grateful for a welcoming place to decompress after a tough day. But that's all it is. This is how I live. I complete a project, move on to the next. That's it.'

He bent his head to mine, eyes burning through the darkness, the scent of him enough to send my head spinning. 'You think that's all this is? Another brief pit stop to avoid whatever it is you're running away from?'

'Yes. I was clear. No dating. No commitments. Even if you weren't Hattie's cousin, I couldn't... I don't... I'm not running away.'

He looked at me, waiting.

'I can't fall for you, Gideon,' I breathed, even as my heart called out the lie. 'Please don't try to make this into something it's not, and never will be.'

His wide lips curled into a smile, those kind eyes crinkling as if I'd said exactly what he'd wanted to hear.

'Oh, I can promise you I won't try to make this anything it isn't already,' he murmured, moving closer so slowly that he had plenty of time to judge whether or not I wanted him to stop. The inch my traitorous body swayed forwards was enough permission for him to softly press his lips against mine.

Oh, my goodness.

The *promise* in that kiss.

It was a second, no more. Long enough for a dozen scenarios to flash through my head, like lightning bolts.

Our non-date. The second. The first I love yous. A proposal on the riverbank. Wedding on the Riverbend lawn, JoJo and Aaliyah bridesmaids as Ezra walks me down the aisle. Summers in the forest. Winters by the fire. Babies. Grandbabies. Rocking chairs.

Everything I had never dared to dream of yet, since the moment we'd met, suddenly didn't know how I could live without.

I stumbled backwards, practically gasping for air.

Gideon's eyes remained closed for a moment longer. When he opened them, they contained a lifetime of certainty. He gave a firm nod as he began to smile. 'I won't make this anything that it hasn't been since I pulled you out of that puddle.' He started to back away. 'Like I said, I'm a patient man. I can wait for you to admit you know exactly what this is.'

His smile became a full-blown grin. 'I'll see you on Friday. Unless you want to come over sooner.'

17

Thank goodness the Gals came over on Thursday evening to stop me obsessing over what was, in reality, barely more than a peck, accompanied by some cryptic statements that, in the cold light of Thursday morning's rainy walk, meant nothing.

I'd spent the afternoon on my laptop, looking for local museums and stately homes who might be interested in displaying any of the attic items in upcoming exhibitions. I also completed some more research into Riverbend and Langford/Hood history, which I could pretend was to assist me in the project but was more because I was curious and also questioning whether Leonard was indirectly guilty of murdering his wife.

I spoke to Ezra about potential culpability but, given the NDA, I was asking questions in such a roundabout way, it was impossible for him to give me a concrete answer.

All in all, I was relieved more than nervous when, after a quick evening meal, it was time to head to the studio. My brain felt as if it might burst if I didn't art some of the tougher stuff out.

Hattie was already there, finishing up what had been the Changelings' final session, and getting ready for our next one. I'd barely seen her all day. She'd slept in after staying late at the studio the night before, and Lizzie had told me at lunch that, having found Hattie asleep at her desk, she'd sent her back to bed. She must have slipped out to the studio while I was changing into my art scruffs.

The rest of the Gals arrived a few minutes later.

'Got your waterproof mascara on, Gals?' Kalani asked, draping her leather jacket on the coat-stand.

'Like I had time to put make-up on, in between driving Archie to his street-dancing class and Flora – or should I say Arolf? – to hang about with hormonal boys at that dangerously ill-supervised youth club,' Laurie said, propping her crocodile umbrella against the wall. 'Before feeding those bloomin' pigeons, feeding Dad and figuring out what I'm going to feed everyone with tomorrow. Ooh, hang on, though.' She stopped and looked at Deirdre. 'You look different. I didn't spot that in the car.'

'Different, how?' Deirdre asked, tugging on a long, auburn curl. 'Good different or bad different?'

'Different as in you've had your hair and eyebrows done, put on a full face of make-up and are a whole lot orangier than you were last week,' Kalani said. 'I'm pretty sure you aren't so sloth-like that someone did all that while you were sleeping.'

'You missed my nails,' Deirdre said, holding out her fingers to show glittery acrylics. 'I've bought some new clothes, too, but I didn't want to risk getting them messy.'

'You have been busy,' Hattie said, sticking both hands in her jeans pockets.

'Good busy, or bad busy?' Deirdre asked.

'Bad different! Bad busy!' Kalani said, crossing her arms. She was wearing zebra-print velvet trousers with a white blouse that made her look ready for a power-meeting in a New York skyscraper.

'What?' Deirdre's face crumpled.

'Kalani, that's overly harsh, even for you,' Laurie chided. 'Deirdre looks fab. You look fab! Well, apart from the spray tan, maybe. But that'll tone down in time.'

'I know she looks fab but, Deirdre, how *dare* you undergo a makeover with anyone apart from the Gals?' Kalani appeared genuinely upset. 'Did one of those drones from your boring job go with you, because if you'd trusted us, we'd never have let you end up looking like a pumpkin. And I know your mum had nothing to do with it; no offence but her taste got stuck back somewhere in the fluorescent eighties.'

'Saying no offence doesn't stop it being offensive,' Laurie interjected.

'Well, sorry, but it's a lot less offensive than going for a makeover without us! My incredible taste is one of my biggest strengths and if I'm no good for that, then what's the point of being friends with me? Who else in this village is a better shopper than me?'

'No one!' Deirdre practically yelled back. 'No one is. We all know you could have your own TV show transforming boring women like me into something... not so boring. But I wanted to do this without you, okay? Without all of you.'

'So who did go with you?' Laurie asked, trying not to sound hurt.

'Is it so impossible to believe that I did this myself?' Deirdre cried. 'It wasn't about the haircut, or the nails or what lipstick suits me best. The point was I got off my backside, made some decisions and started taking control of my own life, for once. And yes, I know I look like an overripe apricot, there's no need to keep going on about it. I'd rather get a disastrous spray tan than never do anything, ever. Besides, Kurt Frinton in the butcher's told me I looked hot, with a capital H, and slipped a free chorizo in with my chicken breasts.'

'I'll bet he did.' Kalani smirked.

'I think it's brilliant,' I said, and couldn't have meant it more. 'How are we going to ever know what we like, how we want to present ourselves to the world, if we don't experiment a bit along the way? It's absolutely good different. You should be really proud of yourself.'

'Thanks, Soph!'

'Anyone else made any positive changes since last week that they'd like to share?' Hattie asked.

'Yes, actually,' Kalani said, causing us all to turn to her, expectantly. 'I spoke to my parents.'

'Don't you call them every Monday after Pilates?' Laurie asked.

'I drove over on Sunday and I told them that I'd been groped.' She paused, then tried again. 'That I'd been sexually assaulted by a lecturer at university. See? I'm getting better at saying it out loud. I told them everything.'

'How did that go?' Hattie asked.

'Mum was a bit freaked out. She went into the kitchen and started bashing spices into smithereens in her pestle and mortar. Dad...' She stopped to gather herself. 'Dad gave me a hug and told me he was sorry, and it wasn't my fault, and he wished I'd felt able to tell him sooner but understood why I hadn't. He... he cried. Then Mum came back and she cried, too. It was really hard to see them so upset, especially when Mum asked if that's why I haven't got married. It was awful, but positive at the same time, if you know what I mean. I feel a little bit lighter – *cleaner* – than I have in years. I've got the details for a support group and thought I might try it some time. See if that helps, too. Because ever since I made that bloody collage, I've been having the worst nightmares, and it's ruining my complexion. Besides, I think I might want to trust Tye enough to properly get to know him, and I can't do that unless I dare let him get to know me, too.'

'I knew you were dating Tye!' Deirdre crowed.

Laurie went on to tell us that she'd signed up to do online food shopping. 'To be honest, it took longer than driving to the supermarket in person, and I forgot so many things I ended up going there anyway. But it's a start.'

'Albeit a rubbish one,' Kalani said. As usual, she was harsh but truthful.

'Maybe today's art will help,' Hattie said, encouragingly. 'It's a three-part project so there's plenty to think about. Firstly, you've got fifteen minutes to paint your animal from last week. Then, I'm allowing you half an hour to create something that represents your home. As it is, not as you pretend or hope it to be. Take a moment to honestly think about what your home means to you. How do you feel when you are in there? Create that.'

'What about you, Hattie?' Deirdre asked. 'Are you ever going to join in with this?'

'I completed mine last night,' Hattie said, gesturing to an easel in the corner. We quickly clustered round to take a look at the large canvas.

'Wowzers,' Laurie said, which summed it up as well as any of us could.

Hattie had created the Riverbend estate. She'd painted the main house in thick, yellow oil paint, then added real twigs and leaves to cleverly represent the trees. Moss denoted the lawn, and there were tiny petals dotted in the flower beds. The river was in the forefront, stunning swirls of blues, greens, greys and purples. She'd stuck on tiny feathers, adding beaks and eyes in black pen to turn them into ducks. Flapjack was a patch of yellow fluff with a pink tongue and a piece of feathery yellow grass for his tail. She'd sketched the chapel and the boathouse, decorating them with dozens of tiny sequin hearts.

It was stunning, beautiful. Shimmering with peace and life. It summed up Riverbend perfectly.

That was, except for the top floor of the house. This was slathered in dirt and grit. Blobs of black paint. Splatters of blood red. A rusting razor blade and two nails were embedded in the mud. I even spotted a dead worm. Somehow, she'd swirled the black paint and the dirt so that it looked like screaming mouths. My bones shivered in revulsion.

Hattie was a genius artist. Thank goodness she usually stuck to woodland creatures.

'Okay, enough gawping at mine. Time to get on. Like I said, we've a lot to do.'

With a strict time limit, it was a sorry bunch of slumpy, shabby so-called homes we brought over to the beanbags later that evening. To be fair, I don't think mine would have been much better had I spent all week on it.

The newly confident Deirdre went first.

She'd used a ruler to draw a perfectly straight square in the middle of her paper with a black pen, adding a square door, two windows and a roof.

'That's it?' Kalani asked.

'Yes, and you know why. So we can move on, please. You've

been to my house; you know it has about as much soul as a service-station toilet. Laurie, what have you done?'

I looked at Laurie's picture and had to smother a smile. She'd scribbled all over the page, in as many different colours as there were in Hattie's pen pot. On top of the mess, she'd stuck pictures chopped out of Hattie's magazine stash. Shoes, plates, phones, and of course pigeons, to name a few. Right in the middle, peeking out from under a pile of clothes and crockery, sprawled inside a hand-drawn hamster wheel, was a woman who looked uncannily like Laurie.

'My home is chaos. How does it make me feel? Like I'm being smothered in other people's expectations. Drowning in their petty dramas. On and on and on it goes, and still I never get anywhere. I dread seeing that lovely, sea-green front door I bought last year in the vain hope that walking through it might make me feel a bit less like entering a fiery furnace of other people's crap.'

'Excellent job, Laurie,' Hattie said. 'Who's next?'

Kalani had tipped everything out of one of the cardboard boxes containing the other art materials. She had lined the huge box with foil, and made a shiny, foil-covered bed, chair and bath out of card. In one corner was a tiny pipe-cleaner person with black paper hair stuck on the top and draped in a red piece of fabric, synched tight where the waist would be.

'I did have another dimension to add to my piece,' Kalani said, before kneeling down and shaking the box, so that pipe-cleaner Kalani slid about, bumping into the bed and the chair. 'There I am, rattling about in all my pointless riches. Some nights, I'd give anything to have a pigeon pooping on my lime-stone flooring. It'd be a welcome distraction to have something to argue with.'

'Can we swap houses, please, Kalani?' Laurie asked. 'I mean, not forever but maybe a year or ten?'

I was last. I'd spent almost half of the thirty minutes trying to decide what to do, leaving me fifteen minutes to frantically stick pictures onto a sheet of paper.

'This is how I feel about home,' I said, pointing to the numerous images of different homes stuck along the side of a road I'd drawn in felt-tipped pen, twisting all over the page until it doubled back on itself and ended up at the beginning.

'Tell us about it,' Hattie said, softly. I think she knew what it would cost me to share this.

'This is where I grew up.' I pointed to the first brick house, which so closely resembled the home I'd grown up in, a tear had dropped onto the picture as I'd stuck it down.

'Are those *graves*?' Deirdre asked. 'In the garden?'

There were, indeed, three tiny graves that I'd half-hoped would go unnoticed.

'My parents. And my sister.' I tried to swallow back the painful lump in my throat. 'They aren't buried there, but, well, they were my real home, not the building we lived in.'

Everyone was so still, so quiet, they could probably hear my heart pounding, so I kept on talking.

'Home, for a long time, has been wherever work took me. I have friends who I stay with when I need a few days off, but, really, home has been me, and Muffin, and most recently here.' I showed them the last house on the road before it reached my original home again, which vaguely looked like Riverbend. 'And I've curved the road back to where it started because, I don't know. I've seen a lot of homes over the years. Stayed in a fair few of them. Some bursting with love, others crackling with hostility. But here, for the first time, I've begun to feel that maybe I should find a permanent home again. One day. To have friends who know me living just around the corner, or a butcher who slips a slice of bacon in with my beef because he spotted I'm making some changes. To have a local café where my friend serves me "the usual". I don't know.' I shrugged. 'But I know I can't do that unless I face *this* home, the first one, and what losing it did to me.'

Hattie handed me a tissue, and it was only then that I realised I was crying. It was my turn to be enveloped in the beanbag huddle – although we kept it short, as there was still part two to complete.

One thing I didn't point out on my artwork was a scrunched-up bouquet of roses at the foot of each grave.

Before the rest of the session, Hattie instructed us to grab our art and carry it down the studio staircase and across the lawn, behind the kitchen garden to the fire pit.

'You guessed it, Gals.' Hattie chucked a match onto the pre-built fire as she spoke. 'Chuck those old, ill-serving, too empty or overcrowded homes into the flames. You've outgrown them. Burn those bad boys!'

So we did. Hattie went first, ignoring our pleas that however disturbing her painting might be, it was far too exquisite to burn. Thankfully, they didn't take long to crumble into ashes because we had more arting still to do.

It was no surprise when Hattie explained the second task. This time, think about what we *wanted* home to be, to feel like. For us, and anyone we shared it with. She showed us a second canvas depicting Riverbend, this time with a clean, bright third floor to match the rest.

We got to work.

Deirdre's home was full of chintzy fabrics. There were chickens in the garden, and twin babies tucked up in a cot. A large bed had a big bump underneath the covers.

'My unspecified husband and me. Having fun. Maybe making more babies. I want a home that's so full of affection, I never once have to worry about finding my man with Heidi Sprag in a disabled toilet. And here,' she pointed to a wall, 'are all the photos of our amazing adventures.'

'Is that someone mud-wrestling?' Laurie asked, peering closer.

'I was running out of time!'

We all agreed it was wonderful.

Kalani had crammed another foil-covered box with people, having a party. 'I love my actual house. I just want to learn how to enjoy having other people in it. Trampling in mud or spilling wine on my sofa. Looking at my stuff.'

Laurie had covered a sheet of paper with a drawing of shelves full of folders and storage boxes. She released a blissful sigh. 'Everything in its place. Orderly. Organised. Doable.' The last shelf was empty. 'This is my Sunday shelf. Please note the absence of any pigeons on this shelf. It's for thinking, napping, pottering or doing nothing at all.'

My ideal home? For a few startling seconds, I'd not been able to stop thinking about the boathouse.

In the end, I'd created a garden. Was there a better symbol for putting down roots, allowing time to know a place, and, in doing so, to be known – and loved? To care enough about a place that it would hurt you to leave.

Wasn't *that* what made a home?

'That is incredible!' The Gals gushed, inspecting the hurriedly arranged silk flowers (not roses! Not yet), the tiny plot of vegetables I'd fashioned out of tissue paper, and the hammock I'd hung from two trees made out of twigs draped with more tissue-paper blossom.

'You should do this for a living,' Deirdre said, the others

nodding in agreement. 'When I finally marry the unidentified man under the bedcovers, will you do my flowers?'

Boy, those beanbags had to bear some blubbering that night. We could probably have wrung the tears out of them afterwards.

Instead, we headed to the kitchen to rehydrate with a gorgeous gal or three.

18

Friday morning was perfect spring weather. Clear and bright, with a warm breeze that carried the scent of cow-parsley blossom and meadow grass. I strolled down to the riverbank accompanied by Muffin, Flapjack and the bleat of distant lambs competing with a symphony of songbirds sounding as exuberant to be out and about as I felt. I'd made do with just a cardigan over jeans and a stripy T-shirt. When I spotted Gideon already waiting, my heart did an involuntary jig.

'Look,' he said quietly, eyes dancing as he gestured with his head to where the light sparkled on the water. It took a moment, but then I spotted it – a streak of brown, slipping up to the bank before disappearing into the reeds on the far side.

'An otter?'

He nodded, smiling. 'It's only the third one I've seen since living here. They normally appear at twilight.'

'Let's hope the rest of the day is as rewarding.'

'Anyway, I should have started with hello, but I didn't want you miss it.' He stopped, catching my eyes with his. 'Hello.'

I tried to keep my smile to a reasonable, 'spending the day

with a friend on a non-date' level. I couldn't do anything about the heat burning my cheeks and neck.

'Hi.'

'Can I carry anything?' He nodded to my rucksack.

'No, I'm fine, thanks.' While I'd brought food for our picnic, Gideon had insisted on bringing drinks, lessening the pack on my back.

'We'll head to the bridge first.'

Once we'd crossed over the water – after a pause to stop and admire a clutch of early ducklings bobbing around their anxious-looking mother – we headed into the trees, following a trail I'd not explored before. The dirt path weaved through stately oak and birch trees, their catkins dangling like snoozing caterpillars. It was too early for bluebells, but we passed snow-drops and wild daffodils. We stopped to listen to what Gideon informed me was the frenetic tapping of a woodpecker.

In between looking and listening and absorbing the wonder of English woodland on the cusp of spring, we talked about everything and nothing, keeping conversation as light as the pools of sunshine dappling the forest floor. I shared stories about the more bizarre clients I'd encountered, including the younger woman who expected me to auction off her late husband's human-hair collection to pay for his funeral, and the two triplets who'd kept their brother's ashes in a life-sized model of his head. Gideon repaid this with tales of his wilder youth on the outskirts of Lancaster, and the extreme measures Agnes sometimes employed to yank him back into line.

One of the highlights happened after cresting a hill to discover a gorgeous view spreading down into a valley, where we decided to stop for lunch. To my pride and pleasure, I spotted her in a small clearing further down the slope.

'A deer,' I whispered to Gideon, taking hold of Muffin's

collar, despite the doe being a good fifty metres away and Muffin being far too invested in waiting for a stray crumb of sandwich.

'It's a roe, I think,' he replied, peering at it. 'The red deer are larger. The roe are normally too shy to be seen in the middle of the day.'

Perhaps hearing the muted voices, she lifted her head from the patch of foliage she'd been nibbling, twitched her nose a few times, then bolted into the shadows at the far side of the clearing.

'An otter and a deer. The forest is being generous today.' Gideon grinned. 'I've come up with a far more impressive date than anticipated.'

'Date?'

He leant over and kissed me, another gentle brush of his mouth against mine, which left me longing for more. 'What would you prefer to call it? Two single people, spending time together, holding hands, kissing and sharing lunch?'

I raised my eyebrows. 'I've had more romantic kisses from my nan. And I used to eat lunch with her every other Saturday when I was young.'

'Now that sounds like a challenge...'

A challenge, and a fib. Gideon's kisses were so romantic, it was all I could do not to swoon.

'Okay.' I held up one hand before he moved any closer. 'This is, to all intents and purposes, a date. Despite it now breaking my strict professional rules about clients and their families.' I took a deep breath. 'But that's still all this is. I don't want to keep going on about it...'

'Then don't?' he asked, a twinge of pain in his eyes.

'I don't want to mess you about. To end up hurting anyone. We need to keep... *this*... casual.'

'It doesn't matter how casual we pretend it is,' he said, a hint of steel in his tone as he snapped a cluster of grapes off the large bunch I'd brought. 'If you decide to go, it will hurt.'

'Gideon, I've known you for two weeks.'

He looked at me from under his brow. 'I know that.'

'I've already got emails lined up from clients wanting help once I'm finished here. Clients in Dundee, St Ives, central London.'

'I didn't realise there were so many people out there needing the services of a historical author.'

I froze for a millisecond.

'You'd be surprised how many people need to share the story of their family history with someone.'

'And, what, then you write it into a book? Can't you do that from anywhere with an Internet connection?'

'It's not that simple. And I can hardly finish up with Hattie and then decide to keep living on her driveway. This is how my business works. Please don't patronise me by assuming you can come along with a better idea of how to run it.'

I was getting defensive because, inside, my very bones were screaming at me to say yes. Yes to more kissing, more getting to know this man. Yes to Riverbend. Yes to finally coming home.

Yes to not being hurt. Because I knew he was right; I'd let myself fall far enough that I was going to miss him, and I had too many missing people in my heart to add another.

'Can I make a proposal?' he asked, after a silence that would have been awkward if it was with anyone except him.

'If you promise to accept my first answer to whatever that might be.' I took a nervous sip of the home-made cider he'd brought.

'This is easy. It's lovely.' He watched me carefully. 'You haven't contradicted what I've said about it being something special, what's growing between us. So I'm working on that assumption.'

I gave a tentative nod.

'Like I said, either way, when – *if* – you leave, and decide not to invest in a relationship that's long-distance, then we're going to be sad. So, we might as well make the most of this while you're here. Stop faffing about, backing off, avoiding facing how we really feel. Why not spend the next however long it is just enjoying it?'

'You don't think that'll make it harder?'

He shrugged. 'Potentially. I'm willing to bet it'll be worth it.'

I took a couple of shaky breaths. How could I begin to explain that the reason I'd structured my life this way was precisely to avoid this type of situation?

'I don't know if I can do that. I don't know *how* to form a proper connection with someone without being on guard, ready to run if things start to get too intimate. To be honest, even thinking about it scares me.' I steeled myself and did the bravest thing I'd done since adopting Muffin: reaching out and wrapping my trembling hand around his. 'But if you can be patient with me, no pushing for promises, no commitment beyond the day I drive away from here, I would really like to enjoy spending more time with you, without pretending we don't care about each other, and seeing how that goes.'

'I can do that.' He nodded, eyes crinkling. 'I would love to do that.'

We sealed the deal with a kiss, until Flapjack wedged his head between us and stole the last piece of cheese.

The rest of the day was bliss. We found the Major Oak, where Robin Hood supposedly hid from the evil Sheriff of Nottingham, walked to the visitor centre, where we shared a giant piece of cake in the dog-friendly café. My pulse skittered every time Gideon took hold of my hand or smiled at me. When he wrapped his arms gently around me from behind while we read the information signs or admired the view, it felt like heaven.

Part of me wanted to jump in my motorhome and speed the heck out of there. The part that didn't want this to ever stop fought that scaredy-cat part and won.

We arrived at the boathouse to find Agnes snoozing on the sofa, a book resting on her lap. After more tea, more cake and a lot more conversation, Gideon drove to a nearby restaurant, Scarlett's, to pick up what he promised was the best takeaway pizza I'd ever eat, and we settled in to watch a film. Halfway through, Agnes decided she'd had enough and went to bed, so Gideon took her place on the sofa, putting his arm around my shoulders.

'Okay? Is this being patient enough?'

I rested back against his chest, eyes closing in contentment. 'Yes. That's more than okay.'

If those pesky thoughts about how this would all end had stopped interrupting, it would have been perfect.

Monday morning, I was supposed to be meeting Hattie to spend more time on the project. She'd spent Saturday resting and Sunday in the studio, so I'd caught up on some washing, finished a book and, after exchanging a ridiculous number of messages, given up and gone to hang out with Gideon and Agnes at the boathouse for a few hours, returning to Riverbend after an evening meal.

However, before I'd had a chance to meet Hattie as planned, I found her in the woods, bent double on a fallen log,

Flapjack waiting patiently beside her until Muffin came to say hello.

'Are you all right?' I asked, although the answer was obvious.

'Oh, Sophie.' She did her best to straighten up, but her pallid face was covered in a sheen of sweat, and she clutched her stomach as if in agony. 'I didn't see you there.'

'Can I help?'

'Oh, it's cramps. A menopause thing.' She shook her head as if it were nothing. 'I really need to up my HRT dose.'

'Does it happen often?' I really wanted to believe that the exhaustion, wobbly legs and lack of appetite were down to the menopause.

'Often enough.' She tried to laugh. 'It'll pass in a minute. Please, don't keep Muffin waiting.'

Muffin was perfectly happy sniffing a clump of grass.

'How about I take both the dogs for a quick run, and if you're still struggling when I get back, I can help you to the house?'

'Thank you, that's very kind. But like I said, I'll be fine by then. I could head back and make us both some brunch?'

I couldn't help smiling, knowing that, for Hattie, making brunch would mean turning on the coffee machine, even if she wasn't in the grip of stomach cramps.

'Okay, we'll see you in a bit.'

It was the shortest walk I could get away with without seeming too obvious, although the dogs spent so much time chasing each other that Muffin must have run twice as far as usual. As we made our way back up the path towards the house, I could see Hattie's hunched frame heaving on the boot-room door as if it were made of solid lead, before semi-collapsing inside.

We spent another five minutes playing with a ball on the

lawn, a few more wiping muddy paws off, and then found Hattie in the kitchen.

'There you are.' She beamed, tucking a stray curl into her headscarf. 'That seemed like a quick walk.'

'How are you feeling?'

'Oh.' She flapped a hand at me. 'Like I said, an irritating cramp. I'm fine now.'

She opened the fridge and stared at the contents for a few seconds.

'It might be worth speaking to your doctor, if it's happening often.'

She closed the fridge again. 'You're right. I'll get straight onto it on Monday, see if she can adjust my patches. Now, I don't know about you but I'm dying for a coffee.'

We spent the rest of the morning avoiding the subject, although I found it impossible to avoid discreetly scrutinising Hattie for any further signs of pain or illness. She eagerly grilled me about Friday's date while we ate bacon, eggs and avocado, and I did a sterling job of describing the walk while successfully omitting any mention of our conversation or kisses.

'I'm so pleased you had a lovely day,' she said, squeezing my hand. 'It must have been a welcome relief from hearing about my wretched story.'

'You're sure you don't mind me spending time with Gideon?' I asked. 'It's not a conflict of interest, given the project?'

'After our conversation about the NDA cleared up any confusion, I'm assuming I can trust you.' Her eyes glittered like polished topaz.

'Of course.'

'Then Gideon could do with a friend who shares his hobbies. And from what you've told me, you could do with one, too.'

I wanted to ask Hattie if she was up to working on the project today, as she picked at her brunch and visibly winced when she stood up to clear the plates. I would have asked when her fingers gripped the banister as she pulled herself up the stairs, or when she paused, as usual, outside the attic door to brace herself.

But I was growing increasingly anxious that she might have a deadline to this project, for the worst possible reasons, so I would do my best to help her push on through. And today, it turned out, was nothing to shy away from. Hattie opened a few boxes before pausing by one that contained a carved wooden deer, a stash of handwritten letters, tied up with a posy of dried flowers, and a painting of a young man. And so began one of the best chapters in Riverbend's story.

19

RIVERBEND

Harriet had known Aidan Hunter all her life. They'd sat beside each other at lunchtime in the tiny village school, and after Verity had heard that he always came empty-handed, she'd started packing extra sandwiches in Harriet's bag, so they could share. Once Harriet moved to the private school, he became a face hovering on the fringes of the Riverbend bonfire night, or picnics. However, when Harriet found a trout wrapped in brown paper on their doorstep, a chunk of fresh rabbit meat or a bowl of wild mushrooms, she knew who it was from.

Her mother knew too. She always reciprocated by sending Harriet to the Hunters' ramshackle cottage on the edge of Middlebeck with a basket of eggs or a carton of plums and the assurance that the Hunters would be doing a favour taking them off her hands; with Mr Langford away, they couldn't possibly eat them all.

Harriet knew from the musty stench that hovered behind Aidan or his siblings when they opened the door that their house wasn't like hers. The windows were peeling and so thick with grime, it was impossible to see through them. The scrubby patch of front garden was mainly weeds, with a pile of rusted scrap metal heaped against the rickety fence. The Hunters never invited her in like other families, let alone offered her a glass of orange squash or a biscuit. As she grew older, she understood that they were poor. Not poor like her and her mother, but poor as in bony wrists poking out of threadbare coat sleeves, and shoes held together with string.

Aidan's three siblings roamed the village with the pinched look of growing boys who never got enough food. They were frequently in fights, often in trouble, and when his eldest brother was convicted for stealing, everyone said that it would only be a matter of time before the next one joined him in Nottingham Prison.

Aidan, however, was more likely to be found in the company of his rangy dog than with the 'Hunter rabble'. He had far less to say than the rest of them and was far slower to speak with his fists – although it had been known. But he was still a Hunter. That family were a scourge on the village and even if you did feel a bit sorry for the youngest, who didn't stand a chance being raised by those criminals, you'd be foolish to do any more than pass him the time of day.

Harriet wasn't sure about that. Aidan had been quiet when they'd sat next to each other at primary school but he'd never been mean. He'd accepted her spare sandwiches with a cautious nod, and once, when she'd got home from school, she'd found a scratched metal yo-yo in her lunchbox, the string frayed and dirty. Anyone else would have probably laughed at this pitiful token of thanks, but Harriet treasured it.

Long before Verity had died, she'd stopped taking baskets to the village. Once Leonard no longer kept leaving on his mysterious trips, the parcels on the doorstep also ceased. Although Harriet missed the unspoken gesture of solidarity, she was grateful that Aidan realised Leonard would have sooner eaten his own socks than accept charity from a villager. If he'd had known the benefactor was a Hunter, he'd have probably fetched his shotgun.

But now, here Aidan was, leaning on the gate and watching Harriet while she drew, his scruffy dog by his feet. When Aidan saw her looking, he rose one slender hand in a slow greeting and began ambling towards her.

'Can I see?' he asked, nodding at her sketchbook once he'd come to a stop a couple of metres away.

Harriet studied him in much the same way she'd contemplated the buttercups. At some point in recent months, Aidan Hunter had grown into his wiry limbs and sharp nose. His hair, once the colour of marmalade, was now a rich russet that hung in curtains past his jawline. She dropped her gaze from his clear, hazel eyes to the grey T-shirt highlighting the frame of someone who spent his life outdoors. His jeans were frayed, rips in each knee and covered in grass stains. His tan boots had one black lace, one brown.

Tentatively, she held out the sketchbook. No one had seen her sketches since her mother died. She believed that she wasn't a terrible artist, but it suddenly mattered more than anything that his boy she'd barely spoken to in years thought that, too.

He studied each page, forehead creased in concentration as her hands plucked at a loose thread on her cotton dress. After what seemed like forever, he handed the book back, the faintest hint of a smile lightening his sun-kissed features.

'Thank you.'

Harriet squinted at him in disbelief. 'That's it? No further comment?'

In one fluid movement, Aidan sat down, still maintaining his distance as he draped an arm around his dog's shoulders. He reminded Harriet of the grey heron who often stood sentinel on the riverbank.

'I don't know anything about art.' His words were soft, but his eyes as warm as the sunshine dancing over the meadow. 'But to me, they're beautiful.'

'Really?' She couldn't help the beam of delight spreading over her face.

'I liked the hare best.'

'Thank you.'

'Do you mind if I sit here while you finish the buttercups?'

'Um...' Did she mind? Harriet wasn't sure she could breathe, let alone draw while this boy sat watching. But she thought about asking him to go and found that she minded that a great deal more. She picked up her pencil. 'It's not my meadow. You can sit where you choose.'

'Oh, I don't know about that.' Aidan tipped his head back, closing his eyes against the sun's glare. 'This was always River-bend land. Might be on loan to Jim Kirk, but you'll get it back one day.'

'My father can barely scrape together enough money to keep the land we still have.'

'True. But I wasn't talking about him.'

Harriet's mouth fell open. It was only when he opened his eyes again and gave her that tiny, not quite there smile that she hurriedly switched her gaze to the flowers.

'I never said how sorry I was about your mother.' Aidan interrupted the chirrup of grasshoppers just as she'd relaxed enough to start focussing properly.

She dropped her pencil.

'I would have called around. At least paid my respects at the funeral. But I didn't want to cause any trouble with your dad.'

He picked up the pencil and leaned closer to hand it to her.

When his fingers brushed hers, her heart felt as though it would burst out of her chest.

'That's okay. I didn't really notice who was there, to be honest.'

'It must have been hard. Since.'

Harriet gripped her pencil so tightly, her knuckles shone white. 'It has, yes.'

'I'm sorry.'

She took her time shading in every last petal and adding a tiny beetle but, despite her desire to prolong this unexpected moment, it was impossible to keep drawing once she knew the picture was finished.

'Here,' she said, ripping out her favourite picture of a hare and holding it out when Aidan turned to face her.

'I can keep it?'

She did her best to give a nonchalant shrug. 'I can always draw another one.'

As she started clambering to her feet, limbs stiff from sitting in the same position so long, he jumped up, taking her hand to help her.

'Will you be here tomorrow?' he asked.

Harriet took a deep breath. 'Yes.'

Another almost smile, a quick flick of his wrist towards the dog, and he had gone.

* * *

The following day, Harriet got up ridiculously early. She threw a load of washing in the machine, then swept the downstairs floors and chopped a pile of vegetables before hanging the wet clothes on the line. She was stuffing a hastily packed lunch into her art bag just as her father stumbled

down the stairs, still blinking away the whisky from the night
before.

'You're late for school,' he growled.

'My final exam was last week. I'm on holiday now until
September,' she said, hooking the bag over the back of a chair
and applying quaking fingers to her sandal straps.

'And you thought you'd spend it pleasing yourself, while I'm
working to keep a roof over our heads.'

Her jaw clenched, but she forced her voice to remain light.
'I'll be back to fetch in the washing and make a cottage pie for
supper.'

'You're what, sixteen? More than old enough for a summer
job.'

'Yes, but with everything I have to do here, the garden, cooking, keeping the house clean... I don't really have time.'

One hand darted out, shockingly fast for someone with a
horrendous hangover, and swiped the canvas bag from the
chair.

'If you stopped messing about with this nonsense, you'd find
the time.'

He flipped the bag upside down and started shaking it, her
precious art supplies clattering across the tiles, sandwiches and
two apples tumbling out with them.

'Oh, so you don't have time to contribute to your mother's
money-pit, but you're happy to steal from it.' He kicked one of
the apples so hard, it smashed into pieces against the skirting
board. 'Get out of here. And don't come back without a job.'

Everything in Harriet screamed out in protest, as her father
ground a heel into the tin of pastels that she'd bought after
weeks picking wild blackberries and selling the jam at the
village Christmas fair.

But she'd learned a long time ago that protesting was not

only futile, but dangerous. She'd have to hope that the mess remained strewn across the kitchen until it was safe to salvage what she could once he'd passed out in his study that evening.

'Get out!'

Another roar, and she fled while her legs were still brave enough to carry her.

* * *

When she returned in the early evening, the art equipment was nowhere to be seen. Her father's sneer that she could earn it back was not enough to pop the bubble of happiness that spending a day with Aidan had brought.

Aidan had spread a blanket on the grass – full of holes, but clean – and they'd lain back, staring at the clouds. 'God's doodles', he'd called them. He'd not said much in the hours they'd spent together, wandering beneath the oak trees, drifting downstream in the old rowing boat, but every syllable was honest, and kind, and the cadence of his words beat in time with her own heart.

When he'd cradled her cheek with his hand, as softly as if she were a baby bird, and called her 'Hattie', she'd known right then that she'd fallen in love.

She'd told him about needing to find work. He'd nodded carefully and asked if he could borrow her sketchbook. Anyone else, she'd have said no, but seeing the sincerity in the depths of his hazel eyes, she'd have given him anything.

Three days later, he handed her a letter from their old teacher, Mrs Armitage, who now worked at a busy craft centre beside Sherwood Forest.

'She wants to use my drawings for cards?' Harriet gasped. 'And sell them in the gift shop?'

'Do you think you can do that?' Aidan asked. 'You might need quite a few.'

She thought about the piles of watercolour pictures stashed in folders in the bottom of her wardrobe and under the bed. 'I don't know. I think so.'

What Harriet did know was that she'd give her all, trying.

Mrs Armitage gave her ten pounds for thirty wildlife paintings, carefully chopped using the village-hall guillotine and neatly glued onto stiff card. As the summer wore on, Harriet – Hattie, as she now thought of herself – started selling framed prints, for a lot more money than the cards. With Aidan's encouragement, she cycled to other tourist venues, most of whom immediately snapped up her stock. By the middle of August, she'd made enough money to stop her father sniping at her, and also began stashing savings underneath the loose floorboard.

Even better, Leonard thought she was working in a local tearoom. It was the perfect excuse to spend her long summer drifting in a haze of young love through the forest with Aidan.

And then September arrived. Sixth form. Hattie had stayed on with the hope of studying art at university. Father agreed as long as she kept up her job at weekends and holidays.

Aidan had defied his family and also decided to complete his A levels. He wanted to enter the police force but he wouldn't mention that to any of the Hunters until he was already on the bus to the academy.

Two years until they could finally be free.

Or so they thought.

On wet days, they'd started to meet after school and at weekends in Riverbend's chapel, seeing as it was one place Leonard would never go. They'd snuck in an old armchair that Aidan had found at a garage sale, along with a camping stove, a blanket and other small home comforts. Hattie considered it the perfect place to meet. Their love was sacred, and they even went as far as kneeling before the tiny wooden altar and exchanging vows, of sorts, with a promise that one day they would stand there and make them official. Most days after school, they would meet to do homework, play cassette tapes on Aidan's battered portable stereo and dream about their future.

One morning in November, Hattie confessed that the sudden bout of nausea that sent her stumbling outside had been plaguing her all week. Aidan came from a big family. He had accumulated several nephews and nieces over the years, and he knew exactly what Hattie's rounder curves and glossy complexion meant.

Harriet Langford was pregnant.

* * *

We were jolted out of the past by a sharp knock on the attic door.

'Who's that?' Hattie asked me, jerking around in shock.

'Shall I go and see?' We'd both frozen in place, Hattie perched on the bare mattress, me as usual squatting by the box we were working through.

'Nobody's allowed up here. They know that.'

'Who is it?' I called, seeing as Hattie appeared too startled to ask.

'It's me,' Lizzie's familiar voice replied. 'Is Hattie in there?'

'I don't want her coming in,' Hattie said, eyes scouring the room frantically, so I went and opened the door, slipping out and closing it behind me.

'Blummin' 'eck, Sophie. What are you doing in there, more naked therapy?'

'Clearly not.' I gave an apologetic smile, glancing down at my jeans and jumper. 'But you know Hattie doesn't want anyone else in the attic.'

'I do. What I don't know is why.' Lizzie blinked, hard, her apparent vulnerability contrasting with the image of a woman brandishing a battle-axe on her T-shirt. 'How can she trust me with running her whole life, but not this?'

'I don't know but, if it makes you feel any better, she doesn't trust her own family with it, either. I'm not allowed to mention it.'

'Has she done something horrific?'

'No!' I paused and decided to reframe my response. 'Not that I know of, anyway.'

'Right. Well. If she has, don't tell me. I don't want to have to find a new job. There aren't that many millionaire artists looking for a PA around Middlebeck.'

'Okay.' I waited a few seconds. 'Did you need Hattie for something?'

Lizzie's eyebrows shot up beneath her fringe. 'Yes. She was due in a meeting ten minutes ago. I tried calling but she left her phone in the kitchen.' She paused, letting out an exasperated huff as she turned to go. 'Please tell her that the twonk, and the twonk's boss, are waiting. I've told them she's been delayed on a call with a major furniture manufacturer in Los Angeles and will be there as soon as possible. If she can spare the time, she has a business that needs running.'

20

After the meeting, Lizzie accompanied her boss into the kitchen, where I was stirring a pot of tomatoey meatballs.

'Good meeting?' I asked, although one glance at Hattie suggested otherwise.

'Fine. The usual. I need a shower, though, after being confronted with the twonk's smirking face for ninety minutes. I'll eat later, if you don't mind saving me some.'

'I'll stay, if that's okay,' Lizzie said. 'Joss is out with his mates tonight and meatballs are my favourite.'

Given that Lizzie had made them, I could hardly refuse. We dished up two bowls of pasta, added the meatballs and a good sprinkling of cheese, and set aside a third bowl for Hattie.

'Did they mind her being late?' I asked, once we were eating.

Lizzie pulled a grim face. 'Not the first few times, but it's started happening often enough that people are losing patience. I know organisation isn't her strong point but that's why she employs me. If I can't even reach her, I can't do my job. The odd creative session where she loses track of time is par for the course, but this whole book thing is taking all of her focus, and far too much energy. She's falling asleep at her desk, skipping meals. Barely has the strength to walk Flapjack. And she signed a contract to design three new Christmas prints. So far, she's submitted a crow who looks as if Santa's forgotten to bring him any presents. It's too much. You need to speak to her, Sophie. Slow it down or something. Find a better balance.' She stuffed in a spoonful of pasta. 'I mean, what's with this book anyway? It's not as if she needs the money. If she wants to talk about her past, then she should know better than anyone to book in some private therapy. Art it out. Don't spill her guts to a stranger who'll then sell it on to as many people as possible. Is a stupid book worth a nervous breakdown?' Lizzie gave a sideways glance. 'No offence or anything.'

'I'll make sure she's got her phone, in future. And I can prompt her to check her calendar before we arrange anything. Perhaps the three of us should sit down and schedule the next few sessions in advance, at a pace we can all agree on?'

As Lizzie had talked, I'd been wrestling with whether or not to tell her that Hattie blamed the menopause for her current state but, even if that wasn't betraying my client's confidence, I couldn't see any point when I didn't believe it.

I also couldn't help wishing I could mention Verity and the vague mishmash of symptoms that, according to her teenage daughter's recollection, included loss of appetite and exhaustion. Was Hattie slipping into clinical depression? Could that also explain her stomach pains and brain fog?

If so, did I have a responsibility to end the project early? Or was she right, and facing the past was in fact the best way to heal?

I examined the NDA until satisfied it allowed for discussions with my business partner, then gave him a call.

His advice was clear, and simple. Nothing good would come

from chattering behind Hattie's back. If I was genuinely worried, I needed to try talking to her again, myself.

While I agreed it was the right answer, it definitely wasn't an easy one. I was used to being direct with my clients and had learned how to communicate difficult information when they were in a troubled state of mind. What I wasn't used to was talking openly and honestly with a friend. I could try to persuade myself that it was none of my business, and if Hattie didn't want to discuss what was wrong, there was nothing I could do about it.

Or I could take inspiration from my new art therapist and ask a carefully phrased question or two next time the Gals were gathered.

For the next few days, I barely saw Hattie, as she secluded herself in her studio, working on the overdue designs. I spent some time on the Riverbend database, filing a few boxes of paperwork into different categories and compiling a reference list, walked both dogs every morning and took Agnes to Laurie's café for lunch when Gideon was working too far away to pop back to check on her. I also did my best to avoid Lizzie, who took every opportunity to describe how much her boss had eaten that day, everything she'd done and how tired or distracted she seemed while she'd done it. There was a fine line between concern and gossip, and Lizzie was clearly prone to overstepping it.

On Wednesday, I ate dinner with Gideon and Agnes, and afterwards, Gideon and I walked into Middlebeck and had a drink at the pub. It was as lovely as our date in Sherwood Forest. Apart from two tiny blips.

'Tell me about your family,' Gideon asked as we cosied up on a bench seat in the corner. A perfectly reasonable question.

Especially since I was finding out all sorts of secrets about his. 'You haven't mentioned your parents.'

Oh dear.

I'd already talked about my family having died in art therapy last week. Prior to arriving at Riverbend, I hadn't discussed it in years. Occasionally, I mentioned to clients that I had lost close family members, if I felt it would help them to know. But I didn't even bring it up with Ezra any more.

I really didn't want to go there again. Even if it was Gideon asking. I didn't want to taint our limited time together with my old wounds.

So, I mumbled an excuse and ran away to the ladies' room. When I returned, several splashes of cold water and deep breaths later, Gideon was talking to a vaguely familiar woman about landscaping her garden.

'Really? You again?' the woman huffed, her sharp voice immediately identifying her as Jen, the Changeling who'd accused me of spying.

'Oh, have you already met Sophie?' Gideon asked, ignoring the sudden dip in temperature.

'Twice.'

'So, how do you two know each other?'

There was a prolonged silence while the Changeling's eyes darted around the room as she opened and closed her mouth again. Just as I nearly cracked and said that we'd met in the café, she blurted out, 'I'm a menopausal woman, and I'm no longer ashamed to say it!'

Before Gideon could choke on his mouthful of beer, she'd disappeared out of the door.

* * *

By the time we set off for home, the temperature had plummeted to freezing. As we huddled together for warmth, our torches glittering off the frosty path, he asked another question that sent my stomach halfway up my throat.

'The day I showed you around Riverbend...'

Ugh. Here it came...

'When you left, quite suddenly, you looked distraught. Had I said something to upset you?'

The silence hung heavy between us as we continued down the footpath providing a shortcut back to Riverbend.

'No. It wasn't you.'

'Okay. That's a relief.' He tugged gently on my gloved hand, but the conversation wasn't over. 'I had wondered if it was a panic attack. I mean, don't talk about it if you don't want to. I don't want to pry, or make you feel uncomfortable...'

'What, and make me panic?'

I felt his smile through the shadows. 'Precisely.'

I took a few more strides to decide how much to tell him. I wanted to tell Gideon everything. But the way my heart flinched at the question – I simply wasn't able to let him into such a fragile part of me, when in a few weeks, I'd have to push him out again.

'It was a sort of panic attack, yes. They don't happen very often, and I can usually handle them. I'm hoping the art sessions with Hattie and the Gals will help. Honestly, just being here seems to help.'

'What, here?' Gideon asked, grinning as he opened the gate leading through the Riverbend boundary wall.

'Or here?' In one deft movement, he pulled me through the gate and into his arms.

'Both.' I giggled, stretching up on my tiptoes to kiss his ice-cold lips.

We tightened the embrace as what I'd intended to be a peck rapidly deepened. I still held back, could not open up and show this man the depth of passion he sparked within me, but with each date, he coaxed me into revealing that little bit more.

'I have a really great suggestion, given that being here, with me, helps so much,' he whispered against my mouth. 'Stay.'

The moment broken, I stepped back into the increasingly cold and lonely place that was not-with-Gideon.

He screwed up his face. 'I know it goes against our deal to even mention it but it is so hard not to try and fight for this. For you.'

'If you want to fight for us, you need to go slower.'

He shook his head, clearly frustrated. 'What I want is to not be the only one fighting for something that we both know is worth it.'

I pressed both hands over my face, unable to cope with the intensity in his gaze. 'Right now, the only thing I'm fighting is another panic attack.'

Gideon was silent for a few moments, until I felt a tentative hand rest on one of mine. I twisted my hand around to clutch his fingers.

'Did I tell you that I'm visiting a local nature reserve with a new colony of beavers?' he said, which was about the most perfect way to distract me.

I lowered my hands from my face and we began walking through the trees towards the fire pit. 'Tell me more.'

'I probably won't see any, but the ranger will show me how they're improving the local habitat.'

By the time we'd reached the boot-room door, I'd heard all about Gideon's dream to reintroduce beavers to Riverbend, and the positive ways they could impact the environment. The previous panic had deflated to a twinge of disquiet.

'Maybe... maybe if you do, I can come back to visit some time and you can show me their dam.'

'Camp out by the river and see if we can spot one?'

'Sounds good.'

He kissed me goodnight.

'It's a date.'

* * *

On Thursday, the Gals arrived much earlier than usual, bearing a Chinese takeaway and a bottle of wine.

'Don't worry,' Kalani said, starting to unpack the cartons. 'The booze is for once we've finished the blubbering.'

'What's all this?' Hattie said, wandering into the dining room in paint-splattered jeans and her usual grey top. 'Therapy is at seven. And unless my phone is broken, it's only six.'

'It's dinner. We arranged it on the Gals WhatsApp.' Deirdre frowned at her. 'Soph invited us.'

'I don't think I read those messages.' Hattie squinted at her phone.

'We assumed you and Sophie would have spoken about it,' Laurie said. 'We agreed it on Monday.'

'Sorry.' I pretended to be embarrassed, but this was the perfect chance to bring up Hattie's health. 'We've not had a chance to speak properly this week.'

'Haven't you been working on the project?' Deirdre asked.

'Hattie's been creating some new designs, and, well, she's not been feeling great so we haven't been eating dinner together, either.'

'Not feeling great?' Three women instantly spun towards Hattie, scrutinising her pale skin, sunken eyes and limp ponytail.

'Phooey.' She waved a half-hearted hand at them. 'You Gals know what I'm like when the inspiration starts flowing. It won't be interrupted with trivial matters like food and sleep.'

'Or a shower.' Kalani winked.

'Not when I'm overdue on a deadline!'

'Well, I hope a takeaway will be a good chance for you to stop and refuel,' I said. 'Sorry, Hattie, I thought you'd read the messages.'

'At the risk of sounding like Kalani, you do look like crap,' Laurie said, once we'd loaded our plates and started eating.

'Thank you for pointing it out.' Hattie sat back, the tiny strand of noodle dangling off her fork quivering.

'You've lost weight,' Kalani said, the soft concern in her voice catching everyone's attention. 'And you were a skinny little thing already.'

'It's not just that,' Laurie said. 'Your posture's changed. Like you're curling in on yourself. It's how Dad looked when his bowels were bad.'

'So, now you're comparing me to your elderly dad with bad bowels?' The noodle slipped off her fork.

'What's going on?' Kalani asked. 'And don't fob us off with the "artist at work" excuse. We've seen you after a week of long days in the studio and you still light the room up.'

'Is this what this meal is about?' Hattie turned to me, bristling beneath her exhaustion. 'Bully Hattie into revealing her private medical information?'

I gave an apologetic shrug. 'Sort of, yes.'

'I already told you.' Her glare swept across the rest of the table. 'I already told her! I'm fifty-five. It's the menopause. Sore joints, sleepless nights, exhausted days, brain fog. Bloated stomach so I'm not eating as much. Would you like to grill me on my dry vagina or horrible wind while we're at it?'

'The menopause can do all that?' Deirdre's expression was simultaneously doubtful and appalled.

'Laurie?' Hattie turned to the only one of us likely to know for themselves.

'Have you forgotten my hot flushes?' Laurie winced at the memory. 'Or the time a customer mentioned that the croissants looked a bit dry and I threw one at his head? Hattie, why on earth haven't you got yourself to the doctor? I'd be in prison by now if I didn't have HRT.'

'I did. She prescribed me some patches and I'm already starting to feel better. But she warned me it could take a few months.'

'You're what, fifty-five, though?' Laurie mused. 'Pretty late for such drastic symptoms to be starting.'

Hattie shrugged. 'That's the joy of the menopause, isn't it? Does what it likes, when it likes, and it's anyone's guess what it'll do next.'

'Ain't that the truth?' Laurie nodded, glumly, before taking a large bite of a spring roll.

'If things don't improve, make sure you go back and speak to her, won't you?' Deirdre said, eyebrows furrowing. 'I don't think it's normal to be that bad.'

'Nothing about this is normal,' Hattie said, pulling a face. 'Anyway, enough ambushing me and my hormonal horrors. Why are we eating this takeaway here, and not at your house, Kalani? What happened to inviting us over at last?'

Kalani shifted in her seat. 'I'm working on it. I wanted to get some new sofa covers before having anyone round.'

'Kalani, we're the Gals!' Laurie said, affronted. 'We aren't "anyone".'

'No, you're four women who like to dance about with a

gorgeous gal in one hand and a plate of greasy food in the other. Invitations will be sent out when I'm ready.'

'It better be soon.' Hattie nodded at me. 'Sophie is ignoring everything she arted out last week about needing a permanent home and still insists she's moving on as soon as the project is done.'

'What?' The others all looked at me, mouths dropping open. 'Why on earth would you want to do that?'

'That's how my business works.' I shrank back into my seat. 'I have to move to wherever the next client is.'

'Can't you find a client close enough to commute each day?' Laurie asked, face creased with consternation. 'You said you wanted to come into a café and have the usual. I've ordered a latte mug with "Soph" on it for your lunches with Agnes.'

'Commute from where?' I swallowed back the ache clogging my throat at the thought of the mug. 'I can't park the motorhome just anywhere.'

'You could move in with Kalani,' Deirdre joked. 'Once she's got her sofa covers.'

'Dogs will not be allowed on the sofas, at any point, ever,' Kalani replied.

'You'll visit, though?' Laurie asked. 'You're a Gal now.'

I took a deep breath. Felt my insides stiffen.

'I've already promised Gideon that I'll be back to visit.'

Well, that turned the conversation in a whole new direction.

'Come on,' I said, eventually, once we'd all laughed so hard that even Hattie's face glowed. 'Let's go and do some art.'

* * *

'Today, something a bit different.' Hattie held out five Post-it notes, folded in half. 'Instead of creating something for ourselves, we are focussing on each other. Pick a name, find a table, and start thinking about that woman, because you're going to be making them something really special.'

'Please don't expect me to hang something one of you lot have made on my wall. Except you, Hattie, of course. I've already got one of your prints in my bathroom.'

'In the bathroom?' Deirdre wrinkled her nose on Hattie's behalf.

'Well, the animals are all very nice and cute and everything, but they don't really fit my aesthetic.' Kalani gave a sympathetic smile to Laurie, who today had worn a long-sleeved top displaying the image of a cartoon cow, and mustard trousers covered in chickens. 'Sorry, Laurie, but you know I don't do creatures who can't flush a toilet.'

Laurie snorted. 'I was having a conversation with my darling son about that very topic only yesterday.'

'What are we making?' I asked, in an attempt to get us back on track.

'A superhero cape!' Hattie announced. 'So, consider carefully what superhero qualities this person possesses. Nothing too obvious, please. What do you see in them that they may not realise about themselves?'

I shrivelled up at the thought of one of these vibrant women picking my name. They'd known each other for years. Gone through family troubles, relationship break-ups and all sorts of ups and downs. What did they know about me apart from a fake story about me being an author? Oh, and that my family had died and I'd been on the run ever since.

Some superhero.

I picked Laurie.

Following my art therapist's instructions, I considered carefully Laurie's superhero qualities, and got to work.

21

An hour later, we sank onto the beanbags in a cloud of nervous anticipation.

Hattie offered to go first but we turned her down on the basis that seeing her creation would only make us feel more self-conscious about showing our own.

Instead, Deirdre held up the cape she'd made for Kalani.

Kalani looked it up and down, eyes narrowing.

'Don't pretend you don't get it.' Deirdre smirked. 'You're Pumpkin Gal.'

Onto a black, sparkly background she'd stuck a painting of a giant pumpkin carved into a scary grimace like a jack-o'-lantern.

'I don't celebrate Halloween.' Kalani shook her head. 'I don't even especially like pumpkin.'

'No, but you are one.'

'Um, what?' Kalani pulled back her chin.

'All tough and hard on the outside.' Deirdre laughed.

'A big, hard, orange ball on the outside?' Kalani muttered, unappeased.

'*Strong* on the outside. But inside, soft and lovely and just enough spice. Plus, pumpkin seeds, right at the centre, are really good for you. Your honesty is so healthy for a people-pleaser like me, Kalani. If you know what I mean.'

'Um, not really?'

'We know full well that you would die for every one of us. Including Muffin and Flapjack. And you pretend to not even like dogs. You might not invite us over for a Gals' night in, but you'd happily carve out your own kidney if we needed one. Hence the pumpkin being carved. When I found Heidi and Gavin together...'

'May her towels always be damp,' Laurie mumbled.

'You sat with me, in that preposterously expensive designer jumpsuit you'd bought especially for the party, on the pee-stained toilet floor, while I cried onto your leather jacket. You slept on my lumpy old sofa for three nights, and I know you turned down a massive work contract to take care of me. I also know you abandoned your Valentine's mini break because I phoned you up in a state. And being fun might not seem important but, for someone struggling with despair, your spice makes all the difference. You pretend to be tough, Kalani Hale, but you are my hero.'

'You do know that pumpkin spice isn't made of pumpkin?' Kalani asked, before promptly bursting into tears.

I went next while Kalani was composing herself, mopping her eyes on the new cape draped around her shoulders.

'Blanket Gal,' I said. Thankfully, people were more prepared to keep an open mind after Pumpkin Gal.

To the outside of Laurie's cape I'd stapled pictures chopped out of Hattie's magazine stash. A roll of bandages, a chef, a taxi, multi-purpose cleaning spray and numerous others.

'This is what people might see on the outside. A giving, capable woman who is many things to many different people.

But we don't love you because of what you do, Laurie.' I tried not to choke on my confession of loving someone. Hattie had no idea what a major step forward that was in my therapy. 'It's brilliant, but it's not why people treasure you.'

I flipped the cape over to reveal the inside was covered in feathers, fur and other pieces of soft fabric, stuck on in squares like a patchwork quilt. 'Occasionally, we meet the kind of person who is instantly trustworthy. Who doesn't have to say anything, but people feel safer just being with them. The kind of person you want around on a bad day. You're like a comfort blanket in human form, and goodness knows we all need one of those.'

Laurie was speechless, but the strength of her hug as I handed her the cape said it all.

Kalani showed me my cape.

She'd covered a square of red fabric with a diamanté shield, leaving an empty heart-shaped space in the middle.

'Going-for-it Gal,' she said, solemnly wrapping it around my shoulders. 'Sophie, you have a backbone of solid diamond. The toughest element on earth. I don't know the ins and outs of your story. But I know it took guts to forge a life for yourself after losing your family. And now, you're summoning a whole new level of courage and exposing your heart again, to love and friendship and to definitely not chickening out of finding a home near Middlebeck.'

She flicked off one of the diamantés, the dogs pricking their ears up as it skittered across the floor. 'You were downright standoffish when you rocked up here in that motorhome. Now look at you, snort-laughing with the Gals and snogging Gideon Langford in the bushes. Daring to let people in again makes you a superhero in my book. You inspire me to do the same.'

This was why I'd never done therapy, my quivering bones

reminded me as Laurie explained Hattie's Sunshine Gal cape, and Hattie wowed us all with her Adventurer's Cape for Deirdre. This was why I kept my distance. *Exposing my heart?* The realisation that I'd allowed this to happen, one tiny diamanté flicking off my shield at a time, made my stomach churn.

How could I ever go back to my old life now?

Perhaps it was in that moment that my newly exposed heart, while blinking in the sudden glare of light, decided to stay. For a little bit longer, at least.

We cleared up the mess and trooped back to the house to open the wine and slosh out the gorgeous gals. Hattie sipped at her drink while slumped in an armchair enfolded in her cape, looking as if she'd spent the evening wrestling crocodiles, not eating Chinese and painting a map onto a piece of fabric.

Noticing her friend's drooping eyes, Kalani nudged Laurie, who downed her cocktail and reminded Deirdre in a loud voice that some of them had to be opening up a bakery in a few hours.

It told me everything I needed to know when, after hugging Hattie goodbye, as she slipped out of the doorway, Laurie muttered to herself, 'Menopause, my arse.'

After a night thrashing about in my super-soft duvet, wondering whether Hattie was lying to herself, or just the rest of us, the problem was solved for me.

The dogs and I cut short our walk as a sprinkling of snow

had appeared overnight, and, although it wasn't deep, it didn't take much prancing about in the dusting for their paws to become encrusted in ice. Once we'd towelled off and I'd changed into warm, dry clothes, I went to the kitchen to get some tea. Lizzie sprang out of the office as I walked past.

'Flapjack's wet. Did you walk him?'

'Oh, hi, Lizzie. Yes, I've been walking him with Muffin while Hattie's busy in the studio.'

'Then she's nowhere.'

'Hattie? What do you mean?'

'She's not anywhere in the house. I've checked her bedroom, the bathroom.' She started counting on her fingers. 'I even had a peep in yours because I was frantic. I broke her precious rules and knocked on the attic door again.'

'Didn't you check the studio?'

'That was the first place I looked. And from the looks of things, if that's where she's been all week, she's not been working. I cleaned in there on Monday, and nothing's been touched. Her paintbrushes, pens and pastels are all exactly where I left them. The same sheet of paper with half an indecipherable squiggle is on her desk, and the easels are empty.'

'Really?'

'Has she been fobbing me off pretending to be working on the designs, while really you've been in the attic?'

'No.' Panic started creeping up my back. 'No. She's not been in there. She gave me the key, said I might as well have it as she'd be in the studio all week.'

'So where is she?'

'Could she have gone out, or to see Agnes? Perhaps she wanted to do some sketches of the snow?'

'Her car's still in the drive. I've called Agnes. Maybe one of her friends picked her up and they went out, but she'd already rearranged a one-on-one therapy session today because she knew we had this phone interview at twelve. I messaged her a reminder at nine and she replied with a thumbs-up, but she's not answered any messages or calls since.' Lizzie's eyes widened.

It was hard to think clearly through the fog of dread. Where else would Hattie go? Somewhere near enough to walk, and to return in time for her interview.

'Have you tried the chapel?'

Lizzie squinted at me. 'Why on earth would she be there?'

I grabbed my still-soaking wet coat, hooked on Flapjack's lead, in case he could sniff out what I couldn't spot, and headed back into the snow.

* * *

We picked up a trail of footprints about halfway between the house and the chapel. Soon after that, Flapjack must have heard her. Ears pricking up, he began straining at the lead, dragging me the last few metres to the chapel door. I heard her too, once we'd tumbled inside and the door had swung shut behind us.

I dropped Flapjack's lead and he raced over to the far corner, where a crumpled heap twitched and groaned in response to his fretful licking.

'Hattie!' I swiftly followed him as she began clumsily pushing herself up, releasing a hiss of pain.

'Lizzie will be fuming,' she groaned as I bent down to help her into a sitting position.

'She was worried about you.' Searching for Lizzie's number in my phone, I hurriedly sent her a message to confirm I'd found Hattie.

'Do you have any meds I can get you?'

Hattie, hunched over her middle, grey curls hanging over her face, shook her head.

'Okay, so are you able to tell me what's going on? Or should I call 999?'

'Give me a minute.' Her hand was surprisingly strong as she reached out to grip mine. I sat down beside her, leaning against the cold chapel wall as Hattie rocked back and forth, clearly in absolute agony.

After what felt like the longest two minutes of my life, she blew out a long sigh and straightened up a few inches.

'I think it's probably time I told you,' she said, her voice hoarse. If I'd taken time to think, I'd have brought some water. 'This isn't all the menopause.'

'Yes. I had worked that out.'

'It appears as though I'm dying.'

I'd been expecting it, but the blow knocked the air out of my chest all the same.

'If you could help me back to the house, I think it's time to call my doctor. And then I need to make up some excuse to Lizzie about my ditziness derailing yet another meeting.'

'She doesn't know?'

A bead of sweat trickled down Hattie's face as together, we hauled her to her feet.

'I'll tell her when I'm ready.'

'I think—'

'I'm not ready.' Her jaw clamped shut, ending the conversation.

'What about the Gals?' I asked as we hobbled back, gripping each other's hands and avoiding the icier patches where we could.

'I think Laurie's guessed something's up, but she knows I'll tell her *when I'm ready*.'

'Gideon?'

Nothing but a grim shake of her head.

'Well, I'm pleased you've told me. But, I mean... what...?' I couldn't utter the worst question – *when*?

'I will tell you. But let me get this interview over with, please?'

'Of course.'

'Let's meet this afternoon. I'll lug myself up to the attic.'

As soon as we entered the house, Hattie pushed back her shoulders, lifted her chin and softened her face into an apologetic smile. The transformation was startling.

She hurried through the hallway into the office, where Lizzie was leaning back in her chair, scowling at her laptop. 'I'm so sorry.'

Lizzie folded her arms, waiting for the explanation.

'There was a stray dog in the garden, but every time I got near it, the poor thing darted away. I would have called, but my phone was in my other coat pocket. Then I slipped on the snow into a gatepost... I am so, so sorry, Lizzie.'

'Sophie said you were in the chapel.'

'Well, yes. I was by the chapel when I fell, so I nipped in to sit down and rest my ankle for a moment.'

'And the dog?'

'The dog? Oh, yes. They disappeared, back towards the river path. We can only hope the owner found them.'

'Perhaps you should put something on the Middlebeck Facebook page? In case it's still lost.' Lizzie kept her face impassive, but her tone was steel.

'Oh, of course. Good idea. I'll do that as soon as we've finished the interview.'

'The interview's cancelled. The radio station said they

couldn't stall any longer. But they'll let you know if another slot becomes free.'

'Oh. Okay. Is there anything else scheduled for today?'

'The Christmas designs are the main priority for now. Presuming they aren't finished yet.' Lizzie's pierced eyebrow flickered. 'Here. I'll take your wet coat. It looks like you need to get changed.'

Hattie handed Lizzie her cream coat, then started to climb the stairs. As I crossed the hallway to follow her, needing to change my own clothes, Lizzie bumped something against my wrist.

Twisting around, I saw Hattie's phone.

'It was in her pocket.'

'Ah.'

'You know what? I think I'm done for the day.' She thrust the phone into my hand. 'Unless you want to tell me what's really going on?'

'I found Hattie in the chapel, like she said.'

Lizzie stared at me for a long minute. 'If she doesn't sort out whatever the hell's up, if she doesn't trust me enough to share it, then I can't do my job. Perhaps you could tell her that, seeing as she's no longer listening to me.' She gave a bitter shrug, backing off towards the office. 'I love my boss, but I'm not prepared to take much more of this crap.'

* * *

After helping myself to some lunch, I decided to wait for Hattie in the kitchen. It was almost three by the time she came downstairs. I poured us both a coffee and we settled onto a sofa in the sunroom. The sun had come out, melting all but the stubbornest snow patches, and the beautiful space was living up to its name, bathed in warmth.

'Did you call the doctor?' I asked.

Hattie nodded. 'I've an appointment on Wednesday.'

We drank our coffee for a while, watching the birds pecking at the soggy lawn, before she continued.

'It's a very rare kind of lymphoma. I was diagnosed two weeks before my fiftieth birthday, after tests for something else. It was low grade, symptomless apart from some tiredness, so, after removing my spleen, I've been on what they call "watch and wait". Tests every six months and looking out for signs it might have turned aggressive. Including exhaustion, stomach pain, confusion, night-sweats.' Her voice began to break. 'I really wanted it to be the menopause. In the first couple of years, I convinced myself that every headache was this sleeping monster starting to stir. But there was only a 10, maybe 20 per cent chance it ever would, so I'd started to hope, to allow myself to believe that it would be fine. It's just the menopause!'

She stopped again, fighting furiously to maintain her composure. 'I think watching and waiting is over. But I'm not ready, Sophie. I'm just not damn well ready.'

I could have offered some platitudes. Reassurances that, with such a small chance, maybe it was the menopause, or something else simple and straightforward to treat.

But even in the three weeks since arriving at Riverbend, I'd seen Hattie changing. Becoming weaker, slower, the spark that had entranced me when we'd first met growing dimmer.

'Would you like me to come with you to the doctor?'

'Oh, darling, that is definitely not part of the job description.'

I reached across and took hold of her hand. 'No. But it's part of being a friend.'

22

'Right.' Hattie managed a smile once we'd cried, and chatted some more about the potential prognosis, and what that would mean going forwards. 'Let's get back to the project before I'm too enfeebled to manage the stairs.'

It took a lot of hunting through the remaining boxes before Hattie found what she'd been looking for. Wrapped up in tissue paper, tucked inside an old plastic bag. A blanket, the exact same colour as Hattie's eyes. Riverbend blue.

'It was for my baby. The only thing I had to give them, apart from, you know, stuff like bones and blood and ten fingers and toes. But then, here it is, and here I am. Once again, I have my father to thank for a Riverbend loss.'

* * *

Riverbend

Hattie was torn in two. Aidan's baby growing inside her was like a secret promise. The hope of a future together, away from her father and the Hunter family in a place where the three of them could be free.

But whenever she indulged these fantasies, the ugly, sticky truth would eventually seep in. How could two sixteen-year-olds fend for themselves, let alone care for a child?

Occasionally, Aidan would try to discuss it. He would get a job. She could sell more paintings. They'd move far away, find a cheap place to rent...

'We can do it, Hattie,' he urged, clasping her hands tightly, eyes shining. 'We've both learned how to live on next to nothing. You, me, and our baby.' He couldn't help smiling. 'I know the timing isn't great, but maybe this is the incentive we need to get away from them.'

'I don't know.' The lump of anxiety pushing at her ribs – a constant companion these days – made it difficult to get the words out. 'Babies need a lot of things. If I'm going to paint, I need a lot. What are we supposed to do: simply jump on a train, get off somewhere and then knock on doors until we find a place to rent?'

'Once we've decided where to go, we can look at the rental ads in local newspapers. I'll go first, find us something. If we save what we can between now and then, we can pay a deposit and have enough left over to buy what we need.'

As the weeks went by, and Hattie's constant nausea was replaced with the soft flutters of tiny limbs, their discussions intensified. She felt certain her father would never let her remain at Riverbend with a baby even if she'd wanted to. And there was no space at the Hunter's dilapidated cottage, even if raising their child amongst career criminals was an option.

She wondered if there was anyone else who could help.

There was no one on her mother's side of the family, and she rarely saw her uncle Chester and his wife. Besides, Uncle Chester had a serious illness. Leonard always made snide remarks about how he wouldn't be around that long. The last thing they needed was their estranged pregnant niece turning up on their doorstep, let alone the uproar that would follow once Leonard found out.

Aidan was right. The only answer was to disappear. She honestly believed her father wouldn't even care, if it weren't for losing out on the money she handed over each week.

But leaving Riverbend? The forest and the fields? Her mother's kitchen garden, and the sunset on the water?

Leaving it in the callous hands of her excuse for a father would be unbearable, if it weren't for the sake of her and Aidan's baby.

More days than not, she simply wished that he would drink himself to death. Then Riverbend would be hers, and all their problems answered. But as a back-up plan, all they could do was keep squirrelling away every penny they could scrape together. Hattie had started to sketch baby animals – it didn't take a genius to figure out why – and the ducklings, fox cubs and tiny otters were proving so popular that, alongside her studies and the ongoing challenge of living with her father, she could barely keep up with demand. However, for the first time, tension hovered between her and Aidan. His restless optimism clashed with the weary hopelessness that dogged her every step.

He did his best to lift her spirits, arriving at the chapel with gifts such as a handful of bath salts to soothe her backache, a book he'd found at a jumble sale or a posy of autumn foliage. He showed her pictures of tiny, terraced cottages with handkerchief gardens in faraway places such as Northumberland or Norfolk. One day, after his sister-in-law had a clear-out, he brought a binbag of newborn clothes and other baby things.

Hattie took one look at a wooden rattle covered in teeth marks and burst into tears.

'I'm so tired,' she wept as Aidan cradled her on his lap, squashed into the armchair. 'Tired of feeling like, however hard I try, it's never going to be enough. I know what it's like to be hungry and cold, and worried all the time. I don't want that for my baby.'

'Our baby,' Aidan whispered, reminding her that she wasn't alone.

'I can't believe I was so stupid,' she sobbed. 'I just want to go back to how it was. I can't do this, Aidan. I can't be a mother!'

His whole body stiffened. 'What are you saying?'

She sat up, twisting around to face him, shaking her head as she pressed a trembling hand against his cheek. 'Not that. I want this baby. Our baby. I love them already.' Her other hand drifted to the tiny swell of her belly. 'I'm just scared. It all feels impossible.'

'I know we can do this.' Aidan covered the hand resting on his face with his own. 'We're strong, you and me. We know how to survive.'

'I don't want to just survive any more. Surviving sucks.' She shook her head, voice breaking on the words.

'I'm not pretending it won't be hard, at first. But I believe in us. As long as we work hard, stick together, we can make it through.' He lowered his face to meet her eyes. 'One day, we'll have land of our own for our children to play in. Picnics and bonfires. Full plates with plenty of leftovers. I'll build you an art studio in the garden, with giant windows to let the light in. And even if we don't have much, our home will be full of love. Like it was with you and your mum. That's enough, isn't it? We can be happy, as long as we're together.'

* * *

Only, as winter slipped into spring, past Aidan turning seventeen and Hattie starting to wear baggy jumpers and letting out the seams on her school skirts, even Aidan started to accept that it wasn't going to be enough.

The lump of anxiety grew to a constant pulse of panic. Aidan tried to reassure her that they would be okay, he'd find a way, but the fear in his eyes told her the truth.

Until, one day, he arrived at the chapel with a grim set to his jaw, the look he gave one of bleak resolve.

'I'll not be able to meet you for a few days.'

'What?' Hattie sat up from where she'd been leaning against his chest, his hand idly stroking her bump. 'Are you going to find us a house?'

He shook his head. 'Not yet. I've got something I need to do first.'

'What do you mean?' Hattie said, unnerved by his evasiveness. 'What do you need to do?'

He wouldn't look at her.

Apprehension tightened around her stomach.

'It's nothing.'

'If it's nothing, then why can't you tell me?'

His face twisted up.

'I just can't. Okay? You have to trust me on this. I... it's better if you don't know.'

Then it hit her.

'It's your family, isn't it?' The brief flicker across his features was answer enough. 'What are they making you do?'

'They aren't—'

She didn't let him finish, gabbling now because she knew this couldn't be good.

'Because you don't have to do it. You mustn't do it.'

'Hattie, you don't understand...'

'No, I do understand! I understand that they're bullies, and criminals, who don't care about who they hurt or get into trouble, and they expect you to go along with it because you're a Hunter. But you owe them nothing. Nothing! They might be your family, and need your help, but whatever they're up to, it won't be good. And I'm your family now.' She grabbed his hand, pressing it against her rounded middle. 'We're your family, we're what matters. Aidan, what are they making you do?'

'They aren't making me do anything! Please don't worry. It can't be good for the baby.'

'How can I not worry when you're going away and won't tell me why?' Her face crumpled into a sob. 'When you won't even look at me?'

He took a deep breath. Eventually dragged his eyes off the floor and turned to face her.

'I am helping my family with something. But it's not dangerous, there's no chance of anyone getting hurt, or finding out. And it'll make us enough money to finally get out of here. That's what I was going to tell you. As soon as I get back, we can leave. You've got three or four days. Can you be ready by then?'

'I... I don't know. I can try. But I don't want you to do this, Aidan. Please, I'm begging you not to do it. What if something goes wrong, and you end up in prison like your brother? What will we do without you?'

Before he could answer, Aidan's dog sat up, ears swivelling towards the door.

'Oh no.'

The chapel door flew open.

Leonard's head wobbled on its neck as he scanned the room. 'Who the hell are you?'

He took two stumbling steps forwards, face contorting in anger. 'What's a runt doing in my chapel with my daughter?'

Even if words could have made any difference at this point, Hattie was too stricken to speak. Aidan, quite possibly unaware of how awful this was, stood up and held out one hand as if to shake her father's in greeting. A bubble of hysteria started rising up her throat.

'I'm Aidan, sir. Pleased to meet you. Harriet and I are doing some schoolwork together.'

Leonard glanced at the proffered hand and instantly dismissed it. 'Harriet. Get inside.'

'No, Father, please. We weren't doing anything. It's just a quiet place to study, that's all…'

'I won't tell you again.'

Any pathetic scrap of hope that this situation could be anything other than a nightmare vanished when Leonard narrowed his eyes.

'Hang on a minute. You're one of them, aren't you? Hunter scum.' He shook his head, spittle flying. 'And you have the audacity to come on my land, put your grubby paws on my daughter.' He swayed, nearly falling into one of the pews. 'I'm going to bloody kill you.'

'No!' Hattie cried, trying to grab his arm as it swung wildly, even as Aidan, well used to drunken fists, stepped away.

'I told you to get inside the house!' Leonard yelled, clamping the arm around her with the intention of propelling her outside.

It was then that he felt the solid, round mass beneath her unbuttoned cardigan.

Despite being soaked in alcohol, his addled brain somehow made the connection. He froze in shock, allowing Hattie to slip out of the cardigan and duck away.

'Go!' Aidan called, and as she turned to him, chest near exploding in a torrent of fear and distress, he mouthed at her: *Four days. Midnight. The riverbank.*

She wouldn't have left him, except that she knew Aidan had learned how to protect himself from violent men. He was stronger and fitter than her father, and crucially, he wasn't hampered by half a bottle of whisky.

However, the most important reason that she ran was that for now, at least, she had to protect their baby.

For the next four days, all she had to do was protect their baby.

Lungs heaving, feet slipping as she hurtled to the comparative safety of her bedroom, she understood why Aidan was prepared to get involved with his family's plans, because in that moment, she knew that she wouldn't only risk prison for this child, she would die for them.

Four days.

It might as well have been forever.

Hattie and I shared a new-found intimacy over the next few days. Reluctant to press on with the next chapter of her story, she instead talked about happier times of her childhood as we worked through more crates of documents, spending Sunday evening burning those that were of no use or value. She reluctantly allowed me to take care of her over the weekend, bringing drinks and meals to where she lay tucked under a blanket in the sunroom, and offering no resistance to me insisting on walking

Flapjack from now on. There were no in-depth conversations about her health, as she'd decided to do her best to put it to one side until she'd spoken to the doctor, but the freedom to make the odd joke about her aching bones or befuddled mind, to not have to try to hide the sudden bouts of agony or desperate exhaustion, was clearly a huge relief to her.

We spent as much time apart as we did together, her in the studio or sleeping, me walking and hanging out at the boathouse with Gideon, who also brought Agnes round for Sunday lunch, but an unspoken agreement had evolved between us. I was no longer simply here for the project. I would be staying for as long as my friend needed me.

It was terrifying. Monumental. Precious.

* * *

I was sitting in my tartan chair, staring at the rose-garden wall out of the window, when Kalani sent a message to the Gals, accompanied with a picture of a karaoke machine.

I only went and bought this. No going back now. The mics go live on Saturday at 7. Feel free to bring drinks. Preferably in travel mugs to prevent spillage.

After a few back and forths about Laurie's kids needing lifts to various places, and Deirdre having a family party, plus a million and one other things these busy women had to do, we eventually settled on swapping Thursday's art therapy to Friday music therapy at Kalani's. I hadn't done karaoke since a night out with my housemates in Leeds, when my sister, Lilly, had come up to visit.

I swallowed down my alarm and firmly told myself that it was about time I gave 'We Are Family' another go, then.

I would sing it for my sister.

And maybe, if these new becoming sisters sang it with me, I would make it past the first line.

23

It was a long day on Wednesday, while Hattie was scanned and biopsied and drained of multiple vials of blood. I sat in the private hospital waiting room, reading the same three lines in a book over and over, letting mugs of coffee go cold and hoping and praying that this would end with a rueful smile and a sigh of relief.

The woman who finally walked out of the doctor's room at the end of the day was not smiling. Her hands shook as she tried stuffing a wodge of papers into her bag, eyes darting around for something that wasn't there.

I gently led her to the passenger seat of her car, anticipating that she might not be up to driving, and waited until we were well on the way home before I asked.

'I have to wait for the test results to be sure. But I've had enough practice reading faces to know that Dr Ambrose is sure enough. It'll be chemo. More medication. But it's probably just delaying tactics at this point. And I really like my hair.'

'I'm so sorry.'

'What do I do, Sophie? When I wake up tomorrow, and the

next day, and however many left I've got after that? Do I spend the next few months alternating between a hospital drip, the toilet bowl and my bed, in the hope I have a few more? Or do I spend it soaking up every last second of the place and people I love?'

'You've got time to decide, once you hear the results.'

'And what about my dog?' That was when she started to cry. Loud sobs that ripped through her torso.

I'd heard these sobs countless times before. Cried them myself often enough. There wasn't much more to do than wait for a red traffic light and then take her hand in mine.

'You know I'll have Flapjack, if it comes to it, if you need me to.'

She sucked in a wheezing whoop of half-hysterical laughter as we started up again. 'What, that great big lump in your motorhome? He'd destroy the place with one wag of his tail.'

'He could move into the boathouse. Agnes would love it.'

'If you think Agnes will be around longer than me, I must look worse than I thought.' She rummaged in her bag for a tissue and, after dabbing at her face and adjusting her curls in the mirror, she gave my hand another squeeze. 'Who knows? By the time I'm dead, you might be ready to move into the boathouse with her.'

'You think there's space in there for me, Muffin *and* your enormous dog?'

Hattie sank back into her seat, eyes closing as she smiled. 'If Gideon's bed is anything like his heart, it'll be big enough.'

* * *

When we arrived back at Riverbend, there was a note from Lizzie stuck onto a pile of papers next to a pot of chicken casserole.

This is what needed to be read/signed/sorted today. Hope you had fun at the spa.

'You told her we were at a spa?'

Hattie shrugged. 'There's no point her worrying too until we know what we're worrying about. I have a feeling Lizzie is going to be more concerned about losing her job than her boss.'

'That's not true,' I said, slipping the casserole into the oven. 'She's already worried about you. She thinks you're confiding secrets in me that you won't share with her.'

'Well, she's right. I suppose some people are simply easier to confide in.' She handed me a glass of wine. 'After all, you are one of the Gals.'

'You really need to tell her something soon.'

Hattie pondered that. 'Here's the thing, Sophie: when you find out that your cancer has turned aggressive, and is trying its damnedest to kill you, you suddenly find out what you really need, and I'm not sure that includes telling Lizzie my private problems.'

When, the following day, Lizzie asked to speak to Hattie in the office, I wasn't surprised when she left an hour later with a box of personal items and a furious scowl.

By the time I'd made Hattie a mug of tea and a slice of buttery raisin toast, she was back in the sunroom.

'It was her decision.' Hattie sighed. 'Although I think she

expected me to beg her to stay, to apologise and confess all, despite everything we've done together, and however strongly I trust her to do her job, I don't trust her with this.'

'She'll be devastated when she finds out.' I sat down in the seat beside hers.

'As she ranted on about you, and the attic, and how she absolutely needs to know everything, I realised she'll be more irritated and embarrassed about not being the famous artist's confidante that she's made herself out to be than she is upset about my diagnosis.'

'Are you sure? She's clearly hurt about being kept in the dark, but she loves you, Hattie.'

'Well.' She took a large bite of toast. 'If she's even a *tiny* bit put out about it, I can't be dealing with it. I'm sorry she's upset, but I'm not sorry to lose an assistant who puts her ego above assisting me. I simply don't have the energy. And trying to emotionally blackmail me into sharing information was the final straw. I'd have let her go if she hadn't resigned.'

'It looked as though she'd cleared out her desk. Doesn't she have to work out any notice?'

'We agreed it would be best to make a clean break. I'll pay her for another month, and she can use up her remaining holiday. She's organised enough to have left things in reasonable order.'

'Will you be able to manage?'

Hattie closed her eyes, shrinking back into the seat cushions. 'I don't suppose you can touch-type?'

After confirming that, no, I wasn't going to take on Hattie Hood's PA work, I did then help her spend a couple of hours trying to sort out what work was urgent, important and, as she put it, 'a boring waste of my limited lifetime'.

We paused bookings on all the upcoming art-therapy

courses on her website. If the test results were better than expected, it was simple enough to open them again. After poring over various files and emails, we decided that, alongside her current therapy classes, the only urgent business was to get the new Christmas designs completed.

'Apart from that, I simply have to get my business, personal admin, finances, house and life in order,' she said, with a groan.

'Which is what you're paying me for,' I replied.

She tipped her head towards where I sat at Lizzie's now-empty desk, her voice dropping to little more than a whisper. 'I'm not going to ask you to stay longer than the project requires.'

'I know that.' I lifted my chin until I could meet those turquoise eyes. 'But I'm staying anyway. For as long as you need me.'

She gave a shaky nod.

Later that day, while Hattie slept, I amended my own website to say that I wouldn't be taking on any new clients for the foreseeable future. For Hattie's sake, I desperately hoped that in a week or two, I would be deleting the message.

That evening, I met Gideon by the river. After the last flurry of late snow the week before, spring was now well and truly under way.

'Hey.' He stood up with a grin, pulling me in for a hug and pressing his lips against mine for a sweet kiss that was all too short. 'Good day?'

'Lizzie resigned,' I blurted, before considering whether or not Hattie would want this information shared so soon, even if it was to her cousin. There were so many thoughts and emotions swarming inside my head, I really needed to let some of them out.

'What?' Gideon sat down on the new, much larger camping chair he'd bought at some point in the last week, shifting to one side so I could squeeze in next to him. 'She'd seemed a bit grumpy lately, but she's been working with Hattie since she was a teenager. Has she found another job, or did something happen?'

I rested my head against his shoulder as we watched the woodlark swoop across the water.

'I think it's partly me.'

'She can't be jealous?' He nudged me. 'Well, she can be. You're amazing. But the project has nothing to do with Lizzie's job, or Hattie's business. Does it?'

'No. But she resented what she perceived as Hattie prioritising it over other things.'

'That's Hattie's decision.'

'Yes. And it's not even true. Hattie spent most of last week in the studio, not the attic.' I wasn't sure how much to say about how Hattie had been distracted, disorganised and deceitful about why. 'But Lizzie felt out of the loop, and like she couldn't do her job properly. She made some demands that Hattie wasn't prepared to fulfil.'

'Wow. Hattie will be lost without her.'

'Which is why I've agreed to stay on longer.'

I felt sure that once she had a firmer prognosis, Hattie would confide in her cousin. I could be honest with him then about quite how long for, and why. Now, he turned to face me, his eyes lighting up.

'I'm suddenly feeling a lot less sorry about Lizzie.' Gideon dipped his head. 'Although, maybe Lizzie resigning isn't the only reason to hang around for a bit?'

'Oh? And what possible other reason could there be?' Despite the heart-breaking reasons why, I couldn't help my own smile.

He leant forwards, cradling my chin in his gentle fingers as he softly kissed me again. 'Oh, come on, we both know you can't resist Agnes' hotpot.'

Not when I got to eat it sitting opposite this man who I felt as if I'd known my whole life, I couldn't.

* * *

'No.' Hattie looked me up and down, her nose wrinkling.

I paused for a second, disconcerted, before continuing down the stairs.

'I know this is still fairly new to you, Sophie, but we're going to *Kalani's house*. For a karaoke party. Dressing like a secretary popping to Greggs for a steak bake will simply not do.'

Hattie was wearing her usual uniform of jeans and a T-shirt, but this time the jeans were sleek and a shimmery black, and the T-shirt was bright red with capped sleeves. She also wore a matching necklace and shiny, red ankle boots. She'd even twisted her curls into a loose bun. I tugged at the blouse I'd worn over a pair of dark-grey trousers.

'I can dress for lunch at Greggs, a muddy dog walk or the pub quiz. I don't really have anything else.'

'Please message the Gals and tell them we'll be slightly late. I'll be back in a minute.'

These days, there was no way Hattie would be up to the attic and back in a minute, but when she did return, it was clear that was where she'd been.

It was my turn to say, 'No!'

'Why not? Are you scorning my mother's best dress?'

She held in her hands one of the party dresses we'd neatly packed away a couple of weeks earlier. A rose-coloured tea-dress with a full skirt, narrow straps and a sweetheart neckline; even decades old, it gleamed with elegance and beauty.

'It will complement your hair perfectly.' Hattie held the dress up to me. 'She had dark-blonde hair, too. Did I tell you that?'

I shook my head, hands itching to run my fingers over the embroidered bodice, even as my sense of propriety ordered me not to.

'Oh, go on. It's never going to fit me, is it?'

By the time I'd slipped into the dress, which draped over my curves perfectly, and Hattie had added a swipe of lipstick and swapped my chunky boots for gold sandals, we were about as late as I'd expected her to be.

'Are you going to tell them?' I asked in a hushed voice once we were in the back of the taxi.

Hattie stared out of the window at the sheep as we bumped down the lane. 'This is Kalani's night. I'll not ruin it for her. But I will tell them, soon.'

* * *

As it turned out, if anyone was ruining the night, it was me.

We pulled up to a moderately sized new-build house on a street with half a dozen others, situated on the other side of Middlebeck, where the river curved back towards the village. A wall of first-floor windows looked out over a large balcony to the water beyond. Below it was a garage and, tucked in beside this, a sleek, black front door.

'I've rowed past a few times since this was built, but it's my first time inside.' Hattie wriggled with anticipation as she rang the doorbell.

'Hi!' Deirdre ushered us into a small vestibule and then up smooth, dark wooden stairs to a large, open living space. She paused on the top step. 'Kalani is feeling a little bit... stressed,' she muttered, plucking at her thigh-length, flowery dress.

'Try *extremely* stressed, dangerously overwrought and on the brink of a nervous breakdown!' Kalani shouted from the kitchen area. 'Whose idea was this therapy malarkey? I want my money back! I want my nice, tidy, lonely, spotless house back! Can you all please go away now? Feel free to leave the wine here.'

'Kalani.' Hattie beamed, scanning the stunning room. 'This is fabulous. Thank you so much for inviting us to your karaoke party. We are going to have one hell of a neat and tidy, spill-free evening!'

The room was, indeed, fabulous. White walls with the odd navy accent. Unfussy, dark furniture to match the kitchen, a few tasteful works of art and throws draped over the leather sofa and chairs. All of it designed to be a mere background to the breathtaking view.

'Plus, where's Laurie?' Kalani wheezed, spinning around with a bottle of gin in one hand, an oven glove in the other. 'I expected you two to be late, but she should be here by now. How are we going to do the Spice Girls if she stands us all up?'

Before we could answer, all our phones pinged with a message from Laurie to say that her husband was stuck at work and she needed to drive Flora to a sleepover. She'd be there by 8.30.

'Well, that's just...' Kalani spluttered.

'A shame, but hardly a disaster,' I finished for her, carefully taking both the bottle and the oven gloves from Kalani and putting them down on the work surface. 'Why don't we pour ourselves a drink, then get cracking with the first song?'

'You go ahead,' Kalani stuttered, as if she'd been replaced with a nervous, insecure Kalani clone. 'I need to sort the snacks. I think I should have got fewer cakes and more samosas. And I thought it'd be fun to try beetroot crisps. But seriously, beetroot is bad enough in a salad, let alone as a crisp. Ugh. I knew this was a terrible idea. Stick to your lane, Kalani, and hosting isn't it!'

'Kalani!' Hattie said, sounding like a Victorian headteacher. 'We are your friends. We've come to hang out and have fun, not eat crisps.'

'Okay, then!' Kalani dumped the unopened packet of crisps in the bin.

Deirdre promptly pulled them out again. 'It's fine, this bin is completely empty and cleaner than my fridge.'

Before she could spiral any further into panic, we all hurried over to where Kalani stood, flapping her hands in front of her face, and enfolded her in a wall of hugs.

This was an eye-opener to me: that someone looking that good in a leather jumpsuit could have a comfort zone, and inviting a few friends round pushed her right over the edge of it.

'Okay,' Kalani gasped after a few seconds. 'I'm okay. I know it doesn't matter. It can't be worse than when we went to Laurie's and her waste pipe flooded. But I sort of feel like I've invited you to read my journal.'

'Here,' I said, offering her a glass brimming with gin and tonic.

'That's a martini glass.' Kalani winced.

'Not right now, it isn't.'

'Oh, stop moaning and choose a song,' Hattie said with a laugh, so that's what we did.

* * *

I might have been okay, if I hadn't just wailed my way through 'We Are Family'. The Gals had let me cry as we bopped and hugged and sang the chorus in each other's faces. I'd collapsed onto the sofa, smiling through my tears, marrying the sadness with the hopefulness of this new start, when Laurie arrived.

'Sorry!' She wheezed, having raced up the stairs. 'I know, I'm a work in progress, but you can't be too mad at me because I actually hired an actual professional cleaner this week, and, even better, I've made initial enquiries with a home carer for Dad...'

The encouraging replies from the others were lost on me as Laurie bustled further into the room.

I smelled and saw the flowers in her hands at the same time.

'Here, an apology. I brought white ones so they'd blend in with the décor.'

Roses, of course.

Roses, on top of a large glass of wine and the melody of my sibling's favourite song still echoing in my ears, and I had to knock Deirdre out of my way as I hurtled down the stairs and through the front door, managing to reach a dark corner around the side of the house before retching my guts up.

'Soph?' Deirdre asked, once I'd finally stopped heaving and was standing braced against the rough brick wall. 'Are you okay?'

'She only had one glass,' I heard Kalani say from behind her. 'Do you think it was the crisps?'

'Can I have a minute?' I asked, resting my forehead on the wall. 'Please.'

I heard the Gals shuffle about and mutter between themselves before slipping away.

Sliding to the ground, I pressed a clammy hand to my chest and willed my heart to stop juddering. When that failed, I pulled out my phone and called the one person I wanted to see right then.

In the few minutes it took for Gideon's car to pull into the space beside Kalani's balcony, I had almost stopped trembling, and felt as though my brain was beginning to unscramble.

I moved out of the patch of shadowy wall I'd been leaning on into the light so he could spot me.

'Hey.'

I tried to reply with something normal, like 'thanks for coming' but instead, my face crumpled and I fell into his arms. We stood there in the damp darkness as I wept and, beneath the embarrassment of running out and the sadness, I could only wonder how on earth I'd managed these moments without him.

'Thank you for coming,' I squeaked, eventually.

'Thank you for calling,' he said, pressing a kiss against the top of my head.

'I probably smell.'

'Yep. Like vomit and... is that beetroot?' Instead of drawing away, he pulled me even tighter against his chest.

I think it was then that my heart finally gave in and fell in love with this man. His kindness, his quiet optimism, the deep, strong roots he'd put down in the soil of his family, and his home.

'Do you want to go back inside?'

I shook my head. 'Will you take me back to Riverbend?'

'Of course.'

'Is it okay if you message Hattie and let her know?'

I could feel his smile against my hair. 'Those Gals have been sneaking glances out here every thirty seconds. I think they'll figure it out.'

* * *

After a quick shower and change into my joggers, I found Gideon in the living room with a pot of tea and a plate of toast. Apart from the fire flickering in the grate, the room was in darkness, and we curled up together on the sofa, gazing out of the window at the moon riding the tops of the trees.

'Laurie brought roses.'

'Ah. Okay.'

'Can I tell you why a bunch of flowers has the power to make me throw up?'

'Sophie, you can tell me anything.'

By the time I'd finished talking, including breaks to cry and eat more toast, Laurie had dropped Hattie off. She peeped into the living room, blew us a kiss and went up to bed.

'It's so humiliating.' I sighed, once Gideon knew everything. 'I'm sick of this stupid phobia having such control over me. You should see me scurrying past the flower section in the supermarket.'

'I'm sorry you had to give up something you loved so much. Even just as a hobby.'

I shrugged. 'I don't think I'd have time for it now, alongside my business.'

He frowned. 'It's quite a change, from floristry to a historical author. I assumed you'd need a history degree or something.'

Oh, crap.

I swallowed back the ball of guilt suddenly blocking the air from reaching my lungs.

'My extreme career change is another long story. I'll save that for a different time.' I yawned and stretched, emphasising my point.

It was a fitful night, the relief at having told Gideon about my family warring with my hatred for the lie about my work. I longed for the day when I could finally be honest about my reason for being here. I could only hope that he'd understand and forgive me.

If he didn't, well, I eventually resigned myself, as the clock ticked into the early morning, I'd simply have to do what I always did. Pack up my home and leave, without looking back.

Easier said than done, of course, now that I'd broken all my rules and fallen for him.

24

Saturday, Gideon and I took his kayak onto the river, stopping for lunch at a pub before paddling back to spend the evening playing board games with Agnes and Hattie. I was slowly learning to love life again, to relish new experiences and relationships without feeling as if I were betraying my family or playing with fire by starting to care for people, and it felt better than I'd have dared to imagine.

On Monday, I was sorting through some paperwork in the office, when the phone rang.

'Hello, I'm calling about the job advert that just went up online. For the personal assistant role?'

Hattie had spent Sunday putting together the advert, despite not yet hearing from Dr Ambrose. She didn't expect the advert to yield anything remotely useful, given the required ambiguity of the wording, and she'd reduced the hours to three days a week, now that any future therapy courses were on hold, but she was stressing about managing things alone, so thought it was worth a try.

'If you let me have your name and email address, I'll send you an application form.'

'Before I do, can I ask a couple of questions? The advert was quite cryptic. I don't want to waste our time if it's not the right fit.'

'Um. Yes, of course. What did you want to know?'

'It said it was based in Nottinghamshire. Can I have a more precise location?'

'It's, er, in the Sherwood Forest area.'

'Fantastic! And it mentioned that an interest in creativity would be useful. Are you able to share any more details about that?'

'Well, yes, but it isn't essential, so if you aren't creative don't let it put you off.' Hattie didn't want to be bombarded with random people interested in working for a famous artist, which was why she was keeping the details confidential until she'd whittled it down to a shortlist of candidates. 'I'm sorry, I'm not authorised to provide any more information at this stage. But anyone who fulfils the basic requirements will be carefully considered.'

'Hang on a minute.' The caller's accent suddenly switched from a nineteen-fifties 'telephone voice' to broad Notts. 'Is that Soph?'

'Deirdre?'

'Are you looking for a PA? Because that would be flippin' awesome. We'd work great together.'

My brain instantly went to full-on flap mode. 'Can I call you back in a couple of minutes?'

'Okay. Sure. My lunchbreak runs out in ten, though. I'm calling from the store cupboard.'

I hung up and hurried over to the studio. Hattie was staring at a sketch of more crows. One of them wore a grey, hooded cloak. Another carried a crossbow. It was certainly a different direction from her usual designs.

'We just had a call about the job.'

'Oh? Did it seem like they have potential?'

'It was Deirdre.'

Hattie stuck her pencil in her mouth and chewed it for a few seconds, forehead creasing.

'She's assumed it'll be working for me. I don't have to tell her it's for Lizzie's job,' I suggested.

'If Deirdre is here three days a week, it'll take her no time to figure out that something's up.'

'I think she already has, she just doesn't know what yet.'

Hattie chewed a bit more.

'The key question is, can you trust her?'

Hattie's frown deepened. 'With my life. Whether I can be her boss is another matter.'

She used the pencil to give one of the crows an eyepatch. 'Then again, if I can manage Lizzie, Deirdre should be doable. Would you mind telling her that Lizzie has resigned, and invite her for an informal of-course-you've-got-the-job interview? I've a few more touches to add to this, and I don't want to stop while the inspiration's flowing.' She shook her head. 'Deirdre, of all the people. If my head was working properly, I'd have already asked her, saved bothering with that advert.'

We arranged for Deirdre to come for dinner before therapy on Thursday. She promised to hold off handing in her resignation letter until then.

I felt a wave of relief, as Hattie spent the rest of the afternoon showing me her 'Christmas' crows. Helping out for a few days was one thing, but I had no idea what to say when confronted with a one-legged crow wearing a Santa hat. I couldn't wait to leave it to Deirdre and go back to rummaging through boxes of junk. Plus, once Deirdre knew, the rest of the Gals would surely follow, and Hattie could tell Gideon the truth about me. The waiting felt like an ill-fitting rucksack chafing on my shoulders. I was more than ready to dump it.

Once the designs were safely sent off, Hattie brightened a little. She slept and read most of Tuesday, and by Wednesday morning, was ready to head back up to the attic and continue her story. She settled upon a box of reports from Madam Bourton's School for Young Ladies, accompanied by a portfolio of paintings. I felt my heart sink at the tale that must accompany it.

* * *

Riverbend

Hattie had grabbed a loaf of bread, some cheese and a bag of fruit before racing upstairs to lock her bedroom door. She felt confident that in his current state, her father would pose no risk to Aidan. But the worst thing Hattie had ever fought was the flu.

Having spent a hideous hour attempting to break the solid oak door down, by morning, Leonard had sobered up enough to fetch a screwdriver and simply remove it from the frame. He found Hattie standing behind an old chest, clutching a silver candlestick.

'You dirty little bitch.' He shook his head, the leer far worse than his usual snarl.

She could barely hear him over the adrenaline stampeding through her bloodstream, but kept her eyes fixed on his, every muscle braced for whatever came next.

'Now I know where the money comes from. Selling yourself

to scum like him.'

'No!' She tried to sound brave, but it was a hoarse whisper.

'Well, it isn't from the Oaktree Tearooms. They've never heard of you.'

'I've been selling my paintings.'

'Oh, really? Did a painting do that to you?' His lip curled up in disgust as he nodded at her belly.

'We're in love. It's not dirty.'

'It's Aidan Hunter's bastard,' her father roared. 'It's a bloody disgrace!'

'I... I could marry him,' she garbled, ignoring the peal of contemptuous laughter. 'He's not like the rest of them. Aidan's going to be a policeman, not a criminal.'

The laughter stopped abruptly.

'Is that what he told you, you silly little girl? And you believed him?'

'It's true!'

'He got arrested last night. Caught red-handed robbing the post office.'

Hattie felt as though her body were collapsing in on itself. As if the baby were the only thing keeping her upright. But it was because of the baby that she would stand tall against her father. He was probably lying. Or simply mistaken. Plenty of people got the Hunter brothers mixed up.

Either way, she decided to nod, apologise, comply with whatever her father wanted. For three days, until her real life began.

She did, however, come up with the presence of mind to ensure her baby's safety in the meantime.

'I've seen the doctor, and the midwife,' she said, squashing down her fear as she tilted up her chin. 'They both know I'm six months pregnant, and that me and the baby are healthy.'

She didn't need to add that, after the various rumours about her mother's death, if any harm came to another Riverbend woman, it would raise more than a little suspicion.

He folded his arms. 'Six months? Make the most of the three you've got left carrying that brat, because the sorry day it's born will be the last time you see it.'

He left then, the door still propped against the corridor wall. Hattie tried not to let his threats overwhelm her. Aidan would meet her on the riverbank. She knew he would.

For the next three days, she packed and repacked, trying to prioritise what meagre possessions she could bring with her. Leonard responded to her pleas of remorse with a blank stare or the flicker of a sneer. He ate the meals she cooked and made no comment as she moved about the house, but when she tried to fetch a bunch of parsley from the garden, the boot-room door was locked and the key missing. She soon found that every way out was equally inaccessible.

'I need some vegetables from the garden. The doctor said I have to eat well, for the baby's sake.'

'Why would we care about a brat that, as far as you're concerned, won't exist in a few months?'

'Are you not going to let me into the garden?'

He looked at her. 'I'm not letting you flaunt that Hunter spawn anywhere. It's bad enough the doctor knows.'

'How is anyone going to see me in the garden? I just want some cabbage and parsley to go with our fish pie.'

He smiled, scanning the page of his newspaper. 'You seem to forget that I no longer believe anything you say.'

She would have panicked about meeting Aidan, but Hattie had been climbing trees since she could walk. A baby bump wouldn't stop her escaping through a window.

Eventually, the fourth day came. She waited until the sun

had long since sunk behind the wan April skyline of the forest she loved, and Leonard's snores drifted through the office door.

Using a blanket to muffle the sound, she smashed the largest pane of glass in the dining-room window with a rolling pin, then pushed out a rucksack and a smaller suitcase before climbing on a chair and squeezing through herself.

It was eleven forty-five when she arrived at their spot on the riverbank. Hattie immediately went to the biggest tree, tucked her bags behind it and then sat on the rucksack to wait.

A long, dark, ice-cold age later, she was startled by a hand on her shoulder. She'd never intended to fall asleep, but in the past few weeks, she'd increasingly been overcome by exhaustion, and the gentle burble of the river had been a lullaby her frazzled body couldn't resist.

Before she was fully awake, the same hand grabbed her under the armpit and yanked her to her feet.

'Stupid, stupid bitch.' Leonard ignored her bags, jerking Hattie forwards despite her feet still scrabbling for purchase in the muddy ground. Pushing and shoving her back towards the house. 'I told you, he's not coming. You take that scum's word over mine?'

'I just went for a walk.' She wept, stumbling over a tree root. 'You can't keep me prisoner inside forever. I waited until it was dark so no one would see me.'

'Oh, so nothing to do with your plan to meet at midnight by the river, then?'

Her heart plummeted. He must have seen Aidan mouth the words, and decided to wait and see if her repentance was genuine.

He put her in her mother's old room in the attic. It still had a solid lock on the door from when Verity had been alive, a 'safety measure' her father had insisted upon. Twice a day, the door was unlocked and a bowl of soup or a sloppily made sandwich was dumped on the chest of drawers. After finding a pad of paper and pen in the bedside cabinet she began leaving notes on the dirty plates for the other things she needed. More toilet paper, clean underwear or another blanket. Sometimes he responded, other requests were ignored.

After a couple of weeks, Leonard instructed her to get dressed and brush her hair (she had to ask him for a brush). He then drove her to the doctor's surgery, explaining with a charming smile to the midwife that he'd be accompanying her during the examination as she was scared of all things medical since her mother's tragic passing.

'Shall we talk about a home birth, then, sweetie, if you're afraid of hospitals?' the kind-looking midwife asked after recording the baby's heartrate.

'Yes, please.' She could hardly request a hospital birth when she lived behind a locked door. At least this way, she could hope for some professionals to be present, rather than face giving birth alone on her mother's bed.

As the weeks dragged by, she couldn't help hoping for Aidan. Like in the films, he'd sneak into the house in the middle of the night and rescue her. She spent hours watching out of the attic windows, straining for a glimpse of him, praying he'd catch a glimpse of her.

But still he didn't come.

Had her father been right? Was Aidan also languishing in a prison somewhere? Or had Leonard scared him away, after all?

Still, she waited, and wished, and wondered if she could reach the branches of the chestnut tree if she jumped out of the window. She'd have happily risked it if it hadn't meant risking her baby, too.

And then, one night, when all that was left were swollen

ankles and numb emotions, the pain started.

Her father must have read the note that morning, because a few hours later, he dragged her down the stairs and into her old bedroom.

'Here.' He handed her a clean nightdress and waited for her to swap it for the grubby, oversized T-shirt she'd been living in for the past few weeks, scrubbing it in the attic bathroom sink when the stench of sweat became too much.

By the time the on-call community midwives arrived, Hattie was on all fours in front of the fireplace, readying herself to die as another pain clamped itself around her middle.

'Not long to go now, my love,' the older one murmured in her ear. Hattie vaguely registered a warm hand pressing against the base of her back, the cool cloth wiping her brow. There was nothing but the relentless earthquake consuming her, and all she wanted was for someone to make it stop.

Only, when it did stop. When the groaning and sweating and uncontrollable pushing all stopped. When the briefest, faintest wail had disappeared behind a closed door, and the bloody mess of new life had been deftly replaced with clean sheets, two neat stitches and paracetamol washed down with a mug of sweet tea.

That was when the other pain began.

A deep, primal moan started in her empty belly and rose up through her raw throat and clenched jaw as she fought to haul her trembling muscles off the bed.

'Harriet, you need to rest.' A dim plea, ignored, irrelevant.

Where is my baby?

'Harriet.' Firmer now, as strong hands pressed her back against the pillow. 'We understand this is difficult, but your father has explained the situation. The baby is safe and well. You must let us take care of them.'

Where is my baby?

Then the doctor, and a jab in her flailing arm, and her mind took her to another place.

Her baby was not in that place, either.

Where have you taken my baby?

* * *

Eight weeks later, the empty husk that was once Harriet Langford enrolled at Madam Bourton's School for Young Ladies on the edge of the Peak District. For the first month, she drifted between classrooms, the dormitory and dining hall. Not that she managed to eat more than a measly mouthful or two. She found the best place to cry was in the bath, where she pressed aching cheeks onto her knees and, for a precious few minutes, allowed the pain to trickle out. She did the minimum amount of work needed to avoid getting into trouble in lessons, pretending to pay attention despite finding it impossible to care about century-old battles or trigonometry. The initial curiosity that a new face generated soon ebbed into lack of interest when she either deflected or outright ignored the other girls' attempts to be friendly.

Having spent the past few years in survival mode, Harriet knew that all she needed to do was keep on getting up every morning and putting on the mask of neutrality. Turn up when she needed to be somewhere and find somewhere to be alone when she didn't. Breathe. Eat. Lie awake at night, staring at the crack in the ceiling and praying that when she eventually slumped into sleep, she'd get a precious few moments to dream about her baby.

When her meek behaviour earned her the right to visit the local town on Saturdays, she spent them scouring the microfiche in the library, poring over old newspapers for reports on post office robberies, but there was nothing.

She swapped one of her necklaces for a stamp, sending a letter to the Hunters' address explaining where she was. She didn't mention the baby for fear that someone else in that crowded cottage would open it, but hopefully, Aidan would read it and know that she still loved him.

Would he come for her, even though their baby had gone? Or at least write back?

Still she waited.

Still nothing.

As the autumn faded into winter, she gradually learned to push the pain of her loss deep down inside her. She knew that it was the only way to survive.

Did she long for her baby? With an ache that seared through every nerve in her body.

Did she think about Aidan? Every day.

But she also began to think about painting again, in Madam Bourton's incredible art rooms. When December arrived, she started spending time with the other girls on her corridor, listening to the top forty countdown on the radio as they decorated their bedrooms, backcombing each other's hair into giant puffballs and flouncing into town to buy hot chocolates and flirt with the local boys.

Even better, she received a last-minute invitation to spend Christmas at her friend Camilla's house in London. Here, she discovered that wine, weed and reckless spontaneity could dim the pain to a tolerable background hum. This blissful self-medication carried her through the rest of the school year, including final exams, then on to a fine art degree at art college in Canterbury.

That was when she met Peter.

25

It took me a moment to recognise Deirdre when I opened the front door on Thursday evening.

'Wow.'

'Kalani did it. I can't pull off Lizzie's badass look but wanted to show Hattie that I'm serious about the job. Is it okay, or has she made me ridiculous?'

'Okay?' I ushered her into the hallway. 'You look incredible.'

Deirdre's spray tan had mercifully faded, and the gold highlights added to her thick, wavy hair went perfectly with her outfit. She wore a loose-fitting jacket and trousers covered in Van Gogh sunflower print, with a cerise blouse and a pair of white trainers.

'Is the bag too much?' She held out a Hattie Hood satchel printed with squirrels. 'If it comes across as grovelly, I'll leave it here.'

'Okay, so firstly, this is Hattie. She's never going to mind someone flaunting her designs. And secondly, this is Hattie. One of your best friends. You're going to have to seriously mess this up to not get the job that is basically already yours. Hattie's number one priority right now is someone she can trust.'

'Rather than someone who can admin the heck out of things, because that's kind of all I went on about in the application form.' She pulled a plastic folder out of the rucksack and waved it at me.

'That's not going to hurt, either. I'll let her know you're here.'

I left Hattie and Deirdre in the dining room with a salmon bake I'd cooked earlier, and ate my own plateful at the kitchen table, trying not to splatter fishy sauce on the book Gideon had lent me about gardening.

While I waited for the clock to tick around to our art session, I did my own tiny bit of solo therapy, flicking open to the chapter on roses, squinting at the pictures of my family's favourite flowers until my lungs stopped lurching. I quickly turned to the section on tomatoes, the words and images pointlessly bouncing off my glistening eyeballs, then tried again.

By the time Deirdre poked her head around the door and informed me that it was time to head to the studio, her first task as Hattie Hood's new assistant, I was pressing one finger to a photograph of a pale-pink climbing rose. The world was still turning, and my heart had decided to keep beating after all.

* * *

The Gals stood in the centre of the studio, waiting for Hattie, who'd disappeared into a store cupboard. Kalani was still preening at having made-over Deirdre's previous makeover, only grumbling slightly when her protégé swapped the suit for leggings and an old T-shirt. Laurie was also smiling. She'd spent the first five minutes listing all the dusting, scrubbing and scouring her new cleaner had done that week, with accompanying before and after photographs, until Kalani had tactfully suggested a change of subject by tipping her head up at the ceiling and screeching that, 'Any more of those photos and our eyeballs will need this shocking phenomenon you call a cleaner.'

'She's just excited,' Deirdre said. 'There's no need to be rude.'

'And you're happy to see close-up images of her dirty toilet bowls?'

'Maybe we could just see the after photos, Laurie?'

Laurie looked baffled. 'Then how are you going to tell the difference?'

'We can tell the difference by how bright you look,' I added, trying to be the diplomat. 'It's obvious that the changes you're making are having a real impact.'

'Thanks, Soph!' Laurie looked genuinely touched. 'How about you? Has our therapy made any difference to you? Only, after you ran away the other night, we weren't sure...'

I ignored the shame prickling across my skin. These were my friends. Of course they were going to have discussed my hysterical exit from Kalani's karaoke party. 'Last Friday was a bit of a setback, but it's made me even more determined to keep pressing forwards.'

'Great to hear!' Hattie said, reversing out of the store cupboard, dragging a giant dresser behind her.

I say dresser; the general shape of the object implied that this was its original intention, but the patchy, lopsided lump of furniture with one door missing, the other hanging off, two wonky shelves and a giant hole in the back could more accurately be described as future firewood.

'Is that something you made earlier?' Kalani joked as she helped Hattie position the ex-dresser in the centre of the room.

'It's something *somebody* once made,' Hattie gently chastened. 'Imagined, designed, lovingly crafted, sanded and stained. I found this dumped at the recycling centre. So worn and broken that someone considered it no longer useful.'

'Well, look at it. They weren't wrong,' Deirdre said.

'Really?' Hattie whipped around to aim a piercing gaze at her new assistant. 'It's been mistreated, neglected, discarded, so does that make it irredeemable?'

Deirdre shrugged, looking sheepish. 'I suppose not.'

'Is this some lesson about how Gavin rejected Deirdre and went with Heidi instead?' Laurie asked.

'Um, I'm not falling to bits!' Deirdre stopped then, frowning. 'Not on the outside, at least.'

'All of us have been battered by different things,' I dared to suggest. 'We could all be that dresser, if we think about it.'

'Precisely!' Hattie pointed a finger at me. 'So, what are we going to do about it? Hide in some back room somewhere, consign ourselves to the dump or the bonfire?'

'Well, we clearly aren't doing that, are we?' Kalani huffed. 'I suppose you want us to somehow make-over that hunk of junk like I did Deirdre?'

'No!' Hattie shook her head so hard, her glasses slipped off. 'You chose Deirdre some new clothes and booked her a hair appointment. I want you to make-over this beautiful treasure as if you were throwing it a karaoke party for the first time.' She turned to me again. 'As if it is worthy of being loved. Being a precious part of someone's home, in the heart of their family.'

'So, if Deirdre has the dresser, what do we get?' Laurie asked.

'The dresser does not just represent Deirdre.' Hattie started handing out aprons. 'This is a group activity. You're going to work together on this. Off you go.'

'Well, that's not at all going to end in a verbal brawl, then, is it?' Kalani said.

It turned out that, while we began with a bit of pushing and shoving, an argument that started off being about crystal doorknobs and ended up referring to how even if Laurie's apple pies were a bit dry, it didn't mean Kalani could be mean about it, a few tears and a pot of paint dangerously close to being chucked over Deirdre's new hair, Kalani's prediction was incorrect.

We ended up, as presumably Hattie had hoped, dividing the tasks in line with our individual strengths. Laurie scrubbed and sandpapered, while Deirdre fixed the broken shelves and door with replacement pieces of wood Hattie had sourced from Gideon. Kalani painted each section in colours and patterns to suit our different personalities, and I added various adornments including the knobs and Moroccan tiles in a diamond shape to cover the hole.

The result was vibrant, chaotic. Beautiful.

'Well, who'd have thought it?' Laurie asked as we stood admiring our work.

'Hattie, I suppose,' Deirdre replied.

'No.' Hattie smiled. 'This is even better than I'd envisioned. And I'm an artist. You've excelled yourselves, Gals. You'll definitely be ready by the time we've completed the final two sessions.'

'Only two more?' Kalani exclaimed.

'Do you really think we'll be ready?' Deirdre asked, before screwing up her face. 'Ready for what, though?' she added.

To our surprise, Hattie's eyes flooded with tears. 'Ready for whatever comes next,' she said, softly.

I didn't miss the glances that passed between the others. Kalani looked at me, eyebrows raised in question.

'I don't know about you, but what I'm ready for right now is a gorgeous gal.' I linked one arm through Laurie's, my attempt at innocence failing miserably.

'Absolutely!' Hattie said, sounding even more fake. 'Lead the way, Sophie! I'll see you in there once I've tidied a few bits away.'

We were on our second jug of cocktail before Hattie joined us. Jokes brittle, conversation stilted, the atmosphere didn't improve for the twenty minutes or so before the others made their excuses and left.

I found keeping secrets from Gideon akin to hiding a venomous scorpion in my underwear drawer. Now, these wonderful women knew I was hiding things from them, too. Secrets about their friend, who they'd known for years before I'd showed up. A whole nest of scorpions.

Soon, very soon, someone was going to get stung. One of those people was sure to be me.

* * *

I'd invited Gideon to come on a date with me. I'd been too passive in this relationship for too long. He'd been unfailingly kind, gentle, romantic, *there*. I'd been hesitant, contrary, guarded. I decided I owed him a thank you, and that would take the form of a trip to Chatsworth House in Derbyshire, where one hundred and five acres of landscaped gardens contained waterfalls, sculptures and other points of interest.

Nearly five hundred years and sixteen generations cultivating their family's land. I felt sure Gideon would appreciate it.

It was the last Saturday in March, and we spent a lovely few hours wandering about, admiring the landscaping while the dogs ambled along the river and through the woodland. Together, we soaked up the present as well as the centuries of history. I'd never experienced this before – feeling so comfort-able with someone who at the same time made my heart fizz over with that sense of *knowing*, every time he caught my gaze or brushed up against me.

We stopped to have lunch in the dog-friendly section of the café, and then the direction of our conversation changed.

'Are you okay?' I asked. Gideon had been staring at a chunk of beef pie on the end of his fork for the past minute. I couldn't imagine why he looked so pensive, so it was making me nervous.

'I'm really okay, Sophie.' He put down the fork and sat back with a sigh. 'Way more than okay.'

'You don't especially sound it,' I said, cautiously.

'This has been... the best day. And the other days... the kayaking. Board games. Even coming to pick you up from Kalani's, when you shared about your family. Every day with you is the best day.' He frowned, forehead wrinkling. 'But it kills me that you don't feel the same.'

'I...' I swallowed, hard. 'I do feel the same. This has been the best day for me, too.'

Until now, at least.

'No.' He gave an abrupt shake of his head. 'If you felt like I do about days like this, you'd do anything for them not to end. I know we said no pressure, and you've already decided to stay at Riverbend for longer. But what does longer mean? Every time I see you, I'm wondering if it's going to be the time you tell me you're leaving.'

'But we agreed...'

'I know. I'm breaking our deal. But you asked, and I'm answering as honestly as I can. I can't lie to you, Sophie. I would follow you anywhere, if it wasn't for Mum. I'd at least commit to making it work long-distance until we could figure things out. I know we said what we said, but things change. How I feel about you—'

'I'm thinking about it,' I blurted, before I could stop myself.

Gideon went very still.

'All the time. I think about what it would be like to find somewhere close by to live. To shut down my business, stop spending every day dealing with...' I broke off my sentence, remembering again that he couldn't know I surrounded myself with death. 'To be the kind of person who was brave enough to stay,' I whispered.

He screwed up his face in a grimace. 'I wish I was enough reason for you to stay.'

'If anything could be enough, it's you.' I swiped at the tear tumbling down my cheek. 'I swear to you, I'm thinking about it.'

He reached over, resting a hand on top of mine. 'Just promise you'll tell me once you've made up your mind.'

I nodded. 'Can you be patient with me about one more thing?'

Gideon managed a weak smile. 'I can try.'

'Can we visit the rose garden?'

'I don't know. Can we?'

In the end, I found that we could. Gripping Muffin's lead as if my life depended on it, I approached the section of beautifully manicured garden flanked by yew hedges, with two rows of stone pillars forming a walkway down the centre. I leant against one of the pillars, flower beds either side of me. It helped that it was outside. And absolutely gorgeous, even so early in the season. There weren't many blooms, but I could smell them, as well as see them in my peripheral vision.

'Okay?' Gideon asked, squeezing the hand that wasn't holding the dog lead.

'Not really.' My whole body was trembling, so it was no wonder my voice quaked.

'Keep breathing.'

'Yep. Good idea.'

I stood there for what felt like hours, but Gideon assured me afterwards was mere minutes. I cried. I wobbled. I breathed in roses. I gradually twisted my head to either side and looked at them. And I survived. I *wanted* to survive, even though my precious father, my mother, my angel Lilly, had not.

Then I scuttled back to Gideon's car, Muffin waffling alongside me.

The following week, Hattie had a call from Dr Ambrose, asking how soon she could make an appointment. We pulled into the hospital car park twenty-five minutes later. Although Deirdre had a month's notice to work out at her old job, she'd planned to pop in that day and complete some admin, so Hattie told her that we'd had a last-minute opportunity to interview someone about Riverbend Chapel, and this was the only date they were free.

'Hah!' Hattie laughed, with only a trace of bitterness. 'This information will directly relate to the chapel, and how quickly I need to plan my funeral in there, so it's not even that much of a lie.'

'You think your funeral will fit in the chapel?' I linked my arm through hers as we walked towards the hospital entrance.

'Friends and family, absolutely. Hangers-on, twonky account managers and stalkery fans can satiate their voyeuristic grief at a memorial service later.'

'Sounds like you've been thinking about it.'

She raised an eyebrow. 'I chose my funeral songs the day I got my initial diagnosis. We all use different ways to cope.'

'I know from experience that the more planning done in advance, the easier it is for the family.'

I didn't add anything trite about hoping those plans wouldn't be needed for a very long time. Doctors didn't call people in for urgent appointments if it was good news.

* * *

An hour later, my arm was linked through Hattie's for a whole different reason as we shuffled back to the car. Her lymphoma had transformed. It was now classed as 'high grade'. What did that mean? It meant, amongst other things, chemotherapy, antibody therapy and a whole lot less art therapy for the good people of Sherwood Forest.

'Generally speaking,' Dr Ambrose had assured her, 'although aggressive, this type of cancer is very treatable.'

'With all due respect,' Hattie retorted, 'your face doesn't say "even slightly treatable", let alone "highly".'

He paused, frown lines deepening even further, picked his pen up then put it down again.

'In this case, the spread is extensive. We are going to do everything we can, hit it hard and fast. But. Well.'

'No promises, eh?'

'I never make promises when it comes to cancer.'

'Will you offer me some odds, then?'

'I don't find providing statistics helpful, Hattie. Every case is different, and everyone responds differently to the treatment.'

'And I respond a lot better to knowing what's likely to be up ahead, rather than being fudged about with vague talk and furrowed eyebrows.'

There was more back and forth along these lines, but in the end, Hattie badgered him into revealing what she'd been after. Hattie should update her will, get her things in order, make the most of every day. There was a good enough chance that this was going to be it.

* * *

'Is there anything else I can do?' I asked, once we'd got back to Riverbend and I'd made her a panini to pick at.

'Two things.' Hattie gestured for me to sit beside her on the sunroom sofa. 'Will you help me sort the rest of the house, get as ready as I can to close down my business and bank accounts, all of that stuff?'

'Hattie, let's not approach this as if the outcome is certain. You might have years yet.'

'I want to get things sorted now, while I still can, just in case.'

'Okay. Of course I'll help. What's the second thing?'

Hattie tipped up her chin. 'Before I enter treatment hell, I'm going to throw a birthday party, one to rival the Riverbend Balls of old.'

'Dr Ambrose said you need to start chemo as soon as possible.'

'My birthday's in a month's time. The first of May, which is also the bank holiday Monday. He can do whatever he likes to me after that.'

Sort a lifetime of memories and possessions, as well as a thriving business, organise a party and, at Hattie's insistence, finish a course of art therapy.

It was going to be a busy month.

26

After an early night and quiet morning, Hattie was ready for another afternoon in the attic. The untouched boxes now made for a forlorn little stack in one corner, those we'd sorted into different categories depending upon what Hattie wanted to do with their contents forming neat piles across one side of the room.

After some opening and closing of different containers, she found what she was looking for. A photograph album. A wedding album, stashed alongside an old VHS video, a dried bouquet of flowers, a flouncy veil and tiara, and the kind of miniature bride and groom figurines that traditionally topped a wedding cake.

'You were married?' I asked as Hattie turned the first page of the album to reveal her standing outside a large church, a much older man with his hand on her elbow. 'Who is he?'

'I was. But not to him.' Hattie shuddered. 'That's my darling father, making sure I didn't decide to leave Peter at the altar.' She grimaced. 'It was a close call. Even then, I couldn't help fantasising about Aidan showing up at the crucial moment the vicar reached that bit about "speak now, or forever hold your peace". But, no. Peter was my only option, so I took it. For Riverbend's sake, as much as my own.'

* * *

Riverbend

Harriet – she couldn't bear to be called the name Aidan had given her any longer – met Peter Chillington in her final year of university. Approaching thirty, after a good decade of enjoying too much money and ample time to spend it in, Peter was under pressure to knuckle down, find a wife, and at some point, produce an heir to the family pile in Devon.

His path had crossed Harriet's at a few house-parties, weddings and other events that she'd attended through her closest friends from Madam Bourton's School for Young Ladies. While Harriet wasn't wealthy, or from a family of any particular standing, she'd learned how to hold her own in high-class circles. More importantly, she was known for being what her friends called 'free-spirited', and others referred to as a 'hot mess'. Wild, reckless, up for almost anything. After a night spent smoking joints on his family's private beach together, followed by skinny dipping and bacon sandwiches, Peter's mind was made up. If he had to marry, it might as well be to someone who wasn't boring or unattractive.

Harriet was stunned when Peter invited her out on a proper date. She wasn't the type of girl who men took out to dinner. She was the one they booted out of bed with an apologetic grin and a raging hangover before the girl they were really interested in found out about it.

That first evening, and the whirlwind courtship that followed, felt like an alternate reality. Peter wooed her with sophisticated restaurants, trips to art exhibitions and the theatre. He asked questions about her life – past and present as well as her hopes for the future. After offering an edited version of her childhood, Harriet made no effort to correct his assumption that her erratic lifestyle had been down to the tragic loss of her mother and nothing more.

She felt as though she were holding her breath for the next few weeks, waiting for him to make some throwaway comment, clarifying that this was nothing but a bit of fun before he settled down with someone suitable. To her overwhelming relief, it never came, and she started to wonder if she could actually become the person Peter seemed to believe she was. She did her best to adopt the role of girlfriend, including charming his family and proving to his friends that she could be wifely material, and it seemed to be working. After all, if there was one thing Harriet could do well, it was fight for survival.

Once university was over, she couldn't contemplate returning to Riverbend. She'd killed off any lingering dreams about Aidan after her father assured her that if she had any contact with the Hunters, he'd disinherit her and sell Riverbend to developers wanting to turn it into a golf club. She had no desire to ever set eyes on her father again, and even if Leonard hadn't been there, the reminders of what she'd lost – her mother, Aidan, that which was too painful to name – were more than she could bear. She knew Verity would be heartbroken by how their home was sliding further into ruin, but she numbed that guilt along with her shame and sadness, replacing her previous drugs of choice with the addictive lure of long-term security, and somewhere to belong.

When Peter proposed to Harriet during a dazzlingly sumptuous trip to Venice, love barely came into it. Their casual 'I love you's were no different from how they greeted friends or fellow art students. But they liked each other well enough, and Harriet adored the woods, wildflower meadows and beach where Peter lived. Surely this would soothe the ache of missing Riverbend.

So, Harriet settled for a man she liked, for a home that felt as wild as her heart, and a family who tolerated her as better than nothing. Unable to speak about her past sufferings, she painted them. Her bleak, anguished depictions of the Devon countryside – a dead rabbit lying in blood-stained dust, a blackened tree split down the middle by a lightning strike, grey clouds over a desolate field – started to win her critical acclaim, if limited sales, and she slowly established an existence she could live with.

Of course, their marriage of convenience was going to find its share of trouble. Peter became increasingly frustrated with Harriet's failure to conceive – thanks to the secret stash of contraceptive pills. After her upbringing, there was no way Harriet was bringing a child into a family lacking in love, even if she could endure being pregnant again. He grew tired of what had first attracted him to her – the lack of domesticity and reluctance to embrace the role of demure Country Wife. She felt irritated at his hypocrisy and triggered by behaviour that began to mirror her father's, not least how he'd convinced himself the other women were her fault. She withdrew further into her art, eventually not even bothering to pretend she cared any more.

After ten years of dysfunctional matrimony, Peter

announced that he was divorcing her to marry the woman carrying his baby.

Harriet packed up her possessions and bought a plane ticket to Rome. On her way to the airport, she took a detour of several hundred miles up to Middlebeck. She parked her old Nissan Micra in a layby, hat and sunglasses enough of a disguise that after several hours, when Leonard eventually lurched past on his way into the village, he barely registered the car, let alone the woman inside it.

She felt a jolt of shock and pity at seeing the figure that had once been her proud, charming father, shuffling past. It was no worse than she'd imagined – all too often hoped – but, being confronted with his flaccid face and stooped, spindly frame, for a brief moment, she wondered if she'd done the right thing, leaving him to rot in his own miserable decisions.

When she pulled through the Riverbend gates and up to the disintegrating remains of her childhood home, any trace of guilt or pity hardened into rough, raw anger.

As she snuck through the front door, the key she'd stolen prior to her wedding needing a firm wiggle in the rusting lock, the wave of memories nearly knocked her to her knees.

It took a fraught twenty minutes to carry the boxes of memories and other encumbrances she couldn't take with her, but had nowhere else to leave, up to the attic floor, where she placed them beside the remains of her mother's things. Being there again, in what was once her prison, was like emotional assault. She felt dizzy, frantic, sick to her stomach. She could feel the ghost of her baby writhing inside her.

That man did this.

He deserved everything he got.

Before she left, she took another, shorter, detour, to a tumbledown cottage in the village. She sat outside for so long that the occupants, more observant than her father, came out and asked what she was doing there.

'Blummin' 'eck. Is it Hattie?'

Harriet thought about that for a moment. Was it time to be Hattie again?

'Yes. I just... I was wondering if Aidan...'

'Oh, bless you. He's over in Kirkby now. With his missus, and two littlies. I'll tell him you came round though, said hello, shall I?'

'Um... yes. Thank you.'

'Are you back for long? You could always pop over next time he's visiting.'

'I'm actually moving abroad. My flight's tomorrow morning.'

'No bother, love. I'll tell him you came to say goodbye.'

* * *

That evening, we had our penultimate art therapy session. It was a mild night, feeling more like May than the end of March, and Hattie relocated us to the riverbank.

'This is nice!' Deirdre exclaimed as we set up camping chairs in the spot where Gideon usually watched the sunset. With the lighter evenings, that would be in an hour or so. I felt torn between wanting to see him and not wanting him to see whatever we'd be up to.

'Are we going to be drawing on ourselves?' Laurie asked, frowning at a forlorn plastic tub full of acrylic pens balanced on a tree stump. It appeared to be all Hattie had brought apart from the chairs.

'Or on each other?' Kalani screwed her nose up. 'Not a chance unless you can 100 per cent guarantee that it washes off. My parents are bringing a load of uncles and aunties over for a takeaway tomorrow. I'm not greeting them with Deirdre's BS version of my inner self scrawled over my face.'

'Your family are coming over?' I asked, thrilled that Kalani had made yet another huge step forwards.

'What do you mean, BS?' Deirdre asked, at the same time. 'Humph. Right now, your inner self still needs some work, Kalani. While most of the drawing would be nice, I'd probably still have to add a tiny little witch, or a female dog to make it accurate.'

'No one is drawing on anyone!' Hattie interjected before Kalani could reply. 'If we were, don't you think I'd have brought face paints or make-up rather than acrylic pens?'

'I don't know,' Laurie said. 'You might have wanted us to display it on our face for a few days, hammer home some point or other.'

'Except that these sessions are confidential,' Hattie said, not unkindly. 'No, we're going to be drawing on rocks today. Good, solid, heavy rocks. The kind that weigh you down.'

Hattie wanted us to choose a rock that 'spoke to us', and then cover it in all the things we needed to get rid of, in order to be our best selves. 'Words, images, random scribbles that represent your ugliest emotions and darkest thoughts. Whatever you like. But I want that rock to be covered! We've no time to waste, Gals. Get all of it out.'

What Hattie had failed to mention was that all the decent-sized rocks were in the river. She flat-out dismissed the palm-sized stones we chose, responding with, 'Are your issues the size of a pebble? If your fears could fit in your hand, you wouldn't be doing therapy.'

'Actually, I'm doing therapy because the rest of you emotionally blackmailed me into it,' Kalani muttered, even as she slipped off her leopard-print boots and rolled up her coral trousers.

'Hah. You've never been blackmailed into anything in your life. You needed this more than the rest of us.' Laurie laughed back, sliding down the muddy bank on her now filthy backside.

We spent an exhilarating few minutes wading through the freezing water, which ran quick and clear over the strands of waterweed covering the sandy bed. In the end, it became a competition for who could find the biggest rock, meaning that we all needed to help each other lug our boulders up to the grass.

Too impatient to wait for the moisture to evaporate, we pulled off our jackets and cardigans and used them to dry the rocks as best we could. Still, as we started to draw, the colours bled across the surface of the stone, making it impossible to create anything precise, or particularly legible.

I soon became oblivious to the others, getting lost in my own art as I tried to embrace the project. I started with a wobbly stick woman, surrounded by rolls of barbed wire. Another one, peering out of the top window of a tall tower, like Rapunzel only with shoulder-length, yellowish hair. I drew dark clouds of fear, and a waterfall of tears running into a squishy human heart, representing all the tears I'd seen and heard over the past eight years, and how, despite my attempts at keeping my guard up, every one of them had watered my heart. I depicted a long, empty road snaking all over the rock, leading to nowhere. Along the road, I added three headstones, and then a smaller one beside them – the point at which I started sobbing – because I lived with the dread of Muffin dying in the next few years, and, unless something significant changed, losing her would break me.

I drew a pile of smashed-up dreams, which, it turned out,

looked like dead roses. I finished off with a broken clock because I'd realised over the past few weeks that my life was stuck, and then coloured every space that was left with a beigey colour.

Deirdre had mostly written words on hers, including 'victim', 'invisible', 'rejected', 'stale', 'boring' and 'ugh!'

Kalani had drawn, amongst other things, a tiny bird in a cage, a ripped pair of knickers bearing the word 'shame' and her version of Munch's *The Scream*.

Laurie's rock featured a bent-over woman dragging a giant wheelbarrow. Riding in the wheelbarrow were various other people who I presumed were her family. She'd written 'control freak!' in red across the rest of the rock, along with 'guilt!' and 'never enough!'

'Now, time to haul your lump of negativity into the river,' Hattie said. 'One at a time, off you go.'

Laurie bent down and gave her rock a good shove. It was hard to tell in the twilight, but it might have wobbled a few millimetres.

Hattie raised both eyebrows, waiting for Laurie to have another go.

After two more tries, Kalani stepped over to help. 'I don't care if this isn't allowed. If we try to shift these ourselves, we'll be here all night. Either that or one of us will end up doing our back in. No offence, Laurie, but that's most likely to be you, and you need a working back more than the rest of us.'

'She's got a point,' Deirdre added, coming to add a third pair of hands. 'Is this allowed, Hattie?'

Hattie put her hands on her hips, eyes rolling up to the indigo sky above our heads. 'What, is it okay for friends to help another friend ditch the crap that's too heavy for them to deal with themselves? Honestly, Gals! This is the second-to-last session. Get with the programme!'

It still took plenty of sweaty, grunty minutes for us to roll the rocks back into the river where they belonged. We all had a few grazes and bumps by the end of it, but we supposed that this fitted the metaphor. Before making the final push down the bank, each of us took a moment to consider the words and images we'd drawn, to commit to getting rid of them, even if it did mean swallowing our pride enough to accept help.

'What about you?' Laurie asked Hattie as we tidied up the pens and wiped the sheen off our faces.

'I did mine a few days ago,' Hattie said. 'This was a new session, and I wanted to try it out first.'

'So who helped lug your rock in the river?' Deirdre asked, eyes narrowing.

Hattie glanced at me. 'I grew up on this land. I'm a lot more used to lugging big lumps about than you four.'

'That's not the point though, is it?' Kalani said, her voice soft and serious. 'Why risk hurting yourself, when we're happy to help?'

Hattie picked up the pens, her smile twisting crookedly. 'The point is, it was fine. I was fine. *I am fine.* When I need your help, I promise I'll ask for it.'

I felt the Gals' eyes sliding between my back and Hattie's, all the way back to the house.

* * *

'They aren't going to let up, you know,' I told Hattie once the others had left. 'They feel hurt that you're keeping something from them.'

She shook her head in frustration, empty cake plates clattering as she rammed them into the dishwasher. 'I don't ask them to share anything they don't want to. I specifically said that they could use squiggles and symbols if they preferred to keep things private.'

'Yes, but those things were feelings, thoughts and past experiences. Not a current cancer diagnosis. They know this isn't just the menopause, so they're inevitably thinking and worrying about the worst.'

'Sophie, please.' Hattie sighed, leaning against the worktop. 'I'm taking four weeks to simply be Hattie. To enjoy one more spring, one last birthday party, without having to handle the looks of pity and whispers of "how terrible, how tragic". There'll be plenty of opportunities for them to take care of me later! To treat me like glass as they fake a smile and talk about me as if I'm not there, all of us pretending to ignore my bald head and bloated body. After everything we've been through, they can get over me keeping this to myself for a piddling little month.'

'Even if it means a weird atmosphere at the party?'

She bowed her head. 'I'll tell them something. Not that I'm dying, though!'

I took a deep breath, took a chance. 'Will you tell Gideon and Agnes something, too?'

Her expression turned to concrete. 'Thanks for helping to clear up. I'm going to bed.'

27

I spent most of the weekend finishing off the attic. Hattie came up sporadically to supervise in between naps, sketching woodlice (I wasn't sure if they were worse than the crows) and composing a guest list for her party. I started sending her images of some of the documents and items I wasn't sure whether to keep or dispose of, so she didn't have to exert herself climbing the stairs, but on Sunday afternoon, following a morning alone in the chapel, she made the effort to help me sort through the only box still untouched that contained objects rather than papers.

This one I needed help with, because most of the contents were things I'd never set eyes on before, let alone knew what they were or what they did.

'Aha,' Hattie said, picking up and examining a piece of metal, twisted into what I thought might be a pig. 'This gorgeous goat was created by a fellow artist in Panama. Every item in this box was made by an artist in a different country.'

'There must be at least...'

'Twenty-six.' She gave me a wry smile. 'I went a long way

trying to find myself. Which only goes to show how badly I was lost.'

* * *

Riverbend

Hattie spent two months in Tuscany, another few weeks wandering around the rest of Italy, before she drifted into Slovenia, and then Hungary and, before she knew it, was spending the summer in an artists' commune in Poland. As the season began to change, she packed up her bags and jumped in the back of a van heading for Turkey, and so began a pattern that lasted for the next five years. She determined to relish every moment, each opportunity, to make up for far too long living half asleep. This included breathtaking views, heart-stopping adventures, living from hand to mouth picking up bar work, fruit picking or sketching simple pictures for tourists. Relying on the kindness of strangers, while making new friends in every town and village she passed through. Her resolve to experience everything the world had to offer had been originally designed to keep her demons at bay, but what she found was something different. In each new stunning sunrise, or sky lit with stars, as she stood on mountains and swam in cerulean seas, conversed in clumsy sign language and danced with barefoot children, she realised that, in more places than not, she was able to leave a demon or two behind.

As she painted and sketched new sights and sounds, she learned more about herself, about people, about life, than she had imagined possible. And what she learned was that life was difficult, and painful, and wondrous and mundane and beautiful, no matter where you went or who you were with. People were people. She saw them love and laugh and lie and lose.

And gradually, over the years, instead of painting wounded animals and broken-down buildings, she started to depict the jade of a hummingbird's wing or the wildflowers growing on a rubbish heap.

She drew a cherry tree in blossom, ignoring last year's rotten leaves collecting around the trunk. Her artwork became full of sunshine, not shadows. Life, not loss.

As the years passed, and she lingered longer in each place, felt the urge to keep running less, she found that her heart, too, began to embrace the good again.

On her thirty-eighth birthday, while living with a group of female artists in the Madeiran mountains, she painted a different scene from the one she could see in front of her. One that she knew better than her own face.

A stretch of meadow grass. Broad, sturdy trees – oak and beech and a horse chestnut. She drew the bend in a river, two ducks sailing past.

She rinsed the paintbrush with her tears, and then sold the painting for three times more than anything she'd created before.

Unlike previous work, this one was not signed Harriet Chillington, or even Langford.

This one was drawn by a girl once lost, now found again: Hattie Hood.

Five months later, after an interview in a British newspaper about the new direction for a British artist, a solicitor found her, living in a tiny chalet in Switzerland. He told her he had sad news, and it was. Sad, and thrilling at the same time.

Leonard Langford had died from a heart-attack.

There were two beneficiaries in his will. The first was his nephew, to whom he'd left a modest sum. To the second, his only child, he'd left everything else – which was practically nothing. That was, except for the one and only thing she wanted from the man supposed to be her father.

Riverbend.

* * *

I was out on my weekly shopping and lunch trip with Agnes. We were feeling adventurous, and so we decided to stop for lunch at a different village, rather than Laurie's bakery. I was intrigued to visit Hatherstone, remembering that the original owner of Riverbend had lived at Hatherstone Hall, a large estate bordering the village. We stopped at the restaurant where Gideon had once got us takeaway pizza, Scarlett's, located on a bustling campsite next to the hall. While we were eating our giant paninis, accompanied with crisp slaw and raspberry lemonade, the waitress told us that it was Hatherstone market day, definitely worth a wander round if we had the time.

Most of the vendors lining the main street had embraced the Robin Hood vibe – there were the straight-up souvenir stalls with postcards, bow and arrow sets and the usual touristy keyrings and tea towels. Others included Friar Tuck's beers and cheeses and Much the Miller's son's pies and cakes.

But what caught my attention, naturally, was Maid Marian's Garlands. The entire stall was covered with greenery, ivy twisting around the legs and up a stunning arched canopy. There were garlands, as advertised, but mostly bouquets, buttonholes, hair accessories and centrepieces. I assumed the gaggle of women browsing were planning a wedding.

I couldn't resist running my fingers over the soft leaf of a lilac bush, one of several miniature trees and shrubs arranged artfully around the stall.

'Can I help you?' one of the two stallholders asked, probably noticing the wistful look on my face. The growing queue of customers prevented me from replying with any one of several questions springing unbidden from my memories.

'No, sorry, I'm not looking to buy anything today. I'm just blown away by your designs. I trained as a bridal florist a few years ago, and I've never seen anything like these.'

'Oh, thanks.' The woman flushed. She looked about forty and was wearing a 'Maid Marian's Garlands' apron embroidered with hundreds of flowers, corduroy trousers and a fleece, her dark-brown hair tied in a loose plait. 'We only started the stall a few months ago, but it's really picking up. As you can see.'

She stopped to quickly take a paper slip from a new customer, exchanging it for a box that she opened to confirm it was the correct hairpiece.

'The instructions for keeping it fresh are all in the box. I hope it goes amazingly tomorrow! Send us some pics, won't you?' She waved off a very happy bride-to-be.

'That's a great idea,' I said to Agnes. 'Selling fresh flower hair accessories that they can pick up the day before.'

'Too great!' the stallholder replied. 'We can't keep up with demand. A couple of venues have started using us to dress gazebos for their Sherwood Forest themed weddings, and it's more work than we can handle.'

'Well,' Agnes said, a smile hiding in the wrinkles around her mouth. 'If you're looking for another pair of hands...' She tilted her head in my direction.

I froze, unable to speak.

The woman helped pin a wreath to someone's head, showing how it looked in a mirror, then turned back to me. 'Are you serious? We've had an advert out for a couple of weeks but no one with any relevant training has contacted us.'

'I never actually completed my apprenticeship...' I stammered, not quite sure why I didn't simply explain that I now ran a successful business, and move on.

'Can I ask why not?'

'My parents died suddenly... I had to...'

'Oh, my goodness, I'm so sorry.' The stallholder, to my shock, instead of looking uncomfortable or changing the subject, grabbed both my hands in hers. 'I lost my mine at eighteen. A house fire.'

'That's terrible.'

'Yes. Thank goodness for grandparents.' She nodded and smiled at Agnes.

'Oh, no. Agnes is a friend... I didn't have any grandparents.'

The woman's face dropped.

'It's fine, honestly. It was a good while ago now.'

'Irrelevant. You never stop missing your mum and dad.' She clutched my hands tighter, pressing them against her apron. She smelled of rosemary and fresh lavender, and I could have breathed that scent in for hours.

'Listen, if you're interested in some work, let me know. I'll have to speak to Karen, but, like I said, we've been looking for extra help and it would be far easier to have someone who knows their way around a rosebush.'

I swallowed hard. I did know my way around a rosebush.

'Thanks. I actually have quite a lot on over the next few weeks, but after that... I'll let you know.'

She handed me a card, gave my fingers one last squeeze and went to help someone asking about centrepieces.

'That was a little bit pushy, Agnes,' I chided as we strolled back to where I'd parked Gideon's car.

Agnes tilted her chin in the air. 'I thought you might be looking for a change. One that means *less* change all the time. And less wallowing in people's tragic pasts.'

I wanted to explain that working with flowers would inevitably mean wallowing in my own tragic past. But I'd stood at that stall, roses lined up in the buckets and bouquets in front of me, and I'd almost been able to appreciate how beautiful they were.

Would I want a job working with roses again?

I thought of Gideon, the look in his eyes when he smiled at me. How my chest grew tight when I thought about not seeing him for days at a time. I let myself remember how thrilling it had been to spend my days surrounded by flowers, creating exquisite tributes to love and happiness.

Was it time to leave the world of loss and celebrate joy and hope again?

As soon as I got home, I called Ezra. He had two words for me.

'Absolutely yes!'

* * *

On Thursday, Hattie cancelled art therapy. Or rather, I cancelled it for her, amidst much protest.

After too long going round and round the same conversation, I decided some tough love was needed before she wore herself out even further.

'Hattie, your skin is the colour of actual vomit. You wince whenever you move. If you want the Gals to conclude that you're dying, by all means carry on with the session. I'll be astonished if you can get through it without collapsing.'

'Do I really look that bad?' I'd found her in the sunroom, curled under a blanket.

I grabbed the mirror from its hook above the mantlepiece and showed her.

'Yuck. I was hoping I only felt like the walking dead. I'll put on some make-up, though; that should help hide it.'

'This would be our final session, Hattie. We want you to enjoy it. Right now, you can't stand for more than a few minutes. How are you going to handle us lot for the whole evening?'

She shook her head, face crumpling. 'I'll probably feel even worse by next week.'

'Next week, you can rest properly beforehand. You were standing up for hours at that easel today.'

'All these woodlice were in my head. I needed to get them out.'

'So I'll tell the Gals the final session is postponed?'

She slumped back. 'See if they can come over on Saturday. In the afternoon, when my energy levels tend to be better. It's probably time I told them something, at least.'

It was the Easter weekend, and the Gals were busy seeing family or still recovering from seeing family last weekend, in Kalani's case. Instead, we arranged for an Easter Monday afternoon tea on Kalani's veranda ('I need you Gals to exorcise the cloud of auntie criticism now haunting my private space').

While Hattie rested on Thursday afternoon, I borrowed her car to drop a load of boxes at a local charity shop, and a couple more at the recycling centre. Once back at Riverbend, I added some individual items to online collector sites I'd used before, and then walked over to the boathouse.

After a quick meal with Agnes, Gideon and I climbed into his kayak. I lay back and stared at the branches overhead as he rowed upstream. These trees, which had been here for generations before Hattie, and would still be here for many more after we'd all gone. That had fed from the sunshine above and the decaying mass of once-living things below. Gideon didn't ask about the weight hunching up my shoulders, so I didn't have to lie to him about how my heart ached as I disposed of Hattie's things, even those she wouldn't want to keep if a miracle happened and she survived the lymphoma. But when he'd brought us back to the river's bend, and we'd squeezed into a chair to watch the last ribbons of sunset, in the simple act of his wrapping his arms around me, I felt less alone and more seen than I had in forever.

I ended that sad, sorry day thinking about flowers. Dreaming about hope.

28

The next day, Good Friday, I readied my motorhome, strapped Muffin into her seat belt and battled the bank holiday traffic up to the Peak District.

JoJo and Aaliyah had made a banner, 'Hello Auntie Sophie', which hung between two trees above the farm gate. As soon as we pulled into the drive, the front door flung open and they tumbled out, Ishmael trailing behind them, the teenager trying to play it cool despite the grin plastered across his face.

We made it back inside in a jostle of hugs, tail wags and competing exclamations of who missed who the most. As always, I was immediately handed a mug of tea and piece of cake the kids had made, followed later on by wine and the feast Naomi had prepared.

The six of us talked, laughed and ate until the sun had long set behind the peaks. Then we moved into the living room to light the fire and play silly games until the kids were ready for either sleep or their Xbox, leaving the adults to settle down with another glass of wine and the box of fancy chocolates I'd brought but not wanted to waste on the children.

'You look incredible, Sophie,' Naomi said, curling up beside me on their squishy sofa while Ezra kissed the girls goodnight. 'Working with people who aren't grieving has clearly done you good.'

I couldn't help agreeing. 'Although no one has died yet, it might end up even harder, working with a client this side of bereavement. But it's not just the project that's doing me good.'

'Sophie Potter. I haven't seen that gleam in your eyes for a very long time. Tell me everything, quick.'

I did, although it was impossible to be too quick, and so Ezra heard most of it as well.

'So, what you're telling us is that you've fallen in love—'

'I didn't say love!'

'Darling, I've known you for twenty years. You didn't have to,' Naomi said, arching one immaculate eyebrow. 'You've *obviously* fallen in love, found some friends in a place you adore, and have finally – *finally* – started to get unstuck from your grief. And you still haven't decided whether or not to stay there? What, is this place full of roses, because I can't think of a single other reason why you haven't already started looking for a house there. One that doesn't have wheels or rattle when the wind blows.'

'It has a rose garden,' I admitted. 'But that's something else I've been working on.'

I described the art therapy, and my own rose therapy, and then Ezra made me tell her that Maid Marian's Garlands had offered me a job.

'Seriously, Ezra. A silent partner isn't supposed to be that silent. Why aren't you insisting on dissolving the company?'

Ezra patted his wife on the knee. 'Because it's Sophie's decision. And it's wise to take her time over something this monumental. Closing a successful business to work ad-hoc for a flower stall isn't that straightforward.'

'Hello? Have you looked at her?'

Ezra turned and looked at me. I met his gaze with a shrug.

'We can always spend some time going over the different options. I mean, if you're not sure one way or the other.'

My head wasn't at all sure. My heart, on the other hand? My heart had put its stake in Riverbend soil the first time Gideon grabbed my hands and lifted me out of that muddy puddle.

We stayed up so late that the morning had all but gone by the time I padded downstairs to find a picnic packed, boots ready and some very impatient children plus dog waiting to conquer a peak or two.

Naomi handed me a travel mug of coffee and a croissant and, after another glance at the kids, I offered to consume them in the car.

It was magnificent, soaking up the panoramic view after an exhilarating scramble up a rocky ridge. Muffin had the time of her life, racing the children through empty fields, sniffing the sheep from the safety of her lead as we skirted those that were occupied. We ate cheese and tomato sandwiches, sausage rolls, apples and thick wedges of fudge cake by the side of a mountain stream, and bought ice cream from one of the farms we passed on the way back to the car.

'Auntie Sophie, do you have a boyfriend?' JoJo asked, when we'd arrived back home and were busy arranging toppings on our pizza for tea.

'Why do you ask?' I stammered, stalling for time. I still wasn't completely sure of the answer.

'Because when girls have a boyfriend, they start floating about and smiling all the time, on a magical cloud of love,' she sang, clasping her hands together and fluttering her eyelashes. 'Usually, you look sort of sad even when you're smiling. Now, you're like really, properly happy, right in your eyes. So, I thought maybe it was because you were in love.'

I looked up at the five expectant faces around the table, all of them looking really, properly happy as they waited for me to answer.

'Yes, I have a boyfriend.'

Above the hoots, whistles and dozen or so questions, I didn't think any of them heard me try to explain that Gideon wasn't the reason I was happy...

Once the kids were in bed, Ezra did offer to spend some time discussing the business, but I assured him that all I wanted to do that weekend was relax and enjoy being together.

'Can you even hear yourself?' he asked. 'Who is this Sophie who likes to relax and have fun, and what have you done with my friend?'

'Was I really that bad?' I picked at the tassel decorating the cushion resting on my lap.

'You were who you needed to be, after a tragedy that is impossible for most of us to imagine.' He looked across at me from his armchair. 'But, oh, I have missed this Sophie. I'm not sorry to have her back.'

'Aaliyah wants to know when we can meet your boyfriend,' Naomi said, walking in with a tray of tea.

'Does she?' That made me pause.

'Yes. We're free on the bank holiday Monday, so I thought we could pop down to Nottinghamshire for the day? Stop off for a cup of tea?'

'Um... Hattie's having a birthday party that day. Quite a big one.'

'Well, that's perfect, then, isn't it?' Naomi gave a smug smile. 'You can ask if there's room for a few more.'

After a chilly Easter Sunday barbeque with Ezra's elderly mother, his brother, niece and nephew, I enjoyed a final night in the farmhouse before heading back to Riverbend straight after Muffin's walk.

It felt odd, as the heathland softened into Nottinghamshire's gentle hills. The closer I got to Sherwood Forest, to Riverbend – to Gideon – I felt an expanding glow inside not too dissimilar to how I had felt when heading in the opposite direction a few days earlier.

It felt like I was coming home.

29

I found Hattie asleep in her usual spot on the sunroom sofa, still wearing pyjamas.

'Do you know how draining it is?' she asked, pushing the curls out of her face with a trembling hand once I'd gently woken her. 'Spending a whole day pretending to be fine, when inside, you're disintegrating? I thought it would be easier with just Gideon and Agnes, less effort. But it was worse because they were focussed on me the whole time.'

'That must have been tough.'

I held back any comment about how much easier it would be if she didn't have to pretend.

'Gideon wanted us to walk around Clumber Park, to see the bluebells. Initially, I faked a migraine, but then the stress of it all produced an actual migraine, which conversely made things easier.'

I braved a glance in the kitchen, which to my surprise, was spotless.

'Gideon,' Hattie said, with a wry smile as she shuffled past on her way to get dressed. 'I'd only eaten a few bits and bobs the rest of the weekend, so it wasn't too bad before he got here.'

She paused, resting one hand on my arm. 'You look wonderful. I can't wait to hear all about your weekend. But I'm so glad you're back. Being horribly ill is a lonely business all by yourself.'

This time, I couldn't resist. 'There is a way to solve that.'

'I know. Let me get dressed, and I'll be straight on it.'

* * *

'Hi, Hattie, you look like crap.' Kalani smiled as she flung open the door.

'Believe me, I feel even worse,' Hattie replied, causing Kalani to stiffen in surprise. 'Pour me an Earl Grey and I'll fill you in.'

We spent a tense few minutes bringing out pots of tea and plates of scones, sandwiches and cakes before everyone was sitting down and staring at Hattie, daring her to make them wait any longer.

'You might remember I had my spleen taken out a few years ago.'

They all nodded.

'Well, after lots of tests, last week, the doctor told me that the infection I had then is back. It's pretty nasty, and there's nothing to take out this time so I'm going to have to live with it. They'll start treatment in a few weeks if it doesn't clear up. I didn't tell you because I didn't want to think about it until I knew for sure.'

I stared hard at my teacup, telling myself this was better than nothing.

'A spleen infection in your non-existent spleen?' Deirdre asked.

'An infection in the empty space where my spleen used to be.' Hattie shrugged. 'And a few other places around about it. A few surviving clusters must have been lying in wait, biding their time until I was run-down enough to succumb again.'

'So that explains it,' Laurie said. 'I knew you couldn't be the only woman, ever, who loses weight due to the menopause.'

'What does "pretty nasty" mean?' Kalani asked, her face taut with concern.

'Crippling exhaustion, stomach pains, no appetite and generally feeling like crap warmed up,' Hattie clarified. 'And things may get worse before I get better.'

'You're assistant-less until Deirdre starts,' Laurie said. 'So how can we help?'

Hattie sat back. She'd been waiting for this question. 'Sophie has been amazing, cooking for us, supporting me with work, but what I really need help with is my party.'

'What party? I haven't been invited to a party.' Kalani bristled. 'I didn't know anything about a party.'

'No, because I've been too knackered to send invitations,' Hattie explained. 'I'm having a birthday celebration. A fancy one. And there's a lot to organise.'

'You're going to be, what, fifty-six? Why a big party this time, when you're not well? If you haven't sent out invites yet, you can always postpone,' Deirdre said.

'Like, until you're sixty, and the right age for a big party,' Kalani added.

'I've had fifty-five birthdays already, and not one proper party. I don't see why I should wait until a round number if I feel like having one now. Maybe I want a big party *because* I'm ill, and things are hard, and I want something else to focus on other than how sick and tired I feel.'

'Then of course we'll help,' the Gals agreed.

We spent the next hour or so planning, looking at ideas on Pinterest and assigning tasks.

My main role on the Party Taskforce?

Decorations.

This was going to be a classy affair. Hattie didn't want bunting, balloons and a few fairy lights. She wanted shimmer and sparkle, opulence and elegance.

I would take inspiration from the weddings I'd helped dress all those years ago. I would fill Riverbend and its lawn and terrace with flowers.

Hattie was determined to get most of her things in order before the party and subsequent onset of treatment. I tried to find ways to make it as easy for her as possible – bringing boxes into the sunroom, working through and streamlining as much of her paperwork and admin as I could myself – but she found her lack of stamina increasingly frustrating.

In the end, she confessed that the real issue wasn't her possessions or financial and business affairs. 'It's this story, scraping at the back of my throat, insisting on being told.'

So, I poured us both a gin and tonic, pushed her comfy outdoor sofas into a patch of April early evening sunshine, and gave her story my full attention.

Riverbend

It was the strangest time, coming home. Hattie found Riverbend full of ghostly shadows. But the slow process of clearing away the dirt and decay did something to chase off the echoes of her father's footsteps, his bitter laugh and the thud of her prison door banging shut.

The only time she ventured anywhere near the attic was to sprint up the stairs and check the door was locked, before burying the key in the back of a drawer in the boot room. Instead, she spent those first few days making the downstairs habitable again, scrubbing away years of neglect in the bathroom, kitchen and a spare bedroom with few enough horrible memories to allow some fitful sleep most nights.

The funeral was as depressing as the latter few years of Leonard Langford's life. A smattering of villagers came, alongside a couple of his family's friends, and a distant cousin Hattie knew nothing about. The big, and best, surprise was the grey-haired woman who shuffled into a seat on the back row of the crematorium (there was no way Hattie was having the proceedings in the chapel, given that the only time her father had set foot in there was the day he ruined her life).

As soon as the curtains had closed, and the mourners started filing out, Hattie intercepted the stranger.

'I'm sorry.' The woman ducked her head. 'I'd hoped to slip in unnoticed. I thought there'd be more of a crowd, given how popular Leonard was.'

'Was being the key word.' Hattie grimaced. 'My father's friends disappeared along with his charm and money. May I ask how you knew him?'

Hattie braced herself. Although her father's affairs were hardly a secret, and this person might not have been around until years after her mother died, the thought of being confronted with an old lover gave her goosebumps.

The woman frowned. 'I'm your Auntie Agnes.'

Hattie burst into tears.

With nothing but a lukewarm cup of tea and a plain biscuit in the crematorium foyer to send off a man neither loved nor liked, Agnes accompanied Hattie back to Riverbend. Once Hattie knew, she could see in the familiar curve of cheek and way her aunt clenched her hands around her midriff that this was Uncle Chester's wife.

'My goodness.' Agnes sighed, taking in the tatty façade, overgrown shrubbery and general air of severe neglect. 'Your mother would have been heartbroken. If I'd known, I'd never have stayed away so long.'

The question begged to be asked: why Leonard's sister-in-law, and Hattie's only family, outside of her abusive, neglectful father, had stayed away. Once they'd made a proper pot of tea and settled at the scuffed kitchen table, Agnes was more than happy to answer it.

'You were fifteen the last time we were here. It had been so strange, calling in and finding out your mother had passed. Even before then, things with Leonard had been strained for a long time. He was very... different from Chester.' Agnes shifted on her seat, her discomfort evident. 'They led very separate lives.'

'Please, don't hold back for fear of upsetting me.' Hattie placed a hand over her aunt's and gave it a squeeze. 'I hadn't seen him since I got married. I shan't miss him. I suppose I'm grateful he's the reason I exist. But I'm not sorry that he's dead.'

Agnes looked at her, aghast, but Hattie pressed her lips together, unapologetic. 'Please, carry on.'

'Right. Well. He made it clear we weren't welcome. Chester phoned a few times, drove all the way down here again, but Leonard turned him away at the door. Threatened all sorts of horrible things if we tried to keep in contact. So, that was that. We had enough to deal with, what with Chester's illness, and then Gideon arriving. To be honest, we were glad the pretence was over and we could move on without too much guilt. He made up an excuse to avoid Chester's funeral, and I only knew Leonard had died when the solicitor called about the will. I have to be honest, we were surprised that he'd left Gideon some money. It wasn't like they knew each other.'

'That monster only cared about himself. I don't blame Chester for wanting nothing to do with him. He probably left Gideon the money for appearances' sake. And so I wouldn't get it.'

Agnes furrowed her brow. 'I don't suppose he was an easy man to live with. I'm sorry, Harriet, that we didn't try harder to keep in touch with you, at least. But then, Chester died when Gideon was only four; it was all I could do to look after the two of us.'

'I'm sorry, too. But we can make up for it now, can't we?'

It was Agnes' turn to start crying.

'Tell me about Gideon,' Harriet asked, once they'd dried their eyes and topped up the teapot.

'Oh, he's a bonny lad.' Agnes beamed. 'Just graduated with a degree in landscape architecture! Now he's on a gap year, in South America, otherwise he'd have come to the funeral, of course.'

'Do you have a photo?' Hattie asked, intrigued and excited about a real-life first cousin.

'Oh, no. I didn't think.' Agnes patted her pockets as if one might appear. 'I'll send you one. Or even better, come up and visit some time. Meet him for yourself.'

'I'd love that,' Hattie said, and she meant it. But then, there was so much to do; before she knew it, months and then a year or two had gone by. She'd made it her mission to restore River-bend back to life, but of course that required funds, so she also had to invest time and effort into building a career out of the Sherwood Forest designs that had begun to attract some commercial attention. Still haunted by her past traumas, she retrained as an art therapist, and with one thing and another, it was almost three years before she and Agnes managed more than the odd phone call. Hattie made the trip up to Lancashire one Easter, but Gideon was away with his girlfriend's family, and the intimacy the two women had shared at the funeral had stiffened into the awkwardness of strangers with nothing in common save a horrible man and a heap of regrets.

It was another four years – seven since the funeral – that Hattie tried again, hoping to establish a connection with her cousin, even if things were still a little forced with her aunt.

She made a detour to Lancaster on the way back south after attending an art-therapy conference in Glasgow, meeting them at a restaurant for dinner.

In that moment, everything changed.

30

The final art therapy session was scheduled for the 20 April. Hattie had requested to meet much earlier than usual, at four, so that we had plenty of time to complete our projects then enjoy a celebration dinner afterwards. The Gals had managed to squeeze in a meal at the pub the week before, to discuss party plans, and we'd been in regular communication since, but this still felt like a significant evening. Hattie hadn't promised our problems would be solved after the six sessions, but she had assured us that we should be a lot clearer about what those issues were, and how we wanted to handle them.

It was also Hattie's last professional therapy session. For now, at least. I tried not to cry about that as we spent the morning sorting through her shoe collection, and the afternoon consolidating her different savings into one bank account.

Once we'd gathered in the studio, Hattie gave us the brief before ushering us outside.

'We're making nests.'

'As in, bird nests?' Laurie asked, stroking the goose printed on her jumper.

'Well, what other type of nest is there?' Kalani asked.

'Now you've done it.' Deirdre smirked.

'Rats. Squirrels.' Laurie started counting off on her fingers. 'Wasps, bees and ants. Duck-billed platypus. Snakes and crocodiles...'

'Okay! We get the picture. Although I don't suppose there are many crocodiles in Hattie's river in need of a nest.'

'Gorillas,' Laurie couldn't help adding.

'Are we making a nest for a duck-billed platypus?' I asked Hattie, attempting to move things along before the casserole I'd prepared completely dried out in the slow cooker.

'No, for ourselves.' Hattie pulled out a scrap of paper from her jeans pocket. 'Nests are designed to protect new life. Eggs, or offspring. To provide a safe place for them to grow, until they're ready to fly. What is your new, post-therapy life going to look like, Gals? What does it need to thrive and grow strong enough to fly? How are you going to protect it from predators like busyness, laziness or people who don't care less about your dreams?'

'What?' Deirdre looked pensive. 'Is this like the other tasks, where we did a collage or a picture? We don't have to actually make a stonking big nest, that we can sit in?'

'Oh, no, we are absolutely going to do that.'

'I'm a forty-something human being. Not a duck, Hattie. Or a rat.' Kalani screwed up her nose. 'I can barely get a duvet cover on, how I am supposed to build a nest?'

Hattie smiled, zipping up her jacket. 'I can't wait to find out.'

* * *

How did a bunch of forty-, fifty- and thirty-something humans construct nests in which to hatch their hopes and dreams? Two hours later, all was revealed. Along with the usual explanation for our creations, Hattie asked us to sum up our therapy journey, and, speaking a little louder than usual so we could hear her from where we were squatting in our own nests around the fire pit, Kalani had offered to go first.

She'd lugged four of the logs that were usually placed around the fire pit for seating into a sort of square shape, only angled to leave a large gap on one side. Inside was a haphazard pile of bracken, leaves and grass.

'I'm keeping it simple here, Gals, for the reasons stated before about my lack of nest-building DNA. You all know the journey I've been on already, and what I need to do to keep it going. So, I'm leaving the door to my messy innards a little wider open. I'm mentally trying to become more open to my home becoming a little messier, too. I answered the door to a delivery driver with no make-up on the other day and he didn't scream in horror. I went back to the support group for survivors of sexual assault and I even shared a bit. And...' She took a deep breath. 'I invited Tye round for a meal and he said yes.'

'Of course he blummin' well said yes!' Laurie yelled.

'About time, too!' Deirdre whooped.

Hattie smiled so hard, she almost looked well again.

Laurie's nest was more like a den. A pretty impressive structure of branches all propped up in a point like a tepee. She'd grabbed a blanket from her car to cover the ground, added a flask of coffee and lay back with her eyes closed, a Lizzo song playing on her phone as she talked.

'Gals, these past few weeks have changed my life. Literally. Every single day is different from how it was before. *I'm* completely different. My kids don't recognise this new, non-doormat, ex-control-freak of a mother. This very morning, Flora messaged from school to say she'd forgotten her PE kit and if I didn't bring it in, she'd get a detention, and I replied with, "That's a shame. I'll be out by the time you come back from a detention so I hope you've not forgotten your key, too". Howard is not sorry that his wife has a bit of energy left over when she slides into bed at night, rather than collapsing face first into the pillow. It's small changes, Gals. Hiring a cleaner for a couple of hours. A care assistant for Dad. A washing-up rota. No more clearing up pigeon poop. And a little time and space in a metaphorical tent just for me.'

After cheering Laurie's small-yet-mighty changes, Deirdre showed us her heart-shaped creation.

'Room for someone else in that love nest.' Kalani winked.

'Perhaps,' Deirdre said, with a coy smile. 'But right now, I don't mind either way. I'm learning to love myself again. I know looks aren't what matter most, but I'd given up on myself, and it showed. Somehow, starting with changing the outside helped me realise who I wanted to be, and then make changes on the inside, too. I've got one day left at that tedious job before I get to start working for one of my best mates, Kurt at the butcher's keeps giving me free meat, *and* I bought some new cushions. I'm not doing what's safest, or easiest, or the same old thing I've always done any more. I'm choosing to do the things I love because I'm one of those things. Along with all of you. I'm so grateful you kept loving me even when I was choosing to be totally pathetic.'

It was my turn. The other Gals decided to leave their own nests because they needed a closer look at mine. I wasn't surprised. It was exquisite, if I do say so myself. I'd woven spindly branches into a basic circle structure, then raided both the flower beds and Hattie's studio, creating a sort of giant version of a floral bridal crown. Almost every inch was covered in greenery, interspersed with both real and paper flowers in a range of bright colours, and fairy lights.

At regular intervals around the circle, imitating where the numbers would be if the circle were a clock, were pink and yellow roses. At twelve o'clock, with trembling fingers, I had attached a single white rose.

I took a deep breath, wiped pointlessly at the tears already rolling down my face, and sat up straight inside my nest.

'I think this is the future I want.' I stopped, shook my head. Took another breath. 'That's not true. I *know* it is. It's going to take time, and probably a whole lot more therapy, but I'm not living surrounded by grief any more. Mine or anybody else's. I choose life, and living, and daring to love again. I'm good at my job, but I was *great* at floristry, at creating the perfect designs to celebrate some- one's hopes for the future. Not holding their hand as they mourned the past. I'm going to plant a garden. I'm going to grow roses. I'm not letting fear decide who I am any more. I'm choosing love.'

Whew, we Gals had one raucous, rip-roaring celebration that evening.

We celebrated friendship, and new beginnings, and the power of arting it out.

We celebrated my plans to tell Gideon that I was staying because I loved him.

And if Hattie fell off her kitchen table at one point, well, as she told us once we'd dragged her back off the floor again, 'No shame in falling, as long as you get back up'.

* * *

I decided to wait until the party to tell Gideon that I was going to stay. Partly because I needed to have a lot more conversations with Ezra about how and when I could start dismantling my business, and what kind of funds would be available for me to set up a brand-new life for myself. Hattie had invited me to stay at Riverbend after the project was complete, and I wanted to be there for her, but once our contract was over, it was only right that I paid rent and contributed my fair share of household expenses. I also had to consider what would happen if – *when* – she died. We hadn't got as far as discussing her will yet, but if Riverbend was left to Gideon, her only close relative, I did wonder what would happen to the boathouse.

There was another big reason why I was putting off talking to Gideon. I was acutely aware that he, along with several other people, was expecting some sort of book at the end of this project. I still had the hurdle of him discovering that I wasn't quite who we'd made me out to be and, to make things more complicated, I'd now been keeping Hattie's illness a secret, too. If I waited until he knew about Hattie, then at least we could have an honest conversation about what I might do next.

There was a third, and final reason to delay telling him. Quite frankly, I was still terrified. Terrified of loving someone, of opening up my heart to being broken again, so needing a week or so to steady my nerves was only natural.

The next ten days were full of party planning and floristry designing, taking care of Hattie and our dogs, and loving Gideon while trying to pretend I hadn't quite fallen in love with him yet.

And a coffee at Scarlett's with Stella and Karen, who ran Maid Marian's Garlands. Karen burst out laughing when she saw me. It turned out she'd been one of the Changelings and had found my accidental intrusions into their therapy sessions hilarious.

'Some of those women really need to tone down their paranoia. They'd probably blame it on the menopause, along with every other piddling mistake they've made in the past ten years, but I've known Morag Burrows since primary school, and she's always been like that.' She shook her head, laughing even more. 'That group was fantastic, though, once we got all the whingeing out of the way. We started out feeling like a bunch of has-beens and finished it ready for anything. Isn't Hattie amazing? It's impossible to spend any time with her and not end up the better for it.'

I was hesitant to accept their offer of a permanent job, given how much Hattie might be needing me once her chemotherapy began, but if I was ever up for some work on a freelance basis, I should give them a call, and we could take it from there.

The next day, with a lump in my throat, I gave them a call and booked myself in to help with some bouquets and a floral arch for a wedding in June.

Before I had time to catch my breath, the day of the party was here.

31

The house and gardens were a flurry of activity all day. To our relief, the weather was calm and bright, so the events company had no problem putting up the marquee, which they then filled with round banqueting tables and chairs. Outside, on the lawn, a dance floor was assembled beside a stage for the swing band. Caterers prepared plates of canapés in the kitchen and set up a portable bar and barbeque on the terrace.

The Gals arrived just after lunch to help decorate. We dressed every available surface with simple glass containers filled with Riverbend-blue flowers. Spring blossoms covered the marquee ceiling, alongside shimmering silver lanterns, and we hung curtain lights across the walls. Together, we lugged elegant stands of flowers onto the edges of the lawn and terrace, added yet more lights, a few more sparkly touches and then we were done.

While Laurie, Deirdre and Kalani went home to get dolled up, I fetched Hattie from the boathouse, where we'd insisted she spend the day resting. Once she reached the house, it was all I could do to wrangle her away from oohing and aahing at the visual transformation, and herd her inside.

We had ninety minutes until the party began. Hattie insisted that it would take half an hour to get ready, so we had time for a cup of tea in the sunroom and, it turned out, the final – and most startling – part of her story.

'Did I tell you that I arranged to meet Agnes in a restaurant in Lancaster?'

I nodded. That was where she'd become overwhelmed and had to stop, the last time we'd spoken.

'It almost didn't happen.' Hattie's slender fingers gripped her mug. 'Only an hour or so before I was due to meet Agnes, she messaged to ask if Gideon could come too. Which, of course, I was delighted about. He was my cousin, my closest blood relation.'

She stopped, took a slow, careful breath.

'Only, that's not who he was.'

Her voice was so quiet, I had to lean forwards to hear her.

'When he walked through the door of the Italian restaurant, I knew immediately. That smile. His build. The eyes. Blue, speckled with brown, like my river. Like my Aidan.'

I almost choked on my tea.

'It was as though Aidan was walking towards me.'

A dozen questions fizzed on my tongue, but I swallowed them back, allowing Hattie to continue at her own pace.

'How I got through that meal, I'll never know. Making conversation and smiling while trying to force pasta into a stomach seized up in shock. I just knew. I *knew*. This was my baby. My son. Right here, in front of me, chatting about farming.'

'Gideon is your son?' I mean, I knew that was what she said, but I had to ask.

'When, later on, I could start to wade through the pandemonium that seeing him had unleashed inside my head, it all made sense. Why my father broke off all contact with his brother. The gift to Gideon in his will.'

'Gideon mentioned that Leonard used to send them money.'

Hattie nodded. 'Yes. Agnes told me that later when I had calmed down enough to speak to her. I went back at a time when I knew Gideon was away with his girlfriend. I was so desperate to see him that I almost drove back the day after the restaurant, and every day following that, but I was so raw, in so much turmoil that I knew it would end badly. I needed to speak to Agnes first. The way she'd so casually invited Gideon along, had spoken about him at the funeral, she must have believed I didn't know who he was.'

'Still, she took the risk that when you met him, you would see the resemblance to Aidan and make the connection.'

'Except that she doesn't know.'

'*What?*'

I wasn't so stunned that she *didn't* know, but Hattie had used the present tense. As in, she still didn't.

'Before speaking to her, I realised that if my father had told her the truth, she'd have insisted on me knowing. More than likely, she'd have ensured that I had at least some involvement in my child's upbringing. I thought very carefully about how to raise the topic of Gideon not being her biological child, but in the end, I couldn't find any way that would allow me to be both tactful and truthful. So, I lied about having a medical condition, and that Gideon could also potentially carry the faulty gene, seeing as I inherited it from my father. After trying to fob me off, Agnes eventually confessed that Gideon was adopted, but that he didn't know. It was such a relief for her to finally tell someone, she was almost grateful to explain how and why he came to be their son. It was, of course, more of Leonard's lies.'

Hattie explained, with a grim expression and a glint of steel running through every word, how her father had conned his brother into taking on an illegal adoption. Chester and Agnes had long given up hope of conceiving a child and been resoundingly rejected as potential adopters due to Chester's life-limiting condition. When Leonard contacted them about a young cleaner for the Riverbend estate expecting a married man's child, they were more than willing to help. Hattie's father explained how the man wanted nothing to do with it, and the girl's parents were strict Catholics, so she dared not tell them. Why she decided to tell Leonard Langford of all people was anyone's guess. Chester and Agnes were so thrilled at the prospect of becoming parents that, to Agnes' shame, they didn't ask too many questions.

After sowing the story amongst Agnes' family and their limited circle of friends, followed by a fake extended stay in hospital for Agnes (in reality, she hid in her house for six weeks), the moment Leonard called, they sped down to Sherwood Forest to collect their baby son and his forged birth certificate, with the promise that they would never darken Riverbend's door again.

'You didn't tell her that he was your baby?' I asked Hattie, my head spinning.

Hattie shrugged. 'I thought about it. I wanted to. I wanted to grab my son by his shoulders, look right in his eyes and tell him he was mine. That I'd thought about him, missed him, longed for him every day since he was stolen from me. But here was this frail, lonely old woman, begging me not to tell the man she had raised that she'd lied to him about who he really was his whole life. That she had no idea who his biological parents were, and no way of ever finding out. I was petrified that I'd end up losing him – and her. I couldn't put any of us through the inevitable trauma. So, I decided to wait, at least until Agnes was no longer with us.' Her face twisted into a bitter smile. 'Fool that I am, thinking I would have plenty of time to decide what to do after that. Not considering for one moment that my aunt would outlive me.'

'How did they come to live in the boathouse?'

Hattie smiled properly then, her eyes shimmering with unshed tears. 'As soon as the boathouse was restored, it seemed the obvious thing to do. Gideon had told me about his dream of tending his own land, and Riverbend will be his one day. I offered them a gorgeous cottage in a stunning location, and Gideon his perfect job. I could fill the gaping hole in my heart and form a genuine relationship with my son. I hadn't anticipated how difficult Agnes would find it, accepting what she considered to be yet more charity from a Langford. It never crossed my mind that she'd be afraid of a villager figuring out that Gideon was the child of someone local. But they were minor drawbacks, all things considered.'

'So, what are you going to do now?'

Hattie blew out a long sigh. 'Agnes wouldn't forgive me if I took her son away from her. It would put Gideon in an impossible situation. I've thought about it endlessly over the past few months. Gone round and round in my head. I decided my only option was to write him a letter. Explain everything. If I do die before his mother, then he can decide whether to tell her or not. If she dies before me – and she's seventy-eight, it's not impossible – I can figure out what to do then. If I die suddenly, without a chance to give him the letter...' She paused, looked over at me. 'Then you'll have to show it to him. Please.'

'Where is it?' I asked, trying not to sound as flustered as that statement made me feel.

'In my desk drawer.'

I put down my empty mug and extended my hand towards her. 'Okay. I can do that. For now, let's go upstairs and get ready, because you have a fabulous Riverbend party waiting for you.'

The party started out as sparkling as Hattie had hoped. The air was light and fresh, yet still carrying enough warmth from the day that we were comfortable in our party dresses. Hattie had invited various contacts from the art-therapy world, friends from the village and a scant smattering from the company who manufactured her designs, excluding the slimy account manager. Lizzie and her husband, Joss, had accepted an invitation, and I was a mix of nervous and delighted that Ezra and Naomi were also on their way, having found babysitters for their children.

As I descended the staircase, arm in arm with Hattie, Gideon suddenly appeared through the kitchen door. He stopped dead, gazing up at us both, and for a second, I wasn't sure whether I was holding Hattie up, or her me.

Every man looked different in a suit. Even more so in a dinner jacket with a French navy bow tie that matched his eyes perfectly, the reddish tints in his dark hair glinting in the light from the hallway chandelier.

Seeing him, now knowing who he was, I felt my pulse start cantering for a whole different reason from the pull of attraction.

How Hattie must have felt, looking down on this beautiful, kind, wise man who had no inkling of who she was, I had no idea. I blinked back the ache behind my eyes and tucked Hattie's arm more firmly against my side.

'Wow,' Gideon said, even as the thought flashed through my own mind. 'I can't imagine a Riverbend ball has ever been graced with more dazzling hosts.'

I felt Hattie relax as a beaming smile spread across his face, and we both started moving again.

'Cousin,' Gideon murmured, kissing her on both cheeks once she'd reached the bottom step. 'You look captivating.'

Hattie wore the forest-green dress that had caused such a stir the night Verity met Leonard. The one that originally belonged to Riverbend's first owner, Millicent. She'd hired a dressmaker to remove the ruffles and ribbons and make some tucks to fit her increasingly slender frame. It was also now embroidered with tiny Hattie Hood woodland creatures, including a rabbit randomly poking their nose above the hemline, a dormouse curled around a button and a deer scampering along the waistband. With an emerald clip pinning her grey hair and a matching pendant around her neck, she looked so elegant and radiant, no one would guess that twenty minutes earlier, she'd been bent double in agony.

'And you look positively gorgeous.' Hattie squeezed his hand. 'I want to steal you away to the studio so I can capture it on canvas.'

'Alternatively, you could take a photo.' He smiled.

'Pah. I'm going to walk away and pretend I didn't hear that.'

Gideon waited for Hattie to head into the garden before turning to me.

'Wow.'

'You already said that.' I looked up at him, grinning like a teenager with her prom date.

'I can't seem to think anything else.'

I did feel a tiny bit wow, for the first time in forever. After I'd politely declined Kalani's offer to take me shopping for a party dress, two days earlier, she'd turned up at the house with an armful of swanky carrier bags, having decided the only thing to do was bring the shopping to me.

Every item she'd brought was gorgeous, but she knew full well that there was only one genuine option. I'd chosen a jumpsuit with flattering, wide-legged trousers and a halter neck that added a hint of sexiness. The sage-green satin was embroidered in tiny roses, with pink and green heels to match. I'd curled my hair into soft waves and attempted a dusting of make-up.

Gideon leant forwards and brushed his lips against mine, and, yep, there it was. That feeling as if I knew this man, deep down in my bones, while thrilled and enchanted at the newness of it all.

I love you.

I clamped my mouth shut, not yet able to speak the words, but sure that they must be clear as day in my eyes, my smile, the way my heart strained to get out of my chest and merge with his.

Up until a couple of hours ago, I'd thought this evening would be the time to tell him, both how I felt and that, because of it, I was planning to stay. But with Hattie's story still hovering over my shoulder, my confidence wavered. Still, as Gideon took my hand and we went to join Hattie on the terrace, I decided the best thing to do was enjoy the party and take each moment as it came.

There were a lot of wonderful moments. Laughing, feasting, dancing to old-time classics. Introducing Ezra and Naomi to my new friends. Exchanging stories and catching the man I loved staring at me from across the garden, looking as though he loved me, too.

Some of the Changelings were there, looking positively splendid in a range of vibrant outfits as they unashamedly gave it their all on the dance floor.

I instigated a lacklustre truce with Lizzie. She'd spent most of the evening demonstrating what a fabulous time she was having, making sure everyone heard about her exciting new job opportunities, and how she hoped that Hattie was coping without her, because, well, she loved her old boss and everything, but bigger, better things were calling.

About halfway through the evening, when I popped inside to check how the caterers were getting on, I spotted her slipping out of the office.

'Lizzie.'

She spun around, the look of startlement on her face swiftly replaced with a bright smile.

'Oh. Sophie. I was heading for the bathroom. I hate Portaloos and I didn't think Hattie would mind me using hers, given that it's me. While I was here, I couldn't resist a peek inside.'

'Of course. I'm really glad you came this evening. I hope it's not too strange.'

'I wouldn't have missed it for the world. Hattie wasn't just my boss; she was my friend and my mentor. For fourteen years. I really care about her.'

I nodded. 'It's been a big adjustment, you leaving.'

She smirked. 'I'll bet it has. I heard she's hired Deirdre, though. So I'm sure she'll be fine. Once this mystery project's done with, anyway.'

'She's nearly completed it, so the worst is over.'

'That's good. Find anything interesting?'

I shrugged. 'You know I'm not allowed to say anything.'

'Of course. Well, I'd better get back to Joss.' She gave me another bright smile and left.

* * *

As the sun began to set, casting the whole party in a shimmering glow, Gideon caught hold of my hand and led me away, into the shadows.

'Where are you taking me?' I giggled, feeling a pleasant buzz from a glass or three of wine.

'Somewhere private. I can't stand to look at you a moment longer.'

'Excuse me?' I tried to stop walking, but he kept tugging me forwards.

'A moment longer, without doing this.'

He let us both come to a stop then, gently manoeuvring me around to lean against the brick of the rose-garden wall as he nestled up against me for a long, delicious kiss.

'Good lady, would you allow me to show you my roses? They are particularly fetching this time of year.'

I giggled again, the less squiffy section of my brain marvelling that I could laugh at the mention of roses. 'Is that a euphemism for something else?'

He grinned. 'It is not. But it is an excuse to kiss you some more.'

I followed him into the garden where I'd sprinted away from him less than three months ago with barely a second thought.

'How is it?' he asked, genuine concern in his eyes as I slowly wandered over to a climbing rose.

'It's beautiful,' I breathed, so relieved that I meant it. 'I actually snuck in here the week before last and stole some for my nest.'

'Your what?'

I smiled, waiting for him to come and playfully pull me against his chest. 'I'm sworn to secrecy. All you need to know is that I can now handle a rose without wanting to pass out.'

'So, you're cured?' He pressed his forehead against mine. It was so safe, so lovely, so *right*, that I knew now was the time.

'I don't know about that, but I'm on my way. Which is why I've come to a decision...'

Gideon pulled his head back, eyes boring into mine, wide with hope and brown flecks of fear.

'I'm going to stay.'

'What?' He pulled me over to a bench, where we both sat down. 'You mean, you're not leaving after your work with Hattie is finished?'

'That's what staying is. Not leaving.'

'Tell me everything.'

'I don't... there isn't much to say, except that... I love you.'

Gideon couldn't have looked more stunned if I'd pulled out my own heart and offered it to him. Which, to all intents and purposes, I had.

After opening and shutting his mouth a couple of times, he closed his eyes, took a moment then opened them again, looked right in mine and said, 'I love you, too. Sophie, I have never felt this way about anyone before. From the first time I saw you tumble on your backside in that filthy water, it was as if something inside me just knew. I don't know how else to put it. I am so completely, agonisingly in love with you.' He stopped to release a breathless laugh. 'These past few weeks have been torture. Trying to be all cool and mature. Wanting to throw myself at your feet and beg you to stay. Oh, Sophie. I love you so much it almost killed me.'

'I felt it too,' I said, ducking my head, overwhelmed by the moment. 'That first time. And every time since.'

In between kisses, Gideon peppered me with questions about where I would live, what would happen with my business and how I'd earn money now. I answered as honestly as I could, hanging onto the knowledge that in a couple of days, I could finally be as open as I yearned to be.

'We should get back.' I sighed eventually, aware that, even if no one else missed us, I didn't want to abandon Ezra and Naomi for any longer.

'One second.' Gideon walked over to the far side of the enclosed garden, picking up a pair of secateurs and snipping off a white bloom that he then tucked into my hair. 'Will you carry roses on our wedding day?' he asked.

I nodded, taking hold of his hand. 'Three white roses, for each of my family. The rest will be the brightest colours you can cultivate.'

'So that's a yes?' He smiled, eyebrows shooting up his forehead.

'Gideon Langford. Was that meant to be a proposal?' I looked at him.

He laughed. 'Just putting a feeler out, seeing how the land lies.'

I turned to him as we stepped through the rose-garden door. 'No feelers necessary. Whatever happens next, however things work out with a house and a job, everything else, you can be sure of what I've told you. I love you, Gideon. You are my heart's home. The family I'd tried to convince myself I didn't need. You're everything. No matter what happens, know that.'

'Hey!' Kalani called from across the grass. 'Is Hattie with you? It's time to cut the cake and Laurie's getting antsy about leaving it outside for too long. We can't find her anywhere.'

'Hattie's missing?'

I stomped down my initial prickle of panic and hurried with Kalani back towards the house. Deirdre and Laurie met her on the terrace, both of them breathless from the search.

'Who saw her last?' I asked, scanning the crowd.

'She was on the dance floor but stopped halfway through a song and said she needed a rest. No one noticed which way she went.'

'You've checked the house?'

Deirdre nodded. 'All the downstairs, and her bedroom suite, too.'

'I've been to the studio, it's all locked up,' Laurie added.

'Okay.' The prickle spread to a sharp stab of fear. 'Maybe someone should try the attic, just in case.'

It seemed unlikely that Hattie would have gone up to the attic. We'd completed our work there, shut the ghosts of the past away and moved on. But on the off chance that the party had sparked an impulse to return to her mother's bedroom, someone ought to make sure.

There was one other place where Hattie might be. My main concern was why she'd be there long enough for everyone to miss her.

'I'm going to check the chapel.'

'The chapel? Why on earth would she go there in the middle of her birthday party?' Kalani asked.

'It's just where she goes, when... when she needs a rest.'

'That makes no sense.'

'I'm pretty sure she'll have found a bench in the garden somewhere, ended up chatting with someone and lost track of time,' Deidre said.

I shrugged, not wanting to delay things by arguing with

them, and turned to go. A moment later, Gideon caught up with me.

'You're sure she's there, aren't you?' he asked as I hurried down the path.

'Enough to bother looking.'

'You know what's going on with her.'

He grabbed my elbow as I stumbled, keeping me upright.

'She's going to tell you after the party. I promised I wouldn't say anything until then.'

He gave a grim nod, and we kept on going.

Shoving open the chapel door, Gideon right behind me using the torch on his phone to guide us, I scrambled down the aisle to the crumpled heap in the far corner that, as I grew closer, took the form of my precious friend.

32

Hattie was conscious, just about, but folded in on herself, head resting on her knees and sweat dripping down her face. The hand I cradled in mine was clammy and ice-cold.

I tried asking her a few questions, but all she could manage was an unearthly moan. By the time I turned to Gideon, he'd already started dialling for an ambulance.

'No.' I shook my head. 'We need to call her doctor.'

'She needs A&E, not a GP appointment,' Gideon said, with a curt head-shake.

'Not her GP. Dr Ambrose. Hang on.' I had my phone in my jumpsuit pocket, so it took no time to find the right website and click on the out-of-hours number.

'He's her private doctor. He told us to call in an emergency. He'll know what to do.'

To my immeasurable relief, Dr Ambrose was on call that evening. He listened carefully, asked me for some further specific details and dispatched a private ambulance in under two minutes.

'What's going on, Sophie?' Gideon asked, through a tightly clenched jaw.

Before I could figure out how to answer, Hattie groaned again, straining to lift up her head, so all my attention was focussed on her until the ambulance arrived. By that time, more people had gathered on the grass outside the chapel door. Hattie was stretched out surrounded by anxious faces, unspoken questions and Lizzie's muffled sobs.

Thankfully, those awesome Gals soon took command of the situation, ordering everybody back to the house, where some stayed to help clear up and others made a discreet exit. I found Ezra and Naomi as soon as I could, giving them tight hugs and kisses goodbye before Gideon drove us both to the hospital.

* * *

'We're here to see Harriet Langford,' Gideon told the hospital receptionist, his voice tight with worry.

'Name, please?'

'Gideon Langford.'

The woman typed for a few seconds. 'Ah, yes. You're her next of kin.'

Gideon gave an impatient shrug.

'If you'd like to take a seat, I'll let the doctor know you're here.'

* * *

'Are you going to explain what's happening, or leave me clueless in front of the doctor?'

I couldn't meet Gideon's eye. My insides were a churned-up

mess of guilt and anxiety. I couldn't blame him for sounding brusque.

'She made me promise not to say anything,' I said, speaking barely above a whisper despite there being no one else here. 'I tried persuading her to tell you, but she kept saying she wasn't ready.'

Gideon was vibrating with impatience. I couldn't see any alternative but to keep going.

'She has a rare form of lymphoma. It was diagnosed a few years ago but didn't need any treatment and she didn't even have symptoms after her spleen was taken out. But in the past few months, she's started to feel ill. The cancer has become aggressive.' I hunched over in mortification. 'She starts chemo on Wednesday.'

I glanced up at Gideon. All the blood had drained from his face. He sat back in the chair, eyes blank, jaw slack.

'Aggressive? Is it terminal?'

'It's rare enough that it's hard to say. But the doctor thinks she should prepare for the worst.' I tried my hardest not to start crying again. This wasn't about me.

'When did you find out?'

I sucked in a deep breath. 'A few weeks ago.'

'The Gals?'

'They think she has a nasty infection. She only told me because I found her in agony.'

'Lizzie?'

I shook my head. 'No one knows but me. She wanted to enjoy the party without it hanging over her.'

'So that explains why you've been walking Flapjack.' His face twisted into a bitter smile. 'Why you decided to stay on.'

'No!' I paused, tried to clear my head so I could answer

honestly. 'I mean, I am going to stay for Hattie. But I'm planning on staying longer. For us.'

He dragged his eyes off the floor to look at me, and the desolation in his gaze cracked my anxious heart in two. 'I can't believe you've known for weeks – *weeks*! – that she's dying. And you didn't so much as hint that I should ask how she was.'

'I told you, she made me promise...'

'That's why she hired you to write this book. To tell her story before it's too late?'

I had to grit my teeth to avoid throwing up.

'I signed a non-disclosure about that.'

'About the book?'

It was impossible to stop the tears now. 'There isn't a book. I'm not a historical author. If you search for Sophie Potter, you'll find my business online.'

An endless minute later, he clicked off his phone and slipped it into his pocket.

'Wow.'

'I asked her, repeatedly, to let me tell you my real business. She made it clear that it was non-negotiable.' I stopped, blotted my face and blew my nose, tried desperately to yank myself back together. 'I was going to tell you as soon as she'd shared about the cancer.'

'Okay.' He nodded, wiping his own eyes. 'I get that you couldn't tell me. But it doesn't change the fact that you lied, over and over again.'

'I didn't lie! Every time you asked me, I never lied.'

His face hardened again. 'Even if you didn't outright lie, you dodged and ducked and contorted your answers to make me believe a lie, so that's okay?'

'I know it's not okay!' My hands were shaking. This conversation would have been hard enough back at the house, or while walking through the peace of the forest. Here, with Hattie on the other side of the hospital door, it was hideous. 'But what else could I do? I signed a business contract. You know I tried to keep things casual between us. I told you so many times that I couldn't commit. I dreaded my loyalty ending up torn like this.'

'I just...' Gideon rubbed a hand over his face. 'It's a lot.'

'I know. And I'm so, so sorry.'

He gave a small nod to acknowledge that truth, at least. 'I need some time, to process all this.'

'Of course. I'll see if I can find us a coffee or something.'

* * *

When I arrived back in the waiting room, having found the small café closed but vending machines serving hot chocolates and cereal bars, Gideon wasn't alone.

It wasn't a shock to see Lizzie huddled in the chair beside him, but I stopped dead when I saw the letter in her hand.

Gideon looked at me, his face concrete. 'Did you know about this, too?'

My expression must have said it all.

'That letter was meant for after Hattie died,' I stammered at Lizzie, my voice rising in distress. 'You had no right to take it. Or read it!'

'For all we know, Hattie is dying right now!' Lizzie cried, tipping her chin up in defiance. 'You had no right to keep Gideon from knowing who his real mother is! He's already lost months of whatever precious time they've got left together, and you could have done something about that. You've known Hattie a few weeks; you have no idea what she'd want in this situation.'

'I have more than an idea because she spoke to me about it.

At length.'

'Hattie doesn't know what she wants!' Lizzie bit back. 'She's not been thinking straight for ages, acting strange, making erratic decisions, and now we know why. She's not of sound mind.'

'That's not true.'

'Hello? Her account manager showed me the Christmas crow designs. The woodlice! You are clearly enabling this breakdown she's going through, using her illness to manipulate and control her. Is that what you do? Exploit vulnerable people for money and a place to live and call it a business?'

'What?' I was too appalled to defend myself.

'Deceiving, concealing. Who knows how much money you've siphoned off from the stuff in the attic while Hattie's been too tired and distracted to notice?'

I looked at Gideon, silently begging the man who'd declared his love for me mere hours ago to stand up for me, but he was a statue of devastation, head in his hands, shoulders slumped in shock.

'You're the one who's rifled through her things and stolen a highly confidential letter.'

'I was doing it to protect her from you! I'm the only one who really understands and cares about her, apart from Gideon.'

'Well, clearly you don't understand her that well, because you didn't know she was dying and you didn't know Gideon was her son!'

Gideon lifted his head. 'I think you'd better go.'

'What?'

Before I could protest, a door opened and Dr Ambrose walked in. 'Ah, hello. Gideon? Would you come with me, please?'

Gideon shot to his feet.

'Would you prefer Sophie to come with you? Or... I'm afraid I don't know this young woman's name.'

'No. They're both leaving.'

I was still looking for a suitable place to dump the hot chocolate as the doctor ushered Gideon towards the internal door.

'You're Hattie's cousin, I believe?' Dr Ambrose asked.

There was an awful pause while Lizzie and I both pretended not to be holding our breath.

'No.' Gideon said, sounding like a man choking on a terrible secret. 'I'm her son.'

I'd packed my things, readied the motorhome and was sitting at the kitchen table, wondering what to do about Flapjack, wondering how on earth I'd managed to convince myself that I could handle a serious relationship, genuine friendships, a normal life... when the front door opened, sending both the dogs scampering out to greet whoever it was.

Cautiously following them, I saw Gideon gently helping a hunched-over, drawn-out Hattie through the door.

'Sophie,' Hattie breathed as they both came to a stop, and then she couldn't seem to think of anything more to say.

Which was to be expected, I supposed, as I stood back to allow Gideon to lead her into the sunroom. I was a near-stranger, hired for a project that was now more or less complete. A grain of grit in the mechanism that had kept Riverbend alive throughout this chapter of its story.

Here was a mother, reunited with her lost child.

Beside her was a son and heir, discovering a legacy and a history that had rocked him to his core.

I watched through the doorway as Hattie slowly lowered herself onto the sofa, felt even more like a voyeuristic intruder as Gideon tucked a blanket around her knees, checked that the cushions were positioned comfortably.

Slipping back into the kitchen, I left a note on the table, picked up my bag, gestured to my dog to follow me, and left.

* * *

A mile outside Middlebeck, I pulled over, my body so wracked with sobs that it was all I could do to steady myself enough to message Deirdre.

I don't know what you've heard, but it's best that I leave. I think Hattie's ready to tell you all the truth now, and she'll need your help. Thanks for everything. Say bye to Laurie and Kalani for me. The Gals meant more to me than I could ever explain xxx

33

I spent a couple of weeks with Ezra and Naomi trying to wallow in my pit of misery while surrounded by children who just didn't seem to respect Auntie Sophie's personal crisis. The constant pleas to play a game, braid hair, watch yet another incomprehensible TikTok video eventually ground me down.

It was impossible not to feel better when surrounded by such innocent, unashamedly exuberant life.

'Did you break up with your boyfriend?' JoJo asked one breakfast, unable to conceal her eagerness for gossip.

Had I broken up with my boyfriend? We hadn't spoken since the hospital.

'I guess I have, yes.'

'Did he cheat?'

'He didn't, no.'

'Did he gaslight you?' She patted my arm in sympathy. 'Ooh, did he slide into another woman's DMs, because that's still cheating, you know?'

'He did nothing wrong.'

'Oh.' She licked the lid of her yogurt pot, brow creasing in confusion. 'Why did you break up, then?'

I took a large bite of toast while I thought about how to answer this.

'Maybe Auntie Sophie was the one sliding into someone's DMs,' Ishmael said, eyeing us over his giant cereal bowl. 'It's not always the guy, you know.'

'Or she lied,' Aaliyah added, her mouth sporting a milk moustache.

'Auntie Sophie would never lie!' JoJo retorted.

I studied the remaining corner of toast for a long moment, my appetite vanished.

'Would anyone like to walk Muffin with me later?'

'Can I hold her lead?'

'Can we take her squeaky ball?'

'Last time you held her lead, Aaliyah, you dropped it, remember? I'll hold her lead...'

* * *

I would get over it, a romance lasting less than three months. I'd recover from losing a few friends who were kind enough to message that they understood me not telling them Hattie's illness was so serious. After all, a Gal never betrays another Gal's secret.

They didn't message me again, though.

Should I contact Gideon?

I thought about that. Agonised over it. Wanted to ask Naomi for her opinion but wasn't sure whether or not I was more scared about her insisting I messaged him or badgering me into deleting him from my contacts.

The truth was, I had no idea what to say. I felt ashamed. Not because I'd kept Hattie's secret – that had been the right thing to do – but I had allowed Gideon to fall for me. I felt ashamed that I had run so easily, taken the coward's way out without even saying goodbye, let alone asking him to hear me out. I didn't know how to live with the guilt that I went back on my promise to Hattie, despite knowing she was better off being cared for by people who loved her, and that my presence would have caused tension that everyone could do without.

I had convinced myself that I was a small player, a momentary glitch in the Riverbend story.

But if Gideon really was in love with me, then maybe me disappearing wouldn't have been what he wanted. Maybe he'd have preferred me to stay and work things out so I could support him through this momentous revelation.

The least I could have done was be there for Agnes. The regret about how she must be feeling sat like a bowling ball in my gut.

Ugh.

I had no idea if I'd done the right thing. Or what the right thing was to do now.

So, I did what I'd always done, and tried my best to put it behind me and move on.

As May passed by, the farmland lush with wildflowers, baby rabbits and the joyful bleating of lambs, I started to regather myself, squash down my emotions and gently tend to my re-shattered heart.

After several evenings in the garden with glasses of wine, gazing at the meadows and gently exploring with Ezra and Naomi what I might do next, I decided to continue with shutting down the business, and tentatively investigate floristry apprenticeships. I called Maid Marian's Garlands and explained that I'd left the area due to unforeseen circumstances, and they were gracious about it while making me promise to call if I ever ended up back in Sherwood Forest.

* * *

I also did one more, risky, meddling thing. It was the only way I could think of to make things up to Hattie.

It took only a few hours of research to find the right Aidan Hunter, now living in the Yorkshire Dales, running an outdoor activity centre. After a couple more days of research, I called the centre and asked if I could speak to him and, to my surprise, a few seconds later, I was introducing myself.

'Hi, Sophie, what can I do for you?'

I took a deep breath. I'd considered easing my way into the conversation – pretending I was a historical author researching Middlebeck, or Riverbend, or a journalist writing about Hattie Hood. But knowing where that had got me, I'd decided to risk being honest from the start.

I'd read dozens of reviews on the activity centre website, many of them glowing about how lovely Aidan was. I'd scoured his social media. It hadn't taken long as his posts were few and far between, but looking at his friends, the messages they sent on his birthday, his two children's accounts, they all painted a picture of a solid, decent, well-liked man.

I had also noted that he'd given his ex-wife away at her recent wedding, which spoke volumes about his character. So, I went for it.

'I'm a friend of Hattie Hood. Hattie Langford, as she was when you knew her.'

There was a moment of silence.

'Go on.'

It was impossible to discern anything from his tone, so I went on, as requested.

'She's been spending time recently telling me her story, including her childhood and relationship with you.'

'That was a very long time ago. We've both been married since then.'

'Married and divorced.'

He didn't reply to that.

'I'm calling you now because, well, she's got cancer.'

I could sense him tensing down the phone.

'That's why she's been going over her past. I have a business helping people sort through their possessions and finances, getting their lives in order... Anyway. There's a lot of unanswered questions about what happened. With you. She doesn't know I'm doing this, and I won't tell her if you aren't interested or if you think the answers wouldn't be helpful. But I think she'd really like to see you again. Complete some of the missing pieces in the story.'

'How bad is it?'

I swallowed back the lump in my throat. 'Bad enough.'

'Where is she living now?'

'She's been back at Riverbend for years.'

Another heavy silence.

'Since her father died,' I added.

'Is this the best number to contact you on?'

'Yes.' I held my breath.

'Is there time for me to think about it?'

'Yes.'

'I'll let you know by the end of the week.'

* * *

A few days later, as I was completing an application form for a week-long intensive wedding floristry course, my phone beeped with a text message.

Can you and I meet up first? I also have questions.

That Thursday, 1 June, I met Aidan at a service station just off the M1 motorway, about an hour's drive for both of us. I'd seen his picture on the activity centre website, but the sight of him standing at ease in the Costa queue jolted the breath from my lungs. The resemblance to his son was undeniable. He even wore the same type of jeans and jacket as Gideon.

We found a table in a quiet corner, and Aidan wasted no time on small talk.

'How is she?'

I fumbled for a few seconds, having expected this question, but finding the answers I'd rehearsed had evaporated. 'I'm back home now, so haven't seen her since she started her first round of chemo.'

He nodded, taking that non-information in.

'Can you tell me the prognosis?'

'It's a very rare form of lymphoma, so is tricky to predict.'

'You don't sound hopeful.'

I shrugged. 'Neither did the doctor. But she's getting excellent care from a private clinic.'

Aidan took a few sips of his coffee before changing the subject. 'She told you what happened, with us?'

I gripped my disposable cup tighter. 'What she knew from her side, at least.'

'In all the interviews, profiles, the online stuff, there's never been any mention of a child.'

Oh boy, we were straight into it, then.

For the first time, Aidan appeared unsure of himself. 'If there had been... and the age fitted the dates. I'd have made contact. I need Hattie to know that. I knew she was married, I wouldn't have caused any trouble there, but there is no way I would have passed up on being a father to my child.'

'But you did, though,' I said, bracing myself. 'Back when Hattie needed you, you never turned up.'

Aidan winced. As he prepared to answer, his eyes unfocussed, as if seeing not me, sitting at a rickety table in a service station, but whatever it was that had happened over thirty-five years ago. Even before he'd started speaking, I knew it wouldn't be good.

'I didn't show up when we'd arranged to meet because I was in hospital. Thanks to my brothers, who took umbrage at my last-minute change of heart about being the fall guy for their latest and quite possibly stupidest enterprise.'

'They hurt you?'

He gave a grim nod, his gaze briefly flicking to me before settling back in the past. 'I'd agreed to help them out in return for a share of the haul that would mean Hattie and I could start over. But I knew, deep down, that it wouldn't work out like they'd promised. I also realised that, even for the sake of our baby, I couldn't go through with it. I'd spent my whole life resisting getting sucked into their sordid lifestyle. How could I give in now when I was about to become a father? How was that any way to start our new family, living off stolen money? Constantly having to look over my shoulder because my brothers would drop me in it in a second to get themselves off the hook?

'I wanted to head to Riverbend straight from the hospital, but I was still a mess. I wouldn't have been able to protect Hattie if things turned nasty. So, I left her a letter in the chapel, explaining what had happened, arranging to meet a week later. I didn't have enough money, but I knew we'd figure something out. Only I couldn't go back home in the meantime, so I spent a week sleeping in an empty barn. I tried sheltering one night in the chapel, but I couldn't rest, expecting Langford to burst through the door at any second. I hung around the house a few times, hoping to catch a glimpse of Hattie, but there was no sign of her.

'On the night I'd asked her to meet, I waited for hours. The note had gone, so I felt sure she'd be there.'

'But she wasn't the one who found the note.'

'Really?' Aidan jerked his head up, startled eyes meeting mine. 'Langford told me she'd given it to him.'

I didn't tell him that Hattie was locked up in Riverbend's attic, for fear of disrupting his story.

'What else did he tell you?'

'That Hattie had seen sense, already "got rid of it".' He stopped, blinked back tears. I felt a wave of sadness that, after all this time, it still upset him. 'She wanted nothing to do with me, or my criminal family, most of whom had been arrested after going ahead with the robbery without me. He said that she'd chosen to live with her aunt for the foreseeable future.'

'And you believed him?'

Aidan grimaced. 'Not at first. But I waited, watched, and she wasn't at Riverbend. She'd clearly disappeared. Everyone in the village knew she was staying with her aunt. Where else would she have gone? I had nowhere to live. My parents made it clear I wasn't welcome. My brothers were out on bail, blaming me for tipping off the police. If they caught so much as a whiff of me, they'd do worse than send me to hospital. So, the only solution was to leave.'

He drained the last of his coffee. I'd barely touched mine.

'Eventually, I served eight years in the army, and came straight back to Middlebeck as soon as I got out. My family had found out who shopped them in, so were ready to make amends, but when I heard Hattie was married, I couldn't stay. Eventually, I met someone, had two girls and tried to get on with my life.' He paused, closing his eyes for a moment. 'I never forgot her, though. I never stopped wondering. When I first saw her face on one of those newspaper magazines, it was as though the world stopped turning. Probably didn't help my marriage last any longer than it should have done.' He took a slow, shaky breath. 'But she's divorced now?'

'For quite a while. And like I said, she never forgot you, either.'

'I hope things were good, at her aunt's house. She managed to get away from him, even if it wasn't with me.'

'I'll let her tell you that side of the story.'

Aidan shook his head. 'I don't know. It's been a long time. Why would I want to dredge all that up for her, especially if she's so ill? I'm grateful you got in touch, but I don't think I should meet her.'

I tried not to tell him, but, after failing to persuade him that meeting Hattie was a good idea, I could see no other option.

'She didn't live with her aunt. She spent months locked in Riverbend's attic, believing you'd abandoned her, before Leonard shipped her off to boarding school.'

'What?' Aidan stared at me, eyes wide with shock. 'Why would he do that?'

I shrugged, starting to panic that I'd given too much away. 'To keep her away from you?'

He shook his head, understandably distressed. 'What else did he lie about?'

He'd looked pale before, but as he thought about that, every drop of colour drained from his complexion. 'He was telling the truth about the baby. I already told you, to be absolutely certain Langford hadn't lied about it I read the articles, her online profiles. Hattie Hood doesn't have children.'

'Like I said, I really think you should hear her side of the story.'

Aidan Hunter swore under his breath, picked up his bag, and – I later discovered – drove straight to Riverbend.

* * *

Riverbend

As an artist, Hattie Hood had long prided herself on having a flourishing imagination, but never in her darkest dreams could she have conjured up something as brutal and wretched as her first round of chemotherapy. She'd expected her hair to fall out, although that wasn't as drastic as she'd feared. She'd been warned about the tiredness, possible nausea, various other unpleasant side effects that began to blur together in the mush inside her head.

It was going to be tough. She'd got the message. But it had to be done, so what was the point in fretting when she could be in her studio, sketching herons?

Tough, she laughed bitterly to herself a few days later, as her son gently picked up the bag of bones that had once been her beautiful body and carried her back to bed. Tough was living in a freezing cold attic, when at least you had the strength to get yourself to the bathroom to throw up.

Tough was giving birth without pain relief, and someone

taking your baby at the end of it.

Tough was...

Ugh. She was too sick, too exhausted, too wracked with bone-screaming agony to come up with anything else.

Either way, the only thing keeping her from calling Dr Ambrose and cancelling the remaining five treatments was owing her son every extra week, day, hour that she could give him, having denied him that for so long.

He'd said nothing about his discovery during the three days of chemo, taking her to the hospital and then refusing to leave her side until she was ready to come home again. Heating up the meals the Gals had left, stubbornly neglecting the mother who'd raised him until Hattie summoned enough strength to send him back to the boathouse.

Hattie wasn't fooled for one moment by Sophie's letter explaining that a family emergency had come up. The timing couldn't be coincidental and, even with her mind feeling as though it had been ambushed by Gideon's chainsaw, she struggled to accept that Sophie would either leave without explaining this mysterious emergency or fail to check up on how her treatment was going.

Something had occurred that was big enough to ensure Sophie had left Riverbend with no plans to return.

A week after the first treatment, when she could get herself from the sofa to the kitchen and back without dry-heaving, and her muscles felt as though they were starting to solidify into functioning body parts again, Gideon told her.

She'd have thought herself too weak to cry, but she managed it.

She also found the strength to reply to some of her son's questions that she knew the answers to, along with fervently repeating how much she loved him and how sorry she was, until he replied in no uncertain terms that he knew, and she mustn't waste any more precious energy trying to convince him.

It was a monumental, grief-stricken few days. Gideon and Agnes moved into the main house, although Hattie and Gideon would not reveal the truth to Agnes or anyone else, at least for the time being. They talked, when Hattie was up to it, and when she wasn't, he walked Flapjack or read while she slept.

He found alternative landscaping firms for most of his current clients. Others who knew Hattie were sympathetic about their projects being postponed.

'You're thinking about her, again,' Hattie pointed out as they sat in the garden watching the sunset one evening.

Gideon didn't bother denying it. It was ridiculous how often he thought about her, considering the other, far more important things he had to focus on.

'Give her a call.'

Gideon's brow furrowed. 'I don't know what to say. Even if I did, I don't think I could say it on the phone.'

'Then go and see her.'

He shifted in his chair. 'I'm not leaving you to go and talk to someone who doesn't want to see me, when I don't even know what I want or need to say, just because I still think about her sometimes.'

'Tell her that. You still think about her.' Hattie smiled. 'All the time.'

Gideon gave a dismissive shake of his head and went to fetch his mother a blanket.

* * *

The second round of chemo was, if possible, worse than the first. Bloated thanks to the steroids, now more bald than not, skin the colour of an old dishrag, eyes sunken, mouth blistered and draped in a baggy T-shirt and leggings, the only items she could bear next to her skin, Hattie Hood was slumped on her garden sofa, trying to distract herself by watching a particularly fat bumblebee feasting on her flowers, when she looked up and saw a mirage.

Either the drugs have brought on hallucinations on top of everything else, I've finally lost my mind or I've slipped off to heaven, she thought, staring at the man who, after pulling up his 4 x 4 on her drive, was now striding across the lawn towards her.

'Hattie,' he said, when close enough to speak without raising his voice.

'Aidan,' she whispered in reply, not even bothered that she was too frail that day to haul herself up into a dignified position, because this man, this angel, was looking at her with so much love in his eyes – and not a trace of pity – that nothing else mattered.

'Can I sit down?'

She breathed something akin to a laugh. 'Well, it'll be far less onerous than me trying to stand up.'

Then he sat, smiled, and held her hands, and before they both knew it, he was pressing the soft, strong mouth she'd never forgotten against her papery forehead, before gently enfolding her against his chest. For a blissful, beautiful moment, she forgot that she was dying.

A while later, Gideon found them, and three lives flipped upside down all over again.

Riverbend's curse is broken, was the last coherent thought before she sank into oblivion that night. I'm not alone any more. My love has come back to me.

And this time, a Riverbend man would stay.

34

Almost two weeks had passed since I'd met with Aidan. He'd messaged to thank me for getting in touch, and to say that he'd be spending some time with Hattie and Gideon over the next week or so. They were all very grateful for what I'd done.

I breathed a huge sigh of relief and was able to throw off another load of the guilt clinging to my shoulders.

When Hattie phoned, a couple of days later, I was too freaked out to answer, but she left a voicemail reiterating Aidan's message, thanking me and asking me to call her, or even better to visit. I wept at the tremor in her voice. Cried that, despite me leaving in such a cowardly way, she was the one to reach out to me. Sobbed into my duvet at how much I missed her. Missed Riverbend. Missed everything, and one person more than all the rest put together.

I then dried my eyes, blew my nose and texted a bland reply about how I was still dealing with the (obviously fake) situation at Ezra's, and I hoped the chemo wasn't too awful, making it clear that I was a flaky, cold-hearted quitter who she was better off without.

I pounded the peaks with my unconditionally devoted dog, played with my honorary nieces and nephews, started creating a portfolio of floral designs while waiting to hear back about the wedding-flowers course and stuffed my emotions back down inside the depths of me where I could ignore them.

Until, one day when I arrived back from a particularly gruelling hike, I found Gideon sitting at the kitchen table, listening to Aaliyah explaining why she might actually, really truly be a Madagascan tomato frog.

'Auntie Sophie, your ex-boyfriend is here,' JoJo announced, in case I hadn't noticed him. 'I did try to say he should wait in the car, but Mum told me to stop being so rude and make him a drink.'

'Mum also said that when Sophie got back, we'd probably want to give them some privacy,' Naomi added, raising her eyebrows at me in unspoken question.

'Well, of course we don't *want* to give them privacy!' JoJo huffed. 'We all want to hear what the heartbreaker has to say for himself.'

'JoJo,' Naomi said, in that tone that was enough to send the girls scurrying out of the room.

'Heartbreaker?' Gideon asked, his face a careful mask.

'Do you want another drink?' I flicked on the kettle in a pointless attempt to give me time to calm down enough to think.

'No, thanks.'

He waited patiently while I fumbled and faffed about, making brewing a pot of tea far more convoluted than it needed to be.

When I couldn't put it off any longer, I took a seat opposite him at the table.

'Hi. How are you?' he asked, the sincerity in his voice reassuring me that he wasn't here looking for trouble.

'I can't believe you're here,' I stammered in response. I wanted to sit and drink him in, it was so good to see him, but at the same time, my eyes couldn't settle for more than a split second. 'I can't believe you found me.'

'Your business is registered here. And I would have come sooner but didn't want to leave Hattie.'

'Is it bad?' I asked, dreading the answer.

He nodded. 'The side effects are pretty nasty, so physically, yes, it is bad. Mentally, she's doing better. Thanks to you.'

I managed a hint of a smile. 'She left a message saying Aidan had been to see her. It must have gone okay, then?'

Gideon's smile threatened to eclipse his whole face. 'It has.'

'What about your mum?'

'We had to tell her. I mean, you've seen him. Even with her poor eyesight, it's obvious.'

'It must have been a shock.'

'Of course. And she was very upset Hattie hadn't told her sooner, but it's hard to stay mad at a woman who's battling for her life. They've had some conversations, reached as easy a truce as Mum can manage.'

'Right.' I didn't know what else to say, still discombobulated that he was here.

'Anyway, Aidan is with her today, so I took the opportunity to come and see you, because I wanted to—'

'Gideon, I'm so sorry,' I blurted, interrupting him. 'For everything. The lies, the falling in love with you and especially the disappearing like I did. I didn't know how to make it better, so I reverted to type and ran away.'

'Thank you. I appreciate that. For what it's worth, I'm sorry too. I was upset, and in shock, obviously, but I shouldn't have taken it out on you, and I should have listened to what you had to say.' Gideon shrugged as he leaned back against the chair. 'I never expected you to leave, though. Or to stop being friends with Hattie.'

'The last thing I wanted, or any of you needed, was me complicating things. Making you feel uncomfortable.' I was surprised it had taken me this long, but I finally started to cry. 'I left so you could focus on Hattie.'

'I understand. That's why I'm here, to clear the air so things won't be awkward if you come and see Hattie again. I know she'd like that.'

'And... is... is that the only reason?' I asked, because the only man I'd ever been in love with had come all the way here to see me, so I couldn't let him go again without having asked. 'If you're sorry, and I'm sorry, is there any way we can get past it? Maybe... try again?'

He sat up, his shoulders stiffening, and I realised that I'd said the wrong thing.

'Sophie, I...' He stopped, swallowed and ran a hand through his chestnut hair, which it turned out was just enough time for my heart to break all over again. 'I meant what I said at the party. I was all-in. Completely in love with you.'

Was.

'I believe you thought you meant what you said, too.'

'What? I did mean it!'

'But then, a few hours later, you disappeared, leaving a note on the kitchen table. For Hattie, not me.'

'And I've apologised, explained... you said you understood.'

'I do understand. I understand that, after what's happened to you, you find it impossible to commit. That even when you thought you loved me, the first big issue we encountered, the first time I wasn't patient or perfect, you were gone. That might still be okay, I would take the risk, do the work, trust that eventually, we'll know that you can stick it out, if things were different. But I'm currently caring for my desperately ill birth-mother and getting my head around a birth-father who is alive and wanting to be a part of my life, all while trying to protect the woman I call my mum. Oh, and keep a business I don't have the time or energy to run still running.

'There are too many people who need me. I'm not sure you even want me, deep down. Not long-term. And even if I did have the capacity for long-distance, right now, my heart is in no fit state to risk being broken.' His voice cracked, and I realised he was probably as upset as me. 'I don't trust you not to break my heart again.'

I nodded, unable to find any words, even if I could have forced them past the splinters of shattered hope in my throat.

'Come and see Hattie, though. She's what matters right now.'

Somehow, we managed an awkward sort-of hug, and I was able to resist crumpling into a pathetic heap on the kitchen tiles until after he'd left.

* * *

I thought about my visit from Gideon incessantly, replaying the conversation as it was and fantasising about what I should have said to make him give us another chance.

I rambled to Naomi and Ezra about it a few times. They made sympathetic noises and reminded me to focus on the hugely positive steps I'd made while in Sherwood Forest.

'A big part of you has been stuck—' Naomi said.

'Lost,' Ezra interrupted.

'Stuck *and* lost, for a really long time,' Naomi conceded. 'And now, look at you. Free to love again. To fully *live* again.'

'To stop and smell the roses along the way,' Ezra added.

'You've gained so much; try not to get bogged down in what you lost.'

I tried. I honestly did. I started to think about taking steps forwards. Having been accepted onto the week-long floristry course, I now had to consider where I was going to live. The farmhouse was wonderful, in small doses, but after years in my own space, where I put something down and it was, not only still there, but not even broken or covered in biscuity finger-prints when I came back to it later, I was growing a little claustrophobic.

I joined Naomi's book club and started hanging out with a couple of women I met there who were a similar age to me. They didn't make me pledge allegiance to their gang, or drink a horrible cocktail as an initiation ceremony, but they were fun to be with, and didn't seem bothered by my currently aimless state.

I even arranged an initial session with a counsellor to help me avoid retreating back into old, constrictive habits.

But it was the wisdom of JoJo that made me see sense.

It was a boiling hot Saturday a week before the end of June, almost a fortnight since Gideon had been to visit me, and at least two hours since I'd thought about him, which was progress.

JoJo asked if we could go and get an ice cream, and, having nothing better to do right then, I could hardly say no.

'Did you see that girl in the ice-cream queue, asking for triple scoops of chocolate cookie dough?' she asked, once we'd settled ourselves on a bench looking out across the valley.

'Um, the one with the blonde hair and a crop top?'

JoJo nodded wisely. 'That's Holly. She's in my tutor group. Do you know why she had three scoops?'

'She really likes ice cream?'

'Uh-uh.' JoJo took a long lick of her strawberry cone, giving time for the tension to build. 'She's emotional eating.'

'Oh?'

'Yes.' JoJo adopted her here-comes-gossip pose, and I readied myself for a very long sentence. 'Because Harry broke up with her because he said she can't commit and she was like, "What are you talking about, I'm your girlfriend, how is that not commitment enough, we're exclusive, aren't we? When Kye DM'd me, I deleted it right away", but Harry's like, "Yeah, but commitment isn't words, it's actions" and Holly's all, "What does that even mean, Harry?" and he said, "Well, you always sit with your friends at lunch, you take hours to reply to my Snaps, and when I asked you to hang out on Sunday, you said you were busy but then I saw you with Mika and Rayon and it's no good saying you want to be with me if you don't even act like it..."'

JoJo went on for a while longer, describing how Holly begged for another chance, then Harry said he was done with girls messing him about and was going to play football with his mates, but I'd mostly tuned out.

It had hit me like a bolt of very obvious lightning.

Gideon didn't want a relationship with me because he was afraid I couldn't commit.

I could accept that and keep trying to wade through my rejection until I moved on.

Or I could show him, by my actions, that he had nothing to be scared about.

I tried not to rush JoJo into finishing her ice cream so we could head back to the farmhouse, but those fifteen minutes of social commentary on the romantic complexities of Year Seven girls were the longest quarter-hour of my life.

I had so much to do, and not a moment to lose.

35

Three weeks later, I was walking up the Riverbend drive again. I'd put on my big-girl pants and called Hattie the day after my ice cream with JoJo. We'd talked, cried and even managed to laugh together a few times by the time we hung up. I unmuted the Gals' group chat, and that weekend, we had a video call while everyone was round at Deirdre's for a painting party. Deirdre, Laurie and Kalani painted her living space in bright colours, while Hattie worked on a painting of a Brimstone butterfly to complement the pale-green kitchen cabinets.

'We told you, Soph,' Kalani reminded me in no uncertain terms. 'Once a Gal, always a Gal, unless gross misconduct of a man-stealing kind has occurred. We're just glad you're back, that's all.'

'On video, at least,' Deidre added. 'When are you joining us in person?'

'Well,' I replied. 'I was going to ask you about that...'

The answer they came up with stunned all of us (except maybe Hattie), and Kalani most of all.

* * *

'Here you are!' Hattie cried, waving to me from her garden sofa as Muffin and Flapjack greeted each other with rapturous sniffs and thumping tails.

It was mid-July, the sun was beaming and, despite my summer dress, I was already sticky after the short walk from my car across the lawn. My heart ached at seeing Hattie with a throw over her knees and wearing a knitted cap.

'Oh, don't mind this, it's easier than a wig,' she said, patting her head.

I bent down for a gentle hug before taking a seat next to her.

'Three chemo cycles down, three to go,' I said, once I'd poured myself a glass of lemonade. 'How's it going at the halfway mark?'

'How does it look like it's going?' Hattie grimaced. It looked as if it was going horrendously, but I wasn't about to say it.

'A hundred times a day, I mentally call that sadist of a doctor and tell him to stuff his treatment plan, I'll take my chances.'

'I'm so sorry.'

I'd told her enough times before, but it was all I could think of to say.

'Oh, it is what it is. And all the other amazing and wonderful things happening are helping me drag myself through. I can hardly quit now my first love has turned up out of the blue and actually seems to not find my current husk of a body physically repulsive, can I?'

'So things are going well with Aidan?'

Hattie smiled a slow, sweet smile. 'Whenever he visits, which is most weekends, he lies down beside me every night, until I fall asleep. Which on bad days, is a long time. And then, because I'm not yet used to sharing a bed, he creeps off to another room so he won't disturb me.'

'Wow.'

'Then in the morning, he wakes me up with the best coffee I've ever tasted.' She nudged my arm. 'Some men fade with time, they grow stuffy, stale and romantically stagnant. Aidan has simply grown better.'

'Anyway,' Hattie said, after a few more minutes catching up on Riverbend news. 'Enough about me. What I really want to talk about is you. How are you handling it at Kalani Towers? Is it all snarky comments and passive-aggressive politeness, or are you actually managing to cohabit as mature adults?'

'It's been okay.' A week ago, I moved into Kalani's spare room, on a temporary basis. My first wedding with Maid Marian's Garlands was the previous weekend and I'd realised that house-hunting was far easier when already in the vicinity. 'We've been getting on really well. On my second night, we drew up a list of house rules, and admittedly, Kalani's side of the list was three times longer than mine, but having both been so used to our own space helps. It's not like one of us is oblivious to how annoying it is when someone moves your stuff, or lets the dirty pots pile up in the sink.'

'But?'

'What makes you think there's a but?'

'Darling, I've known Kalani for years. With that woman, there's always a but.'

'Well, I wouldn't hate it if Tye wasn't around quite so often.'

She raised one wispy eyebrow.

'Or, rather, if when he was around, he felt more inclined to wear clothes.'

'He doesn't parade about in the nude?' Hattie leaned forwards, her eyes gleaming.

'In his underwear. His unusually small, tight underwear.'

'A bit awkward.'

'A lot awkward!' I drained the remains of my lemonade. 'Adjusting to sharing a living space with a friend is one thing. A practically naked virtual stranger is a lot for me. Kalani's kitchen doesn't leave heaps of room for manoeuvre. I'm genuinely thrilled for them. It's great that she feels comfortable having him over for meals and films and reading poetry together on the veranda.'

'All in the past week!' Hattie remarked.

'Yeah. But it would be lovely if I can get out of their way sooner rather than later.'

'Are you having any luck with that?'

I topped up our lemonade. 'Not yet. It turns out there aren't that many smallish cottages for sale around here. I'm thinking I'll have to widen the search.'

'People do like living here. They say for a Middlebeck house to come on the market, you have to wait for someone to die.'

'Then I'll definitely start widening the search.'

Hattie smiled. 'Something will turn up. Next topic: are you enjoying your new job?'

Now, this I could answer with an enthusiastic yes. Spending three days preparing then setting up the flowers for a wedding in a nearby village was similar to my apprenticeship days in all the best ways. The job also had the added bonus of working with lovely women who didn't believe in getting stressed because if we secreted cortisol hormones into the atmosphere, it might negatively impact the flowers. We had so many tea breaks, I spent half the afternoon darting between the workshop in Karen's garden and her bathroom.

'Are they going to let you loose with your own designs at any point?'

'They are!' I beamed. 'They loved my portfolio. I'm going to be given creative control for the next couple who book in.'

'I'm so glad things are coming together.' Hattie reached over and patted my knee. 'I'm even more delighted that you chose to make Middlebeck your home.'

'Now you're the one with a but,' I said, even though I already knew what it was.

'Well. It would be easier if we didn't have to meet in secret. I've had enough of those to last a lifetime.' She squinted at me, turning her hand over to take hold of mine. 'Would it be so awful if Gideon knew you were here?'

I sighed. 'I'm not ready yet. But I'm working on it. I have my first non-art therapy session booked in for next week.'

Hattie smiled. 'Sounds dreadfully dull.'

'I know, right? Sitting in a chair talking. Not a stick of glue in sight. But seeing as the top art therapist in the area is taking some much-needed time off, this was the best I could do.'

'Well, you know how enthusiastically I'm rooting for you. I'm sure it will help you complete this journey.' She winked at me. 'I just hope it doesn't take too long. I hate seeing my son lonely and heartbroken. And I'd love to see a Riverbend wedding while I'm still well enough to enjoy it.'

Me not wanting to throw up or run back to the Peak District at that comment only proved how far I'd already come.

I'd be ready to contact Gideon soon. I hoped. Because not seeing him was even harder now I was back, and proving harder every single day.

* * *

July soon ambled into August. It was peak wedding season, so I worked almost every day, which helped the time pass slightly less agonisingly. I continued my fruitless search for a house. Everything within my price range either required DIY skills I didn't possess, lacked a garden – something I wasn't prepared to compromise on – or was miles away from Middlebeck. Kalani did start spending more time at Tye's, which we both found helpful, but I'd begun to grow homesick for the peace and privacy of my motorhome, which I'd sold to provide funds for a house that didn't seem to exist.

My new therapist was fabulous. She lulled me with a warm smile and chocolate brownies but refused to accept any nonsense, victim mentality or self-delusion. At her encouragement, one day, Ezra drove me to Birmingham. After sitting outside my childhood home for a while, I suddenly surprised us both by jumping out of the car and knocking on the front door. The woman who opened it, carrying one small child on her hip, another hanging off her ankle, listened to my brief explanation and promptly waved me inside and left me to wander about while she made us a coffee.

The house had been transformed thanks to light-oak floorboards instead of our carpets, white walls and lots of open shelving and modern furniture. My old room now contained a dinosaur bed and a huge, wooden castle. Lilly's was stuffed with unicorns and sparkles. She'd have hated it.

The garden was almost exactly as my father had left it, except for a trampoline and two guinea pigs.

I walked along the path towards the flower beds and vegetable patch, then stopped in front of an Iceberg rose bush and sobbed my eyes out.

But by the time I'd stopped bawling, I was smiling through the tear streaks, on my cheeks. I knelt down and smelled the roses I'd planted with my father, in honour of my mother, and felt grateful for the years I'd spent here with my beautiful family. I also felt almost, so very nearly, ready to create a new family, and cram it with as much love and happiness as my old one.

In between all this, I squeezed in summer cocktails and picnics with the Gals, more secret visits to Hattie, and of course, hours of walks through the forests and fields with my dog.

So many walks that it was perhaps inevitable that, one day, I'd run into the one person I was trying to avoid.

My allergic-to-BS therapist would no doubt challenge me on whether this was my subconscious hope all along.

My new, enlightened self would have to admit that, yes, it probably was, because otherwise, I would stay 'getting ready' to prove my new-found ability to commit indefinitely.

36

I'd decided to risk a riverside walk, in the Riverbend direction, because I had the Monday off work following both Saturday and Sunday weddings, and I believed it was safe to assume that Gideon would be busy completing his latest landscaping project on the other side of the forest.

It had rained the past few days, and I was navigating a particularly squelchy section of the footpath, keeping one eye on Muffin, who'd been scurrying along, nose to the ground, following some enticing scent or other, when she suddenly stopped, ears pricked, sniffing the air, before shooting down a side path into the trees.

I hurried after her, calling her name a few times even though I knew that if she'd found something she considered remotely edible or a small animal to chase, then she'd be thoroughly deaf to my cries.

It was only when I heard the barks that I started to worry she'd found trouble. I picked up my pace to a bumpy run along the increasingly overgrown and waterlogged trail, the déjà vu only kicking in as I veered around a thick patch of brambles and hurtled straight into a giant puddle.

Four lurching steps into the water, my walking boot caught on a submerged tree root, sending me flying forwards. Thankfully, my arms instinctively shot out to brace my fall, keeping my face above the water as I splashed onto my hands and knees.

I guessed it even before I'd dared to raise my mud-splattered head and look for him.

There, about three metres away on the other side of the puddle, my dog spun in a frenzy of ecstasy with her best friend. A short distance beyond that, Gideon was standing, seemingly frozen in shock.

It was only as I began clambering to my feet that he jolted back to life, not even bothering to skirt around the edge of the puddle but wading straight up to me, placing his hands underneath both shoulders and lifting me upwards until my face was directly in front of his.

'Sophie?' He scanned my features, his expression incredulous, mouth already twitching in a smile.

'Hi.'

'What are you doing here?'

'Walking my dog.'

We looked at each other for a moment, the air suddenly becoming charged. I was acutely aware of his hands still resting against my sides. Slowly, hesitantly, his face drifted an inch or two towards mine, before he tilted it back again, as if unsure.

I knew, in that moment, how completely, utterly sure I was about Gideon Langford.

My head, my past, my hopes and fears had finally caught up with my heart.

I reached up two filthy, dripping hands, wrapped them around his neck, and stretched up to press my lips against his.

He resisted for only a single, stuttering heartbeat before returning the kiss. His arms flung around me, pulling me up against his chest before one hand moved to cradle the back of my head as weeks of mutual longing and withheld passion poured out.

Eventually, we broke off to catch our breath, those river-deep eyes boring into mine before we rested our foreheads against each other, steadying ourselves.

'Oops.' I reached up and wiped a streak of mud from his cheek. Given the state of my hand, that only made things worse.

'Oops yourself.' Gideon grinned, smudging his wet cheek against mine.

'Hold on, I've got a tissue somewhere.'

I looked down at my jeans' pockets, unsure of how to extract a tissue with my dirty hands, but Gideon gently led us out of the puddle then produced a small towel from his rucksack.

We wiped our hands and faces, leaving our sopping-wet shoes and clothes as a lost cause, and found a fallen tree to sit on while the dogs scampered in and out of the bushes.

'Are you here for the day?' Gideon asked, shifting along the trunk until there was a good few inches between us. 'Does Hattie know?'

I took a deep breath. *Here goes everything.*

'Hattie doesn't know I'm walking along the river today. But she knows I'm here in Middlebeck. Or, more specifically... living at Kalani's house.'

He pulled his head back but said nothing.

'I moved in with her a few weeks ago. I've been looking for a house to buy, but nothing's turned up yet.'

He continued watching me, face a careful mask. 'Go on.'

'I accepted the job with Maid Marian's Garlands and have been working there since I moved. My business is officially closed down and I sold the motorhome. I've also been seeing a therapist. I even went to my old house, where I grew up, and back to Leeds, to where I was when my family died.'

'You've been living in Middlebeck for weeks? Have you seen Hattie?'

I nodded. 'I've visited Riverbend a few times.'

He frowned. 'But you didn't want to see me. That explains a lot.'

My pulse was hammering so hard, it made my head spin. What if I couldn't find the right words, if I messed things up again?

'Except for that kiss,' Gideon continued as his gaze softened. 'That was not the kiss of someone who doesn't want anything to do with me.'

I shook my head in agitation. 'I want *everything* to do with you. Absolutely, completely everything. I didn't tell you I was here because I wanted to be ready to prove it. To be able to show you I was both willing and able to commit, with no chance of hurting you again.'

'By renting a room off Kalani and taking a casual job with a local flower stall?' His voice was gentle, but the words were firm. This was too important for either of us to get swept up in the moment.

'No.' I summoned up every last ounce of my new-found courage and looked him straight in the eye, hoping he would see right into my soul and find the truth there. 'By one day standing in front of you and confessing that I not only love you; I will do everything I can to spend the rest of my life with you. I think about you all the time so the truth is, you're with me anyway.'

'And you would take that chance with me, risk being hurt again?'

I shrugged, my eyes filling with tears. 'You're worth it. If I've learned nothing else these past few weeks, it's that I'm stronger than I thought. I was so scared of facing another heartbreak. But I've learned that hearts are living things. With the right help, they can heal.'

'Okay.' His gaze remained steady on mine. 'How's the getting ready going?'

'I wasn't sure.' I closed my eyes, opened them again. Let out a watery laugh. 'That's not true. I was sure. But I was also putting it off because I was equally sure that you'd reject me, and this way, I could still live in my little Sherwood Forest fantasy of maybe getting my happy ever after. But then, the second I saw you... I'm done being a coward. Living in fear of what may never happen, and so losing all the wonderful things that might. I was ready the day I spoke to Aidan Hunter and realised how he'd wasted decades believing Hattie didn't want him. I was even more ready the day you turned up, just to apologise for feeling perfectly natural feelings in a traumatic moment. I was readier still, watching you drive away and thinking that it might be the last time I ever saw you.' I stopped, trying to allow my thoughts to catch up with my mouth.

'That was two months ago.' The doubt was clear in his voice.

'I know. But you said that you don't trust me. I didn't know how to prove you wrong apart from to show that I'm properly committing to staying here. I was meant to buy a house first.' I must have started crying because Gideon reached up and tenderly wiped my tears away with his thumb.

'My heart was yours the moment I saw you. Now I'm offering you the rest of me, as well. No long-distance. No wait and see. Like I said at the party, if you'll have me – even if you won't because honestly, Muffin and I like it here and we wouldn't know where else to go – I'm staying. For good. Putting down roots in this land, and hoping, praying, I'll be able to watch my children, maybe even grandchildren, grow up here, too.'

'Your children?'

'*Our* children.'

It felt as though the only thing moving in the whole forest was the rise and fall of Gideon's chest. I was holding my own breath and even the dogs had stopped gambolling about and found a dry patch of ground to lie on, watching us expectantly.

Eventually, as all the hopes and dreams I'd been carrying for the past few months flashed before my mind's eye, he gave one, decisive nod.

'That sounds like a plan.'

What?

I closed my eyes, swaying with relief so huge, I didn't quite realise until then how much this conversation meant to me.

'I'm so glad you're up for staying.' Gideon shuffled closer and took hold of my hand, steadying me and sending my heart careening inside my chest in the same instant. 'You know how much I love Riverbend. But I love you infinitely more, Sophie. Wherever we end up, wherever life takes us, what matters is we're together.'

'So you believe me?' I asked, overwhelmed.

'You've spent weeks living with Kalani. If that's not commitment, I don't know what is.'

He kissed me again, slow and tender, as if we had all the time in the world. Which I supposed, now, we did have.

EPILOGUE

It was Valentine's Day, near enough a full year since I'd first arrived at Riverbend and walked in on the Changelings stripping off for their art-therapy class. Unlike that day, this one contained perfect skies, clear and bright, with a deliciously fresh nip in the air to complement the excitement thrumming across the Riverbend grounds.

I'd spent the morning directing operations from the renamed and relocated White Rose Floristry, now occupying what was previously the art-therapy side of the Riverbend studio. My assistants – because Karen and Stella had been all too willing to demote themselves and promote me to Managing Director once the business had flourished to the point where stress was no longer an optional-extra – had borne posies, bouquets and a simply stunning floral arch to the chapel. They had also helped me to set up the dining room, where twenty guests would eat, drink and toast the happy couple once the ceremony was over.

Hattie's wish had come true: she was about to partake in a Riverbend wedding. What she'd not foreseen was that she would be the bride. Aidan had proposed to her during her final chemo session in September and, while in many ways wanting to waste no time, he'd wisely insisted that they wait a few months to give her time to recover, and him time to work out his notice at the activity centre and sell his house.

'Recover or die!' Hattie had argued, but the post-treatment test results had been better than anyone had dared hope, including Dr Ambrose. Hattie was still seriously ill. She still had cancer. But, for now, it seemed to be held at bay.

Once the final bloom was perfectly in place, I hurried over to the boathouse – *my* boathouse, which had seemed such an obvious place for me to live, once Gideon had known about me moving back, that I didn't know why Hattie hadn't mentioned it earlier. Grabbing my bag, a bridesmaid's dress and Muffin, I returned to find the rest of the Gals helping Hattie get ready in her bedroom. That was, if 'getting ready' meant plying her with an enormous gorgeous gal.

'Eugh,' she exclaimed, accepting the glass. 'Do we really have to keep on drinking these things forever?'

'Actually,' Laurie said, 'I had a go at tweaking the recipe. See what you think.'

Hattie took a cautious sip, followed by a reckless swig. 'Finally! One of you women have learned that old recipes that leave a bad taste in your mouth are a waste of a beautiful life. A tweak here and there is often for the better.'

I swiftly changed into my Riverbend-blue dress. All the Gals wore the same colour, but individual styles to suit our shapes and taste. Mine fell just above my ankle, with a flowing skirt and lots of ruches, giving it a Greek-goddess vibe. I swept up my hair and added one of White Rose Floristry's fresh-flower clips, a light touch of make-up, and was ready to try the new, improved cocktail myself.

An hour later, we took a slow, energy-conserving stroll to meet Gideon outside the chapel. Being a gentleman, he kissed Hattie and assured her how divine she looked, before turning towards me with an enchanting grin.

'Just when I keep thinking you can't get any more beautiful.'

'You don't scrub up too badly yourself.'

We waited for a few minutes while one of Aidan's daughters took some photographs. The couple had wanted to keep the occasion small, and so we were all chipping in here and there.

I gave Gideon's hand one last squeeze before we took our positions.

'Holding up okay?' I asked. The only thing marring this celebration was the absence of his other mother. Agnes had peacefully passed away in November, and grieving the loss of a mother while adjusting to life with another one hadn't been without its complications.

'I don't know how she'd have handled all this,' he admitted. 'In some ways, it's probably for the best that she's not here to see me give Hattie away. But on the other hand...'

'You'll never stop missing her. Especially on days like this.'

He nodded, bending down to give me another peck on the cheek before we accompanied one of the best women we knew down the aisle.

* * *

The rest of the day was perfect. I had loved the exuberance of Hattie's birthday party, when Riverbend overflowed with cele-bration. However, there was a lot to be said for an intimate group of friends and family who knew each other's quirks and stories, and were able to relax and make themselves at home, no stress or fuss necessary.

We ate, drank and pushed the living-room furniture to one side to make room for dancing. Hattie slipped upstairs with her new husband for a restorative nap once the sun had set in the early evening, and Gideon suggested we take the dogs out for a quick run while she rested.

I donned a fancy white coat I'd bought just for the occasion, leaving my hair uncovered but adding a scarf and gloves to keep the cold at bay and changing into my trainers.

At first, I'd assumed we were randomly ambling across the grounds to nowhere in particular, but we soon started making our way towards the rose garden.

'Is Deirdre having any luck finding somewhere to live?' Gideon asked, his hand in mine.

'Not yet. It's so frustrating that after spending all that time transforming her house into how she likes it, the landlord has decided to move back in. She's got another couple of weeks on the contract. If it comes to it, she can crash with Kalani and Tye for a while.'

'It would make more sense for her to move here,' Gideon said, pausing by the rose-garden door. 'She might not love living so close to work, but it's got a lot of advantages. I was wondering how she'd feel about moving into Riverbend's guest suite.'

'Well, if she did that, what about you?'

Gideon opened the door and stood back, allowing me to enter first.

'I might have come up with a solution to that. Oh, and don't worry about stealing Hattie's thunder. It was her idea to do this today.'

'Oh!'

I stopped, two steps inside the door. I'd walked into a fairy tale. The rose garden had been transformed. Tiny lights had been strung up across the trellises and wound around the larger bushes. Underneath one of the arches was a small table, with an ice bucket containing champagne, and two glasses. Gideon moved past me, walking backwards until he reached the table, where he swiftly dropped to one knee, pulling a ring from his coat pocket.

'I had a fancy speech planned, but I can't remember any of it.'

'I...' I couldn't speak for a moment. Too overjoyed to cry. Too stunned to breathe. I'd known for a long time that this was the person I was meant to be with. I had no doubt that he knew that, too.

But still. A proposal. Maybe I wasn't too happy to cry, after all.

'I don't need fancy. I just want you.'

'Okay, well, then. I'll keep it simple. Will you marry me, Sophie Potter?'

I practically ran up to where he was kneeling, almost toppling us both over as I flung myself into his arms. I waited until we'd both righted ourselves, wrapping both arms around his neck and looking him straight in his eyes.

'Yes. I will.'

Because, after everything, that was all that needed to be said.

ACKNOWLEDGMENTS

As always, I am so thankful to be part of the Boldwood Books family. Being with a publisher who treats their authors the same whether we sell a thousand books or a million is something very special. Thank you so much to everyone who has contributed to this book. An extra big thank you to my editor, Sarah Ritherdon, who was (if possible) even more encouraging than usual, giving me the confidence to really embrace River-bend's story. My agent, Kiran Kataria, continues to be a steadfast ballast – I am so grateful for your help and support with the businessy side of being an author.

I am consistently blown away by the messages, reviews and comments that I get from all you lovely people who read my books. It really does help me stop faffing about online and give these stories my all. Thank you!

While writing this book, my life was turned upside down after meeting some incredible children who stole my heart. I have learned so much about life and love as a result. It has made me a better person, so must have helped me become a better author, too. Thank you for letting me be your mum in all the ways that matter. And a shout out to Joy Taylor – for listening, for 'getting it', for being there and speaking truth to me when I need to hear it. I thank God for you.

Ciara, Joe and Dom – I'm nowhere near a good enough writer to express how proud I am of the woman and men you have become, and the joy that being your mother brings.

And George – whew! Twenty-five years married, and it still just keeps getting better.

ABOUT THE AUTHOR

Beth Moran is the award winning author of ten contemporary fiction novels, including the number one bestselling *Let It Snow*. Her books are set in and around Sherwood Forest, where she can be found most mornings walking with her spaniel Murphy.

Sign up to Beth Moran's mailing list for news, competitions and updates on future books.

Visit Beth's website: https://bethmoranauthor.com/

Follow Beth on social media here:

 facebook.com/bethmoranauthor

twitter.com/bethcmoran

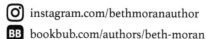 instagram.com/bethmoranauthor

bookbub.com/authors/beth-moran

Boldw⚭d

Boldwood Books is an award-winning fiction publishing company seeking out the best stories from around the world.

Find out more at www.boldwoodbooks.com

Join our reader community for brilliant books, competitions and offers!

Follow us
@BoldwoodBooks
@TheBoldBookClub

Sign up to our weekly deals newsletter

https://bit.ly/BoldwoodBNewsletter

Printed in Great Britain
by Amazon